Hard Press

The Lilac Fairy Book

Edited by Andrew Lang

Contents

'What cases are you engaged in at present?' 'Are you stopping many teeth just now?' 'What people have you converted lately?' Do ladies put these questions to the men—lawyers, dentists, clergymen, and so forth—who happen to sit next them at dinner parties?

I do not know whether ladies thus indicate their interest in the occupations of their casual neighbours at the hospitable board. But if they do not know me, or do not know me well, they generally ask 'Are you writing anything now?' (as if they should ask a painter 'Are you painting anything now?' or a lawyer 'Have you any cases at present?'). Sometimes they are more definite and inquire 'What are you writing now?' as if I must be writing something—which, indeed, is the case, though I dislike being reminded of it. It is an awkward question, because the fair being does not care a bawbee what I am writing; nor would she be much enlightened if I replied 'Madam, I am engaged on a treatise intended to prove that Normal is prior to Conceptional Totemism'--though that answer would be as true in fact as obscure in significance. The best plan seems to be to answer that I have entirely abandoned mere literature, and am contemplating a book on 'The Causes of Early Blight in the Potato,' a melancholy circumstance which threatens to deprive us of our chief esculent root. The inquirer would never be undeceived. One nymph who, like the rest, could not keep off the horrid topic of my occupation, said 'You never write anything but fairy books, do you?' A French gentleman, too, an educationist and expert in portraits of Queen Mary, once sent me a newspaper article in which he had written that I was exclusively devoted to the composition of fairy books, and nothing else. He then came to England, visited me, and found that I knew rather more about portraits of Queen Mary than he did.

In truth I never did write any fairy books in my life, except 'Prince Prigio,' 'Prince Ricardo,' and 'Tales from a Fairy Court'—that of the aforesaid Prigio. I take this opportunity of recommending these fairy books—poor things, but my own—to parents and guardians who may never have heard of them. They are rich in romantic adventure, and the Princes always marry the right Princesses and live happy ever afterwards; while the wicked witches, stepmothers, tutors and governesses are never cruelly punished, but retire to the country on ample pensions. I hate cruelty: I never put a wicked stepmother in a barrel and send her tobogganing down a hill. It is true that Prince Ricardo did kill the Yellow Dwarf; but that was in fair fight, sword in hand, and the dwarf, peace to his ashes! died in harness.

The object of these confessions is not only that of advertising my own fairy books (which are not 'out of print'; if your bookseller says so, the truth is not in him), but of giving credit where credit is due. The fairy books have been almost wholly the work of Mrs. Lang, who has translated and adapted them from the French, German, Portuguese, Italian, Spanish, Catalan, and other languages.

My part has been that of Adam, according to Mark Twain, in the Garden of Eden. Eve worked, Adam superintended. I also superintend. I find out where the stories are, and advise, and, in short, superintend. I do not write the stories out of my own head. The reputation of having written all the fairy books (an European reputation in nurseries and the United States of America) is 'the burden of an honour unto which I was not born.' It weighs upon and is killing me, as the general fash of being the wife of the Lord of Burleigh, Burleigh House by Stamford Town, was too much for the village maiden espoused by that peer.

Nobody really wrote most of the stories. People told them in all parts of the world long before Egyptian hieroglyphics or Cretan signs or Cyprian syllabaries, or alphabets were invented. They are older than reading and writing, and arose like wild flowers before men had any education to quarrel over. The grannies told them to the grandchildren, and when the grandchildren became grannies they repeated the same old tales to the new generation. Homer knew the stories and made up the 'Odyssey' out of half a dozen of them. All the history of Greece till about 800 B.C. is a string of the fairy tales, all about Theseus and Heracles and Oedipus and Minos and Perseus is a Cabinet des Fes, a collection of fairy tales. Shakespeare took them and put bits of them into 'King Lear' and other plays; he could not have made them up himself, great as he was. Let ladies and gentlemen think of this when they sit down to write fairy tales, and have them nicely typed, and send them to Messrs. Longman & Co. to be published. They think that to write a new fairy tale is easy work. They are mistaken: the thing is impossible. Nobody can write a new fairy tale; you can only mix up and dress up the old, old stories, and put the characters into new dresses, as Miss Thackeray did so well in 'Five Old Friends.' If any big girl of fourteen reads this preface, let her insist on being presented with 'Five Old Friends.'

But the three hundred and sixty-five authors who try to write new fairy tales are very tiresome. They always begin with a little boy or girl who goes out and meets the fairies of polyanthuses and gardenias and apple blossoms: 'Flowers and fruits, and other

5

winged things.' These fairies try to be funny, and fail; or they
try to preach, and succeed. Real fairies never preach or talk
slang. At the end, the little boy or girl wakes up and finds that
he has been dreaming.

Such are the new fairy stories. May we be preserved from all the
sort of them!

Our stories are almost all old, some from Ireland, before that
island was as celebrated for her wrongs as for her verdure; some
from Asia, made, I dare say, before the Aryan invasion; some from
Moydart, Knoydart, Morar and Ardnamurchan, where the sea streams
run like great clear rivers and the saw-edged hills are blue, and
men remember Prince Charlie. Some are from Portugal, where the
golden fruits grow in the Garden of the Hesperides; and some are
from wild Wales, and were told at Arthur's Court; and others come
from the firesides of the kinsmen of the Welsh, the Bretons.
There are also modern tales by a learned Scandinavian named
Topelius.

All the stories were translated or adapted by Mrs. Lang, except
'The Jogi's Punishment' and 'Moti,' done by Major Campbell out of
the Pushtoo language; 'How Brave Walter hunted Wolves,' which,
with 'Little Lasse' and 'The Raspberry Worm,' was done from
Topelius by Miss Harding; and 'The Sea King's Gift,' by Miss
Christie, from the same author.

It has been suggested to the Editor that children and parents and
guardians would like ' The Grey True Ghost-Story Book.' He knows
that the children would like it well, and he would gladly give it
to them; but about the taste of fond anxious mothers and kind
aunts he is not quite so certain. Before he was twelve the Editor
knew true ghost stories enough to fill a volume. They were a pure
joy till bedtime, but then, and later, were not wholly a source
of unmixed pleasure. At that time the Editor was not afraid of
the dark, for he thought, ' If a ghost is here, we can't see
him.' But when older and better informed persons said that ghosts
brought their own light with them (which is too true), then one's
emotions were such as parents do not desire the young to endure.
For this reason 'The Grey True Ghost-Story Book' is never likely
to be illustrated by Mr. Ford.

Contents

The Shifty Lad

In the land of Erin there dwelt long ago a widow who had an only son. He was a clever boy, so she saved up enough money to send him to school, and, as soon as he was old enough, to apprentice him to any trade that he would choose. But when the time came, he said he would not be bound to any trade, and that he meant to be a thief.

Now his mother was very sorrowful when she heard of this, but she knew quite well that if she tried to stop his having his own way he would only grow more determined to get it. So all the answer she made was that the end of thieves was hanging at the bridge of Dublin, and then she left him alone, hoping that when he was older he might become more sensible.

One day she was going to church to hear a sermon from a great preacher, and she begged the Shifty Lad, as the neighbours called him from the tricks he played, to

7

come with her. But he only laughed and declared that he did not like sermons, adding:

'However, I will promise you this, that the first trade you hear named after you come out from church shall be my trade for the rest of my life.'

These words gave a little comfort to the poor woman, and her heart was lighter than before as she bade him farewell.

When the Shifty Lad thought that the hour had nearly come for the sermon to be over, he hid himself in some bushes in a little path that led straight to his mother's house, and, as she passed along, thinking of all the good things she had heard, a voice shouted close to her ear 'Robbery! Robbery! Robbery!' The suddenness of it made her jump. The naughty boy had managed to change his voice, so that she did not know it for his, and he had concealed himself so well that, though she peered about all round her, she could see no one. As soon as she had turned the corner the Shifty Lad came out, and by running very fast through the wood he contrived to reach home before his mother, who found him stretched out comfortably before the fire.

'Well, have you got any news to tell me?' asked he.

'No, nothing; for I left the church at once, and did not stop to speak to anyone.'

'Oh, then no one has mentioned a trade to you?' he said in tones of disappointment.

'Ye—es,' she replied slowly. 'At least, as I walked down the path a voice cried out "Robbery! Robbery! Robbery!" but that was all.'

'And quite enough too,' answered the boy. 'What did I tell you? That is going to be my trade.'

'Then your end will be hanging at the bridge of Dublin,' said she. But there was no sleep for her that night, for she lay in the dark thinking about her son.

'If he is to be a thief at all, he had better be a good one. And who is there that can teach him?' the mother asked herself. But an idea came to her, and she arose early, before the sun was up, and set off for the home of the Black Rogue, or Gallows Bird, who was such a wonderful thief that, though all had been robbed by him, no one could catch him.

'Good-morning to you,' said the woman as she reached the place where the Black Gallows Bird lived when he was not away on his business. 'My son has a fancy to learn your trade. Will you be kind enough to teach him?'

8

'If he is clever, I don't mind trying,' answered the Black Gallows Bird; 'and, of course, if *any* one can turn him into a first-rate thief, it is I. But if he is stupid, it is of no use at all; I can't bear stupid people.'

'No, he isn't stupid,' said the woman with a sigh. 'So to-night, after dark, I will send him to you.'

The Shifty Lad jumped for joy when his mother told him where she had been.

'I will become the best thief in all Erin!' he cried, and paid no heed when his mother shook her head and murmured something about 'the bridge of Dublin.'

Every evening after dark the Shifty Lad went to the home of the Black Gallows Bird, and many were the new tricks he learned. By-and-by he was allowed to go out with the Bird and watch him at work, and at last there came a day when his master though that he had grown clever enough to help in a big robbery.

'There is a rich farmer up there on the hill, who has just sold all his fat cattle for much money and has bought some lean ones which will cost him little. Now it happens that, while he has received the money for the fat cattle, he has not yet paid the price of the thin ones, which he has in the cowhouse. To-morrow he will go to the market with the money in his hand, so to-night we must get at the chest. When all is quiet we will hide in the loft.'

There was no moon, and it was the night of Hallowe'en, and everyone was burning nuts and catching apples in a tub of water with their hands tied, and playing all sorts of other games, till the Shifty Lad grew quite tired of waiting for them to get to bed. The Black Gallows Bird, who was more accustomed to the business, tucked himself up on the hay and went to sleep, telling the boy to wake him when the merry-makers had departed. But the Shifty Lad, who could keep still no longer, crept down to the cowshed and loosened the heads of the cattle which were tied, and they began to kick each other and bellow, and made such a noise that the company in the farmhouse ran out to tie them up again. Then the Shifty Lad entered the room and picked up a big handful of nuts, and returned to the loft, where the Black Rogue was still sleeping. At first the Shifty Lad shut his eyes too, but very soon he sat up, and taking a big needle and thread from his pocket, he sewed the hem of the Black Gallows Bird's coat to a heavy piece of bullock's hide that was hanging at his back.

By this time the cattle were all tied up again, but as the people could not find their nuts they sat round the fire and began to tell stories.

'I will crack a nut,' said the Shifty Lad.

'You shall not,' cried the Black Gallows Bird; 'they will hear you.'

'I don't care,' answered the Shifty Lad. 'I never spend Hallowe'en yet without cracking a nut'; and he cracked one.

'Some one is cracking nuts up there,' said one of the merry-makers in the farmhouse. 'Come quickly, and we will see who it is.'

He spoke loudly, and the Black Gallows Bird heard, and ran out of the loft, dragging the big leather hide after him which the Shifty Lad had sewed to his coat.

'He is stealing my hide!' shouted the farmer, and they all darted after him; but he was too swift for them, and at last he managed to tear the hide from his coat, and then he flew like a hare till he reached his old hiding-place. But all this took a long time, and meanwhile the Shifty Lad got down from the loft, and searched the house till he found the chest with the gold and silver in it, concealed behind a load of straw and covered with loaves of bread and a great cheese. The Shifty Lad slung the money bags round his shoulders and took the bread and the cheese under his arm, then set out quietly for the Black Rogue's house.

'Here you are at last, you villain!' cried his master in great wrath. 'But I will be revenged on you.'

'It is all right,' replied the Shifty Lad calmly. 'I have brought what you wanted'; and he laid the things he was carrying down on the ground.

'Ah! you are the better thief,' said the Black Rogue's wife; and the Black Rogue added:

'Yes, it is you who are the clever boy'; and they divided the spoil and the Black Gallows Bird had one half and the Shifty Lad the other half.

A few weeks after that the Black Gallows Bird had news of a wedding that was to be held near the town; and the bridegroom had many friends and everybody sent him a present. Now a rich farmer who lived up near the moor thought that nothing was so useful to a young couple when they first began to keep house as a fine fat sheep, so he bade his shepherd go off to the mountain where the flock were feeding, and bring him back the best he could find. And the shepherd chose out the largest and fattest of the sheep and the one with the whitest fleece; then he tied its feet together and put it across his shoulder, for he had a long way to go.

That day, the Shifty Lad happened to be wandering over the moor, when he saw the man with the sheep on his shoulder walking along the road which led past the Black Rogue's house. The sheep was heavy and the man was in no hurry, so he came slowly and the boy knew that he himself could easily get back to his master before the shepherd was even in sight.

'I will wager,' he cried, as he pushed quickly through the bushes which hid the cabin—'I will wager that I will steal the sheep from the man that is coming before he passes here.'

'Will you indeed?' said the Gallows Bird. 'I will wager you a hundred silver pieces that you can do nothing of the sort.'

'Well, I will try it, anyway,' replied the boy, and disappeared in the bushes. He ran fast till he entered a wood through which the shepherd must go, and then he stopped, and taking off one of his shoes smeared it with mud and set it in the path. When this was done he slipped behind a rock and waited.

Very soon the man came up, and seeing the shoe lying there, he stooped and looked at it.

'It is a good shoe,' he said to himself, 'but very dirty. Still, if I had the fellow, I would be at the trouble of cleaning it'; so he threw the shoe down again and went on.

The Shifty Lad smiled as he heard him, and, picking up the shoe, he crept round by a short way and laid the other shoe on the path. A few minutes after the shepherd arrived, and beheld the second shoe lying on the path.

'Why, that is the fellow of the dirty shoe!' he exclaimed when he saw it. 'I will go back and pick up the other one, and then I shall have a pair of good shoes,' and he put the sheep on the grass and returned to fetch the shoe. Then the Shifty Lad put on his shoes, and, picking up the sheep, carried it home. And the Black Rogue paid him the hundred marks of his wager.

When the shepherd reached the farmhouse that night he told his tale to his master, who scolded him for being stupid and careless, and bade him go the next day to the mountain and fetch him a kid, and he would send that as a wedding gift. But the Shifty Lad was on the look-out, and hid himself in the wood, and the moment the man drew near with the kid on his shoulders began to bleat like a sheep, and no one, not even the sheep's own mother, could have told the difference.

'Why, it must have got its feet loose, and have strayed after all,' thought the man; and he put the kid on the grass and hurried off in the direction of the bleating. Then the boy ran back and picked up the kid, and took it to the Black Gallows Bird.

The shepherd could hardly believe his eyes when he returned from seeking the sheep and found that the kid had vanished. He was afraid to go home and tell the same tale that he had told yesterday; so he searched the wood through and through till night was nearly come. Then he felt that there was no help for it, and he must go home and confess to his master.

Of course, the farmer was very angry at this second misfortune; but this time he told him to drive one of the big bulls from the mountain, and warned him that if he lost *that* he would lose his place also. Again the Shifty Lad, who was on the watch, perceived him pass by, and when he saw the man returning with the great bull he cried to the Black Rogue:

'Be quick and come into the wood, and we will try to get the bull also.'

'But how can we do that?' asked the Black Rogue.

'Oh, quite easily! You hide yourself out there and baa like a sheep, and I will go in the other direction and bleat like a kid. It will be all right, I assure you.'

The shepherd was walking slowly, driving the bull before him, when he suddenly heard a loud baa amongst the bushes far away on one side of the path, and a feeble bleat answering it from the other side.

'Why, it must be the sheep and the kid that I lost,' said he. 'Yes, surely it must'; and tying the bull hastily to a tree, he went off after the sheep and the kid, and searched the wood till he was tired. Of course by the time he came back the two thieves had driven the bull home and killed him for meat, so the man was obliged to go to his master and confess that he had been tricked again.

After this the Black Rogue and the Shifty Lad grew bolder and bolder, and stole great quantities of cattle and sold them and grew quite rich. One day they were returning from the market with a large sum of money in their pockets when they passed a gallows erected on the top of a hill.

'Let us stop and look at that gallows,' exclaimed the Shifty Lad. 'I have never seen one so close before. Yet some say that it is the end of all thieves.'

There was no one in sight, and they carefully examined every part of it.

'I wonder how it feels to be hanged,' said the Shifty Lad. 'I should like to know, in case they ever catch me. I'll try first, and then you can do so.'

As he spoke he fastened the loose cord about his neck, and when it was quite secure he told the Black Rogue to take the other end of the rope and draw him up from the ground.

'When I am tired of it I will shake my legs, and then you must let me down,' said he.

The Black Rogue drew up the rope, but in half a minute the Shifty Lad's legs began to shake, and he quickly let it down again.

'You can't imagine what a funny feeling hanging gives you,' murmured the Shifty Lad, who looked rather purple in the face and spoke in an odd voice. 'I don't think you have every tried it, or you wouldn't have let me go up first. Why, it is the pleasantest thing I have ever done. I was shaking my legs from sheer delight, and if you had been there you would have shaken your legs too.'

'Well, let me try, if it is so nice,' answered the Black Rogue. 'But be sure you tie the knot securely, for I don't want to fall down and break my neck.'

'Oh, I will see to that!' replied the Shifty Lad. 'When you are tired, just whistle, and I'll let you down.'

So the Black Rogue was drawn up, and as soon as he was as high as the rope would allow him to go the Shifty Lad called to him:

'Don't forest to whistle when you want to come down; but if you are enjoying yourself as I did, shake your legs.'

And in a moment the Black Rogue's legs began to shake and to kick, and the Shifty Lad stood below, watching him and laughing heartily.

'Oh, how funny you are! If you could only see yourself! Oh, you *are* funny! But when you have had enough, whistle and you shall be let down'; and he rocked again with laughter.

But no whistle came, and soon the legs ceased to shake and to kick, for the Black Gallows Bird was dead, as the Shifty Lad intended he should be.

Then he went home to the Black Rogue's wife, and told her that her husband was dead, and that he was ready to marry her if she liked. But the woman had been fond of the Black Rogue, thief though he was, and she shrank from the Shifty Lad in horror, and set the people after him, and he had to fly to another part of the country where none knew of his doings.

Perhaps if the Shifty Lad's mother knew anything of this, she may have thought that by this time her son might be tired of stealing, and ready to try some honest trade. But in reality he loved the tricks and danger, and life would have seemed very dull without them. So he went on just as before, and made friends whom he taught to be as wicked as himself, till they took to robbing the king's storehouses, and by the advice of the Wise Man the king sent out soldiers to catch the band of thieves.

For a long while they tried in vain to lay hands on them. The Shifty Lad was too clever for them all, and if they laid traps he laid better ones. At last one night he stole upon some soldiers while they were asleep in a barn and killed them, and persuaded the villagers that if *they* did not kill the other soldiers before morning they would certainly be killed themselves. Thus it happened that when the sun rose not a single soldier was alive in the village.

Of course this news soon reached the king's ears, and he was very angry, and summoned the Wise Man to take counsel with him. And this was the counsel of the Wise Man—that he should invite all the people in the countryside to a ball, and among them the bold and impudent thief would be sure to come, and would be sure to ask the king's daughter to dance with him.

'Your counsel is good,' said the king, who made his feast and prepared for his ball; and all the people of the countryside were present, and the Shifty Lad came with them.

When everyone had eaten and drunk as much as they wanted they went into the ballroom. There was a great throng, and while they were pressing through the doorway the Wise Man, who had a bottle of black ointment hidden in his robes, placed a tiny dot on the cheek of the Shifty Lad near his ear. The Shifty Lad felt nothing, but as he approached the king's daughter to ask her to be his partner he caught sight of the black dot in a silver mirror. Instantly he guessed who had put it there and why, but he said nothing, and danced so beautifully that the princess was quite delighted with him. At the end of the dance he bowed low to his partner and left her, to mingle with the crowd that was filling the doorway. As he passed the Wise Man he contrived not only to steal the bottle but to place two black dots on his face, and one on the faces of twenty other men. Then he slipped the bottle back in the Wise Man's robe.

By-and-by he went up to the king's daughter again, and begged for the honour of another dance. She consented, and while he was stooping to tie the ribbons on his shoe she took out from her pocket another bottle, which the Wizard had given her, and put a black dot on his cheek. But she was not as skilful as the Wise Man, and the Shifty Lad felt the touch of her fingers; so as soon as the dance was over he contrived to place a second black dot on the faces of the twenty men and two more on the Wizard, after which he slipped the bottle into her pocket.

At length the ball came to an end, and then the king ordered all the doors to be shut, and search made for a man with two black dots on his cheek. The chamberlain went among the guests, and soon found such a man, but just as he was going to arrest him and bring him before the king his eye fell on another with the same mark, and another, and another, till he had counted twenty— besides the Wise Man—on whose face were found spots.

Not knowing what to do, the chamberlain hurried back with his tale to the king, who immediately sent for the Wise Man, and then for his daughter.

'The thief must have stolen your bottle,' said the king to the Wizard.

'No, my lord, it is here,' answered the Wise Man, holding it out.

'Then he must have got yours,' he cried, turning to his daughter.

'Indeed, father, it is safe in my pocket,' replied she, taking it out as she spoke; and they all three looked at each other and remained silent.

'Well,' said the king at last, 'the man who has done this is cleverer than most men, and if he will make himself known to me he shall marry the princess and govern half my kingdom while I am alive, and the whole of it when I am dead. Go and announce this in the ballroom,' he added to an attendant, 'and bring the fellow hither.'

So the attendant went into the ballroom and did as the king had bidden him, when, to his surprise, not one man, but twenty, stepped forward, all with black dots on their faces.

'I am the person you want,' they all exclaimed at once, and the attendant, as much bewildered as the chamberlain had been, desired them to follow him into the king's presence.

But the question was too difficult for the king to decide, so he called together his council. For hours they talked, but to no purpose, and in the end they hit upon a plan which they might just as well have thought of at the beginning.

And this was the plan. A child was to be brought to the palace, and next the king's daughter would give her an apple. Then the child was to take the apple and be led into a room where the twenty men with the black dots were sitting in a ring. And to whomsoever the child gave the apple, that man should marry the king's daughter.

'Of course,' said the king, 'it may not be the right man, after all, but then again it *may* be. Anyhow, it is the best we can do.'

The princess herself led the child into the room where the twenty men were now seated. She stood in the centre of the ring for a moment, looking at one man after another, and then held out the apple to the Shifty Lad, who was twisting a shaving of wood round his finger, and had the mouthpiece of a bagpipe hanging from his neck.

'You ought not to have anything which the others have not got,' said the chamberlain, who had accompanied the princess; and he bade the child stand outside for a minute, while he took away the shaving and the mouthpiece, and made the Shifty Lad change his place. Then he called the child in, but the little girl knew him again, and went straight up to him with the apple.

'This is the man whom the child has twice chosen,' said the chamberlain, signing to the Shifty Lad to kneel before the king. 'It was all quite fair; we tried it twice over.'

In this way the Shifty Lad won the king's daughter, and they were married the next day.

A few days later the bride and bridegroom were taking a walk together, and the path led down to the river, and over the river was a bridge.

'And what bridge may this be?' asked the Shifty Lad; and the princess told him that this was the bridge of Dublin.

'Is it indeed?' cried he. 'Well, now, many is the time that my mother has said, when I played her a trick, that my end would be that I should hang on the bridge of Dublin.'

'Oh, if you want to fulfil her prophecies,' laughed the princess, 'you have only to let me tie my handkerchief round your ankle, and I will hold you as you hang over the wall of the bridge.'

'That would be fine fun,' said he; 'but you are not strong enough to hold me up.'

'Oh, yes, I am,' said the princess; 'just try.' So at last he let her bind the handkerchief round his ankle and hang him over the wall, and they both laughed and jested at the strength of the princess.

'Now pull me up again,' called he; but as he spoke a great cry arose that the palace was burning. The princess turned round with a start, and let go her handkerchief, and the Shifty Lad fell, and struck his head on a stone, and died in an instant.

So his mother's prophecy had come true, after all.

West Highland Tales.

16

The False Prince and the True

The king had just awakened from his midday sleep, for it was summer, and everyone rose early and rested from twelve to three, as they do in hot countries. He had dressed himself in cool white clothes, and was passing through the hall on his way to the council chamber, when a number of young nobles suddenly appeared before him, and one amongst them stepped forward and spoke.

'Sire, this morning we were all playing tennis in the court, the prince and this gentleman with the rest, when there broke out some dispute about the game. The prince lost his temper, and said many insulting things to the other, who was playing against him, till at length the gentleman whom you see there struck him violently in the face, so that the blood ran from his mouth and nose. We were all so horrified at the sight, that we should most likely have killed the man then and there, for daring to lay hands on the prince, had not his grandfather the duke stepped between and commanded us to lay the affair before you.'

The king had listened attentively to the story, and when it was ended he said:

'I suppose the prince had no arms with him, or else he would have used them?'

'Yes, sire, he had arms; he always carries a dagger in his belt. But when he saw the blood pouring from his face, he went to a corner of the court and began to cry, which was the strangest thing of all.'

On hearing this the king walked to the window and stood for a few minutes with his back to the room, where the company of young men remained silent. Then he came back, his face white and stern.

'I tell you,' he said, 'and it is the solemn truth, that I would rather you had told me that the prince was dead, though he is my only son, than know that he would suffer such an injury without attempting to avenge it. As for the gentleman who struck him, he will be brought before my judges, and will plead his own cause, but I hardly think he can escape death, after having assaulted the heir to the crown.'

The young man raised his head as if to reply, but the king would not listen, and commanded his guards to put him under arrest, adding, however, that if the prisoner wished to visit any part of the city, he was at liberty to do so properly guarded, and in fifteen days he would be brought to trial before the highest judges in the land.

The young man left the king's presence, surrounded by soldiers, and accompanied by many of his friends, for he was a great favourite. By their advice he spent the fourteen days that remained to him going about to seek counsel from wise men of all sorts, as to how he might escape death, but no one could help him, for none could find any excuse for the blow he had given to the prince.

The fourteenth night had come, and in despair the prisoner went out to take his last walk through the city. He wandered on hardly knowing where he went, and his face was so white and desperate that none of his companions dared speak to him. The sad little procession had passed some hours in this manner, when, near the gate of a monastery, an old woman appeared round a corner, and suddenly stood before the young man. She was bent almost double, and was so wizened and wrinkled that she looked at least ninety; only her eyes were bright and quick as those of a girl.

'Sir,' she said, 'I know all that has happened to you, and how you are seeking if in any wise you can save your life. But there is none that can answer that question save only I myself, if you will promise to do all I ask.'

At her words the prisoner felt as if a load had all at once been rolled off him.

'Oh, save me, and I will do anything!' he cried. 'It is so hard to leave the world and go out into the darkness.'

'You will not need to do that,' answered the old woman, 'you have only got to marry me, and you will soon be free.'

'Marry you?' exclaimed he, 'but—but—I am not yet twenty, and you —why, you must be a hundred at least! Oh, no, it is quite impossible.'

He spoke without thinking, but the flash of anger which darted from her eyes made him feel uncomfortable. However, all she said was:

'As you like; since you reject me, let the crows have you,' and hurried away down the street.

Left to himself, the full horror of his coming death rushed upon the young man, and he understood that he had thrown away his sole chance of life. Well, if he must, he must, he said to himself, and began to run as fast as he could after the old crone, who by this time could scarcely be seen, even in the moonlight. Who would have believed a woman past ninety could walk with such speed? It seemed more like flying! But at length, breathless and exhausted, he reached her side, and gasped out:

'Madam, pardon me for my hasty words just now; I was wrong, and will thankfully accept the offer you made me.'

'Ah, I thought you would come to your senses,' answered she, in rather an odd voice. 'We have no time to lose—follow me at once,' and they went on silently and swiftly till they stopped at the door of a small house in which the priest lived. Before him the old woman bade the prisoner swear that she should be his wife, and this he did in the presence of witnesses. Then, begging the priest and the guards to leave them alone for a little, she told the young man what he was to do, when the next morning he was brought before the king and the judges.

The hall was full to overflowing when the prisoner entered it, and all marvelled at the brightness of his face. The king inquired if he had any excuse to plead for the high treason he had committed by striking the heir to the throne, and, if so, to be quick in setting it forth. With a low bow the youth made answer in a clear voice:

'O my lord and gracious king, and you, nobles and wise men of the land, I leave my cause without fear in your hands, knowing that you will listen and judge rightly, and that you will suffer me to speak to the end, before you give judgment.

'For four years, you, O king, had been married to the queen and yet had no children, which grieved you greatly. The queen saw this, and likewise that your love was going from her, and thought night and day of some plan that might put an end to this evil. At length, when you were away fighting in distant countries, she decided what she would do, and adopted in secret the baby of a poor quarryman, sending a messenger to tell you that you had a son. No one suspected the truth except a priest to whom the queen confessed the truth, and in a few weeks she fell ill and died, leaving the baby to be brought up as became a prince. And now, if your highness will permit me, I will speak of myself.'

'What you have already told me,' answered the king, 'is so strange that I cannot imagine what more there is to tell, but go on with your story.'

'One day, shortly after the death of the queen,' continued the young man, 'your highness was hunting, and outstripped all your attendants while chasing the deer. You were in a part of the country which you did not know, so seeing an orchard all pink and white with apple-blossoms, and a girl tossing a ball in one corner, you went up to her to ask your way. But when she turned to answer you, you were so struck with her beauty that all else fled from your mind. Again and again you rode back to see her, and at length persuaded her to marry you. She only thought you a poor knight, and agreed that as you wished it, the marriage should be kept secret.

'After the ceremony you gave her three rings and a charm with a cross on it, and then put her in a cottage in the forest, thinking to hide the matter securely.

'For some months you visited the cottage every week; but a rebellion broke out in a distant part of the kingdom, and called for your presence. When next you rode up to the cottage, it was empty, and none could inform you whither your bride had gone. That, sire, I can now tell you,' and the young man paused and looked at the king, who coloured deeply. 'She went back to her father the old duke, once your chamberlain, and the cross on her breast revealed at once who you were. Fierce was his anger when he heard his daughter's tale, and he vowed that he would hide her safely from you, till the day when you would claim her publicly as your queen.

'By and bye I was born, and was brought up by my grandfather in one of his great houses. Here are the rings you gave to my mother, and here is the cross, and these will prove if I am your son or not.'

19

As he spoke the young man laid the jewels at the feet of the king, and the nobles and the judges pressed round to examine them. The king alone did not move from his seat, for he had forgotten the hall of justice and all about him, and saw only the apple-orchard, as it was twenty years ago, and the beautiful girl playing at ball. A sudden silence round him made him look up, and he found the eyes of the assembly fixed on him.

'It is true; it is he who is my son, and not the other,' he said with an effort, 'and let every man present swear to acknowledge him as king, after my death.'

Therefore one by one they all knelt before him and took the oath, and a message was sent to the false prince, forbidding him ever again to appear at court, though a handsome pension was granted him.

At last the ceremony was over, and the king, signing to his newly found son to follow him, rose and went into another room.

'Tell me how you knew all that,' he said, throwing himself into a carved chair filled with crimson cushions, and the prince told of his meeting with the old woman who had brought him the jewels from his mother, and how he had sworn before a priest to marry her, though he did not want to do it, on account of the difference in their ages, and besides, he would rather receive a bride chosen by the king himself. But the king frowned, and answered sharply:

'You swore to marry her if she saved your life, and, come what may, you must fulfil your promise.' Then, striking a silver shield that hung close by, he said to the equerry who appeared immediately:

'Go and seek the priest who lives near the door of the prison, and ask him where you can find the old woman who visited him last night; and when you have found her, bring her to the palace.'

It took some time to discover the whereabouts of the old woman, but at length it was accomplished, and when she arrived at the palace with the equerry, she was received with royal honours, as became the bride of the prince. The guards looked at each other with astonished eyes, as the wizened creature, bowed with age, passed between their lines; but they were more amazed still at the lightness of her step as she skipped up the steps to the great door before which the king was standing, with the prince at his side. If they both felt a shock at the appearance of the aged lady they did not show it, and the king, with a grave bow, took her hand, and led her to the chapel, where a bishop was waiting to perform the marriage ceremony.

For the next few weeks little was seen of the prince, who spent all his days in hunting, and trying to forget the old wife at home. As for the princess, no one troubled himself about her, and she passed the days alone in her apartments, for she had absolutely declined the services of the ladies-in-waiting whom the king had appointed for her.

One night the prince returned after a longer chase than usual, and he was so tired that he went up straight to bed. Suddenly he was awakened by a strange noise in the room, and suspecting that a robber might have stolen in, he jumped out of bed, and seized his sword, which lay ready to his hand. Then he perceived that the noise proceeded from the next room, which belonged to the princess, and was lighted by a burning torch. Creeping softly to the door, he peeped through it, and beheld her lying quietly, with a crown of gold and pearls upon her head, her wrinkles all gone, and her face, which was whiter than the snow, as fresh as that of a girl of fourteen. Could that really be his wife—that beautiful, beautiful creature?

The prince was still gazing in surprise when the lady opened her eyes and smiled at him.

'Yes, I really am your wife,' she said, as if she had guessed his thoughts, 'and the enchantment is ended. Now I must tell you who I am, and what befell to cause me to take the shape of an old woman.

'The king of Granada is my father, and I was born in the palace which overlooks the plain of the Vega. I was only a few months old when a wicked fairy, who had a spite against my parents, cast a spell over me, bending my back and wrinkling my skin till I looked as if I was a hundred years old, and making me such an object of disgust to everyone, that at length the king ordered my nurse to take my away from the palace. She was the only person who cared about me, and we lived together in this city on a small pension allowed me by the king.

'When I was about three an old man arrived at our house, and begged my nurse to let him come in and rest, as he could walk no longer. She saw that he was very ill, so put him to bed and took such care of him that by and bye he was as strong as ever. In gratitude for her goodness to him, he told her that he was a wizard and could give her anything she chose to ask for, except life or death, so she answered that what she longed for most in the world was that my wrinkled skin should disappear, and that I should regain the beauty with which I was born. To this he replied that as my misfortune resulted from a spell, this was rather difficult, but he would do his best, and at any rate he could promise that before my fifteenth birthday I should be freed from the enchantment if I could get a man who would swear to marry me as I was.

'As you may suppose, this was not easy, as my ugliness was such that no one would look at me a second time. My nurse and I were almost in despair, as my fifteenth birthday was drawing near, and I had never so much as spoken to a man. At last we received a visit from the wizard, who told us what had happened at court, and your story, bidding me to put myself in your way when you had lost all hope, and offer to save you if you would consent to marry me.

'That is my history, and now you must beg the king to send messengers at once to Granada, to inform my father of our marriage, and I think,' she added with a smile, 'that he will not refuse us his blessing.'

Adapted from the Portuguese.

The Jogi's Punishment

Once upon a time there came to the ancient city of Rahmatabad a jogi[FN#1: A Hindu holy man.] of holy appearance, who took up his abode under a tree outside the city, where he would sit for days at a time fasting from food and drink, motionless except for the fingers that turned restlessly his string of beads. The fame of such holiness as this soon spread, and daily the citizens would flock to see him, eager to get his blessing, to watch his devotions, or to hear his teaching, if he were in the mood to speak. Very soon the rajah himself heard of the jogi, and began regularly to visit him to seek his counsel and to ask his prayers that a son might be vouchsafed to him. Days passed by, and at last the rajah became so possessed with the thought of the holy man that he determined if possible to get him all to himself. So he built in the neighbourhood a little shrine, with a room or two added to it, and a small courtyard closely walled up; and, when all was ready, besought the jogi to occupy it, and to receive no other visitors except himself and his queen and such pupils as the jogi might choose, who would hand down his teaching. To this the jogi consented; and thus he lived for some time upon the king's bounty, whilst the fame of his godliness grew day by day.

Now, although the rajah of Rahmatabad had no son, he possessed a daughter, who as she grew up became the most beautiful creature that eye ever rested upon. Her father had long before betrothed her to the son of the neighbouring rajah of Dilaram, but as yet she had not been married to him, and lived the quiet life proper to a maiden of her beauty and position. The princess had of course heard of the holy man and of his miracles and his fasting, and she was filled with curiosity to see and to speak to him; but this was difficult, since she was not allowed to go out except into the palace grounds, and then was always closely guarded. However, at length she found an opportunity, and made her way one evening alone to the hermit's shrine.

Unhappily, the hermit was not really as holy as he seemed; for no sooner did he see the princess than he fell in love with her wonderful beauty, and began to plot in his heart how he could win her for his wife. But the maiden was not only beautiful, she was also shrewd; and as soon as she read in the glance of the jogi the love that filled his soul, she sprang to her feet, and, gathering her veil about her, ran from the place as fast as she could. The jogi tried to follow, but he was no match for her; so, beside himself with rage at finding that he could not overtake her, he flung at her a lance, which wounded her in the leg. The brave princess stooped for a second to pluck the lance out of the wound, and then ran on until she found herself safe at home again. There she bathed and bound up the wound secretly, and told no one how naughty she had been, for she knew that her father would punish her severely.

Next day, when the king went to visit the jogi, the holy man would neither speak to nor look at him.

'What is the matter?' asked the king. 'Won't you speak to me to-day?'

'I have nothing to say that you would care to hear,' answered the jogi.

'Why?' said the king. 'Surely you know that I value all that you say, whatever it may be.'

But still the jogi sat with his face turned away, and the more the king pressed him the more silent and mysterious he became. At last, after much persuasion, he said:

'Let me tell you, then, that there is in this city a creature which, if you do not put an end to it, will kill every single person in the place.'

The king, who was easily frightened, grew pale.

'What?' he gasped—'what is this dreadful thing? How am I to know it and to catch it? Only counsel me and help me, and I will do all that you advise.'

'Ah!' replied the jogi, 'it is indeed dreadful. It is in the shape of a beautiful girl, but it is really an evil spirit. Last evening it came to visit me, and when I looked upon it its beauty faded into hideousness, its teeth became horrible fangs, its eyes glared like coals of fire, great claws sprang from its slender fingers, and were I not what I am it might have consumed me.'

The king could hardly speak from alarm, but at last he said:

'How am I to distinguish this awful thing when I see it?'

'Search,' said the jogi, 'for a lovely girl with a lance wound in her leg, and when she is found secure her safely and come and tell me, and I will advise you what to do next.'

Away hurried the king, and soon set all his soldiers scouring the country for a girl with a lance wound in her left. For two days the search went on, and then it was somehow discovered that the only person with a lance wound in the leg was the princess herself. The king, greatly agitated, went off to tell the jogi, and to assure him that there must be some mistake. But of course the jogi was prepared for this, and had his answer ready.

'She is not really your daughter, who was stolen away at her birth, but an evil spirit that has taken her form,' said he solemnly. 'You can do what you like, but if you don't take my advice she will kill you all.' And so solemn he appeared, and so unshaken in his confidence, that the king's wisdom was blinded, and he declared that he would do whatever the jogi advised, and believe whatever he said. So the jogi directed him to send him secretly two carpenters; and when they arrived he set them to make a great chest, so cunningly jointed and put together that neither air nor water could penetrate it. There and then the chest was made, and, when it was ready, the jogi bade the king to bring the princess by night; and they two thrust the poor little maiden into the chest and fastened it down with long nails, and between them carried it to the river and pushed it out into the stream.

As soon as the jogi got back from this deed he called two of his pupils, and pretended that it had been revealed to him that there should be found floating on the river a chest with something of great price within it; and he bade them go and watch for it at such a place far down the stream, and when the chest came slowly along, bobbing and turning in the tide, they were to seize it and secretly and swiftly bring it to him, for he was now determined to put the princess to death himself. The pupils set off at once, wondering at the strangeness of their errand, and still more at the holiness of the jogi to whom such secrets were revealed.

It happened that, as the next morning was dawning, the gallant young prince of Dilaram was hunting by the banks of the river, with a great following of wazirs, attendants, and huntsmen, and as he rode he saw floating on the river a large chest, which came slowly along, bobbing and turning in the tide. Raising himself in his saddle, he gave an order, and half a dozen men plunged into the water and drew the chest out on to the river bank, where every one crowded around to see what it could contain. The prince was certainly not the least curious among them; but he was a cautious young man, and, as he prepared to open the chest himself, he bade all but a few stand back, and these few to draw their swords, so as to be prepared in case the chest should hold some evil beast, or djinn, or giant. When all were ready and expectant, the prince with his dagger forced open the lid and flung it back, and there lay, living and breathing, the most lovely maiden he had ever seen in his life.

Although she was half stifled from her confinement in the chest, the princess speedily revived, and, when she was able to sit up, the prince began to question her as to who she was and how she came to be shut up in the chest and set afloat upon the water; and she, blushing and trembling to find herself in the presence of so many strangers, told him that she was the princess of Rahmatabad, and that she had been put into the chest by her own father. When he on his part told her that he was the prince of Dilaram, the astonishment of the young people was unbounded to find that they, who had been betrothed without ever having seen one another, should have actually met for the first time in such strange circumstances. In fact, the prince was so moved by her beauty and modest ways that he called up his wazirs and demanded to be married at once to this lovely lady who had so completely won his heart. And married they were then and there upon the river bank, and went home to the prince's palace, where, when the story was told, they were welcomed by the old rajah, the prince's father, and the remainder of the day was given over to feasting and rejoicing. But when the banquet was over, the bride told her husband that now, on the threshold of their married life, she had more to relate of her adventures than he had given her the opportunity to tell as yet; and then, without hiding anything, she informed him of all that happened to her from the time she had stolen out to visit the wicked jogi.

In the morning the prince called his chief wazir and ordered him to shut up in the chest in which the princess had been found a great monkey that lived chained up in the palace, and to take the chest back to the river and set it afloat once more and watch what became of it. So the monkey was caught and put into the chest, and some of the prince's servants took it down to the river and pushed it off into the water. Then they followed secretly a long way off to see what became of it.

Meanwhile the jogi's two pupils watched and watched for the chest until they were nearly tired of watching, and were beginning to wonder whether the jogi was right after all, when on the second day they spied the great chest coming floating on the river, slowly bobbing and turning in the tide; and instantly a great joy and exultation seized them, for they thought that here indeed was further proof of the wonderful wisdom of their master. With some difficulty they secured the chest, and carried it back as swiftly and secretly as possible to the jogi's house. As soon as they brought in the chest, the jogi, who had been getting very cross and impatient, told them to put it down, and to go outside whilst he opened the magic chest.

'And even if you hear cries and sounds, however alarming, you must on no account enter,' said the jogi, walking over to a closet where lay the silken cord that was to strangle the princess.

And the two pupils did as they were told, and went outside and shut close all the doors. Presently they heard a great outcry within and the jogi's voice crying aloud for help; but they dared not enter, for had they not been told that whatever the noise, they must not come in? So they sat outside, waiting and wondering; and at last all grew still and quiet, and remained so for such a long time that they determined to enter and see if all was well. No sooner had they opened the door leading into the courtyard than they were nearly upset by a huge monkey that came leaping straight to the doorway and escaped past them into the open fields. Then they stepped into the room, and there they saw the jogi's body lying torn to pieces on the threshold of his dwelling!

Very soon the story spread, as stories will, and reached the ears of the princess and her husband, and when she knew that her enemy was dead she made her peace with her father.

From Major Campbell, Feroshepore.

26

The Heart of a Monkey

A long time ago a little town made up of a collection of low huts stood in a tiny green valley at the foot of a cliff. Of course the people had taken great care to build their houses out of reach of the highest tide which might be driven on shore by a west wind, but on the very edge of the town there had sprung up a tree so large that half its boughs hung over the huts and the other half over the deep sea right under the cliff, where sharks loved to come and splash in the clear water. The branches of the tree itself were laden with fruit, and every day at sunrise a big grey monkey might have been seen sitting in the topmost branches having his breakfast, and chattering to himself with delight.

After he had eaten all the fruit on the town side of the tree the monkey swung himself along the branches to the part which hung over the water. While he was looking out for a nice shady place where he might perch comfortably he noticed a shark watching him from below with greedy eyes.

'Can I do anything for you, my friend?' asked the monkey politely.

'Oh! if you only would thrown me down some of those delicious things, I should be so grateful,' answered the shark. 'After you have lived on fish for fifty years you begin to feel you would like a change. And I am so very, very tired of the taste of salt.'

'Well, I don't like salt myself,' said the monkey; 'so if you will open your mouth I will throw this beautiful juicy kuyu into it,' and, as he spoke, he pulled one off the branch just over his head. But it was not so easy to hit the shark's mouth as he supposed, even when the creature had turned on his back, and the first kuyu only struck one of his teeth and rolled into the water. However, the second time the monkey had better luck, and the fruit fell right in.

'Ah, how good!' cried the shark. 'Send me another, please.' And the monkey grew tired of picking the kuyu long before the shark was tired of eating them.

'It is getting late, and I must be going home to my children,' he said, at length, 'but if you are here at the same time to-morrow I will give you another treat.'

'Thank you, thank you,' said the shark, showing all his great ugly teeth as he grinned with delight; 'you can't guess how happy you have made me,' and he swam away into the shadow, hoping to sleep away the time till the monkey came again.

For weeks the monkey and the shark breakfasted together, and it was a wonder that the tree had any fruit left for them. They became fast friends, and told each other about their homes and their children, and how to teach them all they ought to know. By and bye the monkey became rather discontented with his green house in a grove of palms beyond the town, and longed to see the strange things under the sea which he had heard of from the shark. The shark perceived this very clearly, and described greater marvels, and the monkey as he listened grew more and more gloomy.

Matters were in this state when one day the shark said: 'I really hardly know how to thank you for all your kindness to me during these weeks. Here I have nothing of my own to offer you, but if you would only consent to come home with me, how gladly would I give you anything that might happen to take your fancy.'

'I should like nothing better,' cried the monkey, his teeth chattering, as they always did when he was pleased. 'But how could I get there? Not by water. Ugh! It makes me ill to think of it!'

'Oh! don't let that trouble you,' replied the shark, 'you have only to sit on my back and I will undertake that not a drop of water shall touch you.'

So it was arranged, and directly after breakfast next morning the shark swam close up under the tree and the monkey dropped neatly on his back, without even a splash. After a few minutes—for at first he felt a little frightened at his strange position—the monkey began to enjoy himself vastly, and asked the shark a thousand questions about the fish and the sea-weeds and the oddly-shaped things that floated past them, and as the shark always gave him some sort of answer, the monkey never guessed that many of the objects they saw were as new to his guide as to himself.

The sun had risen and set six times when the shark suddenly said, 'My friend, we have now performed half our journey, and it is time that I should tell you something.'

'What is it?' asked the monkey. 'Nothing unpleasant, I hope, for you sound rather grave?'

'Oh, no! Nothing at all. It is only that shortly before we left I heard that the sultan of my country is very ill, and that the only thing to cure him is a monkey's heart.'

'Poor man, I am very sorry for him,' replied the monkey; 'but you were unwise not to tell me till we had started.'

'What do you mean?' asked the shark; but the monkey, who now understood the whole plot, did not answer at once, for he was considering what he should say.

'Why are you so silent?' inquired the shark again.

'I was thinking what a pity it was you did not tell me while I was still on land, and then I would have brought my heart with me.'

'Your heart! Why isn't your heart here?' said the shark, with a puzzled expression.

'Oh, no! Of course not. Is it possible you don't know that when we leave home we always hang up our hearts on trees, to prevent their being troublesome? However, perhaps you won't believe that, and will just think I have invented it because I am afraid, so let us go on to your country as fast as we can, and when we arrive you can look for my heart, and if you find it you can kill me.'

The monkey spoke in such a calm, indifferent way that the shark was quite deceived, and began to wish he had not been in such a hurry.

'But there is no use going on if your heart is not with you,' he said at last. 'We had better turn back to the town, and then you can fetch it.'

Of course, this was just what the monkey wanted, but he was careful not to seem too pleased.

'Well, I don't know,' he remarked carelessly, 'it is such a long way; but you may be right.'

'I am sure I am,' answered the shark, 'and I will swim as quickly as I can,' and so he did, and in three days they caught sight of the kuyu tree hanging over the water.

With a sigh of relief the monkey caught hold of the nearest branch and swung himself up.

'Wait for me here,' he called out to the shark. 'I am so hungry I must have a little breakfast, and then I will go and look for my heart,' and he went further and further into the branches so that the shark could not see him. Then he curled himself up and went to sleep.

'Are you there?' cried the shark, who was soon tired of swimming about under the cliff, and was in haste to be gone.

The monkey awoke with a start, but did not answer.

'Are you there?' called the shark again, louder than before, and in a very cross voice.

'Oh, yes. I am here,' replied the monkey; 'but I wish you had not wakened me up. I was having such a nice nap.'

'Have you got it?' asked the shark. 'It is time we were going.'

'Going where?' inquired the monkey.

'Why, to my country, of course, with your heart. You *can't* have forgotten!'

'My dear friend,' answered the monkey, with a chuckle, 'I think you must be going a little mad. Do you take me for a washerman's donkey?'

'Don't talk nonsense,' exclaimed the shark, who did not like being laughed at. 'What do you mean about a washerman's donkey? And I wish you would be quick, or we may be too late to save the sultan.'

'Did you really never hear of the washerman's donkey?' asked the monkey, who was enjoying himself immensely. 'Why, he is the beast who has no heart. And as I am not feeling very well, and am afraid to start while the sun is so high lest I should get a sunstroke, if you like, I will come a little nearer and tell you his story.'

'Very well,' said the shark sulkily, 'if you won't come, I suppose I may as well listen to that as do nothing.'

So the monkey began.

'A washerman once lived in the great forest on the other side of the town, and he had a donkey to keep him company and to carry him wherever he wanted to go. For a time they got on very well, but by and bye the donkey grew lazy and ungrateful for her master's kindness, and ran away several miles into the heart of the forest, where she did nothing but eat and eat and eat, till she grew so fat she could hardly move.

'One day as she was tasting quite a new kind of grass and wondering if it was as good as what she had had for dinner the day before, a hare happened to pass by.

'"Well, that is a fat creature," thought she, and turned out of her path to tell the news to a lion who was a friend of hers. Now the lion had been very ill, and was not strong enough to go hunting for himself, and when the hare came and told him that a very fat donkey was to be found only a few hundred yards off, tears of disappointment and weakness filled his eyes.

'"What is the good of telling me that?" he asked, in a weepy voice; "you know I cannot even walk as far as that palm."

'"Never mind," answered the hare briskly. "If you can't go to your dinner your dinner shall come to you," and nodding a farewell to the lion she went back to the donkey.

'"Good morning," said she, bowing politely to the donkey, who lifted her head in surprise. "Excuse my interrupting you, but I have come on very important business."

'"Indeed," answered the donkey, "it is most kind of you to take the trouble. May I inquire what the business is?"

30

'"Certainly," replied the hare. "It is my friend the lion who has heard so much of your charms and good qualities that he has sent me to beg that you will give him your paw in marriage. He regrets deeply that he is unable to make the request in person, but he has been ill and is too weak to move."

'"Poor fellow! How sad!" said the donkey. "But you must tell him that I feel honoured by his proposal, and will gladly consent to be Queen of the Beasts."

'"Will you not come and tell him so yourself?" asked the hare.

'Side by side they went down the road which led to the lion's house. It took a long while, for the donkey was so fat with eating she could only walk very slowly, and the hare, who could have run the distance in about five minutes, was obliged to creep along till she almost dropped with fatigue at not being able to go at her own pace. When at last they arrived the lion was sitting up at the entrance, looking very pale and thin. The donkey suddenly grew shy and hung her head, but the lion put on his best manners and invited both his visitors to come in and make themselves comfortable.

'Very soon the hare got up and said, "Well, as I have another engagement I will leave you to make acquaintance with your future husband," and winking at the lion she bounded away.

'The donkey expected that as soon as they were left alone the lion would begin to speak of their marriage, and where they should live, but as he said nothing she looked up. To her surprise and terror she saw him crouching in the corner, his eyes glaring with a red light, and with a loud roar he sprang towards her. But in that moment the donkey had had time to prepare herself, and jumping on one side dealt the lion such a hard kick that he shrieked with the pain. Again and again he struck at her with his claws, but the donkey could bite too, as well as the lion, who was very weak after his illness, and at last a well-planted kick knocked him right over, and he rolled on the floor, groaning with pain. The donkey did not wait for him to get up, but ran away as fast as she could and was lost in the forest.

'Now the hare, who knew quite well what would happen, had not gone to do her business, but hid herself in some bushes behind the cave, where she could hear quite clearly the sounds of the battle. When all was quiet again she crept gently out, and stole round the corner.

'"Well, lion, have you killed her?" asked she, running swiftly up the path.

'"Killed her, indeed!" answered the lion sulkily, "it is she who has nearly killed me. I never knew a donkey could kick like that, though I took care she should carry away the marks of my claws."

'"Dear me! Fancy such a great fat creature being able to fight!" cried the hare. "But don't vex yourself. Just lie still, and your wounds will soon heal," and she bade her friend, good bye, and returned to her family.

'Two or three weeks passed, and only bare places on the donkey's back showed where the lion's claws had been, while, on his side, the lion had recovered from his illness and was now as strong as ever. He was beginning to think that it was almost time for him to begin hunting again, when one morning a rustle was heard in the creepers outside, and the hare's head peeped through.

'"Ah! there is no need to ask how you are," she said. "Still you mustn't overtire yourself, you know. Shall I go and bring you your dinner?"

'"If you will bring me that donkey I will tear it in two," cried the lion savagely, and the hare laughed and nodded and went on her errand.

'This time the donkey was much further than before, and it took longer to find her. At last the hare caught sight of four hoofs in the air, and ran towards them. The donkey was lying on a soft cool bed of moss near a stream, rolling herself backwards and forwards from pleasure.

'"Good morning," said the hare politely, and the donkey got slowly on to her legs, and looked to see who her visitor could be.

'"Oh, it is you, is it?" she exclaimed. "Come and have a chat. What news have you got?"

'"I mustn't stay," answered the hare; "but I promised the lion to beg you to pay him a visit, as he is not well enough to call on you."

'"Well, I don't know," replied the donkey gloomily, "the last time we went he scratched me very badly, and really I was quite afraid."

'"He was only trying to kiss you," said the hare, "and you bit him, and of course that made him cross."

'"If I were sure of that," hesitated the donkey.

'"Oh, you may be quite sure," laughed the hare. "I have a large acquaintance among lions. But let us be quick," and rather unwillingly the donkey set out.

'The lion saw them coming and hid himself behind a large tree. As the donkey went past, followed by the hare, he sprang out, and with one blow of his paw stretched the poor foolish creature dead before him.

'"Take this meat and skin it and roast it," he said to the hare; "but my appetite is not so good as it was, and the only part I want for myself is the heart. The rest you can either eat yourself or give away to your friends."

'"Thank you," replied the hare, balancing the donkey on her back as well as she was able, and though the legs trailed along the ground she managed to drag it to an open space some distance off, where she made a fire and roasted it. As soon as it was cooked the hare took out the heart and had just finished eating it when the lion, who was tired of waiting, came up.

'"I am hungry," said he. "Bring me the creature's heart; it is just what I want for supper."

'"But there is no heart," answered the hare, looking up at the lion with a puzzled face.

'"What nonsense!" said the lion. "As if every beast had not got a heart. What do you mean?"

'"This is a washerman's donkey," replied the hare gravely.

'"Well, and suppose it is?"

'"Oh, fie!" exclaimed the hare. "You, a lion and a grown-up person, and ask questions like that. If the donkey had had a heart would she be here now? The first time she came she knew you were trying to kill her, and ran away. Yet she came back a second time. Well, if she had had a heart would she have come back a second time? Now would she?"

'And the lion answered slowly, "No, she would not."

'So you think I am a washerman's donkey?' said the monkey to the shark, when the story was ended. 'You are wrong; I am not. And as the sun is getting low in the sky, it is time for you to begin your homeward journey. You will have a nice cool voyage, and I hope you will find the sultan better. Farewell!' And the monkey disappeared among the green branches, and was gone.

From 'Swahili Tales,' by Edward Steere, LL.D.

The Fairy Nurse

There was once a little farmer and his wife living near Coolgarrow. They had three children, and my story happened while the youngest was a baby. The wife was a good wife enough, but her mind was all on her family and her farm, and she hardly ever went to her knees without falling asleep, and she thought the time spent in the chapel was twice as long as it need be. So, friends, she let her man and her two children go before her one day to Mass, while she called to consult a fairy man about a disorder one of her cows had. She was late at the chapel, and was sorry all the day after, for her husband was in grief about it, and she was very fond of him.

Late that night he was wakened up by the cries of his children calling out 'Mother! Mother!' When he sat up and rubbed his eyes, there was no wife by his side, and when he asked the little ones what was become of their mother, they said they saw the room full of nice little men and women, dressed in white and red and green, and their mother in the middle of them, going out by the door as if she was walking in her sleep. Out he ran, and searched everywhere round the house but, neither tale nor tidings did he get of her for many a day.

Well, the poor man was miserable enough, for he was as fond of his woman as she was of him. It used to bring the salt tears down his cheeks to see his poor children neglected and dirty, as they often were, and they'd be bad enough only for a kind neighbour that used to look in whenever she could spare time. The infant was away with a nurse.

About six weeks after—just as he was going out to his work one morning—a neighbour, that used to mind women when they were ill, came up to him, and kept step by step with him to the field, and this is what she told him.

'Just as I was falling asleep last night, I heard a horse's tramp on the grass and a knock at the door, and there, when I came out, was a fine-looking dark man, mounted on a black horse, and he told me to get ready in all haste, for a lady was in great want of me. As soon as I put on my cloak and things, he took me by the hand, and I was sitting behind him before I felt myself stirring. "Where are we going, sir?" says I. "You'll soon know," says he; and he drew his fingers across my eyes, and not a ray could I see. I kept a tight grip of him, and I little knew whether he was going backwards or forwards, or how long we were about it, till my hand was taken again, and I felt the ground under me. The fingers went the other way across my eyes, and there we were before a castle door, and in we went through a big hall and great rooms all painted in fine green colours, with red and gold bands and ornaments, and the finest carpets and chairs and tables and window curtains, and grand ladies and gentlemen walking about. At last we came to a bedroom, with a beautiful lady in bed, with a fine bouncing boy beside her. The lady clapped her hands, and in came the Dark Man and kissed her and the baby, and praised me, and gave me a bottle of green ointment to rub the child all over.

'Well, the child I rubbed, sure enough; but my right eye began to smart, and I put up my finger and gave it a rub, and then stared, for never in all my life was I so frightened. The beautiful room was a big, rough cave, with water oozing over the edges of the stones and through the clay; and the lady, and the lord, and the child weazened, poverty-bitten creatures—nothing but skin and bone—and the rich dresses were old rags. I didn't let on that I found any difference, and after a bit says the Dark Man, "Go before me to the hall door, and I will be with you in a few moments, and see you safe home." Well, just as I turned into the outside cave, who should I see watching near the door but poor Molly. She looked round all terrified, and says she to me in a whisper, "I'm brought here to nurse the child of the king and queen of the fairies; but there is one chance of saving me. All the court will pass the cross near Templeshambo next Friday night, on a visit to the fairies of Old Ross. If John can catch me by the hand or cloak when I ride by, and has courage not to let go his grip, I'll be safe. Here's the king. Don't open your mouth to answer. I saw what happened with the ointment."

'The Dark Man didn't once cast his eye towards Molly, and he seemed to have no suspicion of me. When we came out I looked about me, and where do you think we were but in the dyke of the Rath of Cromogue. I was on the horse again, which was nothing but a big rag-weed, and I was in dread every minute I'd fall off; but nothing happened till I found myself in my own cabin. The king slipped five guineas into my hand as soon as I was on the ground, and thanked me, and bade me good night. I hope I'll never see his face again. I got into bed, and couldn't sleep for a long time; and when I examined my five guineas this morning, that I left in the table drawer the last thing, I found five withered leaves of oak—bad luck to the giver!'

Well, you may all think the fright, and the joy, and the grief the poor man was in when the woman finished her story. They talked and they talked, but we needn't mind what they said till Friday night came, when both were standing where the mountain road crosses the one going to Ross.

There they stood, looking towards the bridge of Thuar, in the dead of the night, with a little moonlight shining from over Kilachdiarmid. At last she gave a start, and "By this and by that," says she, "here they come, bridles jingling and feathers tossing!" He looked, but could see nothing; and she stood trembling and her eyes wide open, looking down the way to the ford of Ballinacoola. "I see your wife," says she, "riding on the outside just so as to rub against us. We'll walk on quietly, as if we suspected nothing, and when we are passing I'll give you a shove. If you don't do *your* duty then, woe be with you!"

Well, they walked on easy, and the poor hearts beating in both their breasts; and though he could see nothing, he heard a faint jingle and trampling and rustling, and at last he got the push that she promised. He spread out his arms, and there was his wife's waist within them, and he could see her plain; but such a hullabulloo rose as if there was an earthquake, and he found himself surrounded by horrible-looking things, roaring at him and striving to pull his wife away. But he made the sign of the cross and bid them begone in God's name, and held his wife as if it was iron his arms were made of. Bedad, in one moment everything was as silent as the grave, and the poor woman lying in a faint in the arms of her husband and her good neighbour. Well, all in good time she was minding her family and her business again; and I'll go bail, after the fright she got, she spent more time on her knees, and avoided fairy men all the days of the week, and particularly on Sunday.

It is hard to have anything to do with the good people without getting a mark from them. My brave nurse didn't escape no more than another. She was one Thursday at the market of Enniscorthy, when what did she see walking among the tubs of butter but the Dark Man, very hungry-looking, and taking a scoop out of one tub and out of another. 'Oh, sir,' says she, very foolish, 'I hope your lady is well, and the baby.' 'Pretty well, thank you,' says he, rather frightened like. 'How do I look in this new suit?' says he, getting to one side of her. 'I can't see you plain at all, sir,' says she. 'Well, now?' says he, getting round her back to the other side. 'Musha, indeed, sir, your coat looks no better than a withered dock-leaf.' 'Maybe, then,' says he, 'it will be different now,' and he struck the eye next him with a switch. Friends, she never saw a glimmer after with that one till the day of her death.

'Legendary Fictions of the Irish Celts,' by Patrick Kennedy.

A Lost Paradise

In the middle of a great forest there lived a long time ago a charcoal-burner and his wife. They were both young and handsome and strong, and when they got married, they thought work would never fail them. But bad times came, and they grew poorer and poorer, and the nights in which they went hungry to bed became more and more frequent.

Now one evening the king of that country was hunting near the charcoal-burner's hut. As he passed the door, he heard a sound of sobbing, and being a good-natured man he stopped to listen, thinking that perhaps he might be able to give some help.

'Were there ever two people so unhappy!' said a woman's voice. 'Here we are, ready to work like slaves the whole day long, and no work can we get. And it is all because of the curiosity of old mother Eve! If she had only been like me, who never want to know anything, we should all have been as happy as kings to-day, with plenty to eat, and warm clothes to wear. Why—' but at this point a loud knock interrupted her lamentations.

'Who is there?' asked she.

'I!' replied somebody.

'And who is "I"?'

'The king. Let me in.'

Full of surprise the woman jumped up and pulled the bar away from the door. As the king entered, he noticed that there was no furniture in the room at all, not even a chair, so he pretended to be in too great a hurry to see anything around him, and only said 'You must not let me disturb you. I have no time to stay, but you seemed to be in trouble. Tell me; are you very unhappy?'

'Oh, my lord, we can find no work and have eaten nothing for two days!' answered she. 'Nothing remains for us but to die of hunger.'

'No, no, you shan't do that,' cried the king, 'or if you do, it will be your own fault. You shall come with me into my palace, and you will feel as if you were in Paradise, I promise you. In return, I only ask one thing of you, that you shall obey my orders exactly.'

The charcoal-burner and his wife both stared at him for a moment, as if they could hardly believe their ears; and, indeed, it was not to be wondered at! Then they found their tongues, and exclaimed together:

'Oh, yes, yes, my lord! we will do everything you tell us. How could we be so ungrateful as to disobey you, when you are so kind?'

The king smiled, and his eyes twinkled.

'Well, let us start at once,' said he. 'Lock your door, and put the key in your pocket.'

The woman looked as if she thought this was needless, seeing it was quite, quite certain they would never come back. But she dared not say so, and did as the king told her.

After walking through the forest for a couple of miles, they all three reached the palace, and by the king's orders servants led the charcoal-burner and his wife into rooms filled with beautiful things such as they had never even dreamed of. First they bathed in green marble baths where the water looked like the sea, and then they put on silken clothes that felt soft and pleasant. When they were ready, one of the king's special servants entered, and took them into a small hall, where dinner was laid, and this pleased them better than anything else.

They were just about to sit down to the table when the king walked in.

'I hope you have been attended to properly,' said he, 'and that you will enjoy your dinner. My steward will take care you have all you want, and I wish you to do exactly as you please. Oh, by the bye, there is one thing! You notice that soup-tureen in the middle of the table? Well, be careful on no account to lift the lid. If once you take off the cover, there is an end of your good fortune.' Then, bowing to his guests, he left the room.

'Did you hear what he said?' inquired the charcoal-burner in an awe-stricken voice. 'We are to have what we want, and do what we please. Only we must not touch the soup-tureen.'

'No, of course we won't,' answered the wife. 'Why should we wish to? But all the same it is rather odd, and one can't help wondering what is inside.'

For many days life went on like a beautiful dream to the charcoal- burner and his wife. Their beds were so comfortable, they could hardly make up their minds to get up, their clothes were so lovely they could scarcely bring themselves to take them off; their dinners were so good that they found it very difficult to leave off eating. Then outside the palace were gardens filled with rare flowers and fruits and singing birds, or if they desired to go further, a golden coach, painted with wreaths of forget-me-nots and lined with blue satin, awaited their orders. Sometimes it happened that the king came to see them, and he smiled as he glanced at the man, who was getting rosier and plumper each day. But when his eyes rested on the woman, they took on a look which seemed to say 'I knew it,' though this neither the charcoal-burner nor his wife ever noticed.

'Why are you so silent?' asked the man one morning when dinner had passed before his wife had uttered one word. 'A little while ago you used to be chattering all the day long, and now I have almost forgotten the sound of your voice.'

'Oh, nothing; I did not feel inclined to talk, that was all!' She stopped, and added carelessly after a pause, 'Don't you ever wonder what is in that soup-tureen?'

'No, never,' replied the man. 'It is no affair of ours,' and the conversation dropped once more, but as time went on, the woman spoke less and less, and seemed so wretched that her husband grew quite frightened about her. As to her food, she refused one thing after another.

'My dear wife,' said the man at last, 'you really must eat something. What in the world is the matter with you? If you go on like this you will die.'

'I would rather die than not know what is in that tureen,' she burst forth so violently that the husband was quite startled.

'Is that it?' cried he; 'are you making yourself miserable because of that? Why, you know we should be turned out of the palace, and sent away to starve.'

'Oh no, we shouldn't. The king is too good-natured. Of course he didn't mean a little thing like this! Besides, there is no need to lift the lid off altogether. Just raise one corner so that I may peep. We are quite alone: nobody will ever know.'

The man hesitated: it did seem a 'little thing,' and if it was to make his wife contented and happy it was well worth the risk. So he took hold of the handle of the cover and raised it very slowly and carefully, while the woman stooped down to peep. Suddenly she startled back with a scream, for a small mouse had sprung from the inside of the tureen, and had nearly hit her in the eye. Round and round the room it ran, round and round they both ran after it, knocking down chairs and vases in their efforts to catch the mouse and put it back in the tureen. In the middle of all the noise the door opened, and the mouse ran out between the feet of the king. In one instant both the man and his wife were hiding under the table, and to all appearance the room was empty.

'You may as well come out,' said the king, 'and hear what I have to say.'

'I know what it is,' answered the charcoal-burner, hanging his head. The mouse has escaped.'

'A guard of soldiers will take you back to your hut,' said the king. 'Your wife has the key.'

'Weren't they silly?' cried the grandchildren of the charcoal-burners when they heard the story. 'How we wish that we had had the chance! *We* should never have wanted to know what was in the soup-tureen!'

From 'Litterature Orale de l'Auvergne,' par Paul Sebillot.

How Brave Walter Hunted Wolves

A little back from the high road there stands a house which is called 'Hemgard.' Perhaps you remember the two beautiful mountain ash trees by the reddish-brown palings, and the high gate, and the garden with the beautiful barberry bushes which are always the first to become grown in spring, and which in summer are weighed down with their beautiful berries.

Behind the garden there is a hedge with tall aspens which rustle in the morning wind, behind the hedge is a road, behind the road is a wood, and behind the wood the wide world.

But on the other side of the garden there is a lake, and beyond the lake is a village, and all around stretch meadows and fields, now yellow, now green.

In the pretty house, which has white window-frames, a neat porch and clean steps, which are always strewn with finely-cut juniper leaves, Walter's parents live. His brother Frederick, his sister Lotta, old Lena, Jonah, Caro and Bravo, Putte and Murre, and Kuckeliku.

Caro lives in the dog house, Bravo in the stable, Putte with the stableman, Murre a little here and a little there, and Kuckeliku lives in the hen house, that is his kingdom.

Walter is six years old, and he must soon begin to go to school. He cannot read yet, but he can do many other things. He can turn cartwheels, stand on his head, ride see-saw, throw snowballs, play ball, crow like a cock, eat bread and butter and drink sour milk, tear his trousers, wear holes in his elbows, break the crockery in pieces, throw balls through the windowpanes, draw old men on important papers, walk over the flower-beds, eat himself sick with gooseberries, and be well after a whipping. For the rest he has a good heart but a bad memory, and forgets his father's and his mother's admonitions, and so often gets into trouble and meets with adventures, as you shall hear, but first of all I must tell you how brave he was and how he hunted wolves.

Once in the spring, a little before Midsummer, Walter heard that there were a great many wolves in the wood, and that pleased him. He was wonderfully brave when he was in the midst of his companions or at home with his brothers and sister, then he used often to say 'One wolf is nothing, there ought to be at least four.'

When he wrestled with Klas Bogenstrom or Frithiof Waderfelt and struck them in the back, he would say 'That is what I shall do to a wolf!' and when he shot arrows at Jonas and they rattled against his sheepskin coat he would say: 'That is how I should shoot you if you were a wolf!'

Indeed, some thought that the brave boy boasted a little; but one must indeed believe him since he said so himself. So Jonas and Lena used to say of him 'Look, there goes Walter, who shoots the wolves.' And other boys and girls would say 'Look, there goes brave Walter, who is brave enough to fight with four.'

There was no one so fully convinced of this as Walter himself, and one day he prepared himself for a real wolf hunt. He took with him his drum, which had holes in one end since the time he had climbed up on it to reach a cluster of rowan berries, and his tin sabre, which was a little broken, because he had with incredible courage fought his way through a whole unfriendly army of gooseberry bushes.

He did not forget to arm himself quite to the teeth with his pop-gun, his bow, and his air-pistol. He had a burnt cork in his pocket to blacken his moustache, and a red cock's feather to put in his cap to make himself look fierce. He had besides in his trouser pocket a clasp knife with a bone handle, to cut off the ears of the wolves as soon as he had killed them, for he thought it would be cruel to do that while they were still living.

It was such a good thing that Jonas was going with corn to the mill, for Walter got a seat on the load, while Caro ran barking beside them. As soon as they came to the wood Walter looked cautiously around him to see perchance there was a wolf in the bushes, and he did not omit to ask Jonas if wolves were afraid of a drum. 'Of course they are' (that is understood) said Jonas. Thereupon Walter began to beat his drum with all his might while they were going through the wood.

When they came to the mill Walter immediately asked if there had been any wolves in the neighbourhood lately.

'Alas! yes,' said the miller, 'last night the wolves have eaten our fattest ram there by the kiln not far from here.'

'Ah!' said Walter, 'do you think that there were many?'

'We don't know,' answered the miller.

'Oh, it is all the same,' said Walter. 'I only asked so that I should know if I should take Jonas with me.

'I could manage very well alone with three, but if there were more, I might not have time to kill them all before they ran away.'

'In Walter's place I should go quite alone, it is more manly,' said Jonas.

'No, it is better for you to come too,' said Walter. 'Perhaps there are many.'

'No, I have not time,' said Jonas, 'and besides, there are sure not to be more than three. Walter can manage them very well alone.'

42

'Yes,' said Walter, 'certainly I could; but, you see, Jonas, it might happen that one of them might bite me in the back, and I should have more trouble in killing them. If I only knew that there were not more than two I should not mind, for them I should take one in each hand and give them a good shaking, like Susanna once shook me.'

'I certainly think that there will not be more than two,' said Jonas, 'there are never more than two when they slay children and rams; Walter can very well shake them without me.'

'But, you see, Jonas,' said Walter, 'if there are two, it might still happen that one of them escapes and bites me in the leg, for you see I am not so strong in the left hand as in the right. You can very well come with me, and take a good stick in case there are really two. Look, if there is only one, I shall take him so with both my hands and thrown him living on to his back, and he can kick as much as he likes, I shall hold him fast.'

'Now, when I really think over the thing,' said Jonas, 'I am almost sure there will not be more than one. What would two do with one ram? There will certainly not be more than one.'

'But you should come with me all the same, Jonas,' said Walter. 'You see I can very well manage one, but I am not quite accustomed to wolves yet, and he might tear holes in my new trousers.'

'Well, just listen,' said Jonas, 'I am beginning to think that Walter is not so brave as people say. First of all Walter would fight against four, and then against three, then two, and then one, and now Walter wants help with one. Such a thing must never be; what would people say? Perhaps they would think that Walter is a coward?'

'That's a lie,' said Walter, 'I am not at all frightened, but it is more amusing when there are two. I only want someone who will see how I strike the wolf and how the dust flies out of his skin.'

'Well, then, Walter can take the miller's little Lisa with him. She can sit on a stone and look on,' said Jonas.

'No, she would certainly be frightened,' said Walter, 'and how would it do for a girl to go wolf-hunting? Come with me, Jonas, and you shall have the skin, and I will be content with the ears and the tail.'

'No, thank you,' said Jonas, 'Walter can keep the skin for himself. Now I see quite well that he is frightened. Fie, shame on him!'

This touched Walter's pride very near. 'I shall show that I am not frightened,' he said; and so he took his drum, sabre, cock's feather, clasp-knife, pop-gun and air-pistol, and went off quite alone to the wood to hunt wolves.

It was a beautiful evening, and the birds were singing in all the branches. Walter went very slowly and cautiously. At every step he looked all round him to see if perchance there was anything lurking behind the stones. He quite thought something moved away there in the ditch. Perhaps it was a wolf. 'It is better for me to beat the drum a little before I go there,' thought Walter.

Br-r-r, so he began to beat his drum. Then something moved again. Caw! caw! a crow flew up from the ditch. Walter immediately regained courage. 'It was well I took my drum with me,' he thought, and went straight on with courageous steps. Very soon he came quite close to the kiln, where the wolves had killed the ram. But the nearer he came the more dreadful he thought the kiln looked. It was so gray and old. Who knew how many wolves there might be hidden there? Perhaps the very ones which killed the ram were still sitting there in a corner. Yes, it was not at all safe here, and there were no other people to be seen in the neighbourhood. It would be horrible to be eaten up here in the daylight, thought Walter to himself; and the more he thought about it the uglier and grayer the old kiln looked, and the more horrible and dreadful it seemed to become the food of wolves.

'Shall I go back and say that I struck one wolf and it escaped?' thought Walter. 'Fie!' said his conscience, 'Do you not remember that a lie is one of the worst sins, both in the sight of God and man? If you tell a lie to-day and say you struck a wolf, to-morrow surely it will eat you up.'

'No, I will go to the kiln,' thought Walter, and so he went. But he did not go quite near. He went only so near that he could see the ram's blood which coloured the grass red, and some tufts of wool which the wolves had torn from the back of the poor animal.

It looked so dreadful.

'I wonder what the ram thought when they ate him up,' thought Walter to himself; and just then a cold shiver ran through him from his collar right down to his boots.

'It is better for me to beat the drum,' he thought to himself again, and so he began to beat it. But it sounded horrid, and an echo came out from the kiln that seemed almost like the howl of a wolf. The drumsticks stiffened in Walter's hands, and he thought now they are coming. ...!

Yes, sure enough, just then a shaggy, reddish-brown wolf's head looked out from under the kiln!

What did Walter do now? Yes, the brave Walter who alone could manage four, threw his drum far away, took to his heels and ran, and ran as fast as he could back to the mill.

But, alas! the wolf ran after him. Walter looked back; the wolf was quicker than he and only a few steps behind him. Then Walter ran faster. But fear got the better of him, he neither heard nor saw anything more. He ran over sticks, stones and ditches; he lost drum-sticks, sabre, bow, and air-pistol, and in his terrible hurry he tripped over a tuft of grass. There he lay, and the wolf jumped on to him. ...

It was a gruesome tale! Now you may well believe that it was all over with Walter and all his adventures. That would have been a pity. But do not be surprised if it was not quite so bad as that, for the wolf was quite a friendly one. He certainly jumped on to Walter, but he only shook his coat and rubbed his nose against his face; and Walter shrieked. Yes, he shrieked terribly!

Happily Jonas heard his cry of distress, for Walter was quite near the mill now, and he ran and helped him up.

'What has happened?' he asked. 'Why did Walter scream so terribly?'

'A wolf! A wolf!' cried Walter, and that was all he could say.

'Where is the wolf?' said Jonas. 'I don't see any wolf.'

'Take care, he is here, he has bitten me to death,' groaned Walter.

Then Jonas began to laugh; yes, he laughed so that he nearly burst his skin belt.

Well, well, was that the wolf? Was that the wolf which Walter was to take by the neck and shake and throw down on its back, no matter how much it struggled? Just look a little closer at him: he is your old friend, your own good old Caro. I quite expect he found a leg of the ram in the kiln. When Walter beat his drum, Caro crept out, and when Walter ran away, Caro ran after him, as he so often does when Walter wants to romp and play.

'Down, Caro! you ought to be rather ashamed to have put such a great hero to flight!'

Walter got up feeling very foolish.

'Down, Caro!' he said, both relieved and annoyed.

'It was only a dog, then if it had been a wolf I certainly should have killed him. ...'

'If Walter would listen to my advice, and boast a little less, and do a little more,' said Jonas, consolingly. 'Walter is not a coward, is he?'

'I! You shall see, Jonas, when we next meet a bear. You see I like so much better to fight with bears.'

'Indeed!' laughed Jonas. 'Are you at it again?

'Dear Walter, remember that it is only cowards who boast; a really brave man never talks of his bravery.'

From Z. Topelius.

The King of the Waterfalls

When the young king of Easaidh Ruadh came into his kingdom, the first thing he thought of was how he could amuse himself best. The sports that all his life had pleased him best suddenly seemed to have grown dull, and he wanted to do something he had never done before. At last his face brightened.

'I know!' he said. 'I will go and play a game with the Gruagach.' Now the Gruagach was a kind of wicked fairy, with long curly brown hair, and his house was not very far from the king's house.

But though the king was young and eager, he was also prudent, and his father had told him on his deathbed to be very careful in his dealings with the 'good people,' as the fairies were called. Therefore before going to the Gruagach the king sought out a wise man of the countryside.

'I am wanting to play a game with the curly-haired Gruagach,' said he.

'Are you, indeed?' replied the wizard. 'If you will take my counsel, you will play with someone else.'

'No; I will play with the Gruagach,' persisted the king.

'Well, if you must, you must, I suppose,' answered the wizard; 'but if you win that game, ask as a prize the ugly crop-headed girl that stands behind the door.'

'I will,' said the king.

So before the sun rose he got up and went to the house of the Gruagach, who was sitting outside.

'O king, what has brought you here to-day?' asked the Gruagach. 'But right welcome you are, and more welcome will you be still if you will play a game with me.'

46

'That is just what I want,' said the king, and they played; and sometimes it seemed as if one would win, and sometimes the other, but in the end it was the king who was the winner.

'And what is the prize that you will choose?' inquired the Gruagach.

'The ugly crop-headed girl that stands behind the door,' replied the king.

'Why, there are twenty others in the house, and each fairer than she!' exclaimed the Gruagach.

'Fairer they may be, but it is she whom I wish for my wife, and none other,' and the Gruagach saw that the king's mind was set upon her, so he entered his house, and bade all the maidens in it come out one by one, and pass before the king.

One by one they came; tall and short, dark and fair, plump and thin, and each said 'I am she whom you want. You will be foolish indeed if you do not take me.'

But he took none of them, neither short nor tall, dark nor fair, plump nor thin, till at the last the crop-headed girl came out.

'This is mine,' said the king, though she was so ugly that most men would have turned from her. 'We will be married at once, and I will carry you home.' And married they were, and they set forth across a meadow to the king's house. As they went, the bride stooped and picked a sprig of shamrock, which grew amongst the grass, and when she stood upright again her ugliness had all gone, and the most beautiful woman that ever was seen stood by the king's side.

The next day, before the sun rose, the king sprang from his bed, and told his wife he must have another game with the Gruagach.

'If my father loses that game, and you win it,' said she, 'accept nothing for your prize but the shaggy young horse with the stick saddle.'

'I will do that,' answered the king, and he went.

'Does your bride please you?' asked the Gruagach, who was standing at his own door.

'Ah! does she not!' answered the king quickly. 'Otherwise I should be hard indeed to please. But will you play a game to-day?'

'I will,' replied the Gruagach, and they played, and sometimes it seemed as if one would win, and sometimes the other, but in the end the king was the winner.

'What is the prize that you will choose?' asked the Gruagach.

'The shaggy young horse with the stick saddle,' answered the king, but he noticed that the Gruagach held his peace, and his brow was dark as he led out the horse from the stable. Rough was its mane and dull was its skin, but the king cared nothing for that, and throwing his leg over the stick saddle, rode away like the wind.

On the third morning the king got up as usual before dawn, and as soon as he had eaten food he prepared to go out, when his wife stopped him. 'I would rather,' she said, 'that you did not go to play with the Gruagach, for though twice you have won yet some day he will win, and then he will put trouble upon you.'

'Oh! I must have one more game,' cried the king; 'just this one.' And he went off to the house of the Gruagach.

Joy filled the heart of the Gruagach when he saw him coming, and without waiting to talk they played their game. Somehow or other, the king's strength and skill had departed from him, and soon the Gruagach was the victor.

'Choose your prize,' said the king, when the game was ended, 'but do not be too hard on me, or ask what I cannot give.'

'The prize I choose,' answered the Gruagach, 'is that the crop-headed creature should take thy head and thy neck, if thou dost not get for me the Sword of Light that hangs in the house of the king of the oak windows.'

'I will get it,' replied the young man bravely; but as soon as he was out of sight of the Gruagach he pretended no more, and his face grew dark and his steps lagging.

'You have brought nothing with you to-night,' said the queen, who was standing on the steps awaiting him. She was so beautiful that the king was fain to smile when he looked at her, but then he remembered what had happened, and his heart grew heavy again.

'What is it? What is the matter? Tell me thy sorrow that I may bear it with thee, or, it may be, help thee!' Then the king told her everything that had befallen him, and she stroked his hair the while.

'That is nothing to grieve about,' she said when the tale was finished. 'You have the best wife in Erin, and the best horse in Erin. Only do as I bid you, and all will go well.' And the king suffered himself to be comforted.

He was still sleeping when the queen rose and dressed herself, to make everything ready for her husband's journey; and the first place she went to was the stable, where she fed and watered the shaggy brown horse and put the saddle on it. Most people thought this saddle was of wood, and did not see the little sparkles of gold and silver that were hidden in it. She strapped it lightly on the horse's back, and then led it down before the house, where the king waited.

'Good luck to you, and victories in all your battles,' she said, as she kissed him before he mounted. 'I need not be telling you anything. Take the advice of the horse, and see you obey it.'

So he waved his hand and set out on his journey, and the wind was not swifter than the brown horse—no, not even the March wind which raced it and could not catch it. But the horse never stopped nor looked behind, till in the dark of the night he reached the castle of the king of the oak windows.

'We are at the end of the journey,' said the horse, 'and you will find the Sword of Light in the king's own chamber. If it comes to you without scrape or sound, the token is a good one. At this hour the king is eating his supper, and the room is empty, so none will see you. The sword has a knob at the end, and take heed that when you grasp it, you draw it softly out of its sheath. Now go! I will be under the window.'

Stealthily the young man crept along the passage, pausing now and then to make sure that no man was following him, and entered the king's chamber. A strange white line of light told him where the sword was, and crossing the room on tiptoe, he seized the knob, and drew it slowly out of the sheath. The king could hardly breathe with excitement lest it should make some noise, and bring all the people in the castle running to see what was the matter. But the sword slid swiftly and silently along the case till only the point was left touching it. Then a low sound was heard, as of the edge of a knife touching a silver plate, and the king was so startled that he nearly dropped the knob.

'Quick! quick!' cried the horse, and the king scrambled hastily through the small window, and leapt into the saddle.

'He has heard and he will follow,' said the horse; 'but we have a good start,' And on they sped, on and on, leaving the winds behind them.

At length the horse slackened its pace. 'Look and see who is behind you,' it said; and the young man looked.

'I see a swarm of brown horses racing madly after us,' he answered.

'We are swifter than those,' said the horse, and flew on again.

'Look again, O king! Is anyone coming now?'

'A swarm of black horses, and one has a white face, and on that horse a man is seated. He is the king of the oak windows.'

'That is my brother, and swifter still than I,' said the horse, 'and he will fly past me with a rush. Then you must have your sword ready, and take off the head of the man who sits on him, as he turns and looks at you. And there is no sword in the world that will cut off his head, save only that one.'

'I will do it,' replied the king; and he listened with all his might, till he judged that the white-faced horse was close to him. Then he sat up very straight and made ready.

The next moment there was a rushing noise as of a mighty tempest, and the young man caught a glimpse of a face turned towards him. Almost blindly he struck, not knowing whether he had killed or only wounded the rider. But the head rolled off, and was caught in the brown horse's mouth.

'Jump on my brother, the black horse, and go home as fast as you can, and I will follow as quickly as I may,' cried the brown horse; and leaping forward the king alighted on the back of the black horse, but so near the tail that he almost fell off again. But he stretched out his arm and clutched wildly at the mane and pulled himself into the saddle.

Before the sky was streaked with red he was at home again, and the queen was sitting waiting till he arrived, for sleep was far from her eyes. Glad was she to see him enter, but she said little, only took her harp and sang softly the songs which he loved, till he went to bed, soothed and happy.

It was broad day when he woke, and he sprang up saying:

'Now I must go to the Gruagach, to find out if the spells he laid on me are loose.'

'Have a care,' answered the queen, 'for it is not with a smile as on the other days that he will greet you. Furiously he will meet you, and will ask you in his wrath if you have got the sword, and you will reply that you have got it. Next he will want to know how you got it, and to this you must say that but for the knob you had not got it at all. Then he will raise his head to look at the knob, and you must stab him in the mole which is on the right side of his neck; but take heed, for if you miss the mole with the point of the sword, then my death and your death are certain. He is brother to the king of the oak windows, and sure will he be that the king must be head, or the sword would not be in your hands.' After that she kissed him, and bade him good speed.

'Didst thou get the sword?' asked the Gruagach, when they met in the usual place.

'I got the sword.'

'And how didst thou get it?'

50

'If it had not had a knob on the top, then I had not got it,' answered the king.

'Give me the sword to look at,' said the Gruagach, peering forward; but like a flash the king had drawn it from under his nose and pierced the mole, so that the Gruagach rolled over on the ground.

'Now I shall be at peace,' thought the king. But he was wrong, for when he reached home he found his servants tied together back to back with cloths bound round their mouths, so that they could not speak. He hastened to set them free, and he asked who had treated them in so evil a manner.

'No sooner had you gone than a great giant came, and dealt with us as you see, and carried off your wife and your two horses,' said the men.

'Then my eyes will not close nor will my head lay itself down till I fetch my wife and horses home again,' answered he, and he stopped and noted the tracks of the horses on the grass, and followed after them till he arrived at the wood, when the darkness fell.

'I will sleep here,' he said to himself, 'but first I will make a fire,' And he gathered together some twigs that were lying about, and then took two dry sticks and rubbed them together till the fire came, and he sat by it.

The twigs cracked and the flame blazed up, and a slim yellow dog pushed through the bushes and laid his head on the king's knee, and the king stroked his head.

'Wuf, wuf,' said the dog. 'Sore was the plight of thy wife and thy horses when the giant drove them last night through the forest.'

'That is why I have come,' answered the king; and suddenly his heart seemed to fail him and he felt that he could not go on.

'I cannot fight that giant,' he cried, looking at the dog with a white face. 'I am afraid, let me turn homewards.'

'No, don't do that,' replied the dog. 'Eat and sleep, and I will watch over you.' So the king ate and lay down, and slept till the sun waked him.

'It is time for you to start on your way,' said the dog, 'and if danger presses, call on me, and I will help you.'

'Farewell, then,' answered the king; 'I will not forget that promise,' and on he went, and on, and on, till he reached a tall cliff with many sticks lying about.

'It is almost night,' he thought; 'I will make a fire and rest,' and thus he did, and when the flames blazed up, the hoary hawk of the grey rock flew on to a bough above him.

'Sore was the plight of thy wife and thy horses when they passed here with the giant,' said the hawk.

'Never shall I find them,' answered the king, 'and nothing shall I get for all my trouble.'

'Oh, take heart,' replied the hawk; 'things are never so bad but what they might be worse. Eat and sleep and I will watch thee,' and the king did as he was bidden by the hawk, and by the morning he felt brave again.

'Farewell,' said the bird, 'and if danger presses call to me, and I will help you.'

On he walked, and on and on, till as dusk was falling he came to a great river, and on the bank there were sticks lying about.

'I will make myself a fire,' he thought, and thus he did, and by and bye a smooth brown head peered at him from the water, and a long body followed it.

'Sore was the plight of thy wife and thy horses when they passed the river last night,' said the otter.

'I have sought them and not found them,' answered the king, 'and nought shall I get for my trouble.'

'Be not so downcast,' replied the otter; 'before noon to-morrow thou shalt behold thy wife. But eat and sleep and I will watch over thee.' So the king did as the otter bid him, and when the sun rose he woke and saw the otter lying on the bank.

'Farewell,' cried the otter as he jumped into the water, 'and if danger presses, call to me and I will help you.'

For many hours the king walked, and at length he reached a high rock, which was rent into two by a great earthquake. Throwing himself on the ground he looked over the side, and right at the very bottom he saw his wife and his horses. His heart gave a great bound, and all his fears left him, but he was forced to be patient, for the sides of the rock were smooth, and not even a goat could find foothold. So he got up again, and made his way round through the wood, pushing by trees, scrambling over rocks, wading through streams, till at last he was on flat ground again, close to the mouth of the cavern.

His wife gave a shriek of joy when he came in, and then burst into tears, for she was tired and very frightened. But her husband did not understand why she wept, and he was tired and bruised from his climb, and a little cross too.

'You give me but a sorry welcome,' grumbled he, 'when I have half-killed myself to get to you.'

'Do not heed him,' said the horses to the weeping woman; 'put him in front of us, where he will be safe, and give him food, for he is weary.' And she did as the horses told her, and he ate and rested, till by and bye a long shadow fell over them, and their hearts beat with fear, for they knew that the giant was coming.

'I smell a stranger,' cried the giant, as he entered; but it was dark inside the chasm, and he did not see the king, who was crouching down between the feet of the horses.

'A stranger, my lord! no stranger ever comes here, not even the sun!' and the king's wife laughed gaily as she went up to the giant and stroked the huge hand which hung down by his side.

'Well, I perceive nothing, certainly,' answered he, 'but it is very odd. However, it is time that the horses were fed;' and he lifted down an armful of hay from a shelf of rock and held out a handful to each animal, who moved forward to meet him, leaving the king behind. As soon as the giant's hands were near their mouths they each made a snap, and began to bit them, so that his groans and shrieks might have been heard a mile off. Then they wheeled round and kicked him till they could kick no more. At length the giant crawled away, and lay quivering in a corner, and the queen went up to him.

'Poor thing! poor thing!' she said, 'they seem to have gone mad; it was awful to behold.'

'If I had had my soul in my body they would certainly have killed me,' groaned the giant.

'It was lucky indeed,' answered the queen; 'but tell me, where is thy soul, that I may take care of it?'

'Up there, in the Bonnach stone,' answered the giant, pointing to a stone which was balanced loosely on an edge of rock. 'But now leave me, that I may sleep, for I have far to go to-morrow.'

Soon snores were heard from the corner where the giant lay, and then the queen lay down too, and the horses, and the king was hidden between them, so that none could see him.

Before the dawn the giant rose and went out, and immediately the queen ran up to the Bonnach stone, and tugged and pushed at it till it was quite steady on its ledge, and could not fall over. And so it was in the evening when the giant came home; and when they saw his shadow, the king crept down in front of the horses.

'Why, what have you done to the Bonnach stone?' asked the giant.

'I feared lest it should fall over, and be broken, with your soul in it,' said the queen, 'so I put it further back on the ledge.'

'It is not there that my soul is,' answered he, 'it is on the threshold. But it is time the horses were fed;' and he fetched the hay, and gave it to them, and they bit and kicked him as before, till he lay half dead on the ground.

Next morning he rose and went out, and the queen ran to the threshold of the cave, and washed the stones, and pulled up some moss and little flowers that were hidden in the crannies, and by and bye when dusk had fallen the giant came home.

'You have been cleaning the threshold,' said he.

'And was I not right to do it, seeing that your soul is in it?' asked the queen.

'It is not there that my soul is,' answered the giant. 'Under the threshold is a stone, and under the stone is a sheep, and in the sheep's body is a duck, and in the duck is an egg, and in the egg is my soul. But it is late, and I must feed the horses;' and he brought them the hay, but they only bit and kicked him as before, and if his soul had been within him, they would have killed him outright.

It was still dark when the giant got up and went his way, and then the king and the queen ran forward to take up the threshold, while the horses looked on. But sure enough! just as the giant had said, underneath the threshold was the flagstone, and they pulled and tugged till the stone gave way. Then something jumped out so suddenly, that it nearly knocked them down, and as it fled past, they saw it was a sheep.

'If the slim yellow dog of the greenwood were only here, he would soon have that sheep,' cried the king; and as he spoke, the slim yellow dog appeared from the forest, with the sheep in his mouth. With a blow from the king, the sheep fell dead, and they opened its body, only to be blinded by a rush of wings as the duck flew past.

'If the hoary hawk of the rock were only here, he would soon have that duck,' cried the king; and as he spoke the hoary hawk was seen hovering above them, with the duck in his mouth. They cut off the duck's head with a swing of the king's sword, and took the egg out of its body, but in his triumph the king held it carelessly, and it slipped from his hand, and rolled swiftly down the hill right into the river.

'If the brown otter of the stream were only here, he would soon have that egg,' cried the king; and the next minute there was the brown otter, dripping with water, holding the egg in his mouth. But beside the brown otter, a huge shadow came stealing along— the shadow of the giant.

The king stood staring at it, as if he were turned into stone, but the queen snatched the egg from the otter and crushed it between her two hands. And after that the shadow suddenly shrank and was still, and they knew that the giant was dead, because they had found his soul.

Next day they mounted the two horses and rode home again, visiting their friends the brown otter and the hoary hawk and the slim yellow dog by the way.

From 'West Highland Tales.'

A French Puck

Among the mountain pastures and valleys that lie in the centre of France there dwelt a mischievous kind of spirit, whose delight it was to play tricks on everybody, and particularly on the shepherds and the cowboys. They never knew when they were safe from him, as he could change himself into a man, woman or child, a stick, a goat, a ploughshare. Indeed, there was only one thing whose shape he could not take, and that was a needle. At least, he could transform himself into a needle, but try as he might he never was able to imitate the hole, so every woman would have found him out at once, and this he knew.

Now the hour oftenest chosen by this naughty sprite (whom we will call Puck) for performing his pranks was about midnight, just when the shepherds and cowherds, tired out with their long day's work, were sound asleep. Then he would go into the cowsheds and unfasten the chains that fixed each beast in its own stall, and let them fall with a heavy clang to the ground. The noise was so loud that it was certain to awaken the cowboys, however fatigued they might be, and they dragged themselves wearily to the stable to put back the chains. But no sooner had they returned to their beds than the same thing happened again, and so on till the morning. Or perhaps Puck would spend his night in plaiting together the manes and tails of two of the horses, so that it would take the grooms hours of labour to get them right in the morning, while Puck, hidden among the hay in the loft, would peep out to watch them, enjoying himself amazingly all the time.

One evening more than eighty years ago a man named William was passing along the bank of a stream when he noticed a sheep who was bleating loudly. William thought it must have strayed from the flock, and that he had better take it home with him till he could discover its owner. So he went up to where it was standing, and as it seemed so tired that it could hardly walk, he hoisted it on his shoulders and continued on his way. The sheep was pretty heavy, but the good man was merciful and staggered along as best he could under his load.

'It is not much further,' he thought to himself as he reached an avenue of walnut trees, when suddenly a voice spoke out from over his head, and made him jump.

'Where are you?' said the voice, and the sheep answered:

'Here on the shoulders of a donkey.'

In another moment the sheep was standing on the ground and William was running towards home as fast as his legs would carry him. But as he went, a laugh, which yet was something of a bleat, rang in his ears, and though he tried not to hear, the words reached him, 'Oh, dear! What fun I have had, to be sure!'

Puck was careful not always to play his tricks in the same place, but visited one village after another, so that everyone trembled lest he should be the next victim.

56

After a bit he grew tired of cowboys and shepherds, and wondered if there was no one else to give him some sport. At length he was told of a young couple who were going to the nearest town to buy all that they needed for setting up house. Quite certain that they would forget something which they could not do without, Puck waited patiently till they were jogging along in their cart on their return journey, and changed himself into a fly in order to overhear their conversation.

For a long time it was very dull—all about their wedding day next month, and who were to be invited. This led the bride to her wedding dress, and she gave a little scream.

'Just think! Oh! how could I be so stupid! I have forgotten to buy the different coloured reels of cotton to match my clothes!'

'Dear, dear!' exclaimed the young man. 'That is unlucky; and didn't you tell me that the dressmaker was coming in to-morrow?'

'Yes, I did,' and then suddenly she gave another little scream, which had quite a different sound from the first. 'Look! Look!'

The bridegroom looked, and on one side of the road he saw a large ball of thread of all colours—of all the colours, that is, of the dresses that were tied on to the back of the cart.

'Well, that is a wonderful piece of good fortune,' cried he, as he sprang out to get it. 'One would think a fairy had put it there on purpose.'

'Perhaps she has,' laughed the girl, and as she spoke she seemed to hear an echo of her laughter coming from the horse, but of course that was nonsense.

The dressmaker was delighted with the thread that was given her. It matched the stuffs so perfectly, and never tied itself in knots, or broke perpetually, as most thread did. She finished her work much quicker than she expected and the bride said she was to be sure to come to the church and see her in her wedding dress.

There was a great crowd assembled to witness the ceremony, for the young people were immense favourites in the neighbourhood, and their parents were very rich. The doors were open, and the bride could be seen from afar, walking under the chestnut avenue.

'What a beautiful girl!' exclaimed the men. 'What a lovely dress!' whispered the women. But just as she entered the church and took the hand of the bridegroom, who was waiting for her, a loud noise was heard.

'Crick! crack! Crick! crack!' and the wedding garments fell to the ground, to the great confusion of the wearer.

57

Not that the ceremony was put off for a little thing like that! Cloaks in profusion were instantly offered to the young bride, but she was so upset that she could hardly keep from tears. One of the guests, more curious than the rest, stayed behind to examine the dress, determined, if she could, to find out the cause of the disaster.

'The thread must have been rotten,' she said to herself. 'I will see if I can break it.' But search as she would she could find none.

The thread had vanished!

From 'Litterature Orale de l'Auvergne,' par Paul Sebillot.

The Three Crowns

There was once a king who had three daughters. The two eldest were very proud and quarrelsome, but the youngest was as good as they were bad. Well, three princes came to court them, and two of them were exactly like the eldest ladies, and one was just as lovable as the youngest. One day they were all walking down to a lake that lay at the bottom of the lawn when they met a poor beggar. The king wouldn't give him anything, and the eldest princesses wouldn't give him anything, nor their sweethearts; but the youngest daughter and her true love did give him something, and kind words along with it, and that was better than all.

When they got to the edge of the lake what did they find but the beautifullest boat you ever saw in your life; and says the eldest, 'I'll take a sail in this fine boat'; and says the second eldest, 'I'll take a sail in this fine boat'; and says the youngest, 'I won't take a sail in that fine boat, for I am afraid it's an enchanted one.' But the others persuaded her to go in, and her father was just going in after her, when up sprung on the deck a little man only seven inches high, and ordered him to stand back. Well, all the men put their hands to their swords; and if the same swords were only playthings, they weren't able to draw them, for all strength that was left their arms. Seven Inches loosened the silver chain that fastened the boat, and pushed away, and after grinning at the four men, says he to them. 'Bid your daughters and your brides farewell for awhile. You,' says he to the youngest, 'needn't fear, you'll recover your princess all in good time, and you and she will be as happy as the day is long. Bad people, if they were rolling stark naked in gold, would not be rich. Good-bye.' Away they sailed, and the ladies stretched out their hands, but weren't able to say a word.

Well, they weren't crossing the lake while a cat 'ud be lickin' her ear, and the poor men couldn't stir hand or foot to follow them. They saw Seven Inches handing the three princesses out of the boat, and letting them down by a basket into a draw-well, but king nor princes ever saw an opening before in the same place. When the last lady was out of sight, the men found the strength in their arms and legs again. Round the lake they ran, and never drew rein till they came to the well and windlass; and there was the silk rope rolled on the axle, and the nice white basket hanging to it. 'Let me down,' says the youngest prince. 'I'll die or recover them again.' 'No,' says the second daughter's sweetheart, 'it is my turn first.' And says the other, 'I am the eldest.' So they gave way to him, and in he got into the basket, and down they let him. First they lost sight of him, and then, after winding off a hundred perches of the silk rope, it slackened, and they stopped turning. They waited two hours, and then they went to dinner, because there was no pull made at the rope.

Guards were set till next morning, and then down went the second prince, and sure enough, the youngest of all got himself let down on the third day. He went down perches and perches, while it was as dark about him as if he was in a big pot with a cover on. At last he saw a glimmer far down, and in a short time he felt the ground. Out he came from the big lime-kiln, and, lo! and behold you, there was a wood, and green fields, and a castle in a lawn, and a bright sky over all. 'It's in Tir-na-n-Oge I am,' says he. 'Let's see what sort of people are in the castle.' On he walked, across fields and lawn, and no one was there to keep him out or let him into the castle; but the big hall-door was wide open. He went from one fine room to another that was finer, and at last he reached the handsomest of all, with a table in the middle. And such a dinner as was laid upon it! The prince was hungry enough, but he was too mannerly to eat without being invited. So he sat by the fire, and he did not wait long till he heard steps, and in came Seven Inches with the youngest sister by the hand. Well, prince and princess flew into one another's arms, and says the little man, says he, 'Why aren't you eating?' 'I think, sir,' says the prince, 'it was only good manner to wait to be asked.' 'The other princes didn't think so,' says he. 'Each o' them fell to without leave, and only gave me the rough words when I told them they were making more free than welcome. Well, I don't think they feel much hunger now. There they are, good marble instead of flesh and blood,' says he, pointing to two statues, one in one corner, and the other in the other corner of the room. The prince was frightened, but he was afraid to say anything, and Seven Inches made him sit down to dinner between himself and his bride; and he'd be as happy as the day is long, only for the sight of the stone men in the corner. Well, that day went by, and when the next came, says Seven Inches to him, 'Now, you'll have to set out that way,' pointing to the sun, 'and you'll find the second princess in a giant's castle this evening, when you'll be tired and hungry, and the eldest princess to-morrow evening; and you may as well bring them here with you. You need not ask leave of their masters; and perhaps if they ever get home, they'll look on poor people as if they were flesh and blood like themselves.'

Away went the prince, and bedad! it's tired and hungry he was when he reached the first castle, at sunset. Oh, wasn't the second princess glad to see him! And what a good supper she gave him. But she heard the giant at the gate, and she hid the prince in a closet. Well, when he came in, he snuffed, an' he snuffed, and says he, 'By the life, I smell fresh meat.' 'Oh,' says the princess, 'it's only the calf I got killed to-day.' 'Ay, ay,' says he, 'is supper ready?' 'It is,' says she; and before he rose from the table he ate three-quarters of a calf, and a flask of wine. 'I think,' says he, when all was done, 'I smell fresh meat still.' 'It's sleepy you are,' says she; 'go to bed.' 'When will you marry me?' says the giant. 'You're putting me off too long.' 'St. Tibb's Eve,' says she. 'I wish I knew how far off that is,' says he; and he fell asleep, with his head in the dish.

Next day, he went out after breakfast, and she sent the prince to the castle where the eldest sister was. The same thing happened there; but when the giant was snoring, the princess wakened up the prince, and they saddled two steeds in the stables and rode into the field on them. But the horses' heels struck the stones outside the gate, and up got the giant and strode after them. He roared and he shouted, and the more he shouted, the faster ran the horses, and just as the day was breaking he was only twenty perches behind. But the prince didn't leave the castle of Seven Inches without being provided with something good. He reined in his steed, and flung a short, sharp knife over his shoulder, and up sprung a thick wood between the giant and themselves. They caught the wind that blew before them, and the wind that blew behind them did not catch them. At last they were near the castle where the other sister lived; and there she was, waiting for them under a high hedge, and a fine steed under her.

But the giant was now in sight, roaring like a hundred lions, and the other giant was out in a moment, and the chase kept on. For every two springs the horses gave, the giants gave three, and at last they were only seventy perches off. Then the prince stopped again, and flung the second knife behind him. Down went all the flat field, till there was a quarry between them a quarter of a mile deep, and the bottom filled with black water; and before the giants could get round it, the prince and princesses were inside the kingdom of the great magician, where the high thorny hedge opened of itself to everyone that he chose to let in. There was joy enough between the three sisters, till the two eldest saw their lovers turned into stone. But while they were shedding tears for them, Seven Inches came in, and touched them with his rod. So they were flesh, and blood, and life once more, and there was great hugging and kissing, and all sat down to breakfast, and Seven Inches sat at the head of the table.

When breakfast was over, he took them into another room, where there was nothing but heaps of gold, and silver, and diamonds, and silks, and satins; and on a table there was lying three sets of crowns: a gold crown was in a silver crown, and that was lying in a copper crown. He took up one set of crowns, and gave it to the eldest princess; and another set, and gave it to the second youngest princess; and another, and gave it to the youngest of all; and says he, 'Now you may all go to the bottom of the pit, and you have nothing to do but stir the basket, and the people that are watching above will draw you up. But remember, ladies, you are to keep your crows safe, and be married in them, all the same day. If you be married separately, or if you be married without your crowns, a curse will follow—mind what I say.'

So they took leave of him with great respect, and walked arm-in-arm to the bottom of the draw-well. There was a sky and a sun over them, and a great high wall, covered with ivy, rose before them, and was so high they could not see to the top of it; and there was an arch in this wall, and the bottom of the draw-well was inside the arch. The youngest pair went last; and says the princess to the prince, 'I'm sure the two princes don't mean any good to you. Keep these crowns under your cloak, and if you are obliged to stay last, don't get into the basket, but put a big stone, or any heavy thing inside, and see what will happen.'

As soon as they were inside the dark cave, they put in the eldest princess first, and stirred the basket, and up she went. Then the basket was let down again, and up went the second princess, and then up went the youngest; but first she put her arms round her prince's neck, and kissed him, and cried a little. At last it came to the turn of the youngest prince, and instead of going into the basket he put in a big stone. He drew on one side and listened, and after the basket was drawn up about twenty perches, down came it and the stone like thunder, and the stone was broken into little bits.

Well, the poor prince had nothing for it but to walk back to the castle; and through it and round it he walked, and the finest of eating and drinking he got, and a bed of bog-down to sleep on, and long walks he took through gardens and lawns, but not a sight could he get, high or low, of Seven Inches. He, before a week, got tired of it, he was so lonesome for his true love; and at the end of a month he didn't know what to do with himself.

One morning he went into the treasure room, and took notice of a beautiful snuff-box on the table that he didn't remember seeing there before. He took it in his hands and opened it, and out Seven Inches walked on the table. 'I think, prince,' says he, 'you're getting a little tired of my castle?' 'Ah!' says the other, 'if I had my princess here, and could see you now and then, I'd never know a dismal day.' 'Well, you're long enough here now, and you're wanted there above. Keep your bride's crowns safe, and whenever you want my help, open this snuff-box. Now take a walk down the garden, and come back when you're tired.'

The prince was going down a gravel walk with a quickset hedge on each side, and his eyes on the ground, and he was thinking of one thing and another. At last he lifted his eyes, and there he was outside of a smith's gate that he often passed before, about a mile away from the palace of his betrothed princess. The clothes he had on him were as ragged as you please, but he had his crowns safe under his old cloak.

Then the smith came out, and says he, 'It's a shame for a strong, big fellow like you to be lazy, and so much work to be done. Are you any good with hammer and tongs? Come in and bear a hand, an I'll give you diet and lodging, and a few pence when you earn them.' 'Never say't twice,' says the prince. 'I want nothing but to be busy.' So he took the hammer, and pounded away at the red-hot bar that the smith was turning on the anvil to make into a set of horse-shoes.

They hadn't been long at work when a tailor came in, and he sat down and began to talk. 'You all heard how the two princess were loth to be married till the youngest would be ready with her crowns and her sweetheart. But after the windlass loosened accidentally when they were pulling up her bridegroom that was to be, there was no more sign of a well, or a rope, or a windlass, than there is on the palm of your hand. So the princes that were courting the eldest ladies wouldn't give peace or ease to their lovers nor the king till they got consent to the marriage, and it was to take place this morning. Myself went down out o' curiousity, and to be sure I was delighted with the grand dresses of the two brides, and the three crowns on their heads—gold, silver, and copper, one inside the other. The youngest was standing by mournful enough, and all was ready. The two bridegrooms came in as proud and grand as you please, and up they were walking to the altar rails, when the boards opened two yards wide under their feet, and down they went among the dead men and the coffins in the vaults. Oh, such shrieks as the ladies gave! and such running and racing and peeping down as there was! but the clerk soon opened the door of the vault, and up came the two princes, their fine clothes covered an inch thick with cobwebs and mould.

So the king said they should put off the marriage. 'For,' says he, 'I see there is no use in thinking of it till the youngest gets her three crowns, and is married with the others. I'll give my youngest daughter for a wife to whoever brings three crowns to me like the others; and if he doesn't care to be married, some other one will, and I'll make his fortune.'

'I wish,' says the smith, 'I could do it; but I was looking at the crowns after the princesses got home, and I don't think there's a black or a white smith on the face of the earth that could imitate them.' 'Faint heart never won fair lady,' says the prince. 'Go to the palace and ask for a quarter of a pound of gold, a quarter of a pound of silver, and a quarter of a pound of copper. Get one crown for a pattern, and my head for a pledge, I'll give you out the very things that are wanted in the morning.' 'Are you in earnest?' says the smith. 'Faith, I am so,' says he. 'Go! you can't do worse than lose.'

To make a long story short, the smith got the quarter of a pound of gold, and the quarter of a pound of silver, and the quarter of a pound of copper, and gave them and the pattern crown to the prince. He shut the forge door at nightfall, and the neighbours all gathered in the yard, and they heard him hammering, hammering, hammering, from that to daybreak; and every now and then he'd throw out through the window bits of gold, silver, and copper; and the idlers scrambled for them, and cursed one another, and prayed for the good luck of the workman.

Well, just as the sun was thinking to rise, he opened the door, and brought out the three crowns he got from his true love, and such shouting and huzzaing as there was! The smith asked him to go along with him to the palace, but he refused; so off set the smith, and the whole townland with him; and wasn't the king rejoiced when he saw the crowns! 'Well,' says he to the smith, 'you're a married man. What's to be done?' 'Faith, your majesty, I didn't make them crowns at all. It was a big fellow that took service with me yesterday.' 'Well, daughter, will you marry the fellow that made these crowns?' 'Let me see them first, father,' said she; but when she examined them she knew them right well, and guessed it was her true love that sent them. 'I will marry the man that these crowns came from,' says she.

'Well,' says the king to the elder of the two princes, 'go up to the smith's forge, take my best coaches, and bring home the bridegroom.' He did not like doing this, he was so proud, but he could not refuse. When he came to the forge he saw the prince standing at the door, and beckoned him over to the coach. 'Are you the fellow,' says he, 'that made these crowns?' 'Yes,' says the other. 'Then,' says he, 'maybe you'd give yourself a brushing, and get into that coach; the king wants to see you. I pity the princess.' The young prince got into the carriage, and while they were on the way he opened the snuff-box, and out walked Seven Inches, and stood on his thigh. 'Well,' says he, 'what trouble is on you now?' 'Master,' says the other, 'please let me go back to my forge, and let this carriage be filled with paving stones.' No sooner said than done. The prince was sitting in his forge, and the horses wondered what was after happening to the carriage.

When they came into the palace yard, the king himself opened the carriage door, for respect to his new son-in-law. As soon as he turned the handle, a shower of small stones fell on his powdered wig and his silk coat, and down he fell under them.

There was great fright and some laughter, and the king, after he wiped the blood from his forehead, looked very cross at the eldest prince. 'My lord,' says he, 'I'm very sorry for this accident, but I'm not to blame. I saw the young smith get into the carriage, and we never stopped a minute since.' 'It's uncivil you were to him. Go,' says he to the other prince, 'and bring the young smith here, and be polite.' 'Never fear,' says he.

But there's some people that couldn't be good-natured if they tried, and not a bit civiller was the new messenger than the old, and when the king opened the carriage door a second time, it's shower of mud that came down on him. 'There's no use,' says he, 'going on this way. The fox never got a better messenger than himself.'

So he changed his clothes, and washed himself, and out he set to the prince's forge and asked him to sit along with himself. The prince begged to be allowed to sit in the other carriage, and when they were half-way he opened his snuff-box. 'Master,' says he, 'I'd wish to be dressed now according to my rank.' 'You shall be that,' says Seven Inches. 'And now I'll bid you farewell. Continue as good and kind as you always were; love your wife; and that's all the advice I'll give you.' So Seven Inches vanished; and when the carriage door was opened in the yard, out walks the prince as fine as hands could make him, and the first thing he did was to run over to his bride and embrace her.

Every one was full of joy but the two other princes. There was not much delay about the marriages, and they were all celebrated on the one day. Soon after, the two elder couples went to their own courts, but the youngest pair stayed with the old king, and they were as happy as the happiest married couple you ever heard of in a story.

From 'West Highland Tales.'

The Story of a Very Bad Boy

Once upon a time there lived in a little village in the very middle of France a widow and her only son, a boy about fifteen, whose name was Antoine, though no one ever called him anything but Toueno-Boueno. They were very poor indeed, and their hut shook about their ears on windy nights, till they expected the walls to fall in and crush them, but instead of going to work as a boy of his age ought to do, Toueno-Boueno did nothing but lounge along the street, his eyes fixed on the ground, seeing nothing that went on round him.

'You are very, very stupid, my dear child,' his mother would sometimes say to him, and then she would add with a laugh, 'Certainly you will never catch a wolf by the tail.'

One day the old woman bade Antoine go into the forest and collect enough dry leaves to make beds for herself and him. Before he had finished it began to rain heavily, so he hid himself in the hollow trunk of a tree, where he was so dry and comfortable that he soon fell fast asleep. By and by he was awakened by a noise which sounded like a dog scratching at the door, and he suddenly felt frightened, why he did not know. Very cautiously he raised his head, and right above him he saw a big hairy animal, coming down tail foremost.

'It is the wolf that they talk so much about,' he said to himself, and he made himself as small as he could and shrunk into a corner.

The wolf came down the inside of the tree, slowly, slowly; Antoine felt turned to stone, so terrified was he, and hardly dared to breathe. Suddenly an idea entered his mind, which he thought might save him still. He remembered to have heard from his mother that a wolf could neither bend his back nor turn his head, so as to look behind him, and quick as lightning he stretched up his hand, and seizing the wolf's tail, pulled it towards him.

Then he left the tree and dragged the animal to his mother's house.

'Mother, you have often declared that I was too stupid to catch a wolf by the tail. Now see,' he cried triumphantly.

'Well, well, wonders will never cease,' answered the good woman, who took care to keep at a safe distance. 'But as you really have got him, let us see if we can't put him to some use. Fetch the skin of the ram which died last week out of the chest, and we will sew the wolf up in it. He will make a splendid ram, and to-morrow we will drive him to the fair and sell him.'

Very likely the wolf, who was cunning and clever, may have understood what she said, but he thought it best to give no sign, and suffered the skin to be sewn upon him.

'I can always get away if I choose,' thought he, 'it is better not to be in a hurry;' so he remained quite still while the skin was drawn over his head, which made him very hot and uncomfortable, and resisted the temptation to snap off the fingers or noses that were so close to his mouth.

The fair was at its height next day when Toueno-Boueno arrived with his wolf in ram's clothing. All the farmers crowded round him, each offering a higher price than the last. Never had they beheld such a beautiful beast, said they, and at last, after much bargaining, he was handed over to three brothers for a good sum of money.

It happened that these three brothers owned large flocks of sheep, though none so large and fine as the one they had just bought.

'My flock is the nearest,' observed the eldest brother; 'we will leave him in the fold for the night, and to-morrow we will decide which pastures will be best for him.' And the wolf grinned as he listened, and held up his head a little higher than before.

Early next morning the young farmer began to go his rounds, and the sheep-fold was the first place he visited. To his horror, the sheep were all stretched out dead before him, except one, which the wolf had eaten, bones and all. Instantly the truth flashed upon him. It was no ram that lay curled up in the corner pretending to be asleep (for in reality he could bend back and turn his head as much as he liked), but a wolf who was watching him out of the corner of his eye, and might spring upon him at any moment. So the farmer took no notice, and only thought that here was a fine chance of revenging himself on his next brother for a trick which he had played, and merely told him that the ram would not eat the grass in that field, and it might be well to drive him to the pasture by the river, where his own flock was feeding. The second brother eagerly swallowed the bait, and that evening the wolf was driven down to the field where the young man kept the sheep which had been left him by his father. By the next morning they also were all dead, but the second brother likewise held his peace, and allowed the sheep which belonged to the youngest to share the fate of the other two. Then they met and confessed to each other their disasters, and resolved to take the animal as fast as possible back to Toueno-Boueno, who should get a sound thrashing.

Antoine was sitting on a plum tree belonging to a neighbour, eating the ripe fruit, when he saw the three young farmers coming towards him. Swinging himself down, he flew home to the hut, crying breathlessly, 'Mother, mother, the farmers are close by with the wolf. They have found out all about it, and will certainly kill me, and perhaps you too. But if you do as I tell you, I may be able to save us both. Lie down on the floor, and pretend to be dead, and be sure not to speak, whatever happens.

Thus when the three brothers, each armed with a whip, entered the hut a few seconds later, they found a woman extended on the floor, and Toueno kneeling at her side, whistling loudly into her ears.

'What are you doing now, you rascal?' asked the eldest.

'What am I doing? Oh, my poor friends, I am the most miserable creature in the world! I have lost the best of mothers, and I don't know what will become of me,' and he hid his face in his hands and sobbed again.

'But what are you whistling like that for?'

'Well, it is the only chance. This whistle has been known to bring the dead back to life, and I hoped—' here he buried his face in his hands again, but peeping between his fingers he saw that the brother had opened their six eyes as wide as saucers.

'Look!' he suddenly exclaimed with a cry, 'Look! I am sure I felt her body move! And now her nostrils are twitching. Ah! the whistle has not lost its power after all,' and stooping down, Toueno whistled more loudly than before, so that the old woman's feet and hands showed signs of life, and she soon was able to life her head.

The farmers were so astonished at her restoration, that it was some time before they could speak. At length the eldest turned to the boy and said:

'Now listen to me. There is no manner of doubt that you are a young villain. You sold us a ram knowing full well that it was a wolf, and we came here to-day to pay you out for it. But if you will give us that whistle, we will pardon what you have done, and will leave you alone.'

'It is my only treasure, and I set great store by it,' answered the boy, pretending to hesitate. 'But as you wish for it so much, well, I suppose I can't refuse,' and he held out the whistle, which the eldest brother put in his pocket.

Armed with the precious whistle, the three brothers returned home full of joy, and as they went the youngest said to the others, 'I have such a good idea! Our wives are all lazy and grumbling, and make our lives a burden. Let us give them a lesson, and kill them as soon as we get in. Of course we can restore them to life at once, but they will have had a rare fright.'

'Ah, how clever you are,' answered the other two. 'Nobody else would have thought of that.'

So gaily the three husbands knocked down their three wives, who fell dead to the ground. Then one by one the men tried the whistle, and blew so loudly that it seemed as if their lungs would burst, but the women lay stark and stiff and never moved an eyelid. The husbands grew pale and cold, for they had never dreamed of this, nor meant any harm, and after a while they understood that their efforts were of no use, and that once more the boy had tricked them. With stern faces they rose to their feet, and taking a large sack they retraced their steps to the hut.

This time there was no escape. Toueno had been asleep, and only opened his eyes as they entered. Without a word on either side they thrust him into the sack, and tying up the mouth, the eldest threw it over his shoulder. After that they all set out to the river, where they intended to drown the boy.

But the river was a long way off, and the day was very hot, and Antoine was heavy, heavier than a whole sheaf of corn. They carried him in turns, but even so they grew very tired and thirsty, and when a little tavern came in sight on the roadside, they thankfully flung the sack down on a bench and entered to refresh themselves. They never noticed that a beggar was sitting in the shade at the end of the bench, but Toueno's sharp ears caught the sound of someone eating, and as soon as the farmers had gone into the inn he began to groan softly.

'What is the matter?' asked the beggar, drawing a little nearer. 'Why have they shut you up, poor boy?'

'Because they wanted to make me a bishop, and I would not consent,' answered Toueno.

'Dear me,' exclaimed the beggar, 'yet it isn't such a bad thing to be a bishop.'

'I don't say it is,' replied the young rascal, 'but I should never like it. However, if you have any fancy for wearing a mitre, you need only untie the sack, and take my place.'

'I should like nothing better,' said the man, as he stooped to undo the big knot.

So it was the beggar and not Toueno-Boueno who was flung into the water.

The next morning the three wives were buried, and on returning from the cemetery, their husbands met Toueno-Boueno driving a magnificent flock of sheep. At the sight of him the three farmers stood still with astonishment.

'What! you scoundrel!' they cried at last, 'we drowned you yesterday, and to-day we find you again, as well as ever!'

'It does seem odd, doesn't it?' answered he. 'But perhaps you don't know that beneath this world there lies another yet more beautiful and far, far richer. Well, it was there that you sent me when you flung me into the river, and though I felt a little strange at first, yet I soon began to look about me, and to see what was happening. There I noticed that close to the place where I had fallen, a sheep fair was being held, and a bystander told me that every day horses or cattle were sold somewhere in the town. If I had only had the luck to be thrown into the river on the side of the horse fair I might have made my fortune! As it was, I had to content myself with buying these sheep, which you can get for nothing.'

68

'And do you know exactly the spot in the river which lies over the horse fair?'

'As if I did not know it, when I have seen it with my own eyes.'

'Then if you do not want us to avenge our dead flocks and our murdered wives, you will have to throw us into the river just over the place of the horse fair.'

'Very well; only you must get three sacks and come with me to that rock which juts into the river. I will throw you in from there, and you will fall nearly on to the horses' backs.'

So he threw them in, and as they were never seen again, no one ever knew into which fair they had fallen.

From 'Litterature Orale de L'Auvergne,' par Paul Sebillot.

The Brown Bear of Norway

There was once a king in Ireland, and he had three daughters, and very nice princesses they were. And one day, when they and their father were walking on the lawn, the king began to joke with them, and to ask them whom they would like to be married to. 'I'll have the king of Ulster for a husband,' says one; 'and I'll have the king of Munster,' says another; 'and,' says the youngest, 'I'll have no husband but the Brown Bear of Norway.' For a nurse of hers used to be telling her of an enchanted prince that she called by that name, and she fell in love with him, and his name was the first name on her tongue, for the very night before she was dreaming of him. Well, one laughed, and another laughed, and they joked with the princess all the rest of the evening. But that very night she woke up out of her sleep in a great hall that was lighted up with a thousand lamps; the richest carpets were on the floor, and the walls were covered with cloth of gold and silver, and the place was full of grand company, and the very beautiful prince she saw in her dreams was there, and it wasn't a moment till he was on one knee before her, and telling her how much he loved her, and asking her wouldn't she be his queen. Well, she hadn't the heart to refuse him, and married they were the same evening.

'Now, my darling,' says he, when they were left by themselves, 'you must know that I am under enchantment. A sorceress, that had a beautiful daughter, wished me for her son-in-law; but the mother got power over me, and when I refused to wed her daughter she made me take the form of a bear by day, and I was to continue so till a lady would marry me of her own free will, and endure five years of great trials after.'

Well, when the princess woke in the morning, she missed her husband from her side, and spent the day very sadly. But as soon as the lamps were lighted in the grand hall, where she was sitting on a sofa covered with silk, the folding doors flew open, and he was sitting by her side the next minute. So they spent another happy evening, but he warned her that whenever she began to tire of him, or ceased to have faith in him, they would be parted for ever, and he'd be obliged to marry the witch's daughter.

She got used to find him absent by day, and they spent a happy twelvemonth together, and at last a beautiful little boy was born; and happy as she was before, she was twice as happy now, for she had her child to keep her company in the day when she couldn't see her husband.

At last, one evening, when herself, and himself, and her child were sitting with a window open because it was a sultry night, in flew an eagle, took the infant's sash in his beak, and flew up in the air with him. She screamed, and was going to throw herself out the window after him, but the prince caught her, and looked at her very seriously. She bethought of what he said soon after their marriage, and she stopped the cries and complaints that were on her tongue. She spent her days very lonely for another twelvemonth, when a beautiful little girl was sent to her. Then she thought to herself she'd have a sharp eye about her this time; so she never would allow a window to be more than a few inches open.

70

But all her care was in vain. Another evening, when they were all so happy, and the prince dandling the baby, a beautiful greyhound stood before them, took the child out of the father's hand, and was out of the door before you could wink. This time she shouted and ran out of the room, but there were some of the servants in the next room, and all declared that neither child nor dog passed out. She felt, somehow, as if it was her husband's fault, but still she kept command over herself, and didn't once reproach him.

When the third child was born she would hardly allow a window or a door to be left open for a moment; but she wasn't the nearer to keep the child to herself. They were sitting one evening by the fire, when a lady appeared standing by them. The princess opened her eyes in a great fright and stared at her, and while she was doing so, the lady wrapped a shawl round the baby that was sitting in its father's lap, and either sank through the ground with it or went up through the wide chimney. This time the mother kept her bed for a month.

'My dear,' said she to her husband, when she was beginning to recover, 'I think I'd feel better if I was to see my father and mother and sisters once more. If you give me leave to go home for a few days I'd be glad.' 'Very well,' said he, 'I will do that, and whenever you feel inclined to return, only mention your wish when you lie down at night.' The next morning when she awoke she found herself in her own old chamber in her father's palace. She rang the bell, and in a short time she had her mother and father and married sisters about her, and they laughed till they cried for joy at finding her safe back again.

In time she told them all that had happened to her, and they didn't know what to advise her to do. She was as fond of her husband as ever, and said she was sure that he couldn't help letting the children go; but still she was afraid beyond the world to have another child torn from her. Well, the mother and sisters consulted a wise woman that used to bring eggs to the castle, for they had great faith in her wisdom. She said the only plan was to secure the bear's skin that the prince was obliged to put on every morning, and get it burned, and then he couldn't help being a man night and day, and the enchantment would be at an end.

So they all persuaded her to do that, and she promised she would; and after eight days she felt so great a longing to see her husband again that she made the wish the same night, and when she woke three hours after, she was in her husband's palace, and he himself was watching over her. There was great joy on both sides, and they were happy for many days.

Now she began to think how she never minded her husband leaving her in the morning, and how she never found him neglecting to give her a sweet drink out of a gold cup just as she was going to bed.

One night she contrived not to drink any of it, though she pretended to do so; and she was wakeful enough in the morning, and saw her husband passing out through a panel in the wainscot, though she kept her eyelids nearly closed. The next night she got a few drops of the sleepy posset that she saved the evening before put into her husband's night drink, and that made him sleep sound enough. She got up after midnight, passed through the panel, and found a Beautiful brown bear's hide hanging in the corner. Then she stole back, and went down to the parlour fire, and put the hide into the middle of it till it was all fine ashes. She then lay down by her husband, gave him a kiss on the cheek, and fell asleep.

If she was to live a hundred years she'd never forget how she wakened next morning, and found her husband looking down on her with misery and anger in his face. 'Unhappy woman,' said he, 'you have separated us for ever! Why hadn't you patience for five years? I am now obliged, whether I like or no, to go a three days' journey to the witch's castle, and marry her daughter. The skin that was my guard you have burned it, and the egg-wife that gave you the counsel was the witch herself. I won't reproach you: your punishment will be severe without it. Farewell for ever!'

He kissed her for the last time, and was off the next minute, walking as fast as he could. She shouted after him, and then seeing there was no use, she dressed herself and pursued him. He never stopped, nor stayed, nor looked back, and still she kept him in sight; and when he was on the hill she was in the hollow, and when he was in the hollow she was on the hill. Her life was almost leaving her, when, just as the sun was setting, he turned up a lane, and went into a little house. She crawled up after him, and when she got inside there was a beautiful little boy on his knees, and he kissing and hugging him. 'Here, my poor darling,' says he, 'is your eldest child, and there,' says he, pointing to a woman that was looking on with a smile on her face, 'is the eagle that carried him away.' She forgot all her sorrows in a moment, hugging her child, and laughing and crying over him. The woman washed their feet, and rubbed them with an ointment that took all the soreness out of their bones, and made them as fresh as a daisy. Next morning, just before sunrise, he was up, and prepared to be off, 'Here,' said he to her, 'is a thing which may be of use to you. It's a scissors, and whatever stuff you cut with it will be turned into silk. The moment the sun rises, I'll lose all memory of yourself and the children, but I'll get it at sunset again. Farewell!' But he wasn't far gone till she was in sight of him again, leaving her boy behind. It was the same to-day as yesterday: their shadows went before them in the morning and followed them in the evening. He never stopped, and she never stopped, and as the sun was setting he turned up another lane, and there they found their little daughter. It was all joy and comfort again till morning, and then the third day's journey commenced.

But before he started he gave her a comb, and told her that whenever she used it, pearls and diamonds would fall from her hair. Still he had his memory from sunset to sunrise; but from sunrise to sunset he travelled on under the charm, and never threw his eye behind. This night they came to where the youngest baby was, and the next morning, just before sunrise, the prince spoke to her for the last time. 'Here, my poor wife,' said he, 'is a little hand-reel, with gold thread that has no end, and the half of our marriage ring. If you ever get to my house, and put your half-ring to mine, I shall recollect you. There is a wood yonder, and the moment I enter it I shall forget everything that ever happened between us, just as if I was born yesterday. Farewell, dear wife and child, for ever!' Just then the sun rose, and away he walked towards the wood. She saw it open before him and close after him, and when she came up, she could no more get in than she could break through a stone wall. She wrung her hands and shed tears, but then she recollected herself, and cried out, 'Wood, I charge you by my three magic gifts, the scissors, the comb, and the reel— to let me through'; and it opened, and she went along a walk till she came in sight of a palace, and a lawn, and a woodman's cottage on the edge of the wood where it came nearest the palace.

She went into the lodge, and asked the woodman and his wife to take her into their service. They were not willing at first; but she told them she would ask no wages, and would give them diamonds, and pearls, and silk stuffs, and gold thread whenever they wished for them, and then they agreed to let her stay.

It wasn't long till she heard how a young prince, that was just arrived, was living in the palace of the young mistress. He seldom stirred abroad, and every one that saw him remarked how silent and sorrowful he went about, like a person that was searching for some lost thing.

The servants and conceited folk at the big house began to take notice of the beautiful young woman at the lodge, and to annoy her with their impudence. The head footman was the most troublesome, and at last she invited him to come and take tea with her. Oh, how rejoiced he was, and how he bragged of it in the servants' hall! Well, the evening came, and the footman walked into the lodge, and was shown to her sitting-room; for the lodge-keeper and his wife stood in great awe of her, and gave her two nice rooms for herself. Well, he sat down as stiff as a ramrod, and was talking in a grand style about the great doings at the castle, while she was getting the tea and toast ready. 'Oh,' says she to him, 'would you put your hand out at the window and cut me off a sprig or two of honeysuckle?' He got up in great glee, and put out his hand and head; and said she, 'By the virtue of my magic gifts, let a pair of horns spring out of your head, and sing to the lodge.' Just as she wished, so it was. They sprung from the front of each ear, and met at the back. Oh, the poor wretch! And how he bawled and roared! and the servants that he used to be boasting to were soon flocking from the castle, and grinning, and huzzaing, and beating tunes on tongs and shovels and pans; and he cursing and swearing, and the eyes ready to start out of his head, and he so black in the face, and kicking out his legs behind him like mad.

At last she pitied him, and removed the charm, and the horns dropped down on the ground, and he would have killed her on the spot, only he was as weak as water, and his fellow-servants came in and carried him up to the big house. Well, some way or other the story came to the ears of the prince, and he strolled down that way. She had only the dress of a countrywoman on her as she sat sewing at the window, but that did not hide her beauty, and he was greatly puzzled after he had a good look, just as a body is puzzled to know whether something happened to him when he was young or if he only dreamed it. Well, the witch's daughter heard about it too, and she came to see the strange girl; and what did she find her doing but cutting out the pattern of a gown from brown paper; and as she cut away, the paper became the richest silk she ever saw. The witch's daughter looked on with greedy eyes, and, says she, 'What would you be satisfied to take for that scissors?' 'I'll take nothing,' says she, 'but leave to spend one night outside the prince's chamber.' Well, the proud lady fired up, and was going to say something dreadful; but the scissors kept on cutting, and the silk growing richer and richer every inch. So she promised what the girl had asked her.

When night came on she was let into the palace and lay down till the prince was in such a dead sleep that all she did couldn't awake him. She sung this verse to him, sighing and sobbing, and kept singing it the night long, and it was all in vain:

Four long years I was married to thee; Three sweet babes I bore to thee; Brown Bear of Norway, turn to me.

At the first dawn the proud lady was in the chamber, and led her away, and the footman of the horns put out his tongue at her as she was quitting the palace.

So there was no luck so far; but the next day the prince passed by again and looked at her, and saluted her kindly, as a prince might a farmer's daughter, and passed one; and soon the witch's daughter passed by, and found her combing her hair, and pearls and diamonds dropping from it.

Well, another bargain was made, and the princess spent another night of sorrow, and she left the castle at daybreak, and the footman was at his post and enjoyed his revenge.

The third day the prince went by, and stopped to talk with the strange woman. He asked her could he do anything to serve her, and she said he might. She asked him did he ever wake at night. He said that he often did, but that during the last two nights he was listening to a sweet song in his dreams, and could not wake, and that the voice was one that he must have known and loved in some other world long ago. Says she, 'Did you drink any sleepy posset either of these evenings before you went to bed?' 'I did,' said he. 'The two evenings my wife gave me something to drink, but I don't know whether it was a sleepy posset or not.' 'Well, prince,' said she, 'as you say you would wish to oblige me, you can do it by not tasting any drink to-night.' 'I will not,' says he, and then he went on his walk.

Well, the great lady came soon after the prince, and found the stranger using her hand-reel and winding threads of gold off it, and the third bargain was made.

That evening the prince was lying on his bed at twilight, and his mind much disturbed; and the door opened, and in his princess walked, and down she sat by his bedside and sung:

Four long years I was married to thee; Three sweet babes I bore to thee; Brown Bear of Norway, turn to me.

'Brown Bear of Norway !' said he. 'I don't understand you.' 'Don't you remember, prince, that I was your wedded wife for four years?' 'I do not,' said he, 'but I'm sure I wish it was so.' 'Don't you remember our three babes that are still alive?' 'Show me them. My mind is all a heap of confusion.' 'Look for the half of our marriage ring, that hangs at your neck, and fit it to this.' He did so, and the same moment the charm was broken. His full memory came back on him, and he flung his arms round his wife's neck, and both burst into tears.

Well, there was a great cry outside, and the castle walls were heard splitting and cracking. Everyone in the castle was alarmed, and made their way out. The prince and princess went with the rest, and by the time all were safe on the lawn, down came the building, and made the ground tremble for miles round. No one ever saw the witch and her daughter afterwards. It was not long till the prince and princess had their children with them, and then they set out for their own palace. The kings of Ireland and of Munster and Ulster, and their wives, soon came to visit them, and may every one that deserves it be as happy as the Brown Bear of Norway and his family.

From 'West Highland Tales.'

Little Lasse

There was once a little boy whose name was Lars, and because he was so little he was called Little Lasse; he was a brave little man, for he sailed round the world in a pea-shell boat.

It was summer time, when the pea shells grew long and green in the garden. Little Lasse crept into the pea bed where the pea stalks rose high above his cap, and he picked seventeen large shells, the longest and straightest he could find.

Little Lasse thought, perhaps, that no one saw him; but that was foolish, for God sees everywhere.

Then the gardener came with his gun over his shoulder, and he heard something rustling in the pea bed.

'I think that must be a sparrow,' he said. 'Ras! Ras!' but no sparrows flew out, for Little Lasse had no wings, only two small legs. 'Wait! I will load my gun and shoot the sparrows,' said the gardener.

Then Little Lasse was frightened, and crept out on to the path.

'Forgive me, dear gardener!' he said. 'I wanted to get some fine boats.'

'Well, I will this time,' said the gardener. 'But another time Little Lasse must ask leave to go and look for boats in the pea bed.'

'I will,' answered Lasse; and he went off to the shore. Then he opened the shells with a pin, split them carefully in two, and broke small little bits of sticks for the rowers' seats. Then he took the peas which were in the shells and put them in the boats for cargo. Some of the shells got broken, some remained whole, and when all were ready Lasse had twelve boats. But they should not be boats, they should be large warships. He had three liners, three frigates, three brigs and three schooners. The largest liner was called Hercules, and the smallest schooner The Flea. Little Lasse put all the twelve into the water, and they floated as splendidly and as proudly as any great ships over the waves of the ocean.

And now the ships must sail round the world. The great island over there was Asia; that large stone Africa; the little island America; the small stones were Polynesia; and the shore from which the ships sailed out was Europe. The whole fleet set off and sailed far away to other parts of the world. The ships of the line steered a straight course to Asia, the frigates sailed to Africa, the brigs to America, and the schooners to Polynesia. But Little Lasse remained in Europe, and threw small stones out into the great sea.

Now, there was on the shore of Europe a real boat, father's own, a beautiful white-painted boat, and Little Lasse got into it. Father and mother had forbidden this, but Little Lasse forgot. He thought he should very much like to travel to some other part of the world.

'I shall row out a little way—only a very little way,' he thought. The pea-shell boats had travelled so far that they only looked like little specks on the ocean. 'I shall seize Hercules on the coast of Asia,' said Lasse, 'and then row home again to Europe.'

He shook the rope that held the boat, and, strange to say, the rope became loose. Ditsch, ratsch, a man is a man, and so Little Lasse manned the boat.

Now he would row—and he could row, for he had rowed so often on the step sat home, when the steps pretended to be a boat and father's big stick an oar. But when Little Lasse wanted to row there were no oars to be found in the boat. The oars were locked up in the boat-house, and Little Lasse had not noticed that the boat was empty. It is not so easy as one thinks to row to Asia without oars.

What could Little Lasse do now? The boat was already some distance out on the sea, and the wind, which blew from land, was driving it still further out. Lasse was frightened and began to cry. But there was no one on the shore to hear him. Only a big crow perched alone in the birch tree; and the gardener's black cat sat under the birch tree, waiting to catch the crow. Neither of them troubled themselves in the least about Little Lasse, who was drifting out to sea.

Ah! how sorry Little Lasse was now that he had been disobedient and got into the boat, when father and mother had so often forbidden him to do so! Now it was too late, he could not get back to land. Perhaps he would be lost out on the great sea. What should he do?

When he had shouted until he was tired and no one heard him, he put his two little hands together and said, 'Good God, do not be angry with Little Lasse.' And then he went to sleep. For although it was daylight, old Nukku Matti was sitting on the shores of the 'Land of Nod,' and was fishing for little children with his long fishing rod. He heard the low words which Little Lasse said to God, and he immediately drew the boat to himself and laid Little Lasse to sleep on a bed of rose leaves.

Then Nukku Matti said to one of the Dreams, 'Play with Little Lasse, so that he does not feel lonesome.'

It was a little dream-boy, so little, so little, that he was less than Lasse himself; he had blue eyes and fair hair, a red cap with a silver band, and white coat with pearls on the collar. He came to Little Lasse and said, 'Would you like to sail round the world?'

'Yes,' said Lasse in his sleep, 'I should like to.'

'Come, then,' said the dream-boy, 'and let us sail in your pea-shell boats. You shall sail in Hercules and I shall sail in The Flea.'

So they sailed away from the 'Land of Nod,' and in a little while Hercules and The Flea were on the shores of Asia away at the other end of the world, where the Ice Sea flows through Behring Straits into the Pacific Ocean. A long way off in the winter mist they could see the explorer Nordenskiold with his ship Vega trying to find an opening between the ice. It was so cold, so cold; the great icebergs glittered strangely, and the huge whales now lived under the ice, for they could not make a hole through with their awkward heads. All around on the dreary shore there was snow and snow as far as the eye could see; little grey men in shaggy skins moved about, and drove in small sledges through the snow drifts, but the sledges were drawn by dogs.

'Shall we land here?' asked the dream-boy.

'No,' said Little Lasse. 'I am so afraid that the whales would swallow us up, and the big dogs bite us. Let us sail instead to another part of the world.'

'Very well,' said the dream-boy with the red cap and the silver band; 'it is not far to America'—and at the same moment they were there.

The sun was shining and it was very warm. Tall palm trees grew in long rows on the shore and bore coconuts in their top branches. Men red as copper galloped over the immense green prairies and shot their arrows at the buffaloes, who turned against them with their sharp horns. An enormous cobra which had crept up the stem of a tall palm tree threw itself on to a little llama that was grazing at the foot. Knaps! it was all over the little llama.

'Shall we land here?' asked the dream-boy.

'No,' said Little Lasse. 'I am so afraid that the buffaloes will butt us, and the great serpent eat us up. Let us travel to another part of the world.'

'Very well,' said the dream-boy with the white coat, 'it is only a little way to Polynesia'—and then they were there.

It was very warm there, as warm as in a hot bath in Finland. Costly spices grew on the shores: the pepper plant, the cinnamon tree, ginger, saffron; the coffee plant and the tea plant. Brown people with long ears and thick lips, and hideously painted faces, hunted a yellow-spotted tiger among the high bamboos on the shore, and the tiger turned on them and stuck its claws into one of the brown men. Then all the others took to flight.

'Shall we land here?' asked the dream-boy.

'No,' said Little Lasse. 'Don't you see the tiger away there by the pepper plant? Let us travel to another part of the world.'

'We can do so,' said the dream-boy with the blue eyes. 'We are not far from Africa'—and as he said that they were there.

They anchored at the mouth of a great river where the shores were as green as the greenest velvet. A little distance from the river an immense desert stretched away. The air was yellow; the sun shone so hot, so hot as if it would burn the earth to ashes, and the people were as black as the blackest jet. They rode across the desert on tall camels; the lions roared with thirst, and the great crocodiles with their grey lizard heads and sharp white teeth gaped up out of the river.

'Shall we land here?' asked the dream-boy.

'No,' said Little Lasse. 'The sun would burn us, and the lions and the crocodiles would eat us up. Let us travel to another part of the world.'

'We can travel back to Europe,' said the dream-boy with the fair hair. And with that they were there.

They came to a shore where it was all so cool and familiar and friendly. There stood the tall birch tree with its drooping leaves; at the top sat the old crow, and at its foot crept the gardener's black cat. Not far away was a house which Little Lasse had seen before; near the house there was a garden, and in the garden a pea bed with long pea shells. An old gardener with a green coat walked about and wondered if the cucumbers were ripe. Fylax was barking on the steps, and when he saw Little Lasse he wagged his tail. Old Stina was milking the cows in the farmyard, and there was a very familiar lady in a check woollen shawl on her way to the bleaching green to see if the clothes were bleached. There was, too, a well-known gentleman in a yellow summer coat, with a long pipe in his mouth; he was going to see if the reapers had cut the rye. A boy and a girl were running on the shore and calling out, 'Little Lasse! Come home for bread-and-butter!'

'Shall we land here?' asked the dream-boy, and he blinked his blue eyes roguishly.

'Come with me, and I shall ask mother to give you some bread-and-butter and a glass of milk,' said Little Lasse.

'Wait a little,' said the dream-boy. And now Little Lasse saw that the kitchen door was open, and from within there was heard a low, pleasant frizzling, like that which is heard when one whisks yellow batter with a wooden ladle into a hot frying-pan.

'Perhaps we should sail back to Polynesia now?' said the happy dream-boy.

'No; they are frying pancakes in Europe just now,' said Little Lasse; and he wanted to jump ashore, but he could not. The dream-boy had tied him with a chain of flowers, so that he could not move. And now all the little dreams came about him, thousands and thousands of little children, and they made a ring around him and sang a little song:

> The world is very, very wide,
>   Little Lasse, Lasse,
> And though you've sailed beyond the tide,
> You can never tell how wide
> It is on the other side,
>   Lasse, Little Lasse.
> You have found it cold and hot,
>   Little Lasse, Lasse;
> But in no land is God not,
>   Lasse, Little Lasse.
> Many men live there as here,
> But they all to God are dear,
>   Little Lasse, Lasse.
> When His angel is your guide,
>   Little Lasse, Lasse,
> Then no harm can e'er betide,
> Even on the other side
>   Where the wild beasts wander.
> But tell us now,
>   Whene'er you roam,
>   Do you not find the best is home
> Of all the lands you've looked upon,
>   Lasse, Little Lasse?

When the dreams had sung their song they skipped away, and Nukku Matti carried Lasse back to the boat. He lay there for a long time quite still, and he still heard the frying-pan frizzling at home of the fire, the frizzling was very plain, Little Lasse heard it quite near him; and so he woke up and rubbed his eyes.

There he lay in the boat, where he had fallen asleep. The wind had turned, and the boat had drifted out with one wind and drifted in with another while Little Lasse slept, and what Lasse thought was frizzling in a frying-pan was the low murmur of the waves as they washed against the stones on the shore. But he was not altogether wrong, for the clear blue sea is like a great pan in which God's sun all day makes cakes for good children.

Little Lasse rubbed the sleep out of his eyes and looked around him. Everything was the same as before; the crow in the birch tree, the cat on the grass, and the pea-shell fleet on the shore. Some of the ships had foundered, and some had drifted back to land. Hercules had come back with its cargo from Asia, The Flea had arrived from Polynesia, and the other parts of the world were just where they were before.

Little Lasse did not know what to think. He had so often been in that grotto in the 'Land of Nod' and did not know what tricks dreams can play. But Little Lasse did not trouble his head with such things; he gathered together his boats and walked up the shore back to the house.

His brother and sister ran to meet him, and called out from the distance, 'Where have you been so long, Lasse? Come home and get some bread-and-butter.' The kitchen door stood open, and inside was heard a strange frizzling.

The gardener was near the gate, watering the dill and parsley, the carrots and parsnips.

'Well,' he said, 'where has Little Lasse been so long?'

Little Lasse straightened himself up stiff, and answered: 'I have sailed round the world in a pea-shell boat.'

'Oh!' said the gardener.

He has forgotten Dreamland. But you have not forgotten it; you know that it exists. You know the beautiful grotto and the bright silver walls whose lustre never fades, the sparkling diamonds which never grow dim, the music which never ceases its low, soft murmur through the sweet evening twilight. The airy fairy fancies of happy Dreamland never grow old; they, like the glorious stars above us, are always young. Perhaps you have caught a glimpse of their ethereal wings as they flew around your pillow. Perhaps you have met the same dream-boy with the blue eyes and the fair hair, the one who wore the red cap with the silver band and the white coat with pearls on the collar. Perhaps he has taken you to see all the countries of the world and the peoples, the cold waste lands and the burning deserts, the many coloured men and the wild creatures in the sea and in the woods, so that you may earn many things, but come gladly home again. Yes, who knows? Perhaps you also have sailed round the wide world once in a pea-shell boat.

From Z. Topelius.

'Moti'

Once upon a time there was a youth called Moti, who was very big and strong, but the clumsiest creature you can imagine. So clumsy was he that he was always putting his great feet into the bowls of sweet milk or curds which his mother set out on the floor to cool, always smashing, upsetting, breaking, until at last his father said to him:

'Here, Moti, are fifty silver pieces which are the savings of years; take them and go and make your living or your fortune if you can.'

Then Moti started off one early spring morning with his thick staff over his shoulder, singing gaily to himself as he walked along.

In one way and another he got along very well until a hot evening when he came to a certain city where he entered the travellers' 'serai' or inn to pass the night. Now a serai, you must know, is generally just a large square enclosed by a high wall with an open colonnade along the inside all round to accommodate both men and beasts, and with perhaps a few rooms in towers at the corners for those who are too rich or too proud to care about sleeping by their own camels and horses. Moti, of course, was a country lad and had lived with cattle all his life, and he wasn't rich and he wasn't proud, so he just borrowed a bed from the innkeeper, set it down beside an old buffalo who reminded him of home, and in five minutes was fast asleep.

In the middle of the night he woke, feeling that he had been disturbed, and putting his hand under his pillow found to his horror that his bag of money had been stolen. He jumped up quietly and began to prowl around to see whether anyone seemed to be awake, but, though he managed to arouse a few men and beasts by falling over them, he walked in the shadow of the archways round the whole serai without coming across a likely thief. He was just about to give it up when he overheard two men whispering, and one laughed softly, and peering behind a pillar, he saw two Afghan horsedealers counting out his bag of money! Then Moti went back to bed!

In the morning Moti followed the two Afghans outside the city to the horsemarket in which they horses were offered for sale. Choosing the best-looking horse amongst them he went up to it and said:

'Is this horse for sale? may I try it?' and, the merchants assenting, he scrambled up on its back, dug in his heels, and off they flew. Now Moti had never been on a horse in his life, and had so much ado to hold on with both hands as well as with both legs that the animal went just where it liked, and very soon broke into a break-neck gallop and made straight back to the serai where it had spent the last few nights.

'This will do very well,' thought Moti as they whirled in at the entrance. As soon as the horse had arrived at its table it stopped of its own accord and Moti immediately rolled off; but he jumped up at once, tied the beast up, and called for some breakfast. Presently the Afghans appeared, out of breath and furious, and claimed the horse.

'What do you mean?' cried Moti, with his mouth full of rice, 'it's my horse; I paid you fifty pieces of silver for it—quite a bargain, I'm sure!'

'Nonsense! it is our horse,' answered one of the Afghans beginning to untie the bridle.

'Leave off,' shouted Moti, seizing his staff; 'if you don't let my horse alone I'll crack your skulls! you thieves! I know you! Last night you took my money, so to-day I took your horse; that's fair enough!'

Now the Afghans began to look a little uncomfortable, but Moti seemed so determined to keep the horse that they resolved to appeal to the law, so they went off and laid a complaint before the king that Moti had stolen one of their horses and would not give it up nor pay for it.

Presently a soldier came to summon Moti to the king; and, when he arrived and made his obeisance, the king began to question him as to why he had galloped off with the horse in this fashion. But Moti declared that he had got the animal in exchange for fifty pieces of silver, whilst the horse merchants vowed that the money they had on them was what they had received for the sale of other horses; and in one way and another the dispute got so confusing that the king (who really thought that Moti had stolen the horse) said at last, 'Well, I tell you what I will do. I will lock something into this box before me, and if he guesses what it is, the horse is his, and if he doesn't then it is yours.'

To this Moti agreed, and the king arose and went out alone by a little door at the back of the Court, and presently came back clasping something closely wrapped up in a cloth under his robe, slipped it into the little box, locked the box, and set it up where all might see.

'Now,' said the king to Moti, 'guess!'

It happened that when the king had opened the door behind him, Moti noticed that there was a garden outside: without waiting for the king's return he began to think what could be got out of the garden small enough to be shut in the box. 'Is it likely to be a fruit or a flower? No, not a flower this time, for he clasped it too tight. Then it must be a fruit or a stone. Yet not a stone, because he wouldn't wrap a dirty stone in his nice clean cloth. Then it is a fruit! And a fruit without much scent, or else he would be afraid that I might smell it. Now what fruit without much scent is in season just now? When I know that I shall have guessed the riddle!'

As has been said before, Moti was a country lad, and was accustomed to work in his father's garden. He knew all the common fruits, so he thought he ought to be able to guess right; but so as not to let it seem too easy, he gazed up at the ceiling with a puzzled expression, and looked down at the floor with an air or wisdom and his fingers pressed against his forehead, and then he said, slowly, with his eyes on the king,—

'It is freshly plucked! It is round and it is red! It is a pomegranate!'

Now the king knew nothing about fruits except that they were good to eat; and, as for seasons, he asked for whatever fruit he wanted whenever he wanted it, and saw that he got it; so to him Moti's guess was like a miracle, and clear proof not only of his wisdom but of his innocence, for it was a pomegranate that he had put into the box. Of course when the king marvelled and praised Moti's wisdom, everybody else did so too; and, whilst the Afghans went off crestfallen, Moti took the horse and entered the king's service.

Very soon after this, Moti, who continued to live in the serai, came back one wet and stormy evening to find that his precious horse had strayed. Nothing remained of him but a broken halter cord, and no one knew what had become of him. After inquiring of everyone who was likely to know, Moti seized the cord and his big staff and sallied out to look for him. Away and away he tramped out of the city and into the neighbouring forest, tracking hoof-marks in the mud. Presently it grew late, but still Moti wandered on until suddenly in the gathering darkness he came right upon a tiger who was contentedly eating his horse.

'You thief!' shrieked Moti, and ran up and, just as the tiger, in astonishment, dropped a bone—whack! came Moti's staff on his head with such good will that the beast was half stunned and could hardly breathe or see. Then Moti continued to shower upon him blows and abuse until the poor tiger could hardly stand, whereupon his tormentor tied the end of the broken halter round his neck and dragged him back to the serai.

'If you had my horse,' he said, 'I will at least have you, that's fair enough!' And he tied him up securely by the head and heels, much as he used to tie the horse; then, the night being far gone, he flung himself beside him and slept soundly.

You cannot imagine anything like the fright of the people in the serai, when they woke up and found a tiger—very battered but still a tiger—securely tethered amongst themselves and their beasts! Men gathered in groups talking and exclaiming, and finding fault with the innkeeper for allowing such a dangerous beast into the serai, and all the while the innkeeper was just as troubled as the rest, and none dared go near the place where the tiger stood blinking miserably on everyone, and where Moti lay stretched out snoring like thunder.

At last news reached the king that Moti had exchanged his horse for a live tiger; and the monarch himself came down, half disbelieving the tale, to see if it were really true. Someone at last awaked Moti with the news that his royal master was come; and he arose yawning, and was soon delightedly explaining and showing off his new possession. The king, however, did not share his pleasure at all, but called up a soldier to shoot the tiger, much to the relief of all the inmates of the serai except Moti. If the king, however, was before convinced that Moti was one of the wisest of men, he was now still more convinced that he was the bravest, and he increased his pay a hundredfold, so that our hero thought that he was the luckiest of men.

A week or two after this incident the king sent for Moti, who on arrival found his master in despair. A neighbouring monarch, he explained, who had many more soldiers than he, had declared war against him, and he was at his wits' end, for he had neither money to buy him off nor soldiers enough to fight him—what was he to do?

'If that is all, don't you trouble,' said Moti. 'Turn out your men, and I'll go with them, and we'll soon bring this robber to reason.'

The king began to revive at these hopeful words, and took Moti off to his stable where he bade him choose for himself any horse he liked. There were plenty of fine horses in the stalls, but to the king's astonishment Moti chose a poor little rat of a pony that was used to carry grass and water for the rest of the stable.

'But why do you choose that beast?' said the king.

'Well, you see, your majesty,' replied Moti, 'there are so many chances that I may fall off, and if I choose one of your fine big horses I shall have so far to fall that I shall probably break my leg or my arm, if not my neck, but if I fall off this little beast I can't hurt myself much.'

A very comical sight was Moti when he rode out to the war. The only weapon he carried was his staff, and to help him to keep his balance on horseback he had tied to each of his ankles a big stone that nearly touched the ground as he sat astride the little pony. The rest of the king's cavalry were not very numerous, but they pranced along in armour on fine horses. Behind them came a great rabble of men on foot armed with all sorts of weapons, and last of all was the king with his attendants, very nervous and ill at ease. So the army started.

They had not very far to go, but Moti's little pony, weighted with a heavy man and two big rocks, soon began to lag behind the cavalry, and would have lagged behind the infantry too, only they were not very anxious to be too early in the fight, and hung back so as to give Moti plenty of time. The young man jogged along more and more slowly for some time, until at last, getting impatient at the slowness of the pony, he gave him such a tremendous thwack with his staff that the pony completely lost his temper and bolted. First one stone became untied and rolled away in a cloud of dust to one side of the road, whilst Moti nearly rolled off too, but clasped his steed valiantly by its ragged mane, and, dropping his staff, held on for dear life. Then, fortunately the other rock broke away from his other leg and rolled thunderously down a neighbouring ravine. Meanwhile the advanced cavalry had barely time to draw to one side when Moti came dashing by, yelling bloodthirsty threats to his pony:

'You wait till I get hold of you! I'll skin you alive! I'll wring your neck! I'll break every bone in your body!' The cavalry thought that this dreadful language was meant for the enemy, and were filled with admiration of his courage. Many of their horses too were quite upset by this whirlwind that galloped howling through their midst, and in a few minutes, after a little plunging and rearing and kicking, the whole troop were following on Moti's heels.

Far in advance, Moti continued his wild career. Presently in his course he came to a great field of castor-oil plants, ten or twelve feet high, big and bushy, but quite green and soft. Hoping to escape from the back of his fiery steed Moti grasped one in passing, but its roots gave way, and he dashed on, with the whole plant looking like a young tree flourishing in his grip.

The enemy were in battle array, advancing over the plain, their king with them confident and cheerful, when suddenly from the front came a desperate rider at a furious gallop.

'Sire!' he cried, 'save yourself! the enemy are coming!'

'What do you mean?' said the king.

'Oh, sire!' panted the messenger, 'fly at once, there is no time to lose. Foremost of the enemy rides a mad giant at a furious gallop. He flourishes a tree for a club and is wild with anger, for as he goes he cries, "You wait till I get hold of you! I'll skin you alive! I'll wring your neck! I'll break every bone in your body!" Others ride behind, and you will do well to retire before this whirlwind of destruction comes upon you.'

Just then out of a cloud of dust in the distance the king saw Moti approaching at a hard gallop, looking indeed like a giant compared with the little beast he rode, whirling his castor-oil plant, which in the distance might have been an oak tree, and the sound of his revilings and shoutings came down upon the breeze! Behind him the dust cloud moved to the sound of the thunder of hoofs, whilst here and there flashed the glitter of steel. The sight and the sound struck terror into the king, and, turning his horse, he fled at top speed, thinking that a regiment of yelling giants was upon him; and all his force followed him as fast as they might go. One fat officer alone could not keep up on foot with that mad rush, and as Moti came galloping up he flung himself on the ground in abject fear. This was too much for Moti's excited pony, who shied so suddenly that Moti went flying over his head like a sky rocket, and alighted right on the top of his fat foe.

Quickly regaining his feet Moti began to swing his plant round his head and to shout:

'Where are your men? Bring them up and I'll kill them. My regiments! Come on, the whole lot of you! Where's your king? Bring him to me. Here are all my fine fellows coming up and we'll each pull up a tree by the roots and lay you all flat and your houses and towns and everything else! Come on!'

But the poor fat officer could do nothing but squat on his knees with his hands together, gasping. At last, when he got his breath, Moti sent him off to bring his king, and to tell him that if he was reasonable his life should be spared. Off the poor man went, and by the time the troops of Moti's side had come up and arranged themselves to look as formidable as possible, he returned with his king. The latter was very humble and apologetic, and promised never to make war any more, to pay a large sum of money, and altogether do whatever his conqueror wished.

So the armies on both sides went rejoicing home, and this was really the making of the fortune of clumsy Moti, who lived long and contrived always to be looked up to

86

as a fountain of wisdom, valour, and discretion by all except his relations, who could never understand what he had done to be considered so much wiser than anyone else.

A Pushto Story.

The Enchanted Deer

A young man was out walking one day in Erin, leading a stout cart-horse by the bridle. He was thinking of his mother and how poor they were since his father, who was a fisherman, had been drowned at sea, and wondering what he should do to earn a living for both of them. Suddenly a hand was laid on his shoulder, and a voice said to him:

'Will you sell me your horse, son of the fisherman?' and looking up he beheld a man standing in the road with a gun in his hand, a falcon on his shoulder, and a dog by his side.

'What will you give me for my horse?' asked the youth. 'Will you give me your gun, and your dog, and your falcon?'

'I will give them,' answered the man, and he took the horse, and the youth took the gun and the dog and the falcon, and went home with them. But when his mother heard what he had done she was very angry, and beat him with a stick which she had in her hand.

'That will teach you to sell my property,' said she, when her arm was quite tired, but Ian her son answered her nothing, and went off to his bed, for he was very sore.

That night he rose softly, and left the house carrying the gun with him. 'I will not stay here to be beaten,' thought he, and he walked and he walked and he walked, till it was day again, and he was hungry and looked about him to see if he could get anything to eat. Not very far off was a farm-house, so he went there, and knocked at the door, and the farmer and his wife begged him to come in, and share their breakfast.

'Ah, you have a gun,' said the farmer as the young man placed it in a corner. 'That is well, for a deer comes every evening to eat my corn, and I cannot catch it. It is fortune that has sent you to me.'

'I will gladly remain and shoot the deer for you,' replied the youth, and that night he hid himself and watched till the deer came to the cornfield; then he lifted his gun to his shoulder and was just going to pull the trigger, when, behold! instead of a deer, a woman with long black hair was standing there. At this sight his gun almost dropped from his hand in surprise, but as he looked, there was the deer eating the corn again. And thrice this happened, till the deer ran away over the moor, and the young man after her.

On they went, on and on and one, till they reached a cottage which was thatched with heather. With a bound the deer sprang on the roof, and lay down where none could see her, but as she did so she called out, 'Go in, fisher's son, and eat and drink while

88

you may.' So he entered and found food and wine on the table, but no man, for the house belonged to some robbers, who were still away at their wicked business.

After Ian, the fisher's son, had eaten all he wanted, he hid himself behind a great cask, and very soon he heard a noise, as of men coming through the heather, and the small twigs snapping under their feet. From his dark corner he could see into the room, and he counted four and twenty of them, all big, cross-looking men.

'Some one has been eating our dinner,' cried they, 'and there was hardly enough for ourselves.'

'It is the man who is lying under the cask,' answered the leader. 'Go and kill him, and then come and eat your food and sleep, for we must be off betimes in the morning.'

So four of them killed the fisher's son and left him, and then went to bed.

By sunrise they were all out of the house, for they had far to go. And when they had disappeared the deer came off the roof, to where the dead man lay, and she shook her head over him, and wax fell from her ear, and he jumped up as well as ever.

'Trust me and eat as you did before, and no harm shall happen to you,' said she. So Ian ate and drank, and fell sound asleep under the cask. In the evening the robbers arrived very tired, and crosser than they had been yesterday, for their luck had turned and they had brought back scarcely anything.

'Someone has eaten our dinner again,' cried they.

'It is the man under the barrel,' answered the captain. 'Let four of you go and kill him, but first slay the other four who pretended to kill him last night and didn't because he is still alive.'

Then Ian was killed a second time, and after the rest of the robbers had eaten, they lay down and slept till morning.

No sooner were their faces touched with the sun's rays than they were up and off. Then the deer entered and dropped the healing wax on the dead man, and he was as well as ever. By this time he did not mind what befell him, so sure was he that the deer would take care of him, and in the evening that which had happened before happened again—the four robbers were put to death and the fisher's son also, but because there was no food left for them to eat, they were nearly mad with rage, and began to quarrel. From quarrelling they went on to fighting, and fought so hard that by and bye they were all stretched dead on the floor.

Then the deer entered, and the fisher's son was restored to life, and bidding him follow her, she ran on to a little white cottage where dwelt an old woman and her son, who was thin and dark.

'Here I must leave you,' said the deer, 'but to-morrow meet me at midday in the church that is yonder.' And jumping across the stream, she vanished into a wood.

Next day he set out for the church, but the old woman of the cottage had gone before him, and had stuck an enchanted stick called 'the spike of hurt' in a crack of the door, so that he would brush against it as he stepped across the threshold. Suddenly he felt so sleepy that he could not stand up, and throwing himself on the ground he sank into a deep slumber, not knowing that the dark lad was watching him. Nothing could waken him, not even the sound of sweetest music, nor the touch of a lady who bent over him. A sad look came on her face, as she saw it was no use, and at last she gave it up, and lifting his arm, wrote her name across the side— 'the daughter of the king of the town under the waves.'

'I will come to-morrow,' she whispered, though he could not hear her, and she went sorrowfully away.

Then he awoke, and the dark lad told him what had befallen him, and he was very grieved. But the dark lad did not tell him of the name that was written underneath his arm.

On the following morning the fisher's son again went to the church, determined that he would not go to sleep, whatever happened. But in his hurry to enter he touched with his hand the spike of hurt, and sank down where he stood, wrapped in slumber. A second time the air was filled with music, and the lady came in, stepping softly, but though she laid his head on her knee, and combed his hair with a golden comb, his eyes opened not. Then she burst into tears, and placing a beautifully wrought box in his pocket she went her way.

The next day the same thing befell the fisher's son, and this time the lady wept more bitterly than before, for she said it was the last chance, and she would never be allowed to come any more, for home she must go.

As soon as the lady had departed the fisher's son awoke, and the dark lad told him of her visit, and how he would never see her as long as he lived. At this the fisher's son felt the cold creeping up to his heart, yet he knew the fault had not been his that sleep had overtaken him.

'I will search the whole world through till I find her,' cried he, and the dark lad laughed as he heard him. But the fisher's son took no heed, and off he went, following the sun day after day, till his shoes were in holes and his feet were sore from the journey. Nought did he see but the birds that made their nests in the trees, not so much as a goat or a rabbit. On and on and on he went, till suddenly he came upon a little house, with a woman standing outside it.

'All hail, fisher's son!' said she. 'I know what you are seeking; enter in and rest and eat, and to-morrow I will give you what help I can, and send you on your way.'

Gladly did Ian the fisher's son accept her offer, and all that day he rested, and the woman gave him ointment to put on his feet, which healed his sores. At daybreak he got up, ready to be gone, and the woman bade him farewell, saying:

'I have a sister who dwells on the road which you must travel. It is a long road, and it would take you a year and a day to reach it, but put on these old brown shoes with holes all over them, and you will be there before you know it. Then shake them off, and turn their toes to the known, and their heels to the unknown, and they will come home of themselves.'

The fisher's son did as the woman told him, and everything happened just as she had said. But at parting the second sister said to him, as she gave him another pair of shoes:

'Go to my third sister, for she has a son who is keeper of the birds of the air, and sends them to sleep when night comes. He is very wise, and perhaps he can help you.'

Then the young man thanked her, and went to the third sister.

The third sister was very kind, but had no counsel to give him, so he ate and drank and waited till her son came home, after he had sent all the birds to sleep. He thought a long while after his mother had told him the young man's story, and at last he said that he was hungry, and the cow must be killed, as he wanted some supper. So the cow was killed and the meat cooked, and a bag made of its red skin.

'Now get into the bag,' bade the son, and the young man got in and took his gun with him, but the dog and the falcon he left outside. The keeper of the birds drew the string at the top of the bag, and left it to finish his supper, when in flew an eagle through the open door, and picked the bag up in her claws and carried it through the air to an island. There was nothing to eat on the island, and the fisher's son thought he would die of food, when he remembered the box that the lady had put in his pocket. He opened the lid, and three tiny little birds flew out, and flapping their wings they asked,

'Good master, is there anything we can do for thee?'

'Bear me to the kingdom of the king under the waves,' he answered, and one little bird flew on to his head, and the others perched on each of his shoulders, and he shut his eyes, and in a moment there he was in the country under the sea. Then the birds flew away, and the young man looked about him, his heart beating fast at the thought that here dwelt the lady whom he had sought all the world over.

He walked on through the streets, and presently he reached the house of a weaver who was standing at his door, resting from his work.

'You are a stranger here, that is plain,' said the weaver, 'but come in, and I will give you food and drink.' And the young man was glad, for he knew not where to go, and they sat and talked till it grew late.

'Stay with me, I pray, for I love company and am lonely,' observed the weaver at last, and he pointed to a bed in a corner, where the fisher's son threw himself, and slept till dawn.

'There is to be a horse-race in the town to-day,' remarked the weaver, 'and the winner is to have the king's daughter to wife.' The young man trembled with excitement at the news, and his voice shook as he answered:

'That will be a prize indeed, I should like to see the race.'

'Oh, that is quite easy—anyone can go,' replied the weaver. 'I would take you myself, but I have promised to weave this cloth for the king.'

'That is a pity,' returned the young man politely, but in his heart he rejoiced, for he wished to be alone.

Leaving the house, he entered a grove of trees which stood behind, and took the box from his pocket. He raised the lid, and out flew the three little birds.

'Good master, what shall we do for thee?' asked they, and he answered, 'Bring me the finest horse that ever was seen, and the grandest dress, and glass shoes.'

'They are here, master,' said the birds, and so they were, and never had the young man seen anything so splendid.

Mounting the horse he rode into the ground where the horses were assembling for the great race, and took his place among them. Many good beasts were there which had won many races, but the horse of the fisher's son left them all behind, and he was first at the winning post. The king's daughter waited for him in vain to claim his prize, for he went back to the wood, and got off his horse, and put on his old clothes, and bade the box place some gold in his pockets. After that he went back to the weaver's house, and told him that the gold had been given him by the man who had won the race, and that the weaver might have it for his kindness to him.

Now as nobody had appeared to demand the hand of the princess, the king ordered another race to be run, and the fisher's son rode into the field still more splendidly dressed than he was before, and easily distanced everybody else. But again he left the prize unclaimed, and so it happened on the third day, when it seemed as if all the people in the kingdom were gathered to see the race, for they were filled with curiosity to know who the winner could be.

'If he will not come of his own free will, he must be brought,' said the king, and the messengers who had seen the face of the victor were sent to seek him in every street of the town. This took many days, and when at last they found the young man in the weaver's cottage, he was so dirty and ugly and had such a strange appearance, that they declared he could not be the winner they had been searching for, but a wicked robber who had murdered ever so many people, but had always managed to escape.

'Yes, it must be the robber,' said the king, when the fisher's son was led into his presence; 'build a gallows at once and hang him in the sight of all my subjects, that they may behold him suffer the punishment of his crimes.'

So the gallows was built upon a high platform, and the fisher's son mounted the steps up to it, and turned at the top to make the speech that was expected from every doomed man, innocent or guilt. As he spoke he happened to raise his arm, and the king's daughter, who was there at her father's side, saw the name which she had written under it. With a shriek she sprang from her seat, and the eyes of the spectators were turned towards her.

'Stop! stop!' she cried, hardly knowing what she said. 'If that man is hanged there is not a soul in the kingdom but shall die also.' And running up to where the fisher's son was standing, she took him by the hand, saying,

'Father, this is no robber or murderer, but the victor in the three races, and he loosed the spells that were laid upon me.'

Then, without waiting for a reply, she conducted him into the palace, and he bathed in a marble bath, and all the dirt that the fairies had put upon him disappeared like magic, and when he had dressed himself in the fine garments the princess had sent to him, he looked a match for any king's daughter in Erin. He went down into the great hall where she was awaiting him, and they had much to tell each other but little time to tell it in, for the king her father, and the princes who were visiting him, and all the people of the kingdom were still in their places expecting her return.

'How did you find me out?' she whispered as they went down the passage.

'The birds in the box told me,' answered he, but he could say no more, as they stepped out into the open space that was crowded with people. There the princes stopped.

'O kings!' she said, turning towards them, 'if one of you were killed to-day, the rest would fly; but this man put his trust in me, and had his head cut off three times. Because he has done this, I will marry him rather than one of you, who have come hither to wed me, for many kings here sought to free me from the spells, but none could do it save Ian the fisher's son.'

From 'Popular Tales of the West Highlands.'

A Fish Story

Perhaps you think that fishes were always fishes, and never lived anywhere except in the water, but if you went to Australia and talked to the black people in the sandy desert in the centre of the country, you would learn something quite different. They would tell you that long, long ago you would have met fishes on the land, wandering from place to place, and hunting all sorts of animals, and if you consider how fishes are made, you will understand how difficult this must have been and how clever they were to do it. Indeed, so clever were they that they might have been hunting still if a terrible thing had not happened.

One day the whole fish tribe came back very tired from a hunting expedition, and looked about for a nice, cool spot in which to pitch their camp. It was very hot, and they thought that they could not find a more comfortable place than under the branches of a large tree which grew by the bank of a river. So they made their fire to cook some food, right on the edge of a steep bank, which had a deep pool of water lying beneath it at the bottom. While the food was cooking they all stretched themselves lazily out under the tree, and were just dropping off to sleep when a big black cloud which they had never noticed spread over the sun, and heavy drops of rain began to fall, so that the fire was almost put out, and that, you know, is a very serious thing in savage countries where they have no matches, for it is very hard to light it again. To make matters worse, an icy wind began to blow, and the poor fishes were chilled right through their bodies.

'This will never do,' said Thuggai, the oldest of the fish tribe. 'We shall die of cold unless we can light the fire again,' and he bade his sons rub two sticks together in the hope of kindling a flame, but though they rubbed till they were tired, not a spark could they produce.

'Let me try,' cried Biernuga, the bony fish, but he had no better luck, and no more had Kumbal, the bream, nor any of the rest.

'It is no use,' exclaimed Thuggai, at last. 'The wood is too wet. We must just sit and wait till the sun comes out again and dries it.' Then a very little fish indeed, not more than four inches long and the youngest of the tribe, bowed himself before Thuggai, saying, 'Ask my father, Guddhu the cod, to light the fire. He is skilled in magic more than most fishes.' So Thuggai asked him, and Guddhu stripped some pieces of bark off a tree, and placed them on top of the smouldering ashes. Then he knelt by the side of the fire and blew at it for a long while, till slowly the feeble red glow became a little stronger and the edges of the bark showed signs of curling up. When the rest of the tribe saw this they pressed close, keeping their backs towards the piercing wind, but Guddhu told them they must go to the other side, as he wanted the wind to fan his fire. By and by the spark grew into a flame, and a merry crackling was heard.

'More wood,' cried Guddhi, and they all ran and gathered wood and heaped it on the flames, which leaped and roared and sputtered.

'We shall soon be warm now,' said the people one to another. 'Truly Guddhu is great'; and they crowded round again, closer and closer. Suddenly, with a shriek, a blast of wind swept down from the hills and blew the fire out towards them. They sprang back hurriedly, quite forgetting where they stood, and all fell down the bank, each tumbling over the other, till they rolled into the pool that lay below. Oh, how cold it was in that dark water on which the sun never shone! Then in an instant they felt warm again, for the fire, driven by the strong wind, had followed them right down to the bottom of the pool, where it burned as brightly as ever. And the fishes gathered round it as they had done on the top of the cliff, and found the flames as hot as before, and that fire never went out, like those upon land, but kept burning for ever. So now you know why, if you dive deep down below the cold surface of the water on a frosty day, you will find it comfortable and pleasant underneath, and be quite sorry that you cannot stay there.

Australian Folk Tale.

The Wonderful Tune.

Maurice Connor was the king, and that's no small word, of all the pipers in Munster. He could play jig and reel without end, and Ollistrum's March, and the Eagle's Whistle, and the Hen's Concert, and odd tunes of every sort and kind. But he knew one far more surprising than the rest, which had in it the power to set everything dead or alive dancing.

In what way he learned it is beyond my knowledge for he was mighty cautious about telling how he came by so wonderful a tune. At the very first note of that tune the shoes began shaking upon the feet of all how heard it—old or young, it mattered not—just as if the shoes had the ague; then the feet began going, going, going from under them, and at last up and away with them, dancing like mad, whisking here, there, and everywhere, like a straw in a storm— there was no halting while the music lasted.

Not a fair, nor a wedding, nor a feast in the seven parishes round, was counted worth the speaking of without 'blind Maurice and his pipes.' His mother, poor woman, used to lead him about from one place to another just like a dog.

Down through Iveragh, Maurice Connor and his mother were taking their rounds. Beyond all other places Iveragh is the place for stormy coasts and steep mountains, as proper a spot it is as any in Ireland to get yourself drowned, or your neck broken on the land, should you prefer that. But, notwithstanding, in Ballinskellig Bay there is a neat bit of ground, well fitted for diversion, and down from it, towards the water, is a clean smooth piece of strand, the dead image of a calm summer's sea on a moonlight night, with just the curl of the small waves upon it.

Here is was that Maurice's music had brought from all parts a great gathering of the young men and the young women; for 'twas not every day the strand of Trafraska was stirred up by the voice of a bagpipe. The dance began; and as pretty a dance it was as ever was danced. 'Brave music,' said everybody, 'and well done,' when Maurice stopped.

'More power to your elbow, Maurice, and a fair wind in the bellows,' cried Paddy Dorman, a hump-backed dancing master, who was there to keep order. ''Tis a pity,' said he, 'if we'd let the piper run dry after such music; 'twould be a disgrace to Iveragh, that didn't come on it since the week of the three Sundays.' So, as well became him, for he was always a decent man, says he, 'Did you drink, piper?'

'I will, sir,' said Maurice, answering the question on the safe side, for you never yet knew piper or schoolmaster who refused his drink.

'What will you drink, Maurice?' says Paddy.

'I'm no ways particular,' says Maurice; 'I drink anything, barring raw water; but if it's all the same to you, Mister Dorman, may be you wouldn't lend me the loan of a glass of whisky.'

'I've no glass, Maurice,' said Paddy; 'I've only the bottle.'

'Let that be no hindrance,' answered Maurice; 'my mouth just holds a glass to the drop; often I've tried it sure.'

So Paddy Dorman trusted him with the bottle—more fool was he; and, to his cost, he found that though Maurice's mouth might not hold more than the glass at one time, yet, owing to the hole in his throat, it took many a filling.

'That was no bad whisky neither,' says Maurice, handing back the empty bottle.

'By the holy frost, then!' says Paddy, ''tis but cold comfort there's in that bottle now; and 'tis your word we must take for the strength of the whisky, for you've left us no sample to judge by'; and to be sure Maurice had not.

Now I need not tell any gentleman or lady that if he or she was to drink an honest bottle of whisky at one pull, it is not at all the same thing as drinking a bottle of water; and in the whole course of my life I never knew more than five men who could do so without being the worse. Of these Maurice Connor was not one, though he had a stiff head enough of his own. Don't think I blame him for it; but true is the word that says, 'When liquor's in sense is out'; and puff, at a breath, out he blasted his wonderful tune.

'Twas really then beyond all belief or telling the dancing. Maurice himself could not keep quiet; staggering now on one leg, now on the other, and rolling about like a ship in a cross sea, trying to humour the tune. There was his mother, too, moving her old bones as light as the youngest girl of them all; but her dancing, no, nor the dancing of all the rest, is not worthy the speaking about to the work that was going on down upon the strand. Every inch of it covered with all manner of fish jumping and plunging about to the music, and every moment more and more would tumble in and out of the water, charmed by the wonderful tune. Crabs of monstrous size spun round and round on one claw with the nimbleness of a dancing master, and twirled and tossed their other claws about like limbs that did not belong to them. It was a sight surprising to behold. But perhaps you may have heard of Father Florence Conry, as pleasant a man as one would wish to drink with of a hot summer's day; and he had rhymed out all about the dancing fishes so neatly that it would be a thousand pities not to give you his verses; so here they are in English:

> The big seals in motion,
> Like waves of the ocean,
>   Or gouty feet prancing,
> Came heading the gay fish,
> Crabs, lobsters, and cray-fish,
>   Determined on dancing.
>
> The sweet sounds they followed,
> The gasping cod swallow'd—
>   'Twas wonderful, really;
> And turbot and flounder,
> 'Mid fish that were rounder,
>   Just caper'd as gaily.
>
> John-dories came tripping;
> Dull hake, by their skipping,
>   To frisk it seem'd given;
> Bright mackrel went springing,
> Like small rainbows winging
>   Their flight up to heaven.
>
> The whiting and haddock
> Left salt water paddock
>   This dance to be put in;
> Where skate with flat faces
> Edged out some old plaices;
>   But soles kept their footing.
>
> Sprats and herrings in powers
> Of silvery showers
>   All number out-numbered;
> And great ling so lengthy
> Was there in such plenty
>   The shore was encumber'd.
>
> The scallop and oyster
> Their two shells did roister,

> Like castanets flitting;
> While limpets moved clearly,
> And rocks very nearly
> With laughter were splitting.

Never was such a hullabaloo in this world, before or since; 'twas as if heaven and earth were coming together; and all out of Maurice Connor's wonderful tune!

In the height of all these doings, what should there be dancing among the outlandish set of fishes but a beautiful young woman— as beautiful as the dawn of day! She had a cocked hat upon her head; from under it her long green hair—just the colour of the sea— fell down behind, without hindrance to her dancing. Her teeth were like rows of pearls; her lips for all the world looked like red coral; and she had a shining gown pale green as the hollow of the wave, with little rows of purple and red seaweeds settled out upon it; for you never yet saw a lady, under the water or over the water, who had not a good notion of dressing herself out.

Up she danced at last to Maurice, who was flinging his feet from under him as fast as hops—for nothing in this world could keep still while that tune of his was going on—and says she to him, chanting it out with a voice as sweet as honey:

> I'm a lady of honour
>   Who live in the sea;
> Come down, Maurice Connor,
>   And be married to me.
> Silver plates and gold dishes
>   You shall have, and shall be
> The king of the fishes,
>   When you're married to me.

Drink was strong in Maurice's head, and out he chanted in return for her great civility. It is not every lady, may be, that would be after making such an offer to a blind piper; therefore 'twas only right in him to give her as good as she gave herself, so says Maurice:

> I'm obliged to you, madam:
>   Off a gold dish or plate,
> If a king, and I had 'em,
>   I could dine in great state.
> With your own father's daughter
>   I'd be sure to agree,
> But to drink the salt water
>   Wouldn't do so with me!

The lady looked at him quite amazed, and swinging her head from side to side like a great scholar, 'Well,' says she, 'Maurice, if you're not a poet, where is poetry to be found?'

In this way they kept on at it, framing high compliments; one answering the other, and their feet going with the music as fast as their tongues. All the fish kept dancing, too; Maurice heard the clatter and was afraid to stop playing lest it might be displeasing to the fish, and not knowing what so many of them may take it into their heads to do to him if they got vexed.

Well, the lady with the green hair kept on coaxing Maurice with soft speeches, till at last she over persuaded him to promise to marry her, and be king over the fishes, great and small. Maurice was well fitted to be their king, if they wanted one that could make them dance; and he surely would drink, barring the salt water, with any fish of them all.

When Maurice's mother saw him with that unnatural thing in the form of a green-haired lady as his guide, and he and she dancing down together so lovingly to the water's edge, through the thick of the fishes, she called out after him to stop and come back. 'Oh, then,' says she, 'as if I was not widow enough before, there he is going away from me to be married to that scaly woman. And who knows but 'tis grandmother I may be to a hake or a cod—Lord help and pity me, but 'tis a mighty unnatural thing! And my be 'tis boiling and eating my own grandchild I'll be, with a bit of salt butter, and I not knowing it! Oh, Maurice, Maurice, if there's any love or nature left in you, come back to your own ould mother, who reared you like a decent Christian!' Then the poor woman began to cry and sob so finely that it would do anyone good to hear her.

Maurice was not long getting to the rim of the water. There he kept playing and dancing on as if nothing was the matter, and a great thundering wave coming in towards him ready to swallow him up alive; but as he could not see it, he did not fear it. His mother it was who saw it plainly through the big tears that were rolling down her cheeks; and though she saw it, and her heart was aching as much as ever mother's heart ached for a son, she kept dancing, dancing all the time for the bare life of her. Certain it was she could not help it, for Maurice never stopped playing that wonderful tune of his.

He only turned his ear to the sound of his mother's voice, fearing it might put him out in his steps, and all the answer he made back was, 'Whisht with you mother—— sure I'm going to be king over the fishes down in the sea, and for a token of luck, and a sign that I'm alive and well, I'll send you in, every twelvemonth on this day, a piece of burned wood to Trafraska.' Maurice had not the power to say a word more, for the strange lady with the green hair, seeing the wave just upon them, covered him up with herself in a thing like a cloak with a big hood to it, and the wave curling over twice as high as their heads, burst upon the strand, with a rush and a roar that might be heard as far as Cape Clear.

That day twelvemonth the piece of burned wood came ashore in Trafraska. It was a queer thing for Maurice to think of sending all the way from the bottom of the sea. A gown or a pair of shoes would have been something like a present for his poor mother; but he had said it, and he kept his word. The bit of burned wood regularly came ashore on the appointed day for as good, ay, and better than a hundred years. The day is now forgotten, and may be that is the reason why people say how Maurice Connor has stopped sending the luck-token to his mother. Poor woman, she did not live to get as much as one of them; for what through the loss of Maurice, and the fear of eating her own grandchildren, she died in three weeks after the dance. Some say it was the fatigue that killed her, but whichever it was, Mrs. Connor was decently buried with her own people.

Seafaring people have often heard, off the coast of Kerry, on a still night, the sound of music coming up from the water; and some, who have had good ears, could plainly distinguish Maurice Connor's voice singing these words to his pipes—

Beautiful shore, with thy spreading strand,
Thy crystal water, and diamond sand;
Never would I have parted from thee,
But for the sake of my fair ladie.

From 'Fairy Tales and Traditions of the South of Ireland.'

The Rich Brother and the Poor Brother

There was once a rich old man who had two sons, and as his wife was dead, the elder lived with him, and helped him to look after his property. For a long time all went well; the young man got up very early in the morning, and worked hard all day, and at the end of every week his father counted up the money they had made, and rubbed his hands with delight, as he saw how big the pile of gold in the strong iron chest was becoming. 'It will soon be full now, and I shall have to buy a larger one,' he said to himself, and so busy was he with the thought of his money, that he did not notice how bright his son's face had grown, nor how he sometimes started when he was spoken to, as if his mind was far away.

One day, however, the old man went to the city on business, which he had not done for three years at least. It was market day, and he met with many people he knew, and it was getting quite late when he turned into the inn yard, and bade an ostler saddle his horse, and bring it round directly. While he was waiting in the hall, the landlady came up for a gossip, and after a few remarks about the weather and the vineyards she asked him how he liked his new daughter-in-law, and whether he had been surprised at the marriage.

The old man stared as he listened to her. 'Daughter-in-law? Marriage?' said he. 'I don't know what you are talking about! I've got no daughter-in-law, and nobody has been married lately, that I ever heard of.'

Now this was exactly what the landlady, who was very curious, wanted to find out; but she put on a look of great alarm, and exclaimed:

'Oh, dear! I hope I have not made mischief. I had no idea—or, of course, I would not have spoken—but'—and here she stopped and fumbled with her apron, as if she was greatly embarrassed.

'As you have said so much you will have to say a little more,' retorted the old man, a suspicion of what she meant darting across him; and the woman, nothing loth, answered as before.

'Ah, it was not all for buying or selling that your handsome son has been coming to town every week these many months past. And not by the shortest way, either! No, it was over the river he rode, and across the hill and past the cottage of Miguel the vine-keeper, whose daughter, they say, is the prettiest girl in the whole country side, though she is too white for my taste,' and then the landlady paused again, and glanced up at the farmer, to see how he was taking it. She did not learn much. He was looking straight before him, his teeth set. But as she ceased to talk, he said quietly, 'Go on.'

'There is not much more to tell,' replied the landlady, for she suddenly remembered that she must prepare supper for the hungry men who always stopped at the inn on market days, before starting for home, 'but one fine morning they both went to the little church on top of the hill, and were married. My cousin is servant to the priest, and she found out about it and told me. But good-day to you, sir; here is your horse, and I must hurry off to the kitchen.'

It was lucky that the horse was sure-footed and knew the road, for his bridle hung loose on his neck, and his master took no heed of the way he was going. When the farm-house was reached, the man led the animal to the stable, and then went to look for his son.

'I know everything—you have deceived me. Get out of my sight at once—I have done with you,' he stammered, choking with passion as he came up to the young man, who was cutting a stick in front of the door, whistling gaily the while.

'But, father—'

'You are no son of mine; I have only one now. Begone, or it will be the worse for you,' and as he spoke he lifted up his whip.

The young man shrank back. He feared lest his father should fall down in a fit, his face was so red and his eyes seemed bursting from his head. But it was no use staying: perhaps next morning the old man might listen to reason, though in his heart the son felt that he would never take back his words. So he turned slowly away, and walked heavily along a path which ended in a cave on the side of his hill, and there he sat through the night, thinking of what had happened.

Yes, he had been wrong, there was no doubt of that, and he did not quite know how it had come about. He had meant to have told his father all about it, and he was sure, quite sure, that if once the old man had seen his wife, he would have forgiven her poverty on account of her great beauty and goodness. But he had put it off from day to day, hoping always for a better opportunity, and now this was the end!

If the son had no sleep that night, no more had the father, and as soon as the sun rose, he sent a messenger into the great city with orders to bring back the younger brother. When he arrived the farmer did not waste words, but informed him that he was now his only heir, and would inherit all his lands and money, and that he was to come and live at home, and to help manage the property.

Though very pleased at the thought of becoming such a rich man— for the brothers had never cared much for each other—the younger would rather have stayed where he was, for he soon got tired of the country, and longed for a town life. However, this he kept to himself, and made the best of things, working hard like his brother before him.

In this way the years went on, but the crops were not so good as they had been, and the old man gave orders that some fine houses he was building in the city should be left unfinished, for it would take all the savings to complete them. As to the elder son, he would never even hear his name mentioned, and died at last without ever seeing his face, leaving to the younger, as he had promised, all his lands, as well as his money.

Meanwhile, the son whom he had disinherited had grown poorer and poorer. He and his wife were always looking out for something to do, and never spent a penny that they could help, but luck was against them, and at the time of his father's death they had hardly bread to eat or clothes to cover them. If there had been only himself, he would have managed to get on somehow, but he could not bear to watch his children becoming weaker day by day, and swallowing his pride, at length he crossed the mountains to his old home where his brother was living.

It was the first time for long that the two men had come face to face, and they looked at each other in silence. Then tears rose in the eyes of the elder, but winking them hastily away, he said:

'Brother, it is not needful that I should tell you how poor I am; you can see that for yourself. I have not come to beg for money, but only to ask if you will give me those unfinished houses of yours in the city, and I will make them watertight, so that my wife and children can live in them, and that will save our rent. For as they are, they profit you nothing.'

And the younger brother listened and pitied him, and gave him the houses that he asked for, and the elder went away happy.

For some years things went on as they were, and then the rich brother began to feel lonely, and thought to himself that he was getting older, and it was time for him to be married. The wife he chose was very wealthy, but she was also very greedy, and however much she had, she always wanted more. She was, besides, one of those unfortunate people who invariably fancy that the possessions of other people must be better than their own. Many a time her poor husband regretted the day that he had first seen her, and often her meanness and shabby ways put him to shame. But he had not the courage to rule her, and she only got worse and worse.

After she had been married a few months the bride wanted to go into the city and buy herself some new dresses. She had never been there before, and when she had finished her shopping, she thought she would pay a visit to her unknown sister-in-law, and rest for a bit. The house she was seeking was in a broad street, and ought to have been very magnificent, but the carved stone portico enclosed a mean little door of rough wood, while a row of beautiful pillars led to nothing. The dwelling on each side were in the same unfinished condition, and water trickled down the walls. Most people would have considered it a wretched place, and turned their backs on it as soon as they could, but this lady saw that by spending some money the houses could be made as splendid as they were originally intended to be, and she instantly resolved to get them for herself.

104

Full of this idea she walked up the marble staircase, and entered the little room where her sister-in-law sat, making clothes for her children. The bride seemed full of interest in the houses, and asked a great many questions about them, so that her new relations liked her much better than they expected, and hoped they might be good friends. However, as soon as she reached home, she went straight to her husband, and told him that he must get back those houses from his brother, as they would exactly suit her, and she could easily make them into a palace as fine as the king's. But her husband only told her that she might buy houses in some other part of the town, for she could not have those, as he had long since made a gift of them to his brother, who had lived there for many years past.

At this answer the wife grew very angry. She began to cry, and made such a noise that all the neighbours heard her and put their heads out of the windows, to see what was the matter. 'It was absurd,' she sobbed out, 'quite unjust. Indeed, if you came to think of it, the gift was worth nothing, as when her husband made it he was a bachelor, and since then he had been married, and she had never given her consent to any such thing.' And so she lamented all day and all night, till the poor man was nearly worried to death; and at last he did what she wished, and summoned his brother in a court of law to give up the houses which, he said, had only been lent to him. But when the evidence on both sides had been heard, the judge decided in favour of the poor man, which made the rich lady more furious than ever, and she determined not to rest until she had gained the day. If one judge would not give her the houses another should, and so time after time the case was tried over again, till at last it came before the highest judge of all, in the city of Evora. Her husband was heartily tired and ashamed of the whole affair, but his weakness in not putting a stop to it in the beginning had got him into this difficulty, and now he was forced to go on.

On the same day the two brothers set out on their journey to the city, the rich one on horseback, with plenty of food in his knapsack, the poor one on foot with nothing but a piece of bread and four onions to eat on the way. The road was hilly and neither could go very fast, and when night fell, they were both glad to see some lights in a window a little distance in front of them.

The lights turned out to have been placed there by a farmer, who had planned to have a particularly good supper as it was his wife's birthday, and bade the rich man enter and sit down, while he himself took the horse to the stable. The poor man asked timidly if he might spend the night in a corner, adding that he had brought his own supper with him. Another time permission might have been refused him, for the farmer was no lover of humble folk, but now he gave the elder brother leave to come in, pointing out a wooden chair where he could sit.

Supper was soon served, and very glad the younger brother was to eat it, for his long ride had made him very hungry. The farmer's wife, however, would touch nothing, and at last declared that the only supper she wanted was one of the onions the poor man was cooking at the fire. Of course he gave it to her, though he would gladly have eaten it himself, as three onions are not much at the end of a long day's walk, and soon after they all went to sleep, the poor man making himself as comfortable as he could in his corner.

A few hours later the farmer was aroused by the cries and groans of his wife.

'Oh, I feel so ill, I'm sure I'm going to die,' wept she. 'It was that onion, I know it was. I wish I had not eaten it. It must have been poisoned.'

'If the man has poisoned you he shall pay for it,' said her husband, and seizing a thick stick he ran downstairs and began to beat the poor man, who had been sound asleep, and had nothing to defend himself with. Luckily, the noise aroused the younger brother, who jumped up and snatched the stick from the farmer's hand, saying:

'We are both going to Evora to try a law-suit. Come too, and accuse him there if he has attempted to rob you or murder you, but don't kill him now, or you will get yourself into trouble.'

'Well, perhaps you are right,' answered the farmer, 'but the sooner that fellow has his deserts, the better I shall be pleased,' and without more words he went to the stables and brought out a horse for himself and also the black Andalusian mare ridden by the rich man, while the poor brother, fearing more ill-treatment, started at once on foot.

Now all that night it had rained heavily, and did not seem likely to stop, and in some places the road was so thick with mud that it was almost impossible to get across it. In one spot it was so very bad that a mule laden with baggage had got stuck in it, and tug as he might, his master was quite unable to pull him out. The muleteer in despair appealed to the two horseman, who were carefully skirting the swamp at some distance off, but they paid no heed to his cries, and he began to talk cheerfully to his mule, hoping to keep up his spirits, declaring that if the poor beast would only have a little patience help was sure to come.

And so it did, for very soon the poor brother reached the place, bespattered with mud from head to foot, but ready to do all he could to help with the mule and his master. First they set about finding some stout logs of wood to lay down on the marsh so that they could reach the mule, for by this time his frantic struggles had broken his bridle, and he was deeper in than ever. Stepping cautiously along the wood, the poor man contrived to lay hold of the animal's tale, and with a desperate effort the mule managed to regain his footing on dry ground, but at the cost of leaving his tail in the poor man's hand. When he saw this the muleteer's anger knew no bounds, and forgetting that without the help given him he would have lost his mule altogether, he began to abuse the poor man, declaring that he had ruined his beast, and the law would make him pay for it. Then, jumping on the back of the mule, which was so glad to be out of the choking mud that he did not seem to mind the loss of his tail, the ungrateful wretch rode on, and that evening reached the inn at Evora, where the rich man and the farmer had already arrived for the night.

Meanwhile the poor brother walked wearily along, wondering what other dreadful adventures were in store for him.

'I shall certainly be condemned for one or other of them,' thought he sadly; 'and after all, if I have to die, I would rather choose my own death than leave it to my enemies,' and as soon as he entered Evora he looked about for a place suitable for carrying out the plan he had made. At length he found what he sought, but as it was too late and too dark for him to make sure of success, he curled himself up under a doorway, and slept till morning.

Although it was winter, the sun rose in a clear sky, and its rays felt almost warm when the poor man got up and shook himself. He intended it to be the day of his death, but in spite of that, and of the fact that he was leaving his wife and children behind him, he felt almost cheerful. He had struggled so long, and was so very, very tired; but he would not have minded that if he could have proved his innocence, and triumphed over his enemies. However, they had all been too clever for him, and he had no strength to fight any more. So he mounted the stone steps that led to the battlements of the city, and stopped for a moment to gaze about him.

It happened that an old sick man who lived near by had begged to be carried out and to be laid at the foot of the wall so that the beams of the rising sun might fall upon him, and he would be able to talk with his friends as they passed by to their work. Little did he guess that on top of the battlements, exactly over his head, stood a man who was taking his last look at the same sun, before going to his death that awaited him. But so it was; and as the steeple opposite was touched by the golden light, the poor man shut his eyes and sprang forward. The wall was high, and he flew rapidly through the air, but it was not the ground he touched, only the body of the sick man, who rolled over and died without a groan. As for the other, he was quite unhurt, and was slowly rising to his feet when his arms were suddenly seized and held.

'You have killed our father, do you see? do you see?' cried two young men, 'and you will come with us this instant before the judge, and answer for it.'

'Your father? but I don't know him. What do you mean?' asked the poor man, who was quite bewildered with his sudden rush through the air, and could not think why he should be accused of this fresh crime. But he got no reply, and was only hurried through the streets to the court-house, where his brother, the muleteer, and the farmer had just arrived, all as angry as ever, all talking at once, till the judge entered and ordered them to be silent.

'I will hear you one by one,' he said, and motioned the younger brother to begin.

He did not take long to state his case. The unfinished houses were his, left him with the rest of the property by his father, and his brother refused to give them up. In answer, the poor man told, in a few words, how he had begged the houses from his brother, and produced the deed of gift which made him their owner.

The judge listened quietly and asked a few questions; then he gave his verdict.

'The houses shall remain the property of the man to whom they were given, and to whom they belong. And as you,' he added, turning to the younger brother, 'brought this accusation knowing full well it was wicked and unjust, I order you, besides losing the houses, to pay a thousand pounds damages to your brother.'

The rich man heard the judge with rage in his heart, the poor man with surprise and gratitude. But he was not safe yet, for now it was the turn of the farmer. The judge could hardly conceal a smile at the story, and inquired if the wife was dead before the farmer left the house, and received for answer that he was in such a hurry for justice to be done that he had not waited to see. Then the poor man told his tale, and once more judgment was given in his favour, while twelve hundred pounds was ordered to be paid him. As for the muleteer, he was informed very plainly that he had proved himself mean and ungrateful for the help that had been given him, and as a punishment he must pay to the poor man a fine of fifty pounds, and hand him over the mule till his tail had grown again.

Lastly, there came the two sons of the sick man.

'This is the wretch who killed our father,' they said, 'and we demand that he should die also.'

'How did you kill him?' asked the judge, turning to the accused, and the poor man told how he had leaped from the wall, not knowing that anyone was beneath.

'Well, this is my judgment,' replied the judge, when they had all spoken: 'Let the accused sit under the wall, and let the sons of the dead man jump from the top and fall on him and kill him, and if they will not to this, then they are condemned to pay eight hundred pounds for their false accusation.'

The young men looked at each other, and slowly shook their heads.

'We will pay the fine,' said they, and the judge nodded.

So the poor man rode the mule home, and brought back to his family enough money to keep them in comfort to the end of their days.

Adapted from the Portuguese.

108

The One-Handed Girl

An old couple once lived in a hut under a grove of palm trees, and they had one son and one daughter. They were all very happy together for many years, and then the father became very ill, and felt he was going to die. He called his children to the place where he lay on the floor—for no one had any beds in that country— and said to his son, 'I have no herds of cattle to leave you—only the few things there are in the house—for I am a poor man, as you know. But choose: will you have my blessing or my property?'

'Your property, certainly,' answered the son, and his father nodded.

'And you?' asked the old man of the girl, who stood by her brother.

'I will have blessing,' she answered, and her father gave her much blessing.

That night he died, and his wife and son and daughter mourned for him seven days, and gave him a burial according to the custom of his people. But hardly was the time of mourning over, than the mother was attacked by a disease which was common in that country.

'I am going away from you,' she said to her children, in a faint voice; 'but first, my son, choose which you will have: blessing or property.'

'Property, certainly,' answered the son.

'And you, my daughter?'

'I will have blessing,' said the girl; and her mother gave her much blessing, and that night she died.

When the days of mourning were ended, the brother bade his sister put outside the hut all that belonged to his father and his mother. So the girl put them out, and he took them away, save only a small pot and a vessel in which she could clean her corn. But she had no corn to clean.

She sat at home, sad and hungry, when a neighbour knocked at the door.

'My pot has cracked in the fire, lend me yours to cook my supper in, and I will give you a handful of corn in return.'

And the girl was glad, and that night she was able to have supper herself, and next day another woman borrowed her pot, and then another and another, for never were known so many accidents as befell the village pots at that time. She soon grew quite fat with all the corn she earned with the help of her pot, and then one evening she

109

picked up a pumpkin seed in a corner, and planted it near her well, and it sprang up, and gave her many pumpkins.

At last it happened that a youth from her village passed through the place where the girl's brother was, and the two met and talked.

'What news is there of my sister?' asked the young man, with whom things had gone badly, for he was idle.

'She is fat and well-liking,' replied the youth, 'for the women borrow her mortar to clean their corn, and borrow her pot to cook it in, and for al this they give her more food than she can eat.' And he went his way.

Now the brother was filled with envy at the words of the man, and he set out at once, and before dawn he had reached the hut, and saw the pot and the mortar were standing outside. He slung them over his shoulders and departed, pleased with his own cleverness; but when his sister awoke and sought for the pot to cook her corn for breakfast, she could find it nowhere. At length she said to herself,

'Well, some thief must have stolen them while I slept. I will go and see if any of my pumpkins are ripe.' And indeed they were, and so many that the tree was almost broken by the weight of them. So she ate what she wanted and took the others to the village, and gave them in exchange for corn, and the women said that no pumpkins were as sweet as these, and that she was to bring every day all that she had. In this way she earned more than she needed for herself, and soon was able to get another mortar and cooking pot in exchange for her corn. Then she thought she was quite rich.

Unluckily someone else thought so too, and this was her brother's wife, who had heard all about the pumpkin tree, and sent her slave with a handful of grain to buy her a pumpkin. At first the girl told him that so few were left that she could not spare any; but when she found that he belonged to her brother, she changed her mind, and went out to the tree and gathered the largest and the ripest that was there.

'Take this one,' she said to the slave, 'and carry it back to your mistress, but tell her to keep the corn, as the pumpkin is a gift.'

The brother's wife was overjoyed at the sight of the fruit, and when she tasted it, she declared it was the nicest she had ever eaten. Indeed, all night she thought of nothing else, and early in the morning she called another slave (for she was a rich woman) and bade him go and ask for another pumpkin. But the girl, who had just been out to look at her tree, told him that they were all eaten, so he went back empty-handed to his mistress.

In the evening her husband returned from hunting a long way off, and found his wife in tears.

110

'What is the matter?' asked he.

'I sent a slave with some grain to your sister to buy some pumpkins, but she would not sell me any, and told me there were none, though I know she lets other people buy them.'

'Well, never mind now—go to sleep,' said he, 'and to-morrow I will go and pull up the pumpkin tree, and that will punish her for treating you so badly.'

So before sunrise he got up and set out for his sister's house, and found her cleaning some corn.

'Why did you refuse to sell my wife a pumpkin yesterday when she wanted one?' he asked.

'The old ones are finished, and the new ones are not yet come,' answered the girl. 'When her slave arrived two days ago, there were only four left; but I gave him one, and would take no corn for it.'

'I do not believe you; you have sold them all to other people. I shall go and cut down the pumpkin,' cried her brother in a rage.

'If you cut down the pumpkin you shall cut off my hand with it,' exclaimed the girl, running up to her tree and catching hold of it. But her brother followed, and with one blow cut off the pumpkin and her hand too.

Then he went into the house and took away everything he could find, and sold the house to a friend of his who had long wished to have it, and his sister had no home to go to.

Meanwhile she had bathed her arm carefully, and bound on it some healing leaves that grew near by, and wrapped a cloth round the leaves, and went to hide in the forest, that her brother might not find her again.

For seven days she wandered about, eating only the fruit that hung from the trees above her, and every night she climbed up and tucked herself safely among the creepers which bound together the big branches, so that neither lions nor tigers nor panthers might get at her.

When she woke up on the seventh morning she saw from her perch smoke coming up from a little town on the edge of the forest. The sight of the huts made her feel more lonely and helpless than before. She longed desperately for a draught of milk from a gourd, for there were no streams in that part, and she was very thirsty, but how was she to earn anything with only one hand? And at this thought her courage failed, and she began to cry bitterly.

It happened that the king's son had come out from the town very early to shoot birds, and when the sun grew hot he left tired.

'I will lie here and rest under this tree,' he said to his attendants. 'You can go and shoot instead, and I will just have this slave to stay with me!' Away they went, and the young man fell asleep, and slept long. Suddenly he was awakened by something wet and salt falling on his face.

'What is that? Is it raining?' he said to his slave. 'Go and look.'

'No, master, it is not raining,' answered the slave.

'Then climb up the tree and see what it is,' and the slave climbed up, and came back and told his master that a beautiful girl was sitting up there, and that it must have been her tears which had fallen on the face of the king's son.

'Why was she crying?' inquired the prince.

'I cannot tell—I did not dare to ask her; but perhaps she would tell you.' And the master, greatly wondering, climbed up the tree.

'What is the matter with you?' said he gently, and, as she only sobbed louder, he continued:

'Are you a woman, or a spirit of the woods?'

'I am a woman,' she answered slowly, wiping her eyes with a leaf of the creeper that hung about her.

'Then why do you cry?' he persisted.

'I have many things to cry for,' she replied, 'more than you could ever guess.'

'Come home with me,' said the prince; 'it is not very far. Come home to my father and mother. I am a king's son.'

'Then why are you here?' she said, opening her eyes and staring at him.

'Once every month I and my friends shoot birds in the forest,' he answered, 'but I was tired and bade them leave me to rest. And you—what are you doing up in this tree?'

At that she began to cry again, and told the king's son all that had befallen her since the death of her mother.

'I cannot come down with you, for I do not like anyone to see me,' she ended with a sob.

'Oh! I will manage all that,' said the king's son, and swinging himself to a lower branch, he bade his slave go quickly into the town, and bring back with him four strong men and a curtained litter. When the man was gone, the girl climbed down, and hid herself on the ground in some bushes. Very soon the slave returned with the litter, which was placed on the ground close to the bushes where the girl lay.

'Now go, all of you, and call my attendants, for I do not wish to say here any longer,' he said to the men, and as soon as they were out of sight he bade the girl get into the litter, and fasten the curtains tightly. Then he got in on the other side, and waited till his attendants came up.

'What is the matter, O son of a king?' asked they, breathless with running.

'I think I am ill; I am cold,' he said, and signing to the bearers, he drew the curtains, and was carried through the forest right inside his own house.

'Tell my father and mother that I have a fever, and want some gruel,' said he, 'and bid them send it quickly.'

So the slave hastened to the king's palace and gave his message, which troubled both the king and the queen greatly. A pot of hot gruel was instantly prepared, and carried over to the sick man, and as soon as the council which was sitting was over, the king and his ministers went to pay him a visit, bearing a message from the queen that she would follow a little later.

Now the prince had pretended to be ill in order to soften his parent's hearts, and the next day he declared he felt better, and, getting into his litter, was carried to the palace in state, drums being beaten all along the road.

He dismounted at the foot of the steps and walked up, a great parasol being held over his head by a slave. Then he entered the cool, dark room where his father and mother were sitting, and said to them:

'I saw a girl yesterday in the forest whom I wish to marry, and, unknown to my attendants, I brought her back to my house in a litter. Give me your consent, I beg, for no other woman pleases me as well, even though she has but one hand!'

Of course the king and queen would have preferred a daughter-in-law with two hands, and one who could have brought riches with her, but they could not bear to say 'No' to their son, so they told him it should be as he chose, and that the wedding feast should be prepared immediately.

The girl could scarcely believe her good fortune, and, in gratitude for all the kindness shown her, was so useful and pleasant to her husband's parents that they soon loved her.

By and bye a baby was born to her, and soon after that the prince was sent on a journey by his father to visit some of the distant towns of the kingdom, and to set right things that had gone wrong.

No sooner had he started than the girl's brother, who had wasted all the riches his wife had brought him in recklessness and folly, and was now very poor, chanced to come into the town, and as he passed he heard a man say, 'Do you know that the king's son has married a woman who has lost one of her hands?' On hearing these words the brother stopped and asked, 'Where did he find such a woman?'

'In the forest,' answered the man, and the cruel brother guessed at once it must be his sister.

A great rage took possession of his soul as he thought of the girl whom he had tried to ruin being after all so much better off than himself, and he vowed that he would work her ill. Therefore that very afternoon he made his way to the palace and asked to see the king.

When he was admitted to his presence, he knelt down and touched the ground with his forehead, and the king bade him stand up and tell wherefore he had come.

'By the kindness of your heart have you been deceived, O king,' said he. 'Your son has married a girl who has lost a hand. Do you know why she had lost it? She was a witch, and has wedded three husbands, and each husband she has put to death with her arts. Then the people of the town cut off her hand, and turned her into the forest. And what I say is true, for her town is my town also.'

The king listened, and his face grew dark. Unluckily he had a hasty temper, and did not stop to reason, and, instead of sending to the town, and discovering people who knew his daughter-in-law and could have told him how hard she had worked and how poor she had been, he believed all the brother's lying words, and made the queen believe them too. Together they took counsel what they should do, and in the end they decided that they also would put her out of the town. But this did not content the brother.

'Kill her,' he said. 'It is no more than she deserves for daring to marry the king's son. Then she can do no more hurt to anyone.'

'We cannot kill her,' answered they; 'if we did, our son would assuredly kill us. Let us do as the others did, and put her out of the town. And with this the envious brother was forced to be content.

114

The poor girl loved her husband very much, but just then the baby was more to her than all else in the world, and as long as she had him with her, she did not very much mind anything. So, taking her son on her arm, and hanging a little earthen pot for cooking round her neck, she left her house with its great peacock fans and slaves and seats of ivory, and plunged into the forest.

For a while she walked, not knowing whither she went, then by and bye she grew tired, and sat under a tree to rest and to hush her baby to sleep. Suddenly she raised her eyes, and saw a snake wriggling from under the bushes towards her.

'I am a dead woman,' she said to herself, and stayed quite still, for indeed she was too frightened to move. In another minute the snake had reached her side, and to her surprise he spoke.

'Open your earthen pot, and let me go in. Save me from sun, and I will save you from rain,' and she opened the pot, and when the snake had slipped in, she put on the cover. Soon she beheld another snake coming after the other one, and when it had reached her it stopped and said, 'Did you see a small grey snake pass this way just now?'

'Yes,' she answered, 'it was going very quickly.'

'Ah, I must hurry and catch it up,' replied the second snake, and it hastened on.

When it was out of sight, a voice from the pot said:

'Uncover me,' and she lifted the lid, and the little grey snake slid rapidly to the ground.

'I am safe now,' he said. 'But tell me, where are you going?'

'I cannot tell you, for I do not know,' she answered. 'I am just wandering in the wood.'

'Follow me, and let us go home together,' said the snake, and the girl followed his through the forest and along the green paths, till they came to a great lake, where they stopped to rest.

'The sun is hot,' said the snake, 'and you have walked far. Take your baby and bathe in that cool place where the boughs of the tree stretch far over the water.'

'Yes, I will,' answered she, and they went in. The baby splashed and crowed with delight, and then he gave a spring and fell right in, down, down, down, and his mother could not find him, though she searched all among the reeds.

Full of terror, she made her way back to the bank, and called to the snake, 'My baby is gone!—he is drowned, and never shall I see him again.'

'Go in once more,' said the snake, 'and feel everywhere, even among the trees that have their roots in the water, lest perhaps he may be held fast there.'

Swiftly she went back and felt everywhere with her whole hand, even putting her fingers into the tiniest crannies, where a crab could hardly have taken shelter.

'No, he is not here,' she cried. 'How am I to live without him?' But the snake took no notice, and only answered, 'Put in your other arm too.'

'What is the use of that?' she asked, 'when it has no hand to feel with?' but all the same she did as she was bid, and in an instant the wounded arm touched something round and soft, lying between two stones in a clump of reeds.

'My baby, my baby!' she shouted, and lifted him up, merry and laughing, and not a bit hurt or frightened.

'Have you found him this time?' asked the snake.

'Yes, oh, yes!' she answered, 'and, why—why—I have got my hand back again!' and from sheer joy she burst into tears.

The snake let her weep for a little while, and then he said—

'Now we will journey on to my family, and we will all repay you for the kindness you showed to me.'

'You have done more than enough in giving me back my hand,' replied the girl; but the snake only smiled.

'Be quick, lest the sun should set,' he answered, and began to wriggle along so fast that the girl could hardly follow him.

By and bye they arrived at the house in a tree where the snake lived, when he was not travelling with his father and mother. And he told them all his adventures, and how he had escaped from his enemy. The father and mother snake could not do enough to show their gratitude. They made their guest lie down on a hammock woven of the strong creepers which hung from bough to bough, till she was quite rested after her wanderings, while they watched the baby and gave him milk to drink from the cocoa-nuts which they persuaded their friends the monkeys to crack for them. They even managed to carry small fruit tied up in their tails for the baby's mother, who felt at last that she was safe and at peace. Not that she forgot her

116

husband, for she often thought of him and longed to show him her son, and in the night she would sometimes lie awake and wonder where he was.

In this manner many weeks passed by.

And what was the prince doing?

Well, he had fallen very ill when he was on the furthest border of the kingdom, and he was nursed by some kind people who did not know who he was, so that the king and queen heard nothing about him. When he was better he made his way home again, and into his father's palace, where he found a strange man standing behind the throne with the peacock's feathers. This was his wife's brother, whom the king had taken into high favour, though, of course, the prince was quite ignorant of what had happened.

For a moment the king and queen stared at their son, as if he had been unknown to them; he had grown so thin and weak during his illness that his shoulders were bowed like those of an old man.

'Have you forgotten me so soon?' he asked.

At the sound of his voice they gave a cry and ran towards him, and poured out questions as to what had happened, and why he looked like that. But the prince did not answer any of them.

'How is my wife?' he said. There was a pause.

Then the queen replied:

'She is dead.'

'Dead!' he repeated, stepping a little backwards. 'And my child?'

'He is dead too.'

The young man stood silent. Then he said, 'Show me their graves.'

At these words the king, who had been feeling rather uncomfortable, took heart again, for had he not prepared two beautiful tombs for his son to see, so that he might never, never guess what had been done to his wife? All these months the king and queen had been telling each other how good and merciful they had been not to take her brother's advice and to put her to death. But now, this somehow did not seem so certain.

117

Then the king led the way to the courtyard just behind the palace, and through the gate into a beautiful garden where stood two splendid tombs in a green space under the trees. The prince advanced alone, and, resting his head against the stone, he burst into tears. His father and mother stood silently behind with a curious pang in their souls which they did not quite understand. Could it be that they were ashamed of themselves?

But after a while the prince turned round, and walking past them in to the palace he bade the slaves bring him mourning. For seven days no one saw him, but at the end of them he went out hunting, and helped his father rule his people. Only no one dared to speak to him of his wife and son.

At last one morning, after the girl had been lying awake all night thinking of her husband, she said to her friend the snake:

'You have all shown me much kindness, but now I am well again, and want to go home and hear some news of my husband, and if he still mourns for me!' Now the heart of the snake was sad at her words, but he only said:

'Yes, thus it must be; go and bid farewell to my father and mother, but if they offer you a present, see that you take nothing but my father's ring and my mother's casket.'

So she went to the parent snakes, who wept bitterly at the thought of losing her, and offered her gold and jewels as much as she could carry in remembrance of them. But the girl shook her head and pushed the shining heap away from her.

'I shall never forget you, never,' she said in a broken voice, 'but the only tokens I will accept from you are that little ring and this old casket.'

The two snakes looked at each other in dismay. The ring and the casket were the only things they did not want her to have. Then after a short pause they spoke.

'Why do you want the ring and casket so much? Who has told you of them?'

'Oh, nobody; it is just my fancy,' answered she. But the old snakes shook their heads and replied:

'Not so; it is our son who told you, and, as he said, so it must be. If you need food, or clothes, or a house, tell the ring and it will find them for you. And if you are unhappy or in danger, tell the casket and it will set things right.' Then they both gave her their blessing, and she picked up her baby and went her way.

She walked for a long time, till at length she came near the town where her husband and his father dwelt. Here she stopped under a grove of palm trees, and told the ring that she wanted a house.

118

'It is ready, mistress,' whispered a queer little voice which made her jump, and, looking behind her, she saw a lovely palace made of the finest woods, and a row of slaves with tall fans bowing before the door. Glad indeed was she to enter, for she was very tired, and, after eating a good supper of fruit and milk which she found in one of the rooms, she flung herself down on a pile of cushions and went to sleep with her baby beside her.

Here she stayed quietly, and every day the baby grew taller and stronger, and very soon he could run about and even talk. Of course the neighbours had a great deal to say about the house which had been built so quickly—so very quickly—on the outskirts of the town, and invented all kinds of stories about the rich lady who lived in it. And by and bye, when the king returned with his son from the wars, some of these tales reached his ears.

'It is really very odd about that house under the palms,' he said to the queen; 'I must find out something of the lady whom no one ever sees. I daresay it is not a lady at all, but a gang of conspirators who want to get possession of my throne. To-morrow I shall take my son and my chief ministers and insist on getting inside.'

Soon after sunrise next day the prince's wife was standing on a little hill behind the house, when she saw a cloud of dust coming through the town. A moment afterwards she heard faintly the roll of the drums that announced the king's presence, and saw a crowd of people approaching the grove of palms. Her heart beat fast. Could her husband be among them? In any case they must not discover her there; so just bidding the ring prepare some food for them, she ran inside, and bound a veil of golden gauze round her head and face. Then, taking the child's hand, she went to the door and waited.

In a few minutes the whole procession came up, and she stepped forward and begged them to come in and rest.

'Willingly,' answered the king; 'go first, and we will follow you.'

They followed her into a long dark room, in which was a table covered with gold cups and baskets filled with dates and cocoa-nuts and all kinds of ripe yellow fruits, and the king and the prince sat upon cushions and were served by slaves, while the ministers, among whom she recognised her own brother, stood behind.

'Ah, I owe all my misery to him,' she said to herself. 'From the first he has hated me,' but outwardly she showed nothing. And when the king asked her what news there was in the town she only answered:

'You have ridden far; eat first, and drink, for you must be hungry and thirsty, and then I will tell you my news.'

'You speak sense,' answered the king, and silence prevailed for some time longer. Then he said:

'Now, lady, I have finished, and am refreshed, therefore tell me, I pray you, who you are, and whence you come? But, first, be seated.'

She bowed her head and sat down on a big scarlet cushion, drawing her little boy, who was asleep in a corner, on to her knee, and began to tell the story of her life. As her brother listened, he would fain have left the house and hidden himself in the forest, but it was his duty to wave the fan of peacock's feathers over the king's head to keep off the flies, and he knew he would be seized by the royal guards if he tried to desert his post. He must stay where he was, there was no help for it, and luckily for him the king was too much interested in the tale to notice that the fan had ceased moving, and that flies were dancing right on the top of his thick curly hair.

The story went on, but the story-teller never once looked at the prince, even through her veil, though he on his side never moved his eyes from her. When she reached the part where she had sat weeping in the tree, the king's son could restrain himself no longer.

'It is my wife,' he cried, springing to where she sat with the sleeping child in her lap. 'They have lied to me, and you are not dead after all, nor the boy either.! But what has happened? Why did they lie to me? and why did you leave my house where you were safe?' And he turned and looked fiercely at his father.

'Let me finish my tale first, and then you will know,' answered she, throwing back her veil, and she told how her brother had come to the palace and accused her of being a witch, and had tried to persuade the king to slay her. 'But he would not do that,' she continued softly, 'and after all, if I had stayed on in your house, I should never have met the snake, nor have got my hand back again. So let us forget all about it, and be happy once more, for see! our son is growing quite a big boy.'

'And what shall be done to your brother?' asked the king, who was glad to think that someone had acted in this matter worse than himself.

'Put him out of the town,' answered she.

From 'Swaheli Tales,' by E. Steere.

120

The Bones of Djulung

In a beautiful island that lies in the southern seas, where chains of gay orchids bind the trees together, and the days and nights are equally long and nearly equally hot, there once lived a family of seven sisters. Their father and mother were dead, and they had no brothers, so the eldest girl ruled over the rest, and they all did as she bade them. One sister had to clean the house, a second carried water from the spring in the forest, a third cooked their food, while to the youngest fell the hardest task of all, for she had to cut and bring home the wood which was to keep the fire continually burning. This was very hot and tiring work, and when she had fed the fire and heaped up in a corner the sticks that were to supply it till the next day, she often threw herself down under a tree, and went sound asleep.

One morning, however, as she was staggering along with her bundle on her back, she thought that the river which flowed past their hut looked so cool and inviting that she determined to bathe in it, instead of taking her usual nap. Hastily piling up her load by the fire, and thrusting some sticks into the flame, she ran down to the river and jumped in. How delicious it was diving and swimming and floating in the dark forest, where the trees were so thick that you could hardly see the sun! But after a while she began to look about her, and her eyes fell on a little fish that seemed made out of a rainbow, so brilliant were the colours he flashed out.

'I should like him for a pet,' thought the girl, and the next time the fish swam by, she put out her hand and caught him. Then she ran along the grassy path till she came to a cave in front of which a stream fell over some rocks into a basin. Here she put her little fish, whose name was Djulung-djulung, and promising to return soon and bring him some dinner, she went away.

By the time she got home, the rice for their dinner was ready cooked, and the eldest sister gave the other six their portions in wooden bowls. But the youngest did not finish hers, and when no one was looking, stole off to the fountain in the forest where the little fish was swimming about.

'See! I have not forgotten you,' she cried, and one by one she let the grains of rice fall into the water, where the fish gobbled them up greedily, for he had never tasted anything so nice.

'That is all for to-day,' she said at last, 'but I will come again to-morrow,' and biding him good-bye she went down the path.

Now the girl did not tell her sisters about the fish, but every day she saved half of her rice to give him, and called him softly in a little song she had made for herself. If she sometimes felt hungry, no one knew of it, and, indeed, she did not mind that much, when she saw how the fish enjoyed it. And the fish grew fat and big, but the girl grew thin and weak, and the loads of wood felt heavier every day, and at last her sisters noticed it.

121

Then they took counsel together, and watched her to see what she did, and one of them followed her to the fountain where Djulung lived, and saw her give him all the rice she had saved from her breakfast. Hastening home the sister told the others what she had witnessed, and that a lovely fat fish might be had for the catching. So the eldest sister went and caught him, and he was boiled for supper, but the youngest sister was away in the woods, and did not know anything about it.

Next morning she went as usual to the cave, and sang her little song, but no Djulung came to answer it; twice and thrice she sang, then threw herself on her knees by the edge, and peered into the dark water, but the trees cast such a deep shadow that her eyes could not pierce it.

'Djulung cannot be dead, or his body would be floating on the surface,' she said to herself, and rising to her feet she set out homewards, feeling all of a sudden strangely tired.

'What is the matter with me?' she thought, but somehow or other she managed to reach the hut, and threw herself down in a corner, where she slept so soundly that for days no one was able to wake her.

At length, one morning early, a cock began to crow so loud that she could sleep no longer and as he continued to crow she seemed to understand what he was saying, and that he was telling her that Djulung was dead, killed and eaten by her sisters, and that his bones lay buried under the kitchen fire. Very softly she got up, and took up the large stone under the fire, and creeping out carried the bones to the cave by the fountain, where she dug a hole and buried them anew. And as she scooped out the hole with a stick she sang a song, bidding the bones grow till they became a tree—a tree that reached up so high into the heavens that its leaves would fall across the sea into another island, whose king would pick them up.

As there was no Djulung to give her rice to, the girl soon became fat again, and as she was able to do her work as of old, her sisters did not trouble about her. They never guessed that when she went into the forest to gather her sticks, she never failed to pay a visit to the tree, which grew taller and more wonderful day by day. Never was such a tree seen before. Its trunk was of iron, its leaves were of silk, its flowers of gold, and its fruit of diamonds, and one evening, though the girl did not know it, a soft breeze took one of the leaves, and blew it across the sea to the feet of one of the king's attendants.

'What a curious leaf! I have never beheld one like it before. I must show it to the king,' he said, and when the king saw it he declared he would never rest until he had found the tree which bore it, even if he had to spend the rest of his life in visiting the islands that lay all round. Happily for him, he began with the island that was nearest, and here in the forest he suddenly saw standing before him the iron tree, its boughs covered with shining leaves like the one he carried about him.

122

'But what sort of a tree is it, and how did it get here?' he asked of the attendants he had with him. No one could answer him, but as they were about to pass out of the forest a little boy went by, and the king stopped and inquired if there was anyone living in the neighbourhood whom he might question.

'Seven girls live in a hut down there,' replied the boy, pointing with his finger to where the sun was setting.

'Then go and bring them here, and I will wait,' said the king, and the boy ran off and told the sisters that a great chief, with strings of jewels round his neck, had sent for them.

Pleased and excited the six elder sisters at once followed the boy, but the youngest, who was busy, and who did not care about strangers, stayed behind, to finish the work she was doing. The king welcomed the girls eagerly, and asked them all manner of questions about the tree, but as they had never even heard of its existence, they could tell him nothing. 'And if we, who live close by the forest, do not know, you may be sure no one does,' added the eldest, who was rather cross at finding this was all that the king wanted of them.

'But the boy told me there were seven of you, and there are only six here,' said the king.

'Oh, the youngest is at home, but she is always half asleep, and is of no use except to cut wood for the fire,' replied they in a breath.

'That may be, but perhaps she dreams,' answered the king. 'Anyway, I will speak to her also.' Then he signed to one of his attendants, who followed the path that the boy had taken to the hut.

Soon the man returned, with the girl walking behind him. And as soon as she reached the tree it bowed itself to the earth before her, and she stretched out her hand and picked some of its leaves and flowers and gave them to the king.

'The maiden who can work such wonders is fitted to be the wife of the greatest chief,' he said, and so he married her, and took her with him across the sea to his own home, where they lived happily for ever after.

From 'Folk Lore,' by A. F. Mackenzie.

The Sea King's Gift

There was once a fisherman who was called Salmon, and his Christian name was Matte. He lived by the shore of the big sea; where else could he live? He had a wife called Maie; could you find a better name for her? In winter they dwelt in a little cottage by the shore, but in spring they flitted to a red rock out in the sea and stayed there the whole summer until it was autumn. The cottage on the rock was even smaller than the other; it had a wooden bolt instead of an iron lock to the door, a stone hearth, a flagstaff, and a weather-cock on the roof.

The rock was called Ahtola, and was not larger than the market-place of a town. Between the crevices there grew a little rowan tree and four alder bushes. Heaven only knows how they ever came there; perhaps they were brought by the winter storms. Besides that, there flourished some tufts of velvety grass, some scattered reeds, two plants of the yellow herb called tansy, four of a red flower, and a pretty white one; but the treasures of the rock consisted of three roots of garlic, which Maie had put in a cleft. Rock walls sheltered them on the north side, and the sun shone on them on the south. This does not seem much, but it sufficed Maie for a herb plot.

All good things go in threes, so Matte and his wife fished for salmon in spring, for herring in summer, and for cod in winter. When on Saturdays the weather was fine and the wind favourable, they sailed to the nearest town, sold their fish, and went to church on Sunday. But it often happened that for weeks at a time they were quite alone on the rock Ahtola, and had nothing to look at except their little yellow-brown dog, which bore the grand name of Prince, their grass tufts, their bushes and blooms, the sea bays and fish, a stormy sky and the blue, white-crested waves. For the rock lay far away from the land, and there were no green islets or human habitations for miles round, only here and there appeared a rock of the same red stone as Ahtola, besprinkled day and night with the ocean spray.

Matte and Maie were industrious, hard-working folk, happy and contented in their poor hut, and they thought themselves rich when they were able to salt as many casks of fish as they required for winter and yet have some left over with which to buy tobacco for the old man, and a pound or two of coffee for his wife, with plenty of burned corn and chicory in it to give it a flavour. Besides that, they had bread, butter, fish, a beer cask, and a buttermilk jar; what more did they require? All would have gone well had not Maie been possessed with a secret longing which never let her rest; and this was, how she could manage to become the owner of a cow.

'What would you do with a cow?' asked Matte. 'She could not swim so far, and our boat is not large enough to bring her over here; and even if we had her, we have nothing to feed her on.'

'We have four alder bushes and sixteen tufts of grass,' rejoined Maie.

'Yes, of course,' laughed Matte, 'and we have also three plants of garlic. Garlic would be fine feeding for her.'

'Every cow likes salt herring,' rejoined his wife. 'Even Prince is fond of fish.'

'That may be,' said her husband. 'Methinks she would soon be a dear cow if we had to feed her on salt herring. All very well for Prince, who fights with the gulls over the last morsel. Put the cow out of your head, mother, we are very well off as we are.'

Maie sighed. She knew well that her husband was right, but she could not give up the idea of a cow. The buttermilk no longer tasted as good as usual in the coffee; she thought of sweet cream and fresh butter, and of how there was nothing in the world to be compared with them.

One day as Matte and his wife were cleaning herring on the shore they heard Prince barking, and soon there appeared a gaily painted boat with three young men in it, steering towards the rock. They were students, on a boating excursion, and wanted to get something to eat.

'Bring us a junket, good mother,' cried they to Maie.

'Ah! if only I had such a thing!' sighed Maie.

'A can of fresh milk, then,' said the students; 'but it must not be skim.'

'Yes, if only I had it!' sighed the old woman, still more deeply.

'What! haven't you got a cow?'

Maie was silent. This question so struck her to the heart that she could not reply.

'We have no cow,' Matte answered; 'but we have good smoked herring, and can cook them in a couple of hours.'

'All right, then, that will do,' said the students, as they flung themselves down on the rock, while fifty silvery-white herring were turning on the spit in front of the fire.

'What's the name of this little stone in the middle of the ocean?' asked one of them.

'Ahtola,' answered the old man.

'Well, you should want for nothing when you live in the Sea King's dominion.'

Matte did not understand. He had never read Kalevala and knew nothing of the sea gods of old, but the students proceeded to explain to him.[FN#2: Kalevala is a collection of old Finnish songs about gods and heroes.]

'Ahti,' said they, 'is a mighty king who lives in his dominion of Ahtola, and has a rock at the bottom of the sea, and possesses besides a treasury of good things. He rules over all fish and animals of the deep; he has the finest cows and the swiftest horses that ever chewed grass at the bottom of the ocean. He who stands well with

Ahti is soon a rich man, but one must beware in dealing with him, for he is very changeful and touchy. Even a little stone thrown into the water might offend him, and then as he takes back his gift, he stirs up the sea into a storm and drags the sailors down into the depths. Ahti owns also the fairest maidens, who bear the train of his queen Wellamos, and at the sound of music they comb their long, flowing locks, which glisten in the water.'

'Oh!' cried Matte, 'have your worships really seen all that?'

'We have as good as seen it,' said the students. 'It is all printed in a book, and everything printed is true.'

'I'm not so sure of that,' said Matte, as he shook his head.

But the herring were now ready, and the students ate enough for six, and gave Prince some cold meat which they happened to have in the boat. Prince sat on his hind legs with delight and mewed like a pussy cat. When all was finished, the students handed Matte a shining silver coin, and allowed him to fill his pipe with a special kind of tobacco. They then thanked him for his kind hospitality and went on their journey, much regretted by Prince, who sat with a woeful expression and whined on the shore as long as he could see a flip of the boat's white sail in the distance.

Maie had never uttered a word, but thought the more. She had good ears, and had laid to heart the story about Ahti. 'How delightful,' thought she to herself, 'to possess a fairy cow! How delicious every morning and evening to draw milk from it, and yet have no trouble about the feeding, and to keep a shelf near the window for dishes of milk and junkets! But this will never be my luck.'

'What are you thinking of?' asked Matte.

'Nothing,' said his wife; but all the time she was pondering over some magic rhymes she had heard in her childhood from an old lame man, which were supposed to bring luck in fishing.

'What if I were to try?' thought she.

Now this was Saturday, and on Saturday evenings Matte never set the herring-net, for he did not fish on Sunday. Towards evening, however, his wife said:

'Let us set the herring-net just this once.'

'No,' said her husband, 'it is a Saturday night.'

'Last night was so stormy, and we caught so little,' urged his wife; 'to-night the sea is like a mirror, and with the wind in this direction the herring are drawing towards land.'

'But there are streaks in the north-western sky, and Prince was eating grass this evening,' said the old man.

'Surely he has not eaten my garlic,' exclaimed the old woman.

'No; but there will be rough weather by to-morrow at sunset,' rejoined Matte.

'Listen to me,' said his wife, 'we will set only one net close to the shore, and then we shall be able to finish up our half-filled cask, which will spoil if it stands open so long.'

The old man allowed himself to be talked over, and so they rowed out with the net. When they reached the deepest part of the water, she began to hum the words of the magic rhyme, altering the words to suit the longing of her heart:

> Oh, Ahti, with the long, long beard,
>   Who dwellest in the deep blue sea,
> Finest treasures have I heard,
>   And glittering fish belong to thee.
> The richest pearls beyond compare
>   Are stored up in thy realm below,
> And Ocean's cows so sleek and fair
>   Feed on the grass in thy green meadow.

> King of the waters, far and near,
>   I ask not of thy golden store,
> I wish not jewels of pearl to wear,
>   Nor silver either, ask I for,
> But one is odd and even is two,
>   So give me a cow, sea-king so bold,
> And in return I'll give to you
>   A slice of the moon, and the sun's gold.

'What's that you're humming?' asked the old man.

'Oh, only the words of an old rhyme that keeps running in my head,' answered the old woman; and she raised her voice and went on:

> Oh, Ahti, with the long, long beard,
>   Who dwellest in the deep blue sea,
> A thousand cows are in thy herd,
>   I pray thee give one onto me.

127

'That's a stupid sort of song,' said Matte. 'What else should one beg of the sea-king but fish? But such songs are not for Sunday.'

His wife pretended not to hear him, and sang and sang the same tune all the time they were on the water. Matte heard nothing more as he sat and rowed the heavy boat, while thinking of his cracked pipe and the fine tobacco. Then they returned to the island, and soon after went to bed.

But neither Matte nor Maie could sleep a wink; the one thought of how he had profaned Sunday, and the other of Ahti's cow.

About midnight the fisherman sat up, and said to his wife:

'Dost thou hear anything?'

'No,' said she.

'I think the twirling of the weathercock on the roof bodes ill,' said he; 'we shall have a storm.'

'Oh, it is nothing but your fancy,' said his wife.

Matte lay down, but soon rose again.

'The weathercock is squeaking now,' said he.

'Just fancy! Go to sleep,' said his wife; and the old man tried to.

For the third time he jumped out of bed.

'Ho! how the weather-cock is roaring at the pitch of its voice, as if it had a fire inside it! We are going to have a tempest, and must bring in the net.'

Both rose. The summer night was as dark as if it had been October, the weather-cock creaked, and the storm was raging in every direction. As they went out the sea lay around them as white as now, and the spray was dashing right over the fisher-hut. In all his life Matte had never remembered such a night. To launch the boat and put to sea to rescue the net was a thing not to be thought of. The fisherman and his wife stood aghast on the doorstep, holding on fast by the doorpost, while the foam splashed over their faces.

'Did I not tell thee that there is no luck in Sunday fishing?' said Matte sulkily; and his wife was so frightened that she never even once thought of Ahti's cows.

As there was nothing to be done, they went in. Their eyes were heavy for lack of slumber, and they slept as soundly as if there had not been such a thing as an angry sea roaring furiously around their lonely dwelling. When they awoke, the sun was high in the heavens, the tempest had cased, and only the swell of the sea rose in silvery heavings against the red rock.

'What can that be?' said the old woman, as she peeped out of the door.

'It looks like a big seal,' said Matte.

'As sure as I live, it's a cow!' exclaimed Maie. And certainly it was a cow, a fine red cow, fat and flourishing, and looking as if it had been fed all its days on spinach. It wandered peacefully up and down the shore, and never so much as even looked at the poor little tufts of grass, as if it despised such fare.

Matte could not believe his eyes. But a cow she seemed, and a cow she was found to be; and when the old woman began to milk her, every pitcher and pan, even to the baler, was soon filled with the most delicious milk.

The old man troubled his head in vain as to how she came there, and sallied forth to seek for his lost net. He had not proceeded far when he found it cast up on the shore, and so full of fish that not a mesh was visible.

'It is all very fine to possess a cow,' said Matte, as he cleaned the fish; 'but what are we going to feed her on?'

'We shall find some means,' said his wife; and the cow found the means herself. She went out and cropped the seaweed which grew in great abundance near the shore, and always kept in good condition. Every one Prince alone excepted, thought she was a clever beast; but Prince barked at her, for he had now got a rival.

From that day the red rock overflowed with milk and junkets, and every net was filled with fish. Matte and Maie grew fat on this fine living, and daily became richer. She churned quantities of butter, and he hired two men to help him in his fishing. The sea lay before him like a big fish tank, out of which he hauled as many as he required; and the cow continued to fend for herself. In autumn, when Matte and Maie went ashore, the cow went to sea, and in spring, when they returned to the rock, there she stood awaiting them.

'We shall require a better house,' said Maie the following summer; 'the old one is too small for ourselves and the men.'

'Yes,' said Matte. So he built a large cottage, with a real lock to the door, and a store-house for fish as well; and he and his men caught such quantities of fish that they sent tons of salmon, herring, and cod to Russian and Sweden.

'I am quite overworked with so many folk,' said Maie; 'a girl to help me would not come amiss.'

'Get one, then,' said her husband; and so they hired a girl.

Then Maie said: 'We have too little milk for all these folk. Now that I have a servant, with the same amount of trouble she could look after three cows.'

'All right, then,' said her husband, somewhat provoked, 'you can sing a song to the fairies.'

This annoyed Maie, but nevertheless she rowed out to sea on Sunday night and sang as before:

> Oh, Ahti, with the long, long beard,
>   Who dwellest in the deep blue sea,
> A thousand cows are in thy herd,
>   I pray thee give three unto me.

The following morning, instead of one, three cows stood on the island, and they all ate seaweed and fended for themselves like the first one.

'Art thou satisfied now?' said Matte to his wife.

'I should be quite satisfied,' said his wife, 'if only I had two servants to help, and if I had some finer clothes. Don't you know that I am addressed as Madam?'

'Well, well,' said her husband. So Maie got several servants and clothes fit for a great lady.

'Everything would now be perfect if only we had a little better dwelling for summer. You might build us a two-storey house, and fetch soil to make a garden. Then you might make a little arbour up there to let us have a sea-view; and we might have a fiddler to fiddle to us of an evening, and a little steamer to take us to church in stormy weather.'

'Anything more?' asked Matte; but he did everything that his wife wished. The rock Ahtola became so grand and Maie so grand that all the sea-urchins and herring were lost in wonderment. Even Prince was fed on beefsteaks and cream scones till at last he was as round as a butter jar.

'Are you satisfied now?' asked Matte.

'I should be quite satisfied,' said Maie, 'if only I had thirty cows. At least that number is required for such a household.'

130

'Go to the fairies,' said Matte.

His wife set out in the new steamer and sang to the sea-king. Next morning thirty cows stood on the shore, all finding food for themselves.

'Know'st thou, good man, that we are far too cramped on this wretched rock, and where am I to find room for so many cows?'

'There is nothing to be done but to pump out the sea.'

'Rubbish!' said his wife. 'Who can pump out the sea?'

'Try with thy new steamer, there is a pump in it.'

Maie knew well that her husband was only making fun of her, but still her mind was set upon the same subject. 'I never could pump the sea out,' thought she, 'but perhaps I might fill it up, if I were to make a big dam. I might heap up sand and stones, and make our island as big again.'

Maie loaded her boat with stones and went out to sea. The fiddler was with her, and fiddled so finely that Ahti and Wellamos and all the sea's daughters rose to the surface of the water to listen to the music.

'What is that shining so brightly in the waves?' asked Maie.

'That is sea foam glinting in the sunshine,' answered the fiddler.

'Throw out the stones,' said Maie.

The people in the boat began to throw out the stones, splash, splash, right and left, into the foam. One stone hit the nose of Wellamos's chief lady-in-waiting, another scratched the sea queen herself on the cheek, a third plumped close to Ahti's head and tore off half of the sea-king's beard; then there was a commotion in the sea, the waves bubbled and bubbled like boiling water in a pot.

'Whence comes this gust of wind?' said Maie; and as she spoke the sea opened and swallowed up the steamer. Maie sank to the bottom like a stone, but, stretching out her arms and legs, she rose to the surface, where she found the fiddler's fiddle, and used it as a float. At the same moment she saw close beside her the terrible head of Ahti, and he had only half a beard!'

'Why did you throw stones at me?' roared the sea-king.

'Oh, your majesty, it was a mistake! Put some bear's grease on your beard and that will soon make it grow again.'

'Dame, did I not give you all you asked for—nay, even more?'

'Truly, truly, your majesty. Many thanks for the cows.'

'Well, where is the gold from the sun and the silver from the moon that you promised me?'

'Ah, your majesty, they have been scattered day and night upon the sea, except when the sky was overcast,' slyly answered Maie.

'I'll teach you!' roared the sea-king; and with that he gave the fiddle such a 'puff' that it sent the old woman up like a sky-rocket on to her island. There Prince lay, as famished as ever, gnawing the carcase of a crow. There sat Matte in his ragged grey jacket, quite alone, on the steps of the old hut, mending a net.

'Heavens, mother,' said he, 'where are you coming from at such a whirlwind pace, and what makes you in such a dripping condition?'

Maie looked around her amazed, and said, 'Where is our two-storey house?'

'What house?' asked her husband.

'Our big house, and the flower garden, and the men and the maids, and the thirty beautiful cows, and the steamer, and everything else?'

'You are talking nonsense, mother,' said he. 'The students have quite turned your head, for you sang silly songs last evening while we were rowing, and then you could not sleep till early morning. We had stormy weather during the night, and when it was past I did not wish to waken you, so rowed out alone to rescue the net.'

'But I've seen Ahti,' rejoined Maie.

'You've been lying in bed, dreaming foolish fancies, mother, and then in your sleep you walked into the water.'

'But there is the fiddle,' said Maie.

'A fine fiddle! It is only an old stick. No, no, old woman, another time we will be more careful. Good luck never attends fishing on a Sunday.'

From Z. Topelius.

132

The Raspberry Worm

'Phew!' cried Lisa.

'Ugh!' cried Aina.

'What now?' cried the big sister.

'A worm!' cried Lisa.

'On the raspberry!' cried Aina.

'Kill it!' cried Otto.

'What a fuss over a poor little worm!' said the big sister scornfully.

'Yes, when we had cleaned the raspberries so carefully,' said Lisa.

'It crept out from that very large one,' put in Aina.

'And supposing someone had eaten the raspberry,' said Lisa.

'Then they would have eaten the worm, too,' said Aina.

'Well, what harm?' said Otto.

'Eat a worm!' cried Lisa.

'And kill him with one bite!' murmured Aina.

'Just think of it!' said Otto laughing.

'Now it is crawling on the table,' cried Aina again.

'Blow it away!' said the big sister.

'Tramp on it!' laughed Otto.

But Lisa took a raspberry leaf, swept the worm carefully on to the leaf and carried it out into the yard. Then Aina noticed that a sparrow sitting on the fence was just ready to pounce on the poor little worm, so she took up the leaf, carried it out into the wood and hid it under a raspberry bush where the greedy sparrow could not find it. Yes, and what more is there to tell about a raspberry worm? Who would give three straws for such a miserable little thing? Yes, but who would not like to live in

133

such a pretty home as it lives in; in such a fresh fragrant dark-red cottage, far away in the quiet wood among flowers and green leaves!

Now it was just dinner time, so they all had a dinner of raspberries and cream. 'Be careful with the sugar, Otto,' said the big sister; but Otto's plate was like a snowdrift in winter, with just a little red under the snow.

Soon after dinner the big sister said: 'Now we have eaten up the raspberries and we have none left to make preserve for the winter; it would be fine if we could get two baskets full of berries, then we could clean them this evening, and to-morrow we could cook them in the big preserving pan, and then we should have raspberry jam to eat on our bread!'

'Come, let us go to the wood and pick,' said Lisa.

'Yes, let us,' said Aina. 'You take the yellow basket and I will take the green one.'

'Don't get lost, and come back safely in the evening,' said the big sister.

'Greetings to the raspberry worm,' said Otto, mockingly. 'Next time I meet him I shall do him the honour of eating him up.'

So Aina and Lisa went off to the wood. Ah! how delightful it was there, how beautiful! It was certainly tiresome sometimes climbing over the fallen trees, and getting caught in the branches, and waging war with the juniper bushes and the midges, but what did that matter? The girls climbed well in their short dresses, and soon they were deep in the wood.

There were plenty of bilberries and elder berries, but no raspberries. They wandered on and on, and at last they came ... No, it could not be true! ... they came to a large raspberry wood. The wood had been on fire once, and now raspberry bushes had grown up, and there were raspberry bushes and raspberry bushes as far as the eye could see. Every bush was weighted to the ground with the largest, dark red, ripe raspberries, such a wealth of berries as two little berry pickers had never found before!

Lisa picked, Aina picked. Lisa ate, Aina ate, and in a little while their baskets were full.

'Now we shall go home,' said Aina. 'No, let us gather a few more,' said Lisa. So they put the baskets down on the ground and began to fill their pinafores, and it was not long before their pinafores were full, too.

'Now we shall go home,' said Lina. 'Yes, now we shall go home,' said Aina. Both girls took a basket in one hand and held up her apron in the other and then turned to go home. But that was easier said than done. They had never been so far in the great

134

wood before, they could not find any road nor path, and soon the girls noticed that they had lost their way.

The worst of it was that the shadows of the tress were becoming so long in the evening sunlight, the birds were beginning to fly home, and the day was closing in. At last the sun went down behind the pine tops, and it was cool and dusky in the great wood.

The girls became anxious but went steadily on, expecting that the wood would soon end, and that they would see the smoke from the chimneys of their home.

After they had wandered on for a long time it began to grow dark. At last they reached a great plain overgrown with bushes, and when they looked around them, they saw, as much as they could in the darkness, that they were among the same beautiful raspberry bushes from which they had picked their baskets and their aprons full. Then they were so tired that they sat down on a stone and began to cry.

'I am so hungry,' said Lisa.

'Yes,' said Aina, 'if we had only two good meat sandwiches now.'

As she said that, she felt something in her hand, and when she looked down, she saw a large sandwich of bread and chicken, and at the same time Lisa said: 'How very queer! I have a sandwich in my hand.'

'And I, too,' said Aina. 'Will you dare to eat it?'

'Of course I will,' said Lisa. 'Ah, if we only had a good glass of milk now!'

Just as she said that she felt a large glass of milk between her fingers, and at the same time Aina cried out, 'Lisa! Lisa! I have a glass of milk in my hand! Isn't it queer?'

The girls, however, were very hungry, so they ate and drank with a good appetite. When they had finished Aina yawned, stretched out her arms and said: 'Oh, if only we had a nice soft bed to sleep on now!'

Scarcely had she spoken before she felt a nice soft bed by her side, and there beside Lisa was one too. This seemed to the girls more and more wonderful, but tired and sleepy as they were, they thought no more about it, but crept into the little beds, drew the coverlets over their heads and were soon asleep.

When they awoke the sun was high in the heavens, the wood was beautiful in the summer morning, and the birds were flying about in the branches and the tree tops.

At first the girls were filled with wonder when they saw that they had slept in the wood among the raspberry bushes. They looked at each other, they looked at their beds, which were of the finest flax covered over with leaves and moss. At last Lisa said: 'Are you awake, Aina?'

'Yes,' said Aina.

'But I am still dreaming,' said Lisa.

'No,' said Aina, 'but there is certainly some good fairy living among these raspberry bushes. Ah, if we had only a hot cup of coffee now, and a nice piece of white bread to dip into it!'

Scarcely had she finished speaking when she saw beside her a little silver tray with a gilt coffee-pot, two cups of rare porcelain, a sugar basin of fine crystal, silver sugar tongs, and some good fresh white bread. The girls poured out the beautiful coffee, put in the cream and sugar, and tasted it; never in their lives had they drunk such beautiful coffee.

'Now I should like to know very much who has given us all this,' said Lisa gratefully.

'I have, my little girls,' said a voice just then from the bushes.

The children looked round wonderingly, and saw a little kind-looking old man, in a white coat and a red cap, limping out from among the bushes, for he was lame in his left foot; neither Lisa nor Aina could utter a word, they were so filled with surprise.

'Don't be afraid, little girls,' he said smiling kindly at them; he could not laugh properly because his mouth was crooked. 'Welcome to my kingdom! Have you slept well and eaten well and drunk well?' he asked.

'Yes, indeed we have,' said both the girls, 'but tell us ...' and they wanted to ask who the old man was, but were afraid to.

'I will tell you who I am,' said the old man; 'I am the raspberry king, who reigns over all this kingdom of raspberry bushes, and I have lived here for more than a thousand years. But the great spirit who rules over the woods, and the sea, and the sky, did not want me to become proud of my royal power and my long life. Therefore he decreed that one day in every hundred years I should change into a little raspberry worm, and live in that weak and helpless form from sunrise to sunset. During that time my life is dependent on the little worm's life, so that a bird can eat me, a child can pick me with the berries and trample under foot my thousand years of life. Now yesterday was just my transformation day, and I was taken with the raspberry and would have been trampled to death if you had not saved my life. Until sunset I lay helpless in the grass, and when I was swept away from your table I

136

twisted one of my feet, and my mouth became crooked with terror; but when evening came and I could take my own form again, I looked for you to thank you and reward you. Then I found you both here in my kingdom, and tried to meet you both as well as I could without frightening you. Now I will send a bird from my wood to show you the way home. Good-bye, little children, thank you for your kind hearts; the raspberry king can show that he is not ungrateful.' The children shook hands with the old man and thanked him, feeling very glad that they had saved the little raspberry worm. They were just going when the old man turned round, smiled mischievously with his crooked mouth, and said: 'Greetings to Otto from me, and tell him when I meet him again I shall do him the honour of eating him up.'

'Oh, please don't do that,' cried both the girls, very frightened.

'Well, for your sake I will forgive him,' said the old man, 'I am not revengeful. Greetings to Otto and tell him that he may expect a gift from me, too. Good-bye.'

The two girls, light of heart, now took their berries and ran off through the wood after the bird; and soon it began to get lighter in the wood and they wondered how they could have lost their way yesterday, it seemed so easy and plain now.

One can imagine what joy there was when the two reached home. Everyone had been looking for them, and the big sister had not been able to sleep, for she thought the wolves had eaten them up.

Otto met them; he had a basket in his hand and said: 'Look, here is something that an old man has just left for you.'

When the girls looked into the basket they saw a pair of most beautiful bracelets of precious stones, dark red, and made in the shape of a ripe raspberry and with an inscription: 'To Lisa and Aina'; beside them there was a diamond breast pin in the shape of a raspberry worm: on it was inscribed 'Otto, never destroy the helpless!'

Otto felt rather ashamed: he quite understood what it meant, but he thought that the old man's revenge was a noble one.

The raspberry king had also remembered the big sister, for when she went in to set the table for dinner, she found eleven big baskets of most beautiful raspberries, and no one knew how they had come there, but everyone guessed.

And so there was such a jam-making as had never been seen before, and if you like to go and help in it, you might perhaps get a little, for they must surely be making jam still to this very day.

From Z. Topelius.

The Stones of Plouhinec

Perhaps some of you may have read a book called 'Kenneth; or the Rear-Guard of the Grand Army' of Napoleon. If so, you will remember how the two Scotch children found in Russia were taken care of by the French soldiers and prevented as far as possible from suffering from the horrors of the terrible Retreat. One of the soldiers, a Breton, often tried to make them forget how cold and hungry they were by telling them tales of his native country, Brittany, which is full of wonderful things. The best and warmest place round the camp fire was always given to the children, but even so the bitter frost would cause them to shiver. It was then that the Breton would begin: 'Plouhinec is a small town near Hennebonne by the sea,' and would continue until Kenneth or Effie would interrupt him with an eager question. Then he forgot how his mother had told him the tale, and was obliged to begin all over again, so the story lasted a long while, and by the time it was ended the children were ready to be rolled up in what ever coverings could be found, and go to sleep. It is this story that I am going to tell to you.

Plouhinec is a small town near Hennebonne by the sea. Around it stretches a desolate moor, where no corn can be grown, and the grass is so coarse that no beast grows fat on it. Here and there are scattered groves of fir trees, and small pebbles are so thick on the ground that you might almost take it for a beach. On the further side, the fairies, or korigans, as the people called them, had set up long long ago two rows of huge stones; indeed, so tall and heavy were they, that it seemed as if all the fairies in the world could not have placed them upright.

Not far off them this great stone avenue, and on the banks of the little river Intel, there lived a man named Marzinne and his sister Rozennik. They always had enough black bread to eat, and wooden shoes or sabots to wear, and a pig to fatten, so the neighbours thought them quite rich; and what was still better, they thought themselves rich also.

Rozennik was a pretty girl, who knew how to make the best of everything, and she could, if she wished, have chosen a husband from the young men of Plouhinec, but she cared for none of them except Bernez, whom she had played with all her life, and Bernez, though he worked hard, was so very very poor that Marzinne told him roughly he must look elsewhere for a wife. But whatever Marzinne might say Rozennik smiled and nodded to him as before, and would often turn her head as she passed, and sing snatches of old songs over her shoulder.

Christmas Eve had come, and all the men who worked under Marzinne or on the farms round about were gathered in the large kitchen to eat the soup flavoured with honey followed by rich puddings, to which they were always invited on this particular night. In the middle of the table was a large wooden bowl, with wooden spoons placed in a circle round it, so that each might dip in his turn. The benches were filled, and Marzinne was about to give the signal, when the door was suddenly thrown open, and an old man came in, wishing the guests a good appetite for their supper. There was a pause, and some of the faces looked a little frightened; for the new comer was well known to them as a beggar, who was also said to be a wizard who cast spells over the cattle, and caused the corn to grow black, and old people to die, of what, nobody knew. Still, it was Christmas Eve, and besides it was as well not to offend him, so the farmer invited him in, and gave him a seat at the table and a wooden spoon like the rest.

There was not much talk after the beggar's entrance, and everyone was glad when the meal came to an end, and the beggar asked if he might sleep in the stable, as he should die of cold if he were left outside. Rather unwillingly Marzinne gave him leave, and bade Bernez take the key and unlock the door. There was certainly plenty of room for a dozen beggars, for the only occupants of the stable were an old donkey and a thin ox; and as the night was bitter, the wizard lay down between them for warmth, with a sack of reeds for a pillow.

He had walked far that day, and even wizards get tired sometimes, so in spite of the hard floor he was just dropping off to sleep, when midnight struck from the church tower of Plouhinec. At this sound the donkey raised her head and shook her ears, and turned towards the ox.

'Well, my dear cousin,' said she, 'and how have you fared since last Christmas Eve, when we had a conversation together?'

Instead of answering at once, the ox eyed the beggar with a long look of disgust.

'What is the use of talking,' he replied roughly, 'when a good-for-nothing creature like that can hear all we say?'

'Oh, you mustn't lose time in grumbling,' rejoined the donkey gaily, 'and don't you see that the wizard is asleep?'

'His wicked pranks do not make him rich, certainly,' said the ox, 'and he isn't even clever enough to have found out what a piece of luck might befall him a week hence.'

'What piece of luck?' asked the donkey.

'Why, don't you know,' inquired the ox, 'that once very hundred years the stones on Plouhinec heath go down to drink at the river, and that while they are away the treasures underneath them are uncovered?'

'Ah, I remember now,' replied the donkey, 'but the stones return so quickly to their places, that you certainly would be crushed to death unless you have in your hands a bunch of crowsfoot and of five-leaved trefoil.'

'Yes, but that is not enough,' said the ox; 'even supposing you get safely by, the treasure you have brought with you will crumble into dust if you do not give in

139

exchange a baptised soul. It is needful that a Christian should die before you can enjoy the wealth of Plouhinec.'

The donkey was about to ask some further questions, when she suddenly found herself unable to speak: the time allowed them for conversation was over.

'Ah, my dear creatures,' thought the beggar, who had of course heard everything, 'you are going to make me richer than the richest men of Vannes or Lorient. But I have no time to lose; to-morrow I must begin to hunt for the precious plants.'

He did not dare to seek too near Plouhinec, lest somebody who knew the story might guess what he was doing, so he went away further towards the south, where the air was softer and the plants are always green. From the instant it was light, till the last rays had faded out of the sky, he searched every inch of ground where the magic plants might grow; he scarcely gave himself a minute to eat and drink, but at length he found the crowsfoot in a little hollow! Well, that was certainly a great deal, but after all, the crowsfoot was of no use without the trefoil, and there was so little time left.

He had almost give up hope, when on the very last day before it was necessary that he should start of Plouhinec, he came upon a little clump of trefoil, half hidden under a rock. Hardly able to breathe from excitement, he sat down and hunted eagerly through the plant which he had torn up. Leaf after leaf he threw aside in disgust, and he had nearly reached the end when he gave a cry of joy— the five-leaved trefoil was in his hand.

The beggar scrambled to his feet, and without a pause walked quickly down the road that led northwards. The moon was bright, and for some hours he kept steadily on, not knowing how many miles he had gone, nor even feeling tired. By and bye the sun rose, and the world began to stir, and stopping at a farmhouse door, he asked for a cup of milk and slice of bread and permission to rest for a while in the porch. Then he continued his journey, and so, towards sunset on New Year's Eve, he came back to Plouhinec.

As he was passing the long line of stones, he saw Bernez working with a chisel on the tallest of them all.

'What are you doing there?' called the wizard, 'do you mean to hollow out for yourself a bed in that huge column?'

'No,' replied Bernez quietly, 'but as I happened to have no work to do to-day, I thought I would just carve a cross on this stone. The holy sign can never come amiss.'

'I believe you think it will help you to win Rozennik,' laughed the old man.

Bernez ceased his task for a moment to look at him.

'Ah, so you know about that,' replied he; 'unluckily Marzinne wants a brother-in-law who has more pounds than I have pence.'

'And suppose I were to give you more pounds than Marzinne ever dreamed of?' whispered the sorcerer glancing round to make sure that no one overheard him.

'You?'

'Yes, I.'

'And what am I to do to gain the money,' inquired Bernez, who knew quite well that the Breton peasant gives nothing for nothing.

'What I want of you only needs a little courage,' answered the old man.

'If that is all, tell me what I have got to do, and I will do it,' cried Bernez, letting fall his chisel. 'If I have to risk thirty deaths, I am ready.'

When the beggar knew that Bernez would give him no trouble, he told him how, during that very night, the treasures under the stones would be uncovered, and how in a very few minutes they could take enough to make them both rich for life. But he kept silence as to the fate that awaited the man who was without the crowsfoot and the trefoil, and Bernez thought that nothing but boldness and quickness were necessary. So he said:

'Old man, I am grateful, indeed, for the chance you have given me, and there will always be a pint of my blood at your service. Just let me finish carving this cross. It is nearly done, and I will join you in the fir wood at whatever hour you please.'

'You must be there without fail an hour before midnight,' answered the wizard, and went on his way.

As the hour struck from the great church at Plouhinec, Bernez entered the wood. He found the beggar already there with a bag in each hand, and a third slung round his neck.

'You are punctual,' said the old man, 'but we need not start just yet. You had better sit down and think what you will do when your pockets are filled with gold and silver and jewels.'

'Oh, it won't take me long to plan out that,' returned Bernez with a laugh. 'I shall give Rozennik everything she can desire, dresses of all sorts, from cotton to silk, and good things of all kinds to eat, from white bread to oranges.'

'The silver you find will pay for all that, and what about the gold?'

'With the gold I shall make rich Rozennik's relations and every friend of hers in the parish,' replied he.

'So much for the gold; and the jewels?'

'Then,' cried Bernez, 'I will divide the jewels amongst everybody in the world, so that they may be wealthy and happy; and I will tell them that it is Rozennik who would have it so.'

'Hush! it is close on midnight—we must go,' whispered the wizard, and together they crept to the edge of the wood.

With the first stroke of twelve a great noise arose over the silent heath, and the earth seemed to rock under the feet of the two watchers. The next moment by the light of the moon they beheld the huge stones near them leave their places and go down the slope leading to the river, knocking against each other in their haste. Passing the spot where stood Bernez and the beggar, they were lost in the darkness. It seemed as if a procession of giants had gone by.

'Quick,' said the wizard, in a low voice, and he rushed towards the empty holes, which even in the night shone brightly from the treasures within them. Flinging himself on his knees, the old man began filling the wallets he had brought, listening intently all the time for the return of the stones up the hill, while Bernez more slowly put handfuls of all he could see into his pockets.

The sorcerer had just closed his third wallet, and was beginning to wonder if he could carry away any more treasures when a low murmur as of a distant storm broke upon his ears.

The stones had finished drinking, and were hastening back to their places.

On they came, bent a little forward, the tallest of them all at their head, breaking everything that stood in their way. At the sight Bernez stood transfixed with horror, and said,

'We are lost! They will crush us to death.'

'Not me!' answered the sorcerer, holding up the crowsfoot and the five-leaved trefoil, 'for these will preserve me. But in order to keep my riches, I was obliged to sacrifice a Christian to the stones, and an evil fate threw you in my way.' And as he spoke he stretched out the magic herbs to the stones, which were advancing rapidly. As if acknowledging a power greater than theirs, the monstrous things instantly parted to the right and left of the wizard, but closed their ranks again as they approached Bernez.

142

The young man did not try to escape, he knew it was useless, and sank on his knees and closed his eyes. But suddenly the tall stone that was leading stopped straight in front of Bernez, so that no other could get past.

It was the stone on which Bernez had carved the cross, and it was now a baptized stone, and had power to save him.

So the stone remained before the young man till the rest had taken their places, and then, darting like a bird to its own hole, came upon the beggar, who, thinking himself quite safe, was staggering along under the weight of his treasures.

Seeing the stone approaching, he held out the magic herbs which he carried, but the baptized stone was no longer subject to the spells that bound the rest, and passed straight on its way, leaving the wizard crushed into powder in the heather.

Then Bernez went home, and showed his wealth to Marzinne, who this time did not refuse him as a brother-in-law, and he and Rozennik were married, and lived happy for ever after.

From 'Le Royer Breton,' par Emile Souvestre.

The Castle of Kerglas

Peronnik was a poor idiot who belonged to nobody, and he would have died of starvation if it had not been for the kindness of the village people, who gave him food whenever he chose to ask for it. And as for a bed, when night came, and he grew sleepy, he looked about for a heap of straw, and making a hole in it, crept in, like a lizard. Idiot though he was, he was never unhappy, but always thanked gratefully those who fed him, and sometimes would stop for a little and sing to them. For he could imitate a lark so well, that no one knew which was Peronnik and which was the bird.

He had been wandering in a forest one day for several hours, and when evening approached, he suddenly felt very hungry. Luckily, just at that place the trees grew thinner, and he could see a small farmhouse a little way off. Peronnik went straight towards it, and found the farmer's wife standing at the door holding in her hands the large bowl out of which her children had eaten their supper.

'I am hungry, will you give me something to eat?' asked the boy.

'If you can find anything here, you are welcome to it,' answered she, and, indeed, there was not much left, as everybody's spoon had dipped in. But Peronnik ate what was there with a hearty appetite, and thought that he had never tasted better food.

'It is made of the finest flour and mixed with the richest milk and stirred by the best cook in all the countryside,' and though he said it to himself, the woman heard him.

'Poor innocent,' she murmured, 'he does not know what he is saying, but I will cut him a slice of that new wheaten loaf,' and so she did, and Peronnik ate up every crumb, and declared that nobody less than the bishop's baker could have baked it. This flattered the farmer's wife so much that she gave him some butter to spread on it, and Peronnik was still eating it on the doorstep when an armed knight rode up.

'Can you tell me the way to the castle of Kerglas?' asked he.

'To Kerglas? are you really going to Kerglas?' cried the woman, turning pale.

'Yes; and in order to get there I have come from a country so far off that it has taken me three months' hard riding to travel as far as this.'

'And why do you want to go to Kerglas?' said she.

'I am seeking the basin of gold and the lance of diamonds which are in the castle,' he answered. Then Peronnik looked up.

'The basin and the lance are very costly things,' he said suddenly.

'More costly and precious than all the crowns in the world,' replied the stranger, 'for not only will the basin furnish you with the best food that you can dream of, but if you drink of it, it will cure you of any illness however dangerous, and will even bring the dead back to life, if it touches their mouths. As to the diamond lance, that will cut through any stone or metal.'

'And to whom do these wonders belong?' asked Peronnik in amazement.

'To a magician named Rogear who lives in the castle,' answered the woman. 'Every day he passes along here, mounted on a black mare, with a colt thirteen months old trotting behind. But no one dares to attack him, as he always carries his lance.'

'That is true,' said the knight, 'but there is a spell laid upon him which forbids his using it within the castle of Kerglas. The moment he enters, the basin and lance are put away in a dark cellar which no key but one can open. And that is the place where I wish to fight the magician.'

'You will never overcome him, Sir Knight,' replied the woman, shaking her head. 'More than a hundred gentlemen have ridden past this house bent on the same errand, and not one has ever come back.'

'I know that, good woman,' returned the knight, 'but then they did not have, like me, instructions from the hermit of Blavet.'

'And what did the hermit tell you?' asked Peronnik.

'He told me that I should have to pass through a wood full of all sorts of enchantments and voices, which would try to frighten me and make me lose my way. Most of those who have gone before me have wandered they know not where, and perished from cold, hunger, or fatigue.'

'Well, suppose you get through safely?' said the idiot.

'If I do,' continued the knight, 'I shall then meet a sort of fairy armed with a needle of fire which burns to ashes all it touches. This dwarf stands guarding an apple-tree, from which I am bound to pluck an apple.'

'And next?' inquired Peronnik.

'Next I shall find the flower that laughs, protected by a lion whose mane is formed of vipers. I must pluck that flower, and go on to the lake of the dragons and fight the black man who holds in his hand the iron ball which never misses its mark and returns of its own accord to its master. After that, I enter the valley of pleasure, where some who conquered all the other obstacles have left their bones. If I can win through this, I shall reach a river with only one ford, where a lady in black will be seated. She will mount my horse behind me, and tell me what I am to do next.'

145

He paused, and the woman shook her head.

'You will never be able to do all that,' said she, but he bade her remembered that these were only matters for men, and galloped away down the path she pointed out.

The farmer's wife sighed and, giving Peronnik some more food, bade him good-night. The idiot rose and was opening the gate which led into the forest when the farmer himself came up.

'I want a boy to tend my cattle,' he said abruptly, 'as the one I had has run away. Will you stay and do it?' and Peronnik, though he loved his liberty and hated work, recollected the good food he had eaten, and agreed to stop.

At sunrise he collected his herd carefully and led them to the rich pasture which lay along the borders of the forest, cutting himself a hazel wand with which to keep them in order.

His task was not quite so easy as it looked, for the cows had a way of straying into the wood, and by the time he had brought one back another was off. He had gone some distance into the trees, after a naughty black cow which gave him more trouble than all the rest, when he heard the noise of horse's feet, and peeping through the leaves he beheld the giant Rogear seated on his mare, with the colt trotting behind. Round the giant's neck hung the golden bowl suspended from a chain, and in his hand he grasped the diamond lance, which gleamed like fire. But as soon as he was out of sight the idiot sought in vain for traces of the path he had taken.

This happened not only once but many times, till Peronnik grew so used to him that he never troubled to hide. But on each occasion he saw him the desire to possess the bowl and the lance became stronger.

One evening the boy was sitting alone on the edge of the forest, when a man with a white beard stopped beside him. 'Do you want to know the way to Kerglas?' asked the idiot, and the man answered 'I know it well.'

'You have been there without being killed by the magician?' cried Peronnik.

'Oh! he had nothing to fear from me,' replied the white-bearded man, 'I am Rogear's elder brother, the wizard Bryak. When I wish to visit him I always pass this way, and as even I cannot go through the enchanted wood without losing myself, I call the colt to guide me.' Stooping down as he spoke he traced three circles on the ground and murmured some words very low, which Peronnik could not hear. Then he added aloud:

Colt, free to run and free to eat.
Colt, gallop fast until we meet,

146

and instantly the colt appeared, frisking and jumping to the wizard, who threw a halter over his neck and leapt on his back.

Peronnik kept silence at the farm about this adventure, but he understood very well that if he was ever to get to Kerglas he must first catch the colt which knew the way. Unhappily he had not heard the magic words uttered by the wizard, and he could not manage to draw the three circles, so if he was to summon the colt at all he must invent some other means of doing it.

All day long, while he was herding the cows, he thought and thought how he was to call the colt, for he felt sure that once on its back he could overcome the other dangers. Meantime he must be ready in case a chance should come, and he made his preparations at night, when everyone was asleep. Remembering what he had seen the wizard do, he patched up an old halter that was hanging in a corner of the stable, twisted a rope of hemp to catch the colt's feet, and a net such as is used for snaring birds. Next he sewed roughly together some bits of cloth to serve as a pocket, and this he filled with glue and lark's feathers, a string of beads, a whistle of elder wood, and a slice of bread rubbed over with bacon fat. Then he went out to the path down which Rogear, his mare, and the colt always rode, and crumbled the bread on one side of it.

Punctual to their hour all three appeared, eagerly watched by Peronnik, who lay hid in the bushes close by. Suppose it was useless; suppose the mare, and not the colt, ate the crumbs? Suppose—but no! the mare and her rider went safely by, vanishing round a corner, while the colt, trotting along with its head on the ground, smelt the bread, and began greedily to lick up the pieces. Oh, how good it was! Why had no one ever given it that before, and so absorbed was the little beast, sniffing about after a few more crumbs, that it never heard Peronnik creep up till it felt the halter on its neck and the rope round its feet, and—in another moment—some one on its back.

Going as fast as the hobbles would allow, the colt turned into one of the wildest parts of the forest, while its rider sat trembling at the strange sights he saw. Sometimes the earth seemed to open in front of them and he was looking into a bottomless pit; sometimes the trees burst into flames and he found himself in the midst of a fire; often in the act of crossing a stream the water rose and threatened to sweep him away; and again, at the foot of a mountain, great rocks would roll towards him, as if they would crush him and his colt beneath their weight. To his dying day Peronnik never knew whether these things were real or if he only imagined them, but he pulled down his knitted cap so as to cover his eyes, and trusted the colt to carry him down the right road.

At last the forest was left behind, and they came out on a wide plain where the air blew fresh and strong. The idiot ventured to peep out, and found to his relief that the enchantments seemed to have ended, though a thrill of horror shot through him as he noticed the skeletons of men scattered over the plain, beside the skeletons of their horses. And what were those grey forms trotting away in the distance? Were they—could they be—wolves?

But vast through the plain seemed, it did not take long to cross, and very soon the colt entered a sort of shady park in which was standing a single apple-tree, its branches bowed down to the ground with the weight of its fruit. In front was the korigan— the little fairy man—holding in his hand the fiery sword, which reduced to ashes everything it touched. At the sight of Peronnik he uttered a piercing scream, and raised his sword, but without appearing surprised the youth only lifted his cap, though he took care to remain at a little distance.

'Do not be alarmed, my prince,' said Peronnik, 'I am just on my way to Kerglas, as the noble Rogear has begged me to come to him on business.'

'Begged you to come!' repeated the dwarf, 'and who, then, are you?'

'I am the new servant he has engaged, as you know very well,' answered Peronnik.

'I do not know at all,' rejoined the korigan sulkily, 'and you may be a robber for all I can tell.'

'I am so sorry,' replied Peronnik, 'but I may be wrong in calling myself a servant, for I am only a bird-catcher. But do not delay me, I pray, for his highness the magician expects me, and, as you see, has lent me his colt so that I may reach the castle all the quicker.'

At these words the korigan cast his eyes for the first time on the colt, which he knew to be the one belonging to the magician, and began to think that the young man was speaking the truth. After examining the horse, he studied the rider, who had such an innocent, and indeed vacant, air that he appeared incapable of inventing a story. Still, the dwarf did not feel quite sure that all was right, and asked what the magician wanted with a bird-catcher.

'From what he says, he wants one very badly,' replied Peronnik, 'as he declares that all his grain and all the fruit in his garden at Kerglas are eaten up by the birds.'

'And how are you going to stop that, my fine fellow?' inquired the korigan; and Peronnik showed him the snare he had prepared, and remarked that no bird could possible escape from it.

'That is just what I should like to be sure of,' answered the korigan. 'My apples are completely eaten up by blackbirds and thrushes. Lay your snare, and if you can manage to catch them, I will let you pass.'

'That is a fair bargain,' and as he spoke Peronnik jumped down and fastened his colt to a tree; then, stopping, he fixed one end of the net to the trunk of the apple tree, and called to the korigan to hold the other while he took out the pegs. The dwarf did as he was bid, when suddenly Peronnik threw the noose over his neck and drew it close, and the korigan was held as fast as any of the birds he wished to snare.

148

Shrieking with rage, he tried to undo the cord, but he only pulled the knot tighter. He had put down the sword on the grass, and Peronnik had been careful to fix the net on the other side of the tree, so that it was now easy for him to pluck an apple and to mount his horse, without being hindered by the dwarf, whom he left to his fate.

When they had left the plain behind them, Peronnik and his steed found themselves in a narrow valley in which was a grove of trees, full of all sorts of sweet-smelling things—roses of every colour, yellow broom, pink honeysuckle—while above them all towered a wonderful scarlet pansy whose face bore a strange expression. This was the flower that laughs, and no one who looked at it could help laughing too. Peronnik's heart beat high at the thought that he had reached safely the second trial, and he gazed quite calmly at the lion with the mane of vipers twisting and twirling, who walked up and down in front of the grove.

The young man pulled up and removed his cap, for, idiot though he was, he knew that when you have to do with people greater than yourself, a cap is more useful in the hand than on the head. Then, after wishing all kinds of good fortune to the lion and his family, he inquired if he was on the right road to Kerglas.

'And what is your business at Kerglas?' asked the lion with a growl, and showing his teeth.

'With all respect,' answered Peronnik, pretending to be very frightened, 'I am the servant of a lady who is a friend of the noble Rogear and sends him some larks for a pasty.'

'Larks?' cried the lion, licking his long whiskers. 'Why, it must be a century since I have had any! Have you a large quantity with you?'

'As many as this bag will hold,' replied Peronnik, opening, as he spoke, the bag which he had filled with feathers and glue; and to prove what he said, he turned his back on the lion and began to imitate the song of a lark.

'Come,' exclaimed the lion, whose mouth watered, 'show me the birds! I should like to see if they are fat enough for my master.'

'I would do it with pleasure,' answered the idiot, 'but if I once open the bag they will all fly away.'

'Well, open it wide enough for me to look in,' said the lion, drawing a little nearer.

Now this was just what Peronnik had been hoping for, so he held the bag while the lion opened it carefully and put his head right inside, so that he might get a good mouthful of larks. But the mass of feathers and glue stuck to him, and before he could pull his head out again Peronnik had drawn tight the cord, and tied it in a knot

149

that no man could untie. Then, quickly gathering the flower that laughs, he rode off as fast as the colt could take him.

The path soon led to the lake of the dragons, which he had to swim across. The colt, who was accustomed to it, plunged into the water without hesitation; but as soon as the dragons caught sight of Peronnik they approached from all parts of the lake in order to devour him.

This time Peronnik did not trouble to take off his cap, but he threw the beads he carried with him into the water, as you throw black corn to a duck, and with each bead that he swallowed a dragon turned on his back and died, so that the idiot reached the other side without further trouble.

The valley guarded by the black man now lay before him, and from afar Peronnik beheld him, chained by one foot to a rock at the entrance, and holding the iron ball which never missed its mark and always returned to its master's hand. In his head the black man had six eyes that were never all shut at once, but kept watch one after the other. At this moment they were all open, and Peronnik knew well that if the black man caught a glimpse of him he would cast his ball. So, hiding the colt behind a thicket of bushes, he crawled along a ditch and crouched close to the very rock to which the black man was chained.

The day was hot, and after a while the man began to grow sleepy. Two of his eyes closed, and Peronnik sang gently. In a moment a third eye shut, and Peronnik sang on. The lid of a fourth eye dropped heavily, and then those of the fifth and the sixth. The black man was asleep altogether.

Then, on tiptoe, the idiot crept back to the colt which he led over soft moss past the black man into the vale of pleasure, a delicious garden full of fruits that dangled before your mouth, fountains running with wine, and flowers chanting in soft little voices. Further on, tables were spread with food, and girls dancing on the grass called to him to join them.

Peronnik heard, and, scarcely knowing what he did drew the colt into a slower pace. He sniffed greedily the smell of the dishes, and raised his head the better to see the dancers. Another instant and he would have stopped altogether and been lost, like others before him, when suddenly there came to him like a vision the golden bowl and the diamond lance. Drawing his whistle from his pocket, he blew it loudly, so as to drown the sweet sounds about him, and ate what was left of his bread and bacon to still the craving of the magic fruits. His eyes he fixed steadily on the ears of the colt, that he might not see the dancers.

In this way he was able to reach the end of the garden, and at length perceived the castle of Kerglas, with the river between them which had only one ford. Would the lady be there, as the old man had told him? Yes, surely that was she, sitting on a rock, in a black satin dress, and her face the colour of a Moorish woman's. The idiot

150

rode up, and took off his cap more politely than ever, and asked if she did not wish to cross the river.

'I was waiting for you to help me do so,' answered she. 'Come near, that I may get up behind you.'

Peronnik did as she bade him, and by the help of his arm she jumped nimbly on to the back of the colt.

'Do you know how to kill the magician?' asked the lady, as they were crossing the ford.

'I thought that, being a magician, he was immortal, and that no one could kill him,' replied Peronnik.

'Persuade him to taste that apple, and he will die, and if that is not enough I will touch him with my finger, for I am the plague,' answered she.

'But if I kill him, how am I to get the golden bowl and the diamond lance that are hidden in the cellar without a key?' rejoined Peronnik.

'The flower that laughs opens all doors and lightens all darkness,' said the lady; and as she spoke, they reached the further bank, and advanced towards the castle.

In front of the entrance was a sort of tent supported on poles, and under it the giant was sitting, basking in the sun. As soon as he noticed the colt bearing Peronnik and the lady, he lifted his head, and cried in a voice of thunder:

'Why, it is surely the idiot, riding my colt thirteen months old!'

'Greatest of magicians, you are right,' answered Peronnik.

'And how did you manage to catch him?' asked the giant.

'By repeating what I learnt from your brother Bryak on the edge of the forest,' replied the idiot. 'I just said—

Colt, free to run and free to eat,
Colt, gallop fast until we meet,

and it came directly.'

'You know my brother, then?' inquired the giant. 'Tell me why he sent you here.'

'To bring you two gifts which he has just received from the country of the Moors,' answered Peronnik: 'the apple of delight and the woman of submission. If you eat the apple you will not desire anything else, and if you take the woman as your servant you will never wish for another.'

'Well, give me the apple, and bid the woman get down,' answered Rogear.

The idiot obeyed, but at the first taste of the apple the giant staggered, and as the long yellow finger of the woman touched him he fell dead.

Leaving the magician where he lay, Peronnik entered the palace, bearing with him the flower that laughs. Fifty doors flew open before him, and at length he reached a long flight of steps which seemed to lead into the bowels of the earth. Down these he went till he came to a silver door without a bar or key. Then he held up high the flower that laughs, and the door slowly swung back, displaying a deep cavern, which was as bright as the day from the shining of the golden bowl and the diamond lance. The idiot hastily ran forward and hung the bowl round his neck from the chain which was attached to it, and took the lance in his hand. As he did so, the ground shook beneath him, and with an awful rumbling the palace disappeared, and Peronnik found himself standing close to the forest where he led the cattle to graze.

Though darkness was coming on, Peronnik never thought of entering the farm, but followed the road which led to the court of the duke of Brittany. As he passed through the town of Vannes he stopped at a tailor's shop, and bought a beautiful costume of brown velvet and a white horse, which he paid for with a handful of gold that he had picked up in the corridor of the castle of Kerglas. Thus he made his way to the city of Nantes, which at that moment was besieged by the French.

A little way off, Peronnik stopped and looked about him. For miles round the country was bare, for the enemy had cut down every tree and burnt every blade of corn; and, idiot though he might be, Peronnik was able to grasp that inside the gates men were dying of famine. He was still gazing with horror, when a trumpeter appeared on the walls, and, after blowing a loud blast, announced that the duke would adopt as his heir the man who could drive the French out of the country.

On the four sides of the city the trumpeter blew his blast, and the last time Peronnik, who had ridden up as close as he might, answered him.

'You need blow no more,' said he, 'for I myself will free the town from her enemies.' And turning to a soldier who came running up, waving his sword, he touched him with the magic lance, and he fell dead on the spot. The men who were following stood still, amazed. Their comrade's armour had not been pierced, of that they were sure, yet he was dead, as if he had been struck to the heart. But before they had time to recover from their astonishment, Peronnik cried out:

152

'You see how my foes will fare; now behold what I can do for my friends,' and, stooping down, he laid the golden bowl against the mouth of the soldier, who sat up as well as ever. Then, jumping his horse across the trench, he entered the gate of the city, which had opened wide enough to receive him.

The news of these marvels quickly spread through the town, and put fresh spirit into the garrison, so that they declared themselves able to fight under the command of the young stranger. And as the bowl restored all the dead Bretons to life, Peronnik soon had an army large enough to drive away the French, and fulfilled his promise of delivering his country.

As to the bowl and the lance, no one knows what became of them, but some say that Bryak the sorcerer managed to steal them again, and that any one who wishes to possess them must seek them as Peronnik did.

From 'Le Foyer Breton,' par Emile Souvestre.

The Battle of the Birds

There was to be a great battle between all the creatures of the earth and the birds of the air. News of it went abroad, and the son of the king of Tethertown said that when the battle was fought he would be there to see it, and would bring back word who was to be king. But in spite of that, he was almost too late, and every fight had been fought save the last, which was between a snake and a great black raven. Both struck hard, but in the end the snake proved the stronger, and would have twisted himself round the neck of the raven till he died had not the king's son drawn his sword, and cut off the head of the snake at a single blow. And when the raven beheld that his enemy was dead, he was grateful, and said:

'For thy kindness to me this day, I will show thee a sight. So come up now on the root of my two wings.' The king's son did as he was bid, and before the raven stopped flying, they had passed over seven bens and seven glens and seven mountain moors.

'Do you see that house yonder?' said the raven at last. 'Go straight for it, for a sister of mine dwells there, and she will make you right welcome. And if she asks, "Wert thou at the battle of the birds?" answer that thou wert, and if she asks, "Didst thou see my likeness?" answer that thou sawest it, but be sure thou meetest me in the morning at this place.'

The king's son followed what the raven told him and that night he had meat of each meat, and drink of each drink, warm water for his feet, and a soft bed to lie in.

Thus it happened the next day, and the next, but on the fourth meeting, instead of meeting the raven, in his place the king's son found waiting for him the handsomest youth that ever was seen, with a bundle in his hand.

'Is there a raven hereabouts?' asked the king's son, and the youth answered:

'I am that raven, and I was delivered by thee from the spells that bound me, and in reward thou wilt get this bundle. Go back by the road thou camest, and lie as before, a night in each house, but be careful not to unloose the bundle till thou art in the place wherein thou wouldst most wish to dwell.'

Then the king's son set out, and thus it happened as it had happened before, till he entered a thick wood near his father's house. He had walked a long way and suddenly the bundle seemed to grow heavier; first he put it down under a tree, and next he thought he would look at it.

The string was easy to untie, and the king's son soon unfastened the bundle. What was it he saw there? Why, a great castle with an orchard all about it, and in the orchard fruit and flowers and birds of very kind. It was all ready for him to dwell in, but instead of being in the midst of the forest, he did wish he had left the bundle unloosed till he had reached the green valley close to his father's palace. Well, it was no use wishing, and with a sigh he glanced up, and beheld a huge giant coming towards him.

'Bad is the place where thou hast built thy house, king's son,' said the giant.

'True; it is not here that I wish to be,' answered the king's son.

'What reward wilt thou give me if I put it back in the bundle?' asked the giant.

'What reward dost thou ask?' answered the king's son.

'The first boy thou hast when he is seven years old,' said the giant.

'If I have a boy thou shalt get him,' answered the king's son, and as he spoke the castle and the orchard were tied up in the bundle again.

'Now take thy road, and I will take mine,' said the giant. 'And if thou forgettest thy promise, I will remember it.'

Light of heart the king's son went on his road, till he came to the green valley near his father's palace. Slowly he unloosed the bundle, fearing lest he should find nothing but a heap of stones or rags. But no! all was as it had been before, and as he opened the castle door there stood within the most beautiful maiden that ever was seen.

'Enter, king's son,' said she, 'all is ready, and we will be married at once,' and so they were.

The maiden proved a good wife, and the king's son, now himself a king, was so happy that he forgot all about the giant. Seven years and a day had gone by, when one morning, while standing on the ramparts, he beheld the giant striding towards the castle. Then he remembered his promise, and remembered, too, that he had told the queen nothing about it. Now he must tell her, and perhaps she might help him in his trouble.

The queen listened in silence to his tale, and after he had finished, she only said:

'Leave thou the matter between me and the giant,' and as she spoke, the giant entered the hall and stood before them.

'Bring out your son,' cried he to the king, 'as you promised me seven years and a day since.'

The king glanced at his wife, who nodded, so he answered:

'Let his mother first put him in order,' and the queen left the hall, and took the cook's son and dressed him in the prince's clothes, and led him up to the giant, who held his hand, and together they went out along the road. They had not walked far when the giant stopped and stretched out a stick to the boy.

'If your father had that stick, what would he do with it?' asked he.

'If my father had that stick, he would beat the dogs and cats that steal the king's meat,' replied the boy.

'Thou art the cook's son!' cried the giant. 'Go home to thy mother'; and turning his back he strode straight to the castle.

'If you seek to trick me this time, the highest stone will soon be the lowest,' said he, and the king and queen trembled, but they could not bear to give up their boy.

'The butler's son is the same age as ours,' whispered the queen; 'he will not know the difference,' and she took the child and dressed him in the prince's clothes, and the giant let him away along the road. Before they had gone far he stopped, and held out a stick.

'If thy father had that rod, what would he do with it?' asked the giant.

'He would beat the dogs and cats that break the king's glasses,' answered the boy.

'Thou art the son of the butler!' cried the giant. 'Go home to thy mother'; and turning round he strode back angrily to the castle.

'Bring out thy son at once,' roared he, 'or the stone that is highest will be lowest,' and this time the real prince was brought.

But though his parents wept bitterly and fancied the child was suffering all kinds of dreadful things, the giant treated him like his own son, though he never allowed him to see his daughters. The boy grew to be a big boy, and one day the giant told him that he would have to amuse himself alone for many hours, as he had a journey to make. So the boy wandered to the top of the castle, where he had never been before. There he paused, for the sound of music broke upon his ears, and opening a door near him, he beheld a girl sitting by the window, holding a harp.

'Haste and begone, I see the giant close at hand,' she whispered hurriedly, 'but when he is asleep, return hither, for I would speak with thee.' And the prince did as he was bid, and when midnight struck he crept back to the top of the castle.

'To-morrow,' said the girl, who was the giant's daughter, 'to-morrow thou wilt get the choice of my two sisters to marry, but thou must answer that thou wilt not take either, but only me. This will anger him greatly, for he wishes to betroth me to the son of the king of the Green City, whom I like not at all.'

Then they parted, and on the morrow, as the girl had said, the giant called his three daughters to him, and likewise the young prince to whom he spoke.

'Now, O son of the king of Tethertown, the time has come for us to part. Choose one of my two elder daughters to wife, and thou shalt take her to your father's house the day after the wedding.'

'Give me the youngest instead,' replied the youth, and the giant's face darkened as he heard him.

'Three things must thou do first,' said he.

'Say on, I will do them,' replied the prince, and the giant left the house, and bade him follow to the byre, where the cows were kept.

'For a hundred years no man has swept this byre,' said the giant, 'but if by nightfall, when I reach home, thou has not cleaned it so that a golden apple can roll through it from end to end, thy blood shall pay for it.'

All day long the youth toiled, but he might as well have tried to empty the ocean. At length, when he was so tired he could hardly move, the giant's youngest daughter stood in the doorway.

'Lay down thy weariness,' said she, and the king's son, thinking he could only die once, sank on the floor at her bidding, and fell sound asleep. When he woke the girl had disappeared, and the byre was so clean that a golden apple could roll from end to end of it. He jumped up in surprise, and at that moment in came the giant.

'Hast thou cleaned the byre, king's son?' asked he.

'I have cleaned it,' answered he.

'Well, since thou wert so active to-day, to-morrow thou wilt thatch this byre with a feather from every different bird, or else thy blood shall pay for it,' and he went out.

Before the sun was up, the youth took his bow and his quiver and set off to kill the birds. Off to the moor he went, but never a bird was to be seen that day. At last he got so tired with running to and fro that he gave up heart.

'There is but one death I can die,' thought he. Then at midday came the giant's daughter.

'Thou art tired, king's son?' asked she.

'I am,' answered he; 'all these hours have I wandered, and there fell but these two blackbirds, both of one colour.'

'Lay down thy weariness on the grass,' said she, and he did as she bade him, and fell fast asleep.

When he woke the girl had disappeared, and he got up, and returned to the byre. As he drew near, he rubbed his eyes hard, thinking he was dreaming, for there it was, beautifully thatched, just as the giant had wished. At the door of the house he met the giant.

'Hast thou thatched the byre, king's son?'

'I have thatched it.'

'Well, since thou hast been so active to-day, I have something else for thee! Beside the loch thou seest over yonder there grows a fir tree. On the top of the fir tree is a magpie's nest, and in the nest are five eggs. Thou wilt bring me those eggs for breakfast, and if one is cracked or broken, thy blood shall pay for it.'

Before it was light next day, the king's son jumped out of bed and ran down to the loch. The tree was not hard to find, for the rising sun shone red on the trunk, which was five hundred feet from the ground to its first branch. Time after time he walked round it, trying to find some knots, however small, where he could put his feet, but the bark was quite smooth, and he soon saw that if he was to reach the top at all, it must be by climbing up with his knees like a sailor. But then he was a king's son and not a sailor, which made all the difference.

However, it was no use standing there staring at the fir, at least he must try to do his best, and try he did till his hands and knees were sore, for as soon as he had struggled up a few feet, he slid back again. Once he climbed a little higher than before, and hope rose in his heart, then down he came with such force that his hands and knees smarted worse than ever.

'This is no time for stopping,' said the voice of the giant's daughter, as he leant against the trunk to recover his breath.

'Alas! I am no sooner up than down,' answered he.

'Try once more,' said she, and she laid a finger against the tree and bade him put his foot on it. Then she placed another finger a little higher up, and so on till he reached the top, where the magpie had built her nest.

158

'Make haste now with the nest,' she cried, 'for my father's breath is burning my back,' and down he scrambled as fast as he could, but the girl's little finger had caught in a branch at the top, and she was obliged to leave it there. But she was too busy to pay heed to this, for the sun was getting high over the hills.

'Listen to me,' she said. 'This night my two sisters and I will be dressed in the same garments, and you will not know me. But when my father says 'Go to thy wife, king's son,' come to the one whose right hand has no little finger.'

So he went and gave the eggs to the giant, who nodded his head.

'Make ready for thy marriage,' cried he, 'for the wedding shall take place this very night, and I will summon thy bride to greet thee.' Then his three daughters were sent for, and they all entered dressed in green silk of the same fashion, and with golden circlets round their heads. The king's son looked from one to another. Which was the youngest? Suddenly his eyes fell on the hand of the middle one, and there was no little finger.

'Thou hast aimed well this time too,' said the giant, as the king's son laid his hand on her shoulder, 'but perhaps we may meet some other way'; and though he pretended to laugh, the bride saw a gleam in his eye which warned her of danger.

The wedding took place that very night, and the hall was filled with giants and gentlemen, and they danced till the house shook from top to bottom. At last everyone grew tired, and the guests went away, and the king's son and his bride were left alone.

'If we stay here till dawn my father will kill thee,' she whispered, 'but thou art my husband and I will save thee, as I did before,' and she cut an apple into nine pieces, and put two pieces at the head of the bed, and two pieces at the foot, and two pieces at the door of the kitchen, and two at the big door, and one outside the house. And when this was done, and she heard the giant snoring, she and the king's son crept out softly and stole across to the stable, where she led out the blue-grey mare and jumped on its back, and her husband mounted behind her. Not long after, the giant awoke.

'Are you asleep?' asked he.

'Not yet,' answered the apple at the head of the bed, and the giant turned over, and soon was snoring as loudly as before. By and bye he called again.

'Are you asleep?'

'Not yet,' said the apple at the foot of the bed, and the giant was satisfied. After a while, he called a third time, 'Are you asleep?'

'Not yet,' replied the apple in the kitchen, but when in a few minutes, he put the question for the fourth time and received an answer from the apple outside the house door, he guessed what had happened, and ran to the room to look for himself.

The bed was cold and empty!

'My father's breath is burning my back,' cried the girl, 'put thy hand into the ear of the mare, and whatever thou findest there, throw it behind thee.' And in the mare's ear there was a twig of sloe tree, and as he threw it behind him there sprung up twenty miles of thornwood so thick that scarce a weasel could go through it. And the giant, who was striding headlong forwards, got caught in it, and it pulled his hair and beard.

'This is one of my daughter's tricks,' he said to himself, 'but if I had my big axe and my wood-knife, I would not be long making a way through this,' and off he went home and brought back the axe and the wood-knife.

It took him but a short time to cut a road through the blackthorn, and then he laid the axe and the knife under a tree.

'I will leave them there till I return,' he murmured to himself, but a hoodie crow, which was sitting on a branch above, heard him.

'If thou leavest them,' said the hoodie, 'we will steal them.'

'You will,' answered the giant, 'and I must take them home.' So he took them home, and started afresh on his journey.

'My father's breath is burning my back,' cried the girl at midday. 'Put thy finger in the mare's ear and throw behind thee whatever thou findest in it,' and the king's son found a splinter of grey stone, and threw it behind him, and in a twinkling twenty miles of solid rock lay between them and the giant.

'My daughter's tricks are the hardest things that ever met me,' said the giant, 'but if I had my lever and my crowbar, I would not be long in making my way through this rock also,' but as he had got them, he had to go home and fetch them. Then it took him but a short time to hew his way through the rock.

'I will leave the tools here,' he murmured aloud when he had finished.

'If thou leavest them, we will steal them,' said a hoodie who was perched on a stone above him, and the giant answered:

'Steal them if thou wilt; there is no time to go back.'

160

'My father's breath is burning my back,' cried the girl; 'look in the mare's ear, king's son, or we are lost,' and he looked, and found a tiny bladder full of water, which he threw behind him, and it became a great lock. And the giant, who was striding on so fast, could not stop himself, and he walked right into the middle and was drowned.

The blue-grey mare galloped on like the wind, and the next day the king's son came in sight of his father's house.

'Get down and go in,' said the bride, 'and tell them that thou hast married me. But take heed that neither man nor beast kiss thee, for then thou wilt cease to remember me at all.'

'I will do thy bidding,' answered he, and left her at the gate. All who met him bade him welcome, and he charged his father and mother not to kiss him, but as he greeted them his old greyhound leapt on his neck, and kissed him on the mouth. And after that he did not remember the giant's daughter.

All that day she sat on a well which was near the gate, waiting, waiting, but the king's son never came. In the darkness she climbed up into an oak tree that shadowed the well, and there she lay all night, waiting, waiting.

On the morrow, at midday, the wife of a shoemaker who dwelt near the well went to draw water for her husband to drink, and she saw the shadow of the girl in the tree, and thought it was her own shadow.

'How handsome I am, to be sure,' said she, gazing into the well, and as she stopped to behold herself better, the jug struck against the stones and broke in pieces, and she was forced to return to her husband without the water, and this angered him.

'Thou hast turned crazy,' said he in wrath. 'Go thou, my daughter, and fetch me a drink,' and the girl went, and the same thing befell her as had befallen her mother.

'Where is the water?' asked the shoemaker, when she came back, and as she held nothing save the handle of the jug he went to the well himself. He too saw the reflection of the woman in the tree, but looked up to discover whence it came, and there above him sat the most beautiful woman in the world.

'Come down,' he said, 'for a while thou canst stay in my house,' and glad enough the girl was to come.

Now the king of the country was about to marry, and the young men about the court thronged the shoemaker's shop to buy fine shoes to wear at the wedding.

'Thou hast a pretty daughter,' said they when they beheld the girl sitting at work.

161

'Pretty she is,' answered the shoemaker, 'but no daughter of mine.'

'I would give a hundred pounds to marry her,' said one.

'And I,' 'And I,' cried the others.

'That is no business of mine,' answered the shoemaker, and the young men bade him ask her if she would choose one of them for a husband, and to tell them on the morrow. Then the shoemaker asked her, and the girl said that she would marry the one who would bring his purse with him. So the shoemaker hurried to the youth who had first spoken, and he came back, and after giving the shoemaker a hundred pounds for his news, he sought the girl, who was waiting for him.

'Is it thou?' inquired she. 'I am thirsty, give me a drink from the well that is yonder.' And he poured out the water, but he could not move from the place where he was; and there he stayed till many hours had passed by.

'Take away that foolish boy,' cried the girl to the shoemaker at last, 'I am tired of him,' and then suddenly he was able to walk, and betook himself to his home, but he did not tell the others what had happened to him.

Next day there arrived one of the other young men, and in the evening, when the shoemaker had gone out and they were alone, she said to him, 'See if the latch is on the door.' The young man hastened to do her bidding, but as soon as he touched the latch, his fingers stuck to it, and there he had to stay for many hours, till the shoemaker came back, and the girl let him go. Hanging his head, he went home, but he told no one what had befallen him.

Then was the turn of the third man, and his foot remained fastened to the floor, till the girl unloosed it. And thankfully, he ran off, and was not seen looking behind him.

'Take the purse of gold,' said the girl to the shoemaker, 'I have no need of it, and it will better thee.' And the shoemaker took it and told the girl he must carry the shoes for the wedding up to the castle.

'I would fain get a sight of the king's son before he marries,' sighed she.

'Come with me, then,' answered he; 'the servants are all my friends, and they will let you stand in the passage down which the king's son will pass, and all the company too.'

Up they went to the castle, and when the young men saw the girl standing there, they led her into the hall where the banquet was laid out and poured her out some wine. She was just raising the glass to drink when a flame went up out of it, and out of the flame sprang two pigeons, one of gold and one of silver. They flew round and round

162

the head of the girl, when three grains of barley fell on the floor, and the silver pigeon dived down, and swallowed them.

'If thou hadst remembered how I cleaned the byre, thou wouldst have given me my share,' cooed the golden pigeon, and as he spoke three more grains fell, and the silver pigeon ate them as before.

'If thou hadst remembered how I thatched the byre, thou wouldst have given me my share,' cooed the golden pigeon again; and as he spoke three more grains fell, and for the third time they were eaten by the silver pigeon.

'If thou hadst remembered how I got the magpie's nest, thou wouldst have given me my share,' cooed the golden pigeon.

Then the king's son understood that they had come to remind him of what he had forgotten, and his lost memory came back, and he knew his wife, and kissed her. But as the preparations had been made, it seemed a pity to waste them, so they were married a second time, and sat down to the wedding feast.

From 'Tales of the West Highlands.'

The Lady of the Fountain.

In the centre of the great hall in the castle of Caerleon upon Usk, king Arthur sat on a seat of green rushes, over which was thrown a covering of flame-coloured silk, and a cushion of red satin lay under his elbow. With him were his knights Owen and Kynon and Kai, while at the far end, close to the window, were Guenevere the queen and her maidens embroidering white garments with strange devices of gold.

'I am weary,' said Arthur, 'and till my food is prepared I would fain sleep. You yourselves can tell each other tales, and Kai will fetch you from the kitchen a flagon of mean and some meat.'

And when they had eaten and drunk, Kynon, the oldest among them, began his story.

'I was the only son of my father and mother, and much store they set by me, but I was not content to stay with them at home, for I thought no deed in all the world was too mighty for me. None could hold me back, and after I had won many adventures in my own land, I bade farewell to my parents and set out to see the world. Over mountains, through deserts, across rivers I went, till I reached a fair valley full of trees, with a path running by the side of a stream. I walked along that path all the day, and in the evening I came to a castle in front of which stood two youths clothed in yellow, each grasping an ivory bow, with arrows made of the bones of the whale, and winged with peacock's feathers. By their sides hung golden daggers with hilts of the bones of the whale.

'Near these young men was a man richly dressed, who turned and went with me towards the castle, where all the dwellers were gathered in the hall. In one window I beheld four and twenty damsels, and the least fair of them was fairer than Guenevere at her fairest. Some took my horse, and others unbuckled my armour, and washed it, with my sword and spear, till it all shone like silver. Then I washed myself and put on a vest and doublet which they brought me, and I and the man that entered with me sat down before a table of silver, and a goodlier feast I never had.

'All this time neither the man nor the damsels had spoken one word, but when our dinner was half over, and my hunger was stilled, the man began to ask who I was. Then I told him my name and my father's name, and why I came there, for indeed I had grown weary of gaining the mastery over all men at home, and sought if perchance there was one who could gain the mastery over me. And at this the man smiled and answered:

'"If I did not fear to distress thee too much, I would show thee what thou seekest." His words made me sorrowful and fearful of myself, which the man perceived, and added, "If thou meanest truly what thou sayest, and desirest earnestly to prove thy valour, and not to boast vainly that none can overcome thee, I have somewhat to show thee. But to-night thou must sleep in the this castle, and in the morning see that thou rise early and follow the road upwards through the valley, until thou reachest a wood. In the wood is a path branching to the right; go along this path until thou comest to a space of grass with a mound in the middle of it. On the top of the mound stands a black man, larger than any two white men; his eye is in the centre of his forehead and he has only one foot. He carries a club of iron, and two white men could hardly lift it. Around him graze a thousand beasts, all of different kinds, for he is the guardian of that wood, and it is he who will tell thee which way to go in order to find the adventure thou art in quest of."

'So spake the man, and long did that night seem to me, and before dawn I rose and put on my armour, and mounted my horse and rode on till I reached the grassy space of which he had told me. There was the black man on top of the mound, as he had said, and in truth he was mightier in all ways than I had thought him to be. As for the club, Kai, it would have been a burden for four of our warriors. He waited for me to speak, and I asked him what power he held over the beasts that thronged so close about him.

'"I will show thee, little man," he answered, and with his club he struck a stag on the head till he brayed loudly. And at his braying the animals came running, numerous as the stars in the sky, so that scarce was I able to stand among them. Serpents were there also, and dragons, and beasts of strange shapes, with horns in places where never saw I horns before. And the black man only looked at them and bade them go and feed. And they bowed themselves before him, as vassals before their lord.

'"Now, little man, I have answered thy question and showed thee my power," said he. "Is there anything else thou wouldest know?" Then I inquired of him my way,

164

but he grew angry, and, as I perceived, would fain have hindered me; but at the last, after I had told him who I was, his anger passed from him.

'"Take that path," said he, "that leads to the head of this grassy glade, and go up the wood till thou reachest the top. There thou wilt find an open space, and in the midst of it a tall tree. Under the tree is a fountain, and by the fountain a marble slab, and on the slab a bowl of silver, with a silver chain. Dip the bowl in the fountain, and throw the water on the slab, and thou wilt hear a might peal of thunder, till heaven and earth seem trembling with the noise. After the thunder will come hail, so fierce that scarcely canst thou endure it and live, for the hailstones are both large and thick. Then the sun will shine again, but every leaf of the tree will by lying on the ground. Next a flight of birds will come and alight on the tree, and never didst thou hear a strain so sweet as that which they will sing. And at the moment in which their song sounds sweetest thou wilt hear a murmuring and complaining coming towards thee along the valley, and thou wilt see a knight in black velvet bestriding a black horse, bearing a lance with a black pennon, and he will spur his steed so as to fight thee. If thou turnest to flee, he will overtake thee. And if thou abidest were thou art, he will unhorse thee. And if thou dost not find trouble in that adventure, thou needest not to seek it during the rest of thy life."

'So I bade the black man farewell, and took my way to the top of the wood, and there I found everything just as I had been told. I went up to the tree beneath which stood the fountain, and filling the silver bowl with water, emptied it on the marble slab. Thereupon the thunder came, louder by far than I had expected to hear it, and after the thunder came the shower, but heavier by far than I had expected to feel it, for, of a truth I tell thee, Kai, not one of those hailstones would be stopped by skin or by flesh till it had reached the bone. I turned my horse's flank towards the shower, and, bending over his neck, held my shield so that it might cover his head and my own. When the hail had passed, I looked on the tree and not a single leaf was left on it, and the sky was blue and the sun shining, while on the branches were perched birds of very kind, who sang a song sweeter than any that has come to my ears, either before or since.

'Thus, Kai, I stood listening to the birds, when lo, a murmuring voice approached me, saying:

'"O knight, what has brought thee hither? What evil have I done to thee, that thou shouldest do so much to me, for in all my lands neither man nor beast that met that shower has escaped alive." Then from the valley appeared the knight on the black horse, grasping the lance with the black pennon. Straightway we charged each other, and though I fought my best, he soon overcame me, and I was thrown to the ground, while the knight seized the bridle of my horse, and rode away with it, leaving me where I was, without even despoiling me of my armour.

'Sadly did I go down the hill again, and when I reached the glade where the black man was, I confess to thee, Kai, it was a marvel that I did not melt into a liquid pool, so great was my shame. That night I slept at the castle where I had been before, and

I was bathed and feasted, and none asked me how I had fared. The next morning when I arose I found a bay horse saddled for me, and, girdling on my armour, I returned to my own court. The horse is still in the stable, and I would not part with it for any in Britain.

'But of a truth, Kai, no man ever confessed an adventure so much to his own dishonour, and strange indeed it seems that none other man have I ever met that knew of the black man, and the knight and the shower.'

'Would it not be well,' said Owen, 'to go and discover the place?'

'By the hand of my friend,' answered Kai, 'often dost thou utter that with thy tongue which thou wouldest not make good with thy deeds.'

'In truth,' said Guenevere the queen, who had listened to the tale, 'thou wert better hanged, Kai, than use such speech towards a man like Owen.'

'I meant nothing, lady,' replied Kai; 'thy praise of Owen is not greater than mine.' And as he spoke Arthur awoke, and asked if he had not slept for a little.

'Yes, lord,' answered Owen, 'certainly thou hast slept.'

'Is it time for us to go to meat?'

'It is, lord,' answered Owen.

Then the horn for washing themselves was sounded, and after that the king and his household sat down to eat. And when they had finished, Owen left them, and made ready his horse and his arms.

With the first rays of the sun he set forth, and travelled through deserts and over mountains and across rivers, and all befell him which had befallen Kynon, till he stood under the leafless tree listening to the song of the birds. Then he heard the voice, and turning to look found the knight galloping to meet him. Fiercely they fought till their lances were broken, and then they drew their swords, and a blow from Owen cut through the knight's helmet, and pierced his skull.

Feeling himself wounded unto death the knight fled, and Owen pursued him till they came to a splendid castle. Here the knight dashed across the bridge that spanned the moat, and entered the gate, but as soon as he was safe inside, the drawbridge was pulled up and caught Owen's horse in the middle, so that half of him was inside and half out, and Owen could not dismount and knew not what to do.

While he was in this sore plight a little door in the castle gate opened, and he could see a street facing him, with tall houses. Then a maiden with curling hair of gold looked through the little door and bade Owen open the gate.

'By my troth!' cried Owen, 'I can no more open it from here than thou art able to set me free.'

'Well,' said she, 'I will do my best to release thee if thou wilt do as I tell thee. Take this ring and put it on with the stone inside thy hand, and close thy fingers tight, for as long as thou dost conceal it, it will conceal thee. When the men inside have held counsel together, they will come to fetch thee to thy death, and they will be much grieved not to find thee. I will stand on the horse block yonder and thou canst see me though I cannot see thee. Therefore draw near and place thy hand on my shoulder and follow me wheresoever I go.'

Upon that she went away from Owen, and when the men came out from the castle to seek him and did not find him they were sorely grieved, and they returned to the castle.

Then Owen went to the maiden and placed his hand on her shoulder, and she guided him to a large room, painted all over with rich colours, and adorned with images of gold. Here she gave him meat and drink, and water to wash with and garments to wear, and he lay down upon a soft bed, with scarlet and fur to cover him, and slept gladly.

In the middle of the night he woke hearing a great outcry, and he jumped up and clothed himself and went into the hall, where the maiden was standing.

'What is it?' he asked, and she answered that the knight who owned the castle was dead, and they were bearing his body to the church. Never had Owen beheld such vast crowds, and following the dead knight was the most beautiful lady in the world, whose cry was louder than the shout of the men, or the braying of the trumpets. And Owen looked on her and loved her.

'Who is she?' he asked the damsel. 'That is my mistress, the countess of the fountain, and the wife of him whom thou didst slay yesterday.'

'Verily,' said Owen, 'she is the woman that I love best.'

'She shall also love thee not a little,' said the maiden.

Then she left Owen, and after a while went into the chamber of her mistress, and spoke to her, but the countess answered her nothing.

'What aileth thee, mistress?' inquired the maiden.

'Why hast thou kept far from me in my grief, Luned?' answered the countess, and in her turn the damsel asked:

'Is it well for thee to mourn so bitterly for the dead, or for anything that is gone from thee?'

'There is no man in the world equal to him,' replied the countess, her cheeks growing red with anger. 'I would fain banish thee for such words.'

'Be not angry, lady,' said Luned, 'but listen to my counsel. Thou knowest well that alone thou canst not preserve thy lands, therefore seek some one to help thee.'

'And how can I do that?' asked the countess.

'I will tell thee,' answered Luned. 'Unless thou canst defend the fountain all will be lost, and none can defend the fountain except a knight of Arthur's court. There will I go to seek him, and woe betide me if I return without a warrior that can guard the fountain, as well as he who kept it before.'

'Go then,' said the countess, 'and make proof of that which thou hast promised.'

So Luned set out, riding on a white palfrey, on pretence of journeying to King Arthur's court, but instead of doing that she hid herself for as many days as it would have taken her to go and come, and then she left her hiding-place, and went into the countess.

'What news from the court?' asked her mistress, when she had given Luned a warm greeting.

'The best of news,' answered the maiden, 'for I have gained the object of my mission. When wilt thou that I present to thee the knight who has returned with me?'

'To-morrow at midday,' said the countess, 'and I will cause all the people in the town to come together.'

Therefore the next day at noon Owen put on his coat of mail, and over it he wore a splendid mantle, while on his feet were leather shoes fastened with clasps of gold. And he followed Luned to the chamber of her mistress.

Right glad was the countess to see them, but she looked closely at Owen and said:

'Luned, this knight has scarcely the air of a traveller.'

'What harm is there in that, lady?' answered Luned.

168

'I am persuaded,' said the countess, 'that this man and no other chased the soul from the body of my lord.'

'Had he not been stronger than thy lord,' replied the damsel, 'he could not have taken his life, and for that, and for all things that are past, there is no remedy.'

'Leave me, both of you,' said the countess, 'and I will take counsel.'

Then they went out.

The next morning the countess summoned her subjects to meet in the courtyard of the castle, and told them that now that her husband was dead there was none to defend her lands.

'So choose you which it shall be,' she said. 'Either let one of you take me for a wife, or give me your consent to take a new lord for myself, that my lands be not without a master.'

At her words the chief men of the city withdrew into one corner and took counsel together, and after a while the leader came forward and said that they had decided that it was best, for the peace and safety of all, that she should choose a husband for herself. Thereupon Owen was summoned to her presence, and he accepted with joy the hand that she offered him, and they were married forthwith, and the men of the earldom did him homage.

From that day Owen defended the fountain as the earl before him had done, and every knight that came by was overthrown by him, and his ransom divided among his barons. In this way three years passed, and no man in the world was more beloved than Owen.

Now at the end of the three years it happened that Gwalchmai the knight was with Arthur, and he perceived the king to be very sad.

'My lord, has anything befallen thee?' he asked.

'Oh, Gwalchmai, I am grieved concerning Owen, whom I have lost these three years, and if a fourth year passes without him I can live no longer. And sure am I that the tale told by Kynon the son of Clydno caused me to lose him. I will go myself with the men of my household to avenge him if he is dead, to free him if he is in prison, to bring him back if he is alive.'

Then Arthur and three thousand men of his household set out in quest of Owen, and took Kynon for their guide. When Arthur reached the castle, the youths were shooting in the same place, and the same yellow man was standing by, and as soon as he beheld Arthur he greeted him and invited him in, and they entered together. So vast was the castle that the king's three thousand men were of no more account than if they had been twenty.

At sunrise Arthur departed thence, with Kynon for his guide, and reached the black man first, and afterwards the top of the wooded hill, with the fountain and the bowl and the tree.

'My lord,' said Kai, 'let me throw the water on the slab, and receive the first adventure that may befall.'

'Thou mayest do so,' answered Arthur, and Kai threw the water.

Immediately all happened as before; the thunder and the shower of hail which killed many of Arthur's men; the song of the birds and the appearance of the black knight. And Kai met him and fought him, and was overthrown by him. Then the knight rode away, and Arthur and his men encamped where they stood.

In the morning Kai again asked leave to meet the knight and to try to overcome him, which Arthur granted. But once more he was unhorsed, and the black knight's lance broke his helmet and pierced the skin even to the bone, and humbled in spirit he returned to the camp.

After this every one of the knights gave battle, but none came out victor, and at length there only remained Arthur himself and Gwalchmai.

'Oh, let me fight him, my lord,' cried Gwalchmai, as he saw Arthur taking up his arms.

'Well, fight then,' answered Arthur, and Gwalchmai threw a robe over himself and his horse, so that none knew him. All that day they fought, and neither was able to throw the other, and so it was on the next day. On the third day the combat was so fierce that they fell both to the ground at once, and fought on their feet, and at last the black knight gave his foe such a blow on his head that his helmet fell from his face.

'I did not know it was thee, Gwalchmai,' said the black knight. 'Take my sword and my arms.'

'No,' answered Gwalchmai, 'it is thou, Owen, who art the victor, take thou my sword'; but Owen would not.

'Give me your swords,' said Arthur from behind them, 'for neither of you has vanquished the other,' and Owen turned and put his arms round Arthur's neck.

The next day Arthur would have given orders to his men to make ready to go back whence they came, but Owen stopped him.

'My lord,' he said, 'during the three years that I have been absent from thee I have been preparing a banquet for thee, knowing full well that thou wouldst come to seek me. Tarry with me, therefore, for a while, thou and thy men.'

So they rode to the castle of the countess of the fountain, and spent three months in resting and feasting. And when it was time for them to depart Arthur besought the countess that she would allow Owen to go with him to Britain for the space of three months. With a sore heart she granted permission, and so content was Owen to be once more with his old companions that three years instead of three months passed away like a dream.

One day Owen sat at meat in the castle of Caerleon upon Usk, when a damsel on a bay horse entered the hall, and riding straight up to the place where Owen sat she stooped and drew the ring from off his hand.

'Thus shall be treated the traitor and the faithless,' said she, and turning her horse's head she rode out of the hall.

At her words Owen remembered all that he had forgotten, and sorrowful and ashamed he went to his own chamber and made ready to depart. At the dawn he set out, but he did not go back to the castle, for his heart was heavy, but he wandered far into wild places till his body was weak and thin, and his hair was long. The wild beasts were his friends, and he slept by their side, but in the end he longed to see the face of a man again, and he came down into a valley and fell asleep by a lake in the lands of a widowed countess.

Now it was the time when the countess took her walk, attended by her maidens, and when they saw a man lying by the lake they shrank back in terror, for he lay so still that they thought he was dead. But when they had overcome their fright, they drew near him, and touched him, and saw that there was life in him. Then the countess hastened to the castle, and brought from it a flask full of precious ointment and gave it to one of her maidens.

'Take that horse which is grazing yonder,' she said, 'and a suit of men's garments, and place them near the man, and pour some of this ointment near his heart. If there is any life in him that will bring it back. But if he moves, hide thyself in the bushes near by, and see what he does.'

The damsel took the flask and did her mistress' bidding. Soon the man began to move his arms, and then rose slowly to his feet. Creeping forward step by step he took the garments from off the saddle and put them on him, and painfully he mounted the horse. When he was seated the damsel came forth and greeted him, and glad was he when he saw her and inquired what castle that was before him.

'It belongs to a widowed countess,' answered the maiden. 'Her husband left her two earldoms, but it is all that remains of her broad lands, for they have been torn from her by a young earl, because she would not marry him.'

'That is a pity,' replied Owen, but he said no more, for he was too weak to talk much. Then the maiden guided him to the castle, and kindled a fire, and brought him food. And there he stayed and was tended for three months, till he was handsomer than ever he was.

At noon one day Owen heard a sound of arms outside the castle, and he asked of the maiden what it was.

'It is the earl of whom I spoke to thee,' she answered, 'who has come with a great host to carry off my mistress.'

'Beg of her to lend me a horse and armour,' said Owen, and the maiden did so, but the countess laughed somewhat bitterly as she answered:

'Nay, but I will give them to him, and such a horse and armour and weapons as he has never had yet, though I know not what use they will be to him. Yet mayhap it will save them from falling into the hands of my enemies.'

The horse was brought out and Owen rode forth with two pages behind him, and they saw the great host encamped before them.

'Where is the earl?' said he, and the pages answered:

'In yonder troop where are four yellow standards.'

'Await me,' said Owen, 'at the gate of the castle, and he cried a challenge to the earl, who came to meet him. Hard did they fight, but Owen overthrew his enemy and drove him in front to the castle gate and into the hall.

'Behold the reward of thy blessed balsam,' said he, as he bade the earl kneel down before her, and made him swear that he would restore all that he had taken from her.

After that he departed, and went into the deserts, and as he was passing through a wood he heard a loud yelling. Pushing aside the bushes he beheld a lion standing on a great mound, and by it a rock. Near the rock was a lion seeking to reach the mound, and each time he moved out darted a serpent from the rock to prevent him. Then Owen unsheathed his sword, and cut off the serpent's head and went on his way, and the lion followed and played about him, as if he had been a greyhound. And much more useful was he than a greyhound, for in the evening he brought large logs in his mouth to kindle a fire, and killed a fat buck for dinner.

172

Owen made his fire and skinned the buck, and put some of it to roast, and gave the rest to the lion for supper. While he was waiting for the meat to cook he heard a sound of deep sighing close to him, and he said:

'Who are thou?'

'I am Luned,' replied a voice from a cave so hidden by bushes and green hanging plants that Owen had not seen it.

'And what dost thou here?' cried he.

'I am held captive in this cave on account of the knight who married the countess and left her, for the pages spoke ill of him, and because I told them that no man living was his equal they dragged me here and said I should die unless he should come to deliver me by a certain day, and that is no further than the day after tomorrow. His name is Owen the son of Urien, but I have none to send to tell him of my danger, or of a surety he would deliver me.'

Owen held his peace, but gave the maiden some of the meat, and bade her be of good cheer. Then, followed by the lion, he set out for a great castle on the other side of the plain, and men came and took his horse and placed it in a manger, and the lion went after and lay down on the straw. Hospitable and kind were all within the castle, but so full of sorrow that it might have been thought death was upon them. At length, when they had eaten and drunk, Owen prayed the earl to tell him the reason of their grief.

'Yesterday,' answered the earl, 'my two sons were seized, while they were hunting, by a monster who dwells on those mountains yonder, and he vows that he will not let them go unless I give him my daughter to wife.'

'That shall never be,' said Owen; 'but what form hath this monster?'

'In shape he is a man, but in stature he is a giant,' replied the earl, 'and it were better by far that he should slay my sons than that I should give up my daughter.'

Early next morning the dwellers in the castle were awakened by a great clamour, and they found that the giant had arrived with the two young men. Swiftly Owen put on his armour and went forth to meet the giant, and the lion followed at his heels. And when the great beast beheld the hard blows which the giant dealt his master he flew at his throat, and much trouble had the monster in beating him off.

'Truly,' said the giant, 'I should find no difficulty in fighting thee, if it were not for that lion.' When he heard that Owen felt shame that he could not overcome the giant with his own sword, so he took the lion and shut him up in one of the towers of the castle, and returned to the fight. But from the sound of the blows the lion knew that the combat was going ill for Owen, so he climbed up till he reached the top of the tower, where there was a door on to the roof, and from the tower he sprang on to the walls, and from the walls to the ground. Then with a loud roar he leaped upon the giant, who fell dead under the blow of his paw.

Now the gloom of the castle was turned into rejoicing, and the earl begged Owen to stay with him till he could make him a feast, but the knight said he had other work to do, and rode back to the place where he had left Luned, and the lion followed at his heels. When he came there he saw a great fire kindled, and two youths leading out the maiden to cast her upon the pile.

'Stop!' he cried, dashing up to them. 'What charge have you against her?'

'She boasted that no man in the world was equal to Owen,' said they, 'and we shut her in a cave, and agreed that none should deliver her but Owen himself, and that if he did not come by a certain day she should die. And now the time has past and there is no sign of him.'

'In truth he is a good knight, and had he but known that the maid was in peril he would have come to save her,' said Owen; 'but accept me in his stead, I entreat you.'

'We will,' replied they, and the fight began.

The youths fought well and pressed hard on Owen, and when the lion saw that he came to help his master. But the youths made a sign for the fight to stop, and said:

'Chieftain, it was agreed we should give battle to thee alone, and it is harder for us to contend with yonder beast than with thee.'

Then Owen shut up the lion in the cave where the maiden had been in prison, and blocked up the front with stones. But the fight with the giant had sorely tried him, and the youths fought well, and pressed him harder than before. And when the lion saw that he gave a loud roar, and burst through the stones, and sprang upon the youths and slew them. And so Luned was delivered at the last.

Then the maiden rode back with Owen to the lands of the lady of the fountain. And he took the lady with him to Arthur's court, where they lived happily till they died.

From the 'Mabinogion.'

174

The Four Gifts

In the old land of Brittany, once called Cornwall, there lived a woman named Barbaik Bourhis, who spent all her days in looking after her farm with the help of her niece Tephany. Early and late the two might be seen in the fields or in the dairy, milking cows, making butter, feeding fowls; working hard themselves and taking care that others worked too. Perhaps it might have been better for Barbaik if she had left herself a little time to rest and to think about other things, for soon she grew to love money for its own sake, and only gave herself and Tephany the food and clothes they absolutely needed. And as for poor people she positively hated them, and declared that such lazy creatures had no business in the world.

Well, this being the sort of person Barbaik was, it is easy to guess at her anger when one day she found Tephany talking outside the cowhouse to young Denis, who was nothing more than a day labourer from the village of Plover. Seizing her niece by the arm, she pulled her sharply away, exclaiming:

'Are you not ashamed, girl, to waste your time over a man who is as poor as a rat, when there are a dozen more who would be only too happy to buy you rings of silver, if you would let them?'

'Denis is a good workman, as you know very well,' answered Tephany, red with anger, 'and he puts by money too, and soon he will be able to take a farm for himself.'

'Nonsense,' cried Barbaik, 'he will never save enough for a farm till he is a hundred. I would sooner see you in your grave than the wife of a man who carries his whole fortune on his back.'

'What does fortune matter when one is young and strong?' asked Tephany, but her aunt, amazed at such words, would hardly let her finish.

'What does fortune matter?' repeated Barbaik, in a shocked voice. 'Is it possible that you are really so foolish as to despise money? If this is what you learn from Denis, I forbid you to speak to him, and I will have him turned out of the farm if he dares to show his face here again. Now go and wash the clothes and spread them out to dry.'

Tephany did not dare to disobey, but with a heavy heart went down the path to the river.

'She is harder than these rocks,' said the girl to herself, 'yes, a thousand times harder. For the rain at least can at last wear away the stone, but you might cry for ever, and she would never care. Talking to Denis is the only pleasure I have, and if I am not to see him I may as well enter a convent.'

Thinking these thoughts she reached the bank, and began to unfold the large packet of linen that had to be washed. The tap of a stick made her look up, and standing before her she saw a little old woman, whose face was strange to her.

'You would like to sit down and rest, granny?' asked Tephany, pushing aside her bundle.

'When the sky is all the roof you have, you rest where you will,' replied the old woman in trembling tones.

'Are you so lonely, then?' inquired Tephany, full of pity. 'Have you no friends who would welcome you into their houses?'

The old woman shook her head.

'They all died long, long ago,' she answered, 'and the only friends I have are strangers with kind hearts.'

The girl did not speak for a moment, then held out the small loaf and some bacon intended for her dinner.

'Take this,' she said; 'to-day at any rate you shall dine well,' and the old woman took it, gazing at Tephany the while.

'Those who help others deserve to be helped,' she answered; 'your eyes are still red because that miser Barbaik has forbidden you to speak to the young man from Plover. But cheer up, you are a good girl, and I will give you something that will enable you to see him once every day.'

'You?' cried Tephany, stupefied at discovering that the beggar knew all about her affairs, but the old woman did not hear her.

'Take this long copper pin,' she went on, 'and every time you stick it in your dress Mother Bourhis will be obliged to leave the house in order to go and count her cabbages. As long as the pin is in your dress you will be free, and your aunt will not come back until you have put it in its case again.' Then, rising, she nodded to Tephany and vanished.

The girl stood where she was, as still as a stone. If it had not been for the pin in her hands she would have thought she was dreaming. But by that token she knew it was no common old woman who had given it to her, but a fairy, wise in telling what would happen in the days to come. Then suddenly Tephany's eyes fell on the clothes, and to make up for lost time she began to wash them with great vigour.

Next evening, at the moment when Denis was accustomed to wait for her in the shadow of the cowhouse, Tephany stuck the pin in her dress, and at the very same instant Barbaik took up her sabots or wooden shoes and went through the orchard and past to the fields, to the plot where the cabbages grew. With a heart as light as her footsteps, the girl ran from the house, and spent her evening happily with Denis. And so it was for many days after that. Then, at last, Tephany began to notice something, and the something made her very sad.

At first, Denis seemed to find the hours that they were together fly as quickly as she did, but when he had taught her all the songs he knew, and told her all the plans he had made for growing rich and a great man, he had nothing more to say to her, for he, like a great many other people, was fond of talking himself, but not of listening to any one else. Sometimes, indeed, he never came at all, and the next evening he would tell Tephany that he had been forced to go into the town on business, but though she never reproached him she was not deceived and saw plainly that he no longer cared for her as he used to do.

Day by day her heart grew heavier and her cheeks paler, and one evening, when she had waited for him in vain, she put her water-pot on her shoulder and went slowly down to the spring. On the path in front of her stood the fairy who had given her the pin, and as she glanced at Tephany she gave a little mischievous laugh and said:

'Why, my pretty maiden hardly looks happier than she did before, in spite of meeting her lover whenever she pleases.'

'He has grown tired of me,' answered Tephany in a trembling voice, 'and he makes excuses to stay away. Ah! granny dear, it is not enough to be able to see him, I must be able to amuse him and to keep him with me. He is so clever, you know. Help me to be clever too.'

'Is that what you want?' cried the old woman. 'Well, take this feather and stick it in your hair, and you will be as wise as Solomon himself.'

Blushing with pleasure Tephany went home and stuck the feather into the blue ribbon which girls always wear in that part of the country. In a moment she heard Denis whistling gaily, and as her aunt was safely counting her cabbages, she hurried out to meet him. The young man was struck dumb by her talk. There was nothing that she did not seem to know, and as for songs she not only could sing those from every part of Brittany, but could compose them herself. Was this really the quiet girl who had been so anxious to learn all he could teach her, or was it somebody else? Perhaps she had gone suddenly mad, and there was an evil spirit inside her. But in any case, night after night he came back, only to find her growing wiser and wiser. Soon the neighbours whispered their surprise among themselves, for Tephany had not been able to resist the pleasure of putting the feather in her hair for some of the people who despised her for her poor clothes, and many were the jokes she made about them. Of course they heard of her jests, and shook their heads saying:

'She is an ill-natured little cat, and the man that marries her will find that it is she who will hold the reins and drive the horse.'

It was not long before Denis began to agree with them, and as he always liked to be master wherever he went, he became afraid of Tephany's sharp tongue, and instead of laughing as before when she made fun of other people he grew red and uncomfortable, thinking that his turn would come next.

So matters went on till one evening Denis told Tephany that he really could not stay a moment, as he had promised to go to a dance that was to be held in the next village.

Tephany's face fell; she had worked hard all day, and had been counting on a quiet hour with Denis. She did her best to persuade him to remain with her, but he would not listen, and at last she grew angry.

'Oh, I know why you are so anxious not to miss the dance,' she said; 'it is because Aziliez of Pennenru will be there.'

Now Aziliez was the loveliest girl for miles round, and she and Denis had known each other from childhood.

'Oh yes, Aziliez will be there,' answered Denis, who was quite pleased to see her jealous, 'and naturally one would go a long way to watch her dance.'

'Go then!' cried Tephany, and entering the house she slammed the door behind her.

Lonely and miserable she sat down by the fire and stared into the red embers. Then, flinging the feather from her hair, she put her head on her hands, and sobbed passionately.

'What is the use of being clever when it is beauty that men want? That is what I ought to have asked for. But it is too late, Denis will never come back.'

'Since you wish it so much you shall have beauty,' said a voice at her side, and looking round she beheld the old woman leaning on her stick.

'Fasten this necklace round your neck, and as long as you wear it you will be the most beautiful woman in the world,' continued the fairy. With a little shriek of joy Tephany took the necklace, and snapping the clasp ran to the mirror which hung in the corner. Ah, this time she was not afraid of Aziliez or of any other girl, for surely none could be as fair and white as she. And with the sight of her face a thought came to her, and putting on hastily her best dress and her buckled shoes she hurried off to the dance.

On the way she met a beautiful carriage with a young man seated in it.

178

'What a lovely maiden!' he exclaimed, as Tephany approached. 'Why, there is not a girl in my own country that can be compared to her. She, and no other, shall be my bride.'

The carriage was large and barred the narrow road, so Tephany was forced, much against her will, to remain where she was. But she looked the young man full in the face as she answered:

'Go your way, noble lord, and let me go mine. I am only a poor peasant girl, accustomed to milk, and make hay and spin.'

'Peasant you may be, but I will make you a great lady,' said he, taking her hand and trying to lead her to the carriage.

'I don't want to be a great lady, I only want to be the wife of Denis,' she replied, throwing off his hand and running to the ditch which divided the road from the cornfield, where he hoped to hide. Unluckily the young man guessed what she was doing, and signed to his attendants, who seized her and put her in the coach. The door was banged, and the horses whipped up into a gallop.

At the end of an hour they arrived at a splendid castle, and Tephany, who would not move, was lifted out and carried into the hall, while a priest was sent for to perform the marriage ceremony. The young man tried to win a smile from her by telling of all the beautiful things she should have as his wife, but Tephany did not listen to him, and looked about to see if there was any means by which she could escape. It did not seem easy. The three great doors were closely barred, and the one through which she had entered shut with a spring, but her feather was still in her hair, and by its aid she detected a crack in the wooden panelling, through which a streak of light could be dimly seen. Touching the copper pin which fastened her dress, the girl sent every one in the hall to count the cabbages, while she herself passed through the little door, not knowing whither she was going.

By this time night had fallen, and Tephany was very tired. Thankfully she found herself at the gate of a convent, and asked if she might stay there till morning. But the portress answered roughly that it was no place for beggars, and bade her begone, so the poor girl dragged herself slowly along the road, till a light and the bark of a dog told her that she was near a farm.

In front of the house was a group of people; two or three women and the sons of the farmer. When their mother heard Tephany's request to be given a bed the good wife's heart softened, and she was just going to invite her inside, when the young men, whose heads were turned by the girl's beauty, began to quarrel as to which should do most for her. From words they came to blows, and the women, frightened at the disturbance, pelted Tephany with insulting names. She quickly ran down the nearest path, hoping to escape them in the darkness of the trees, but in an instant she heard their footsteps behind her. Wild with fear her legs trembled under her, when suddenly she bethought herself of her necklace. With a violent effort she burst the clasp and flung it round the neck of a pig which was grunting in a ditch, and as she did so she heard the footsteps cease from pursuing her and run after the pig, for her charm had vanished.

On she went, scarcely knowing where she was going, till she found herself, to her surprise and joy, close to her aunt's house. For several days she felt so tired and unhappy that she could hardly get through her work, and to make matters worse Denis scarcely ever came near her.

'He was too busy,' he said, 'and really it was only rich people who could afford to waste time in talking.'

As the days went on Tephany grew paler and paler, till everybody noticed it except her aunt. The water-pot was almost too heavy for her now, but morning and evening she carried it to the spring, though the effort to lift it to her shoulder was often too much for her.

'How could I have been so foolish,' she whispered to herself, when she went down as usual at sunset. 'It was not freedom to see Denis that I should have asked for, for he was soon weary of me, nor a quick tongue, for he was afraid of it, nor beauty, for that brought me nothing but trouble, but riches which make life easy both for oneself and others. Ah! if I only dared to beg this gift from the fairy, I should be wiser than before and know how to choose better.'

'Be satisfied,' said the voice of the old woman, who seemed to be standing unseen at Tephany's elbow. 'If you look in your right-hand pocket when you go home you will find a small box. Rub your eyes with the ointment it contains, and you will see that you yourself contain a priceless treasure.'

Tephany did not in the least understand what she meant, but ran back to the farm as fast as she could, and began to fumble joyfully in her right-hand pocket. Sure enough, there was the little box with the precious ointment. She was in the act of rubbing her eyes with it when Barbaik Bourhis entered the room. Ever since she had been obliged to leave her work and pass her time, she did not know why, in counting cabbages, everything had gone wrong, and she could not get a labourer to stay with her because of her bad temper. When, therefore, she saw her niece standing quietly before her mirror, Barbaik broke out:

'So this is what you do when I am out in the fields! Ah! it is no wonder if the farm is ruined. Are you not ashamed, girl, to behave so?'

Tephany tried to stammer some excuse, but her aunt was half mad with rage, and a box on the ears was her only answer. At this Tephany, hurt, bewildered and excited, could control herself no longer, and turning away burst into tears. But what was her surprise when she saw that each tear-drop was a round and shining pearl. Barbaik, who also beheld this marvel, uttered a cry of astonishment, and threw herself on her knees to pick them up from the floor.

She was still gathering them when the door opened and in came Denis.

'Pearls! Are they really pearls?' he asked, falling on his knees also, and looking up at Tephany he perceived others still more beautiful rolling down the girl's cheeks.

'Take care not to let any of the neighbours hear of it, Denis,' said Barbaik. 'Of course you shall have your share, but nobody else shall get a single one. Cry on, my dear, cry on,' she continued to Tephany. It is for your good as well as ours,' and she held out her apron to catch them, and Denis his hat.

But Tephany could hardly bear any more. She felt half choked at the sight of their greediness, and wanted to rush from the hall, and though Barbaik caught her arm to prevent this, and said all sorts of tender words which she thought would make the girl weep the more, Tephany with a violent effort forced back her tears, and wiped her eyes.

'Is she finished already?' cried Barbaik, in a tone of disappointment. 'Oh, try again, my dear. Do you think it would do any good to beat her a little?' she added to Denis, who shook his head.

'That is enough for the first time. I will go into the town and find out the value of each pearl.'

'Then I will go with you,' said Barbaik, who never trusted anyone and was afraid of being cheated. So the two went out, leaving Tephany behind them.

She sat quite still on her chair, her hands clasped tightly together, as if she was forcing something back. At last she raised her eyes, which had been fixed on the ground, and beheld the fairy standing in a dark corner by the hearth, observing her with a mocking look. The girl trembled and jumped up, then, taking the feather, the pin, and the box, she held them out to the old woman.

'Here they are, all of them,' she cried; 'they belong to you. Let me never see them again, but I have learned the lesson that they taught me. Others may have riches, beauty and wit, but as for me I desire nothing but to be the poor peasant girl I always was, working hard for those she loves.'

'Yes, you have learned your lesson,' answered the fairy, 'and now you shall lead a peaceful life and marry the man you love. For after all it was not yourself you thought of but him.'

Never again did Tephany see the old woman, but she forgave Denis for selling her tears, and in time he grew to be a good husband, who did his own share of work.

From 'Le Foyer Breton,' par E. Souvestre.

The Groac'h of the Isle of Lok

In old times, when all kinds of wonderful things happened in Brittany, there lived in the village of Lanillis, a young man named Houarn Pogamm and a girl called Bellah Postik. They were cousins, and as their mothers were great friends, and constantly in and out of each other's houses, they had often been laid in the same cradle, and had played and fought over their games.

'When they are grown up they will marry,' said the mothers; but just as every one was beginning to think of wedding bells, the two mothers died, and the cousins, who had no money, went as servants in the same house. This was better than being parted, of course, but not so good as having a little cottage of their own, where they could do as they liked, and soon they might have been heard bewailing to each other the hardness of their lots.

'If we could only manage to buy a cow and get a pig to fatten,' grumbled Houarn, 'I would rent a bit of ground from the master, and then we could be married.'

'Yes,' answered Bellah, with a deep sigh; 'but we live in such hard times, and at the last fair the price of pigs had risen again.'

'We shall have long to wait, that is quite clear,' replied Houarn, turning away to his work.

Whenever they met they repeated their grievances, and at length Houarn's patience was exhausted, and one morning he came to Bellah and told her that he was going away to seek his fortune.

The girl was very unhappy as she listened to this, and felt sorry that she had not tried to make the best of things. She implored Houarn not to leave her, but he would listen to nothing.

'The birds,' he said, 'continue flying until they reach a field of corn, and the bees do not stop unless they find the honey-giving flowers, and why should a man have less sense than they? Like them, I shall seek till I get what I want—that is, money to buy a cow and a pig to fatten. And if you love me, Bellah, you won't attempt to hinder a plan which will hasten our marriage.'

The girl saw it was useless to say more, so she answered sadly:

'Well, go then, since you must. But first I will divide with you all that my parents left me,' and going to her room, she opened a small chest, and took from it a bell, a knife, and a little stick.

'This bell,' she said, 'can be heard at any distance, however far, but it only rings to warn us that our friends are in great danger. The knife frees all it touches from the spells that have been laid on them; while the stick will carry you wherever you want to go. I will give you the knife to guard you against the enchantments of wizards, and the bell to tell me of your perils. The stick I shall keep for myself, so that I can fly to you if ever you have need of me.'

Then they cried for a little on each other's necks, and Houarn started for the mountains.

But in those days, as in these, beggars abounded, and through every village he passed they followed Houarn in crowds, mistaking him for a gentleman, because there were no holes in his clothes.

'There is no fortune to be made here,' he thought to himself; 'it is a place for spending, and not earning. I see I must go further,' and he walked on to Pont-aven, a pretty little town built on the bank of a river.

He was sitting on a bench outside an inn, when he heard two men who were loading their mules talking about the Groac'h of the island of Lok.

'What is a Groac'h?' asked he. 'I have never come across one.' And the men answered that it was the name given to the fairy that dwelt in the lake, and that she was rich—oh! richer than all the kings in the world put together. Many had gone to the island to try and get possession of her treasures, but no one had ever come back.

As he listened Houarn's mind was made up.

'I will go, and return too,' he said to the muleteers. They stared at him in astonishment, and besought him not to be so mad and to throw away his life in such a foolish manner; but he only laughed, and answered that if they could tell him of any other way in which to procure a cow and a pig to fatten, he would think no more about it. But the men did not know how this was to be done, and, shaking their heads over his obstinacy, left him to his fate.

So Houarn went down to the sea, and found a boatman who engaged to take him to the isle of Lok.

The island was large, and lying almost across it was a lake, with a narrow opening to the sea. Houarn paid the boatman and sent him away, and then proceeded to walk round the lake. At one end he perceived a small skiff, painted blue and shaped like a swan, lying under a clump of yellow broom. As far as he could see, the swan's head was tucked under its wing, and Houarn, who had never beheld a boat of the sort, went quickly towards it and stepped in, so as to examine it the better. But no sooner was he on board than the swan woke suddenly up; his head emerged from under his wing, his feet began to move in the water, and in another moment they were in the middle of the lake.

As soon as the young man had recovered from his surprise, he prepared to jump into the lake and swim to shore. But the bird had guessed his intentions, and plunged beneath the water, carrying Houarn with him to the palace of the Groac'h.

Now, unless you have been under the sea and beheld all the wonders that lie there, you can never have an idea what the Groac'h's palace was like. It was all made of shells, blue and green and pink and lilac and white, shading into each other till you could not tell where one colour ended and the other began. The staircases were of crystal, and every separate stair sang like a woodland bird as you put your foot on it. Round the palace were great gardens full of all the plants that grow in the sea, with diamonds for flowers.

In a large hall the Groac'h was lying on a couch of gold. The pink and white of her face reminded you of the shells of her palace, while her long black hair was intertwined with strings of coral, and her dress of green silk seemed formed out of the sea. At the sight of her Houarn stopped, dazzled by her beauty.

'Come in,' said the Groac'h, rising to her feet. 'Strangers and handsome youths are always welcome here. Do not be shy, but tell me how you found your way, and what you want.'

'My name is Houarn,' he answered, 'Lanillis is my home, and I am trying to earn enough money to buy a little cow and a pig to fatten.'

'Well, you can easily get that,' replied she; 'it is nothing to worry about. Come in and enjoy yourself.' And she beckoned him to follow her into a second hall whose floors and walls were formed of pearls, while down the sides there were tables laden with fruit and wines of all kinds; and as he ate and drank, the Groac'h talked to him and told him how the treasures he saw came from shipwrecked vessels, and were brought to her palace by a magic current of water.

'I do not wonder,' exclaimed Houarn, who now felt quite at home— 'I do not wonder that the people on the earth have so much to say about you.'

'The rich are always envied.'

'For myself,' he added, with a laugh, 'I only ask for the half of your wealth.'

'You can have it, if you will, Houarn,' answered the fairy.

'What do you mean?' cried he.

185

'My husband, Korandon, is dead,' she replied, 'and if you wish it, I will marry you.'

The young man gazed at her in surprise. Could any one so rich and so beautiful really wish to be his wife? He looked at her again, and Bellah was forgotten as he answered:

'A man would be mad indeed to refuse such an offer. I can only accept it with joy.'

'Then the sooner it is done the better,' said the Groac'h, and gave orders to her servants. After that was finished, she begged Houarn to accompany her to a fish-pond at the bottom of the garden.

'Come lawyer, come miller, come tailor, come singer!' cried she, holding out a net of steel; and at each summons a fish appeared and jumped into the net. When it was full she went into a large kitchen and threw them all into a golden pot; but above the bubbling of the water Houarn seemed to hear the whispering of little voices.

'Who is it whispering in the golden pot, Groac'h?' he inquired at last.

'It is nothing but the noise of the wood sparkling,' she answered; but it did not sound the least like that to Houarn.

'There it is again,' he said, after a short pause.

'The water is getting hot, and it makes the fish jump,' she replied; but soon the noise grew louder and like cries.

'What is it?' asked Houarn, beginning to feel uncomfortable.

'Just the crickets on the hearth,' said she, and broke into a song which drowned the cries from the pot.

But though Houarn held his peace, he was not as happy as before. Something seemed to have gone wrong, and then he suddenly remembered Bellah.

'Is it possible I can have forgotten her so soon? What a wretch I am!' he thought to himself; and he remained apart and watched the Groac'h while she emptied the fish into a plate, and bade him eat his dinner while she fetched wine from her cellar in a cave.

Houarn sat down and took out the knife which Bellah had given him, but as soon as the blade touched the fish the enchantment ceased, and four men stood before him.

'Houarn, save us, we entreat you, and save yourself too!' murmured they, not daring to raise their voices.

'Why, it must have been you who were crying out in the pot just now!' exclaimed Houarn.

'Yes, it was us,' they answered. 'Like you, we came to the isle of Lok to seek our fortunes, and like you we consented to marry the Groac'h, and no sooner was the ceremony over than she turned us into fishes, as she had done to all our forerunners, who are in the fish-pond still, where you will shortly join them.'

On hearing this Houarn leaped into the air, as if he already felt himself frizzling in the golden pot. He rushed to the door, hoping to escape that way; but the Groac'h, who had heard everything, met him on the threshold. Instantly she threw the steel net over his head, and the eyes of a little green frog peeped through the meshes.

'You shall go and play with the rest,' she said, carrying him off to the fish-pond.

It was at this very moment that Bellah, who was skimming the milk in the farm dairy, heard the fairy bell tinkle violently.

At the sound she grew pale, for she knew it meant that Houarn was in danger; and, hastily, changing the rough dress she wore for her work, she left the farm with the magic stick in her hand.

Her knees were trembling under her, but she ran as fast as she could to the cross roads, where she drove her stick into the ground, murmuring as she did so a verse her mother had taught her:

Little staff of apple-tree,   Over the earth and over
the sea,
Up in the air be guide to me,   Everywhere to wander
free,

and immediately the stick became a smart little horse, with a rosette at each ear and a feather on his forehead. He stood quite still while Bellah scrambled up, then he started off, his pace growing quicker and quicker, till at length the girl could hardly see the trees and houses as they flashed past. But, rapid as the pace was, it was not rapid enough for Bellah, who stooped and said:

'The swallow is less swift than the wind, the wind is less swift than the lightning. But you, my horse, if you love me, must be swifter than them all, for there is a part of my heart that suffers —the best part of my heart that is in danger.'

And the horse heard her, and galloped like a straw carried along by a tempest till they reached the foot of a rock called the Leap of the Deer. There he stopped, for no horse or mule that ever was born could climb that rock, and Bellah knew it, so she began to sing again:

```
Horse of Leon, given to me,      Over the earth and over
the sea,
Up in the air be guide to me,      Everywhere to wander
free,
```

and when she had finished, the horse's fore legs grew shorter and spread into wings, his hind legs became claws, feathers sprouted all over his body, and she sat on the back of a great bird, which bore her to the summit of the rock. Here she found a nest made of clay and lined with dried moss, and in the centre a tiny man, black and wrinkled, who gave a cry of surprise at the sight of Bellah.

'Ah! you are the pretty girl who was to come and save me!'

'To save you!' repeated Bellah. 'But who are you, my little friend?'

'I am the husband of the Groac'h of the isle of Lok, and it is owing to her that I am here.'

'But what are you doing in this nest?'

'I am sitting on six eggs of stone, and I shall not be set free till they are hatched.'

On hearing this Bellah began to laugh.

'Poor little cock!' she said, 'and how am I to deliver you?'

'By delivering Houarn, who is in the power of the Groac'h.'

'Ah! tell me how I can manage that, and if I have to walk round the whole of Brittany on my bended knees I will do it!'

'Well, first you must dress yourself as a young man, and then go and seek the Groac'h. When you have found her you must contrive to get hold of the net of steel that hangs from her waist, and shut her up in it for ever.'

'But where am I to find a young man's clothes?' asked she.

'I will show you,' he replied, and as he spoke he pulled out three of his red hairs and blew them away, muttering something the while. In the twinkling of an eye the four hairs changed into four tailors, of whom the first carried a cabbage, the second a pair of scissors, the third a needle, and the fourth an iron. Without waiting for orders, they sat down in the nest and, crossing their legs comfortably, began to prepare the suit of clothes for Bellah.

188

With one of the leaves of the cabbage they made her a coat, and another served for a waistcoat; but it took two for the wide breeches which were then in fashion. The hat was cut from the heart of the cabbage, and a pair of shoes from the thick stem. And when Bellah had put them all on you would have taken her for a gentleman dressed in green velvet, lined with white satin.

She thanked the little men gratefully, and after a few more instructions, jumped on the back of her great bird, and was borne away to the isle of Lok. Once there, she bade him transform himself back into a stick, and with it in her hand she stepped into the blue boat, which conducted her to the palace of shells.

The Groac'h seemed overjoyed to see her, and told her that never before had she beheld such a handsome young man. Very soon she led her visitor into the great hall, where wine and fruit were always waiting, and on the table lay the magic knife, left there by Houarn. Unseen by the Groac'h, Bellah hid it in a pocket of her green coat, and then followed her hostess into the garden, and to the pond which contained the fish, their sides shining with a thousand different colours.

'Oh! what beautiful, beautiful creatures!' said she. 'I'm sure I should never be tired of watching them.' And she sat down on the bank, with her elbows on her knees and her chin in her hands, her eyes fixed on the fishes as they flashed past.

'Would you not like to stay here always?' asked the Groac'h; and Bellah answered that she desired nothing better.

'Then you have only to marry me,' said the Groac'h. 'Oh! don't say no, for I have fallen deeply in love with you.'

'Well, I won't say "No,"' replied Bellah, with a laugh, 'but you must promise first to let me catch one of those lovely fish in your net.'

'It is not so easy as it looks,' rejoined the Groac'h, smiling, 'but take it, and try your luck.'

Bellah took the net which the Groac'h held out, and, turning rapidly, flung it over the witch's head.

'Become in body what you are in soul!' cried she, and in an instant the lovely fairy of the sea was a toad, horrible to look upon. She struggled hard to tear the net asunder, but it was no use. Bellah only drew it the tighter, and, flinging the sorceress into a pit, she rolled a great stone across the mouth, and left her.

As she drew near the pond she saw a great procession of fishes advancing to meet her, crying in hoarse tones:

'This is our lord and master, who has saved us from the net of steel and the pot of gold!'

'And who will restore you to your proper shapes,' said Bellah, drawing the knife from her pocket. But just as she was going to touch the foremost fish, her eyes fell on a green frog on his knees beside her, his little paws crossed over his little heart. Bellah felt as if fingers were tightening round her throat, but she managed to cry:

'Is this you, my Houarn? Is this you?'

'It is I,' croaked the little frog; and as the knife touched him he was a man again, and, springing up, he clasped her in his arms.

'But we must not forget the others,' she said at last, and began to transform the fishes to their proper shapes. There were so many of them that it took quite a long time. Just as she had finished there arrived the little dwarf from the Deer's Leap in a car drawn by six cockchafers, which once had been the six stone eggs.

'Here I am!' he exclaimed. 'You have broken the spell that held me, and now come and get your reward,' and, dismounting from his chariot, he led them down into the caves filled with gold and jewels, and bade Bellah and Houarn take as much as they wanted.

When their pockets were full, Bellah ordered her stick to become a winged carriage, large enough to bear them and the men they had rescued back to Lanillis.

There they were married the next day, but instead of setting up housekeeping with the little cow and pig to fatten that they had so long wished for, they were able to buy lands for miles round for themselves, and gave each man who had been delivered from the Groac'h a small farm, where he lived happily to the end of his days.

From 'Le Foyer Breton,' par E. Souvestre.

The Escape of the Mouse

Manawyddan the prince and his friend Pryderi were wanderers, for the brother of Manawyddan had been slain, and his throne taken from him. Very sorrowful was Manawyddan, but Pryderi was stout of heart, and bade him be of good cheer, as he knew a way out of his trouble.

'And what may that be?' asked Manawyddan.

'It is that thou marry my mother Rhiannon and become lord of the fair lands that I will give her for dowry. Never did any lady have more wit than she, and in her youth none was more lovely; even yet she is good to look upon.'

'Thou art the best friend that ever a man had,' said Manawyddan. 'Let us go now to seek Rhiannon, and the lands where she dwells.'

Then they set forth, but the news of their coming ran swifter still, and Rhiannon and Kieva, wife of Pryderi, made haste to prepare a feast for them. And Manawyddan found that Pryderi had spoken the truth concerning his mother, and asked if she would take him for her husband. Right gladly did she consent, and without delay they were married, and rode away to the hunt, Rhiannon and Manawyddan, Kieva and Pryderi, and they would not be parted from each other by night or by day, so great was the love between them.

One day, when they were returned, they were sitting out in a green place, and suddenly the crash of thunder struck loudly on their ears, and a wall of mist fell between them, so that they were hidden one from the other. Trembling they sat till the darkness fled and the light shone again upon them, but in the place where they were wont to see cattle, and herds, and dwellings, they beheld neither house nor beast, nor man nor smoke; neither was any one remaining in the green place save these four only.

'Whither have they gone, and my host also?' cried Manawyddan, and they searched the hall, and there was no man, and the castle, and there was none, and in the dwellings that were left was nothing save wild beasts. For a year these four fed on the meat that Manawyddan and Pryderi killed out hunting, and the honey of the bees that sucked the mountain heather. For a time they desired nothing more, but when the next year began they grew weary.

'We cannot spend our lives thus,' said Manawyddan at last, 'let us go into England and learn some trade by which we may live.' So they left Wales, and went to Hereford, and there they made saddles, while Manawyddan fashioned blue enamel ornaments to put on their trappings. And so greatly did the townsfolk love these saddles, that no others were bought throughout the whole of Hereford, till the saddlers banded together and resolved to slay Manawyddan and his companions.

When Pryderi heard of it, he was very wroth, and wished to stay and fight. But the counsels of Manawyddan prevailed, and they moved by night to another city.

'What craft shall we follow?' asked Pryderi.

'We will make shields,' answered Manawyddan.

'But do we know anything of that craft?' answered Pryderi.

'We will try it,' said Manawyddan, and they began to make shields, and fashioned them after the shape of the shields they had seen; and these likewise they enamelled. And so greatly did they prosper that no man in the town bought a shield except they had made it, till at length the shield-makers banded together as the saddlers had done, and resolved to slay them. But of this they had warning, and by night betook themselves to another town.

'Let us take to making shoes,' said Manawyddan, 'for there are not any among the shoemakers bold enough to fight us.'

'I know nothing of making shoes,' answered Pryderi, who in truth despised so peaceful a craft.

'But I know,' replied Manawyddan, 'and I will teach thee to stitch. We will buy the leather ready dressed, and will make the shoes from it.

Then straightway he sought the town for the best leather, and for a goldsmith to fashion the clasps, and he himself watched till it was done, so that he might learn for himself. Soon he became known as 'The Maker of Gold Shoes,' and prospered so greatly, that as long as one could be bought from him not a shoe was purchased from the shoemakers of the town. And the craftsmen were wroth, and banded together to slay them.

'Pryderi,' said Manawyddan, when he had received news of it, 'we will not remain in England any longer. Let us set forth to Dyved.'

So they journeyed until they came to their lands at Narberth. There they gathered their dogs round them, and hunted for a year as before.

After that a strange thing happened. One morning Pryderi and Manawyddan rose up to hunt, and loosened their dogs, which ran before them, till they came to a small bush. At the bush, the dogs shrank away as if frightened, and returned to their masters, their hair brisling on their backs.

'We must see what is in that bush,' said Pryderi, and what was in it was a boar, with a skin as white as the snow on the mountains. And he came out, and made a stand as the dogs rushed on him, driven on by the men. Long he stood at bay; then at last he betook himself to flight, and fled to a castle which was newly built, in a place where no building had ever been known. Into the castle he ran, and the dogs after him, and long though their masters looked and listened, they neither saw nor heard aught concerning dogs or boar.

'I will go into the castle and get tidings of the dogs,' said Pryderi at last.

'Truly,' answered Manawyddan, 'thou wouldst do unwisely, for whosoever has cast a spell over this land has set this castle here.'

'I cannot give up my dogs,' replied Pryderi, and to the castle he went.

But within was neither man nor beast; neither boar nor dogs, but only a fountain with marble round it, and on the edge a golden bowl, richly wrought, which pleased Pryderi greatly. In a moment he forgot about his dogs, and went up to the bowl and took hold of it, and his hands stuck to the bowl, and his feet to the marble slab, and despair took possession of him.

Till the close of day Manawyddan waited for him, and when the sun was fast sinking, he went home, thinking that he had strayed far.

'Where are thy friend and thy dogs?' said Rhiannon, and he told her what had befallen Pryderi.

'A good friend hast thou lost,' answered Rhiannon, and she went up to the castle and through the gate, which was open. There, in the centre of the courtyard, she beheld Pryderi standing, and hastened towards him.

'What dost thou here?' she asked, laying her hand on the bowl, and as she spoke she too stuck fast, and was not able to utter a word. Then thunder was heard and a veil of darkness descended upon them, and the castle vanished and they with it.

When Kieva, the wife of Pryderi, found that neither her husband nor his mother returned to her, she was in such sorrow that she cared not whether she lived or died. Manawyddan was grieved also in his heart, and said to her:

'It is not fitting that we should stay here, for he have lost our dogs and cannot get food. Let us go into England—it is easier for us to live there.' So they set forth.

'What craft wilt thou follow?' asked Kieva as they went along.

'I shall make shoes as once I did,' replied he; and he got all the finest leather in the town and caused gilded clasps to be made for the shoes, till everyone flocked to buy, and all the shoemakers in the town were idle and banded together in anger to kill him. But luckily Manawyddan got word of it, and he and Kieva left the town one night and proceeded to Narberth, taking with him a sheaf of wheat, which he sowed in three plots of ground. And while the wheat was growing up, he hunted and fished, and they had food enough and to spare. Thus the months passed until the harvest; and one evening Manawyddan visited the furthest of his fields of wheat; and saw that it was ripe.

'To-morrow I will reap this,' said he; but on the morrow when he went to reap the wheat he found nothing but the bare straw.

Filled with dismay he hastened to the second field, and there the corn was ripe and golden.

'To-morrow I will reap this,' he said, but on the morrow the ears had gone, and there was nothing but the bare straw.

'Well, there is still one field left,' he said, and when he looked at it, it was still fairer than the other two. 'To-night I will watch here,' thought he, 'for whosoever carried off the other corn will in like manner take this, and I will know who it is.' So he hid himself and waited.

The hours slid by, and all was still, so still that Manawyddan well-nigh dropped asleep. But at midnight there arose the loudest tumult in the world, and peeping out he beheld a mighty host of mice, which could neither be numbered nor measured. Each mouse climbed up a straw till it bent down with its weight, and then it bit off one of the ears, and carried it away, and there was not one of the straws that had not got a mouse to it.

Full of wrath he rushed at the mice, but he could no more come up with them than if they had been gnats, or birds of the air, save one only which lingered behind the rest, and this mouse Manawyddan came up with. Stooping down he seized it by the tail, and put it in his glove, and tied a piece of string across the opening of the glove, so that the mouse could not escape. When he entered the hall where Kieva was sitting, he lighted a fire, and hung the glove up on a peg.

'What hast thou there?' asked she.

'A thief,' he answered, 'that I caught robbing me.'

'What kind of a thief may it be which thou couldst put in thy glove?' said Kieva.

'That I will tell thee,' he replied, and then he showed her how his fields of corn had been wasted, and how he had watched for the mice.

'And one was less nimble than the rest, and is now in my glove. To-morrow I will hang it, and I only wish I had them all.'

194

'It is a marvel, truly,' said she, 'yet it would be unseemly for a man of thy dignity to hang a reptile such as this. Do not meddle with it, but let it go.'

'Woe betide me,' he cried, 'if I would not hang them all if I could catch them, and such as I have I will hang.'

'Verily,' said she, 'there is no reason I should succour this reptile, except to prevent discredit unto thee.'

'If I knew any cause that I should succour it, I would take thy counsel,' answered Manawyddan, 'but as I know of none, I am minded to destroy it.'

'Do so then,' said Kieva.

So he went up a hill and set up two forks on the top, and while he was doing this he saw a scholar coming towards him, whose clothes were tattered. Now it was seven years since Manawyddan had seen man or beast in that place, and the sight amazed him.

'Good day to thee, my lord,' said the scholar.

'Good greeting to thee, scholar. Whence dost thou come?'

'From singing in England; but wherefore dost thou ask?'

'Because for seven years no man hath visited this place.'

'I wander where I will,' answered the scholar. 'And what work art thou upon?'

'I am about to hang a thief that I caught robbing me!'

'What manner of thief is that?' inquired the scholar. 'I see a creature in thy hand like upon a mouse, and ill does it become a man of thy rank to touch a reptile like this. Let it go free.'

'I will not let it go free,' cried Manawyddan. 'I caught it robbing me, and it shall suffer the doom of a thief.'

'Lord!' said the scholar, 'sooner than see a man like thee at such a work, I would give thee a pound which I have received as alms to let it go free.'

'I will not let it go free, neither will I sell it.'

'As thou wilt, lord,' answered the scholar, and he went his way.

Manawyddan was placing the cross-beam on the two forked sticks, where the mouse was to hang, when a priest rode past.

'Good-day to thee, lord; and what art thou doing?'

'I am hanging a thief that I caught robbing me.'

'What manner of thief, lord?'

'A creature in the form of a mouse. It has been robbing me, and it shall suffer the doom of a thief.'

'Lord,' said the priest, 'sooner than see thee touch this reptile, I would purchase its freedom.'

'I will neither sell it nor set it free.'

'It is true that a mouse is worth nothing, but rather than see thee defile thyself with touching such a reptile as this, I will give thee three pounds for it.'

'I will not take any price for it. It shall be hanged as it deserves.'

'Willingly, my lord, if it is thy pleasure.' And the priest went his way.

Then Manawyddan noosed the string about the mouse's neck, and was about to draw it tight when a bishop, with a great following and horses bearing huge packs, came by.

'What work art thou upon?' asked the bishop, drawing rein.

'Hanging a thief that I caught robbing me.'

'But is not that a mouse that I see in thine hand?' asked the bishop.

'Yes; that is the thief,' answered Manawyddan.

'Well, since I have come at the doom of this reptile, I will ransom it of thee for seven pounds, rather than see a man of thy rank touch it. Loose it, and let it go.'

'I will not let it loose.'

'I will give thee four and twenty pounds to set it free,' said the bishop.

'I will not set it free for as much again.'

196

'If thou wilt not set it free for this, I will give thee all the horses thou seest and the seven loads of baggage.'

'I will not set it free.'

'Then tell me at what price thou wilt loose it, and I will give it.'

'The spell must be taken off Rhiannon and Pryderi,' said Manawyddan.

'That shall be done.'

'But not yet will I loose the mouse. The charm that has been cast over all my lands must be taken off likewise.'

'This shall be done also.'

'But not yet will I loose the mouse till I know who she is.'

'She is my wife,' answered the bishop.

'And wherefore came she to me?' asked Manawyddan.

'To despoil thee,' replied the bishop, 'for it is I who cast the charm over thy lands, to avenge Gwawl the son of Clud my friend. And it was I who threw the spell upon Pryderi to avenge Gwawl for the trick that had been played on him in the game of Badger in the Bag. And not only was I wroth, but my people likewise, and when it was known that thou wast come to dwell in the land, they besought me much to change them into mice, that they might eat thy corn. The first and the second nights it was the men of my own house that destroyed thy two fields, but on the third night my wife and her ladies came to me and begged me to change them also into the shape of mice, that they might take part in avenging Gwawl. Therefore I changed them. Yet had she not been ill and slow of foot, thou couldst not have overtaken her. Still, since she was caught, I will restore thee Pryderi and Rhiannon, and will take the charm from off thy lands. I have told thee who she is; so now set her free.'

'I will not set her free,' answered Manawyddan, 'till thou swear that no vengeance shall be taken for his, either upon Pryderi, or upon Rhiannon, or on me.'

'I will grant thee this boon; and thou hast done wisely to ask it, for on thy head would have lit all the trouble. Set now my wife free.'

'I will not set her free till Pryderi and Rhiannon are with me.'

'Behold, here they come,' said the bishop.

Then Manawyddan held out his hands and greeted Pryderi and Rhiannon, and they seated themselves joyfully on the grass.

'Ah, lord, hast thou not received all thou didst ask?' said the bishop. 'Set now my wife free!'

'That I will gladly,' answered Manawyddan, unloosing the cord from her neck, and as he did so the bishop struck her with his staff, and she turned into a young woman, the fairest that ever was seen.

'Look around upon thy land,' said he, 'and thou wilt see it all tilled and peopled, as it was long ago.' And Manawyddan looked, and saw corn growing in the fields, and cows and sheep grazing on the hill-side, and huts for the people to dwell in. And he was satisfied in his soul, but one more question he put to the bishop.

'What spell didst thou lay upon Pryderi and Rhiannon?'

'Pryderi has had the knockers of the gate of my palace hung about him, and Rhiannon has carried the collars of my asses around her neck,' said the bishop with a smile.

From the 'Mabinogion.'

The Believing Husbands

Once upon a time there dwelt in the land of Erin a young man who was seeking a wife, and of all the maidens round about none pleased him as well as the only daughter of a farmer. The girl was willing and the father was willing, and very soon they were married and went to live at the farm. By and bye the season came when they must cut the peats and pile them up to dry, so that they might have fires in the winter. So on a fine day the girl and her husband, and the father and his wife all went out upon the moor.

They worked hard for many hours, and at length grew hungry, so the young woman was sent home to bring them food, and also to give the horses their dinner. When she went into the stables, she suddenly saw the heavy pack-saddle of the speckled mare just over her head, and she jumped and said to herself:

'Suppose that pack-saddle were to fall and kill me, how dreadful it would be!' and she sat down just under the pack-saddle she was so much afraid of, and began to cry.

Now the others out on the moor grew hungrier and hungrier.

'What can have become of her?' asked they, and at length the mother declared that she would wait no longer, and must go and see what had happened.

198

As the bride was nowhere in the kitchen or the dairy, the old woman went into the stable, where she found her daughter weeping bitterly.

'What is the matter, my dove?' and the girl answered, between her sobs:

'When I came in and saw the pack-saddle over my head, I thought how dreadful it would be if it fell and killed me,' and she cried louder than before.

The old woman struck her hands together: 'Ah, to think of it! if that were to be, what should I do?' and she sat down by her daughter, and they both wrung their hands and let their tears flow.

'Something strange must have occurred,' exclaimed the old farmer on the moor, who by this time was not only hungry, but cross. 'I must go after them.' And he went and found them in the stable.

'What is the matter?' asked he.

'Oh!' replied his wife, 'when our daughter came home, did she not see the pack-saddle over her head, and she thought how dreadful it would be if it were to fall and kill her.'

'Ah, to think of it!' exclaimed he, striking his hands together, and he sat down beside them and wept too.

As soon as night fell the young man returned full of hunger, and there they were, all crying together in the stable.

'What is the matter?' asked he.

'When thy wife came home,' answered the farmer, 'she saw the pack-saddle over her head, and she thought how dreadful it would be if it were to fall and kill her.'

'Well, but it didn't fall,' replied the young man, and he went off to the kitchen to get some supper, leaving them to cry as long as they liked.

The next morning he got up with the sun, and said to the old man and to the old woman and to his wife:

'Farewell: my foot shall not return to the house till I have found other three people as silly as you,' and he walked away till he came to the town, and seeing the door of a cottage standing open wide, he entered. No man was present, but only some women spinning at their wheels.

'You do not belong to this town,' said he.

'You speak truth,' they answered, 'nor you either?'

'I do not,' replied he, 'but is it a good place to live in?'

The women looked at each other.

'The men of the town are so silly that we can make them believe anything we please,' said they.

'Well, here is a gold ring,' replied he, 'and I will give it to the one amongst you who can make her husband believe the most impossible thing,' and he left them.

As soon as the first husband came home his wife said to him:

'Thou art sick!'

'Am I?' asked he.

'Yes, thou art,' she answered; 'take off thy clothes and lie down.'

So he did, and when he was in his bed his wife went to him and said:

'Thou art dead.'

'Oh, am I?' asked he.

'Thou art,' said she; 'shut thine eyes and stir neither hand nor foot.'

And dead he felt sure he was.

Soon the second man came home, and his wife said to him:

'You are not my husband!'

'Oh, am I not?' asked he.

'No, it is not you,' answered she, so he went away and slept in the wood.

When the third man arrived his wife gave him his supper, and after that he went to bed, just as usual. The next morning a boy knocked at the door, bidding him attend the burial of the man who was dead, and he was just going to get up when his wife stopped him.

'Time enough,' said she, and he lay still till he heard the funeral passing the window.

200

'Now rise, and be quick,' called the wife, and the man jumped out of bed in a great hurry, and began to look about him.

'Why, where are my clothes?' asked he.

'Silly that you are, they are on your back, of course,' answered the woman.

'Are they?' said he.

'They are,' said she, 'and make haste lest the burying be ended before you get there.'

Then off he went, running hard, and when the mourners saw a man coming towards them with nothing on but his nightshirt, they forgot in their fright what they were there for, and fled to hide themselves. And the naked man stood alone at the head of the coffin.

Very soon a man came out of the wood and spoke to him.

'Do you know me?'

'Not I,' answered the naked man. 'I do not know you.'

'But why are you naked?' asked the first man.

'Am I naked? My wife told me that I had all my clothes on,' answered he.

'And my wife told me that I myself was dead,' said the man in the coffin.

But at the sound of his voice the two men were so terrified that they ran straight home, and the man in the coffin got up and followed them, and it was his wife that gained the gold ring, as he had been sillier than the other two.

From 'West Highland Tales.'

The Hoodie-Crow.

Once there lived a farmer who had three daughters, and good useful girls they were, up with the sun, and doing all the work of the house. One morning they all ran down to the river to wash their clothes, when a hoodie came round and sat on a tree close by.

'Wilt thou wed me, thou farmer's daughter?' he said to the eldest.

'Indeed I won't wed thee,' she answered, 'an ugly brute is the hoodie.' And the bird, much offended, spread his wings and flew away. But the following day he came back again, and said to the second girl:

'Wilt thou wed me, farmer's daughter?'

'Indeed I will not,' answered she, 'an ugly brute is the hoodie.' And the hoodie was more angry than before, and went away in a rage. However, after a night's rest he was in a better temper, and thought that he might be more lucky the third time, so back he went to the old place.

'Wilt thou wed me, farmer's daughter?' he said to the youngest.

'Indeed I will wed thee; a pretty creature is the hoodie,' answered she, and on the morrow they were married.

'I have something to ask thee,' said the hoodie when they were far away in his own house. 'Wouldst thou rather I should be a hoodie by day and a man by night, or a man by day and a hoodie by night?'

The girl was surprised at his words, for she did not know that he could be anything but a hoodie at all times.

Still she said nothing of this, and only replied, 'I would rather thou wert a man by day and a hoodie by night,' And so he was; and a handsomer man or a more beautiful hoodie never was seen. The girl loved them both, and never wished for things to be different.

By and bye they had a son, and very pleased they both were. But in the night soft music was heard stealing close towards the house, and every man slept, and the mother slept also. When they woke again it was morning, and the baby was gone. High and low they looked for it, but nowhere could they find it, and the farmer, who had come to see his daughter, was greatly grieved, as he feared it might be thought that he had stolen it, because he did not want the hoodie for a son-in-law.

The next year the hoodie's wife had another son, and this time a watch was set at every door. But it was no use. In vain they determined that, come what might, they would not close their eyes; at the first note of music they all fell asleep, and when the farmer arrived in the morning to see his grandson, he found them all weeping, for while they had slept the baby had vanished.

Well, the next year it all happened again, and the hoodie's wife was so unhappy that her husband resolved to take her away to another house he had, and her sisters with her for company. So they set out in a coach which was big enough to hold them, and had not gone very far when the hoodie suddenly said:

'You are sure you have not forgotten anything?'

'I have forgotten my coarse comb,' answered the wife, feeling in her pocket, and as she spoke the coach changed into a withered faggot, and the man became a hoodie again, and flew away.

The two sisters returned home, but the wife followed the hoodie. Sometimes she would see him on a hill-top, and then would hasten after him, hoping to catch him. But by the time she had got to the top of the hill, he would be in the valley on the other side. When night came, and she was tired, she looked about for some place to rest, and glad she was to see a little house full of light straight in front of her, and she hurried towards it as fast as she could.

At the door stood a little boy, and the sight of him filled her heart with pleasure, she did not know why. A woman came out, and bade her welcome, and set before her food, and gave her a soft bed to lie on. And the hoodie's wife lay down, and so tired was she, that it seemed to her but a moment before the sun rose, and she awoke again. From hill to hill she went after the hoodie, and sometimes she saw him on the top; but when she got to the top, he had flown into the valley, and when she reached the valley he was on the top of another hill—and so it happened till night came round again. Then she looked round for some place to rest in, and she beheld a little house of light before her, and fast she hurried towards it. At the door stood a little boy, and her heart was filled with pleasure at the sight of him, she did not know why. After that a woman bade her enter, and set food before her, and gave her a soft bed to lie in. And when the sun rose she got up, and left the house, in search of the hoodie. This day everything befell as on the two other days, but when she reached the small house, the woman bade her keep awake, and if the hoodie flew into the room, to try to seize him.

But the wife had walked far, and was very tired, and strive as she would, she fell sound asleep.

Many hours she slept, and the hoodie entered through a window, and let fall a ring on her hand. The girl awoke with a start, and leant forward to grasp him, but he was already flying off, and she only seized a feather from his wing. And when dawn came, she got up and told the woman.

'He has gone over the hill of poison,' said she, 'and there you cannot follow him without horse-shoes on your hands and feet. But I will help you. Put on this suit of men's clothes, and go down this road till you come to the smithy, and there you can learn to make horse-shoes for yourself.'

The girl thanked her, and put on the cloths and went down the road to do her bidding. So hard did she work, that in a few days she was able to make the horse-shoes. Early one morning she set out for the hill of poison. On her hands and feet she went, but even with the horse-shoes on she had to be very careful not to stumble, lest some poisoned thorns should enter into her flesh, and she should die. But when at last she was over, it was only to hear that her husband was to be married that day to the daughter of a great lord.

Now there was to be a race in the town, and everyone meant to be there, except the stranger who had come over the hill of poison— everyone, that is, but the cook, who was to make the bridal supper. Greatly he loved races, and sore was his heart to think that one should be run without his seeing it, so when he beheld a woman whom he did not know coming along the street, hope sprang up in him.

'Will you cook the wedding feast in place of me?' he said, 'and I will pay you well when I return from the race.'

Gladly she agreed, and cooked the feast in a kitchen that looked into the great hall, where the company were to eat it. After that she watched the seat where the bridegroom was sitting, and taking a plateful of the broth, she dropped the ring and the feather into it, and set if herself before him.

With the first spoonful he took up the ring, and a thrill ran through him; in the second he beheld the feather and rose from his chair.

'Who has cooked this feast?' asked he, and the real cook, who had come back from the race, was brought before him.

'He may be the cook, but he did not cook this feast,' said the bridegroom, and then inquiry was made, and the girl was summoned to the great hall.

'That is my married wife,' he declared, 'and no one else will I have,' and at that very moment the spells fell off him, and never more would he be a hoodie. Happy indeed were they to be together again, and little did they mind that the hill of poison took long to cross, for she had to go some way forwards, and then throw the horse-shoes back for him to put on. Still, at last they were over, and they went back the way she had come, and stopped at the three houses in order to take their little sons to their own home.

But the story never says who had stolen them, nor what the coarse comb had to do with it.

From 'West Highland Tales.'

204

The Brownie of the Lake

Once upon a time there lived in France a man whose name was Jalm Riou. You might have walked a whole day without meeting anyone happier or more contented, for he had a large farm, plenty of money, and above all, a daughter called Barbaik, the most graceful dancer and the best-dressed girl in the whole country side. When she appeared on holidays in her embroidered cap, five petticoats, each one a little shorter than the other, and shoes with silver buckles, the women were all filled with envy, but little cared Barbaik what they might whisper behind her back as long as she knew that her clothes were finer than anyone else's and that she had more partners than any other girl.

Now amongst all the young men who wanted to marry Barbaik, the one whose heart was most set on her was her father's head man, but as his manners were rough and he was exceedingly ugly she would have nothing to say to him, and, what was worse, often made fun of him with the rest.

Jegu, for that was his name, of course heard of this, and it made him very unhappy. Still he would not leave the farm, and look for work elsewhere, as he might have done, for then he would never see Barbaik at all, and what was life worth to him without that?

One evening he was bringing back his horses from the fields, and stopped at a little lake on the way home to let them drink. He was tired with a long day's work, and stood with his hand on the mane of one of the animals, waiting till they had done, and thinking all the while of Barbaik, when a voice came out of the gorse close by.

'What is the matter, Jegu? You mustn't despair yet.'

The young man glanced up in surprise, and asked who was there.

'It is I, the brownie of the lake,' replied the voice.

'But where are you?' inquired Jegu.

'Look close, and you will see me among the reeds in the form of a little green frog. I can take,' he added proudly, 'any shape I choose, and even, which is much harder, be invisible if I want to.'

'Then show yourself to me in the shape in which your family generally appear,' replied Jegu.

'Certainly, if you wish,' and the frog jumped on the back of one of the horses, and changed into a little dwarf, all dressed in green.

This transformation rather frightened Jegu, but the brownie bade him have no fears, for he would not do him any harm; indeed, he hoped that Jegu might find him of some use.

'But why should you take all this interest in me?' asked the peasant suspiciously.

'Because of a service you did me last winter, which I have never forgotten,' answered the little fellow. 'You know, I am sure, that the korigans[FN#3: The spiteful fairies.] who dwell in the White Corn country have declared war on my people, because they say that they are the friends of man. We were therefore obliged to take refuge in distant lands, and to hide ourselves at first under different animal shapes. Since that time, partly from habit and partly to amuse ourselves, we have continued to transform ourselves, and it was in this way that I got to know you.'

'How?' exclaimed Jegu, filled with astonishment.

'Do you remember when you were digging in the field near the river, three months ago, you found a robin redbreast caught in a net?

'Yes,' answered Jegu, 'I remember it very well, and I opened the net and let him go.'

'Well, I was that robin redbreast, and ever since I have vowed to be your friend, and as you want to marry Barbaik, I will prove the truth of what I say by helping you to do so.'

'Ah! my little brownie, if you can do that, there is nothing I won't give you, except my soul.'

'Then let me alone,' rejoined the dwarf, 'and I promise you that in a very few months you shall be master of the farm and of Barbaik.'

'But how are you going to do it?' exclaimed Jegu wonderingly.

'That is my affair. Perhaps I may tell you later. Meanwhile you just eat and sleep, and don't worry yourself about anything.'

Jegu declared that nothing could be easier, and then taking off his hat, he thanked the dwarf heartily, and led his horses back to the farm.

Next morning was a holiday, and Barbaik was awake earlier than usual, as she wished to get through her work as soon as possible, and be ready to start for a dance which was to be held some distance off. She went first to the cow-house, which it was her duty to keep clean, but to her amazement she found fresh straw put down, the racks filled with hay, the cows milked, and the pails standing neatly in a row.

'Of course, Jegu must have done this in the hope of my giving him a dance,' she thought to herself, and when she met him outside the door she stopped and thanked him for his help. To be sure, Jegu only replied roughly that he didn't know what she was talking about, but this answer made her feel all the more certain that it was he and nobody else.

The same thing took place every day, and never had the cow-house been so clean nor the cows so fat. Morning and evening Barbaik found her earthen pots full of milk and a pound of butter freshly churned, ornamented with leaves. At the end of a few weeks she grew so used to this state of affairs that she only got up just in time to prepare breakfast.

Soon even this grew to be unnecessary, for a day arrived when, coming downstairs, she discovered that the house was swept, the furniture polished, the fire lit, and the food ready, so that she had nothing to do except to ring the great bell which summoned the labourers from the fields to come and eat it. This, also, she thought was the work of Jegu, and she could not help feeling that a husband of this sort would be very useful to a girl who liked to lie in bed and to amuse herself.

Indeed, Barbaik had only to express a wish for it to be satisfied. If the wind was cold or the sun was hot and she was afraid to go out lest her complexion should be spoilt, she need only to run down to the spring close by and say softly, 'I should like my churns to be full, and my wet linen to be stretched on the hedge to dry,' and she need never give another thought to the matter.

If she found the rye bread too hard to bake, or the oven taking too long to heat, she just murmured, 'I should like to see my six loaves on the shelf above the bread box,' and two hours after there they were.

If she was too lazy to walk all the way to market along a dirty road, she would say out loud the night before, 'Why am I not already back from Morlaix with my milk pot empty, my butter bowl inside it, a pound of wild cherries on my wooden plate, and the money I have gained in my apron pocket?' and in the morning when she got up, lo and behold! there were standing at the foot of her bed the empty milk pot with the butter bowl inside, the black cherries on the wooden plate, and six new pieces of silver in the pocket of her apron. And she believed that all this was owing to Jegu, and she could no longer do without him, even in her thoughts.

When things had reached this pass, the brownie told the young man that he had better ask Barbaik to marry him, and this time the girl did not turn rudely away, but listened patiently to the end. In her eyes he was as ugly and awkward as ever, but he would certainly make a most useful husband, and she could sleep every morning till breakfast time, just like a young lady, and as for the rest of the day, it would not be half long enough for all she meant to do. She would wear the beautiful dresses that came when she wished for them, and visit her neighbours, who would be dying of envy all the while, and she would be able to dance as much as she wished. Jegu would always be there to work for her and save for her, and watch over her. So, like a well-brought-up girl, Barbaik answered that it should be as her father pleased, knowing quite well that old Riou had often said that after he was dead there was no one so capable of carrying on the farm.

The marriage took place the following month, and a few days later the old man died quite suddenly. Now Jegu had everything to see to himself, and somehow it did not seem so easy as when the farmer was alive. But once more the brownie stepped in, and was better than ten labourers. It was he who ploughed and sowed and reaped, and if, as happened, occasionally, it was needful to get the work done quickly, the brownie called in some of his friends, and as soon as it was light a host of little dwarfs might have been seen in the fields, busy with hoe, fork or sickle. But by the time the people were about all was finished, and the little fellows had disappeared.

And all the payment the brownie ever asked for was a bowl of broth. From the very day of her marriage Barbaik had noted with surprise and rage that things ceased to be done for her as they had been done all the weeks and months before. She complained to Jegu of his laziness, and he only stared at her, not understanding what she was talking about. But the brownie, who was standing by, burst out laughing, and confessed that all the good offices she spoke of had been performed by him, for the sake of Jegu, but that now he had other business to do, and it was high time that she looked after her house herself.

Barbaik was furious. Each morning when she was obliged to get up before dawn to milk the cows and go to market, and each evening when she had to sit up till midnight in order to churn the butter, her heart was filled with rage against the brownie who had caused her to expect a life of ease and pleasure. But when she looked at Jegu and beheld his red face, squinting eyes, and untidy hair, her anger was doubled.

'If it had not been for you, you miserable dwarf!' she would say between her teeth, 'if it had not been for you I should never have married that man, and I should still have been going to dances, where the young men would have brought me present of nuts and cherries, and told me that I was the prettiest girl in the parish. While now I can receive no presents except from my husband. I can never dance, except with my husband. Oh, you wretched dwarf, I will never, never forgive you!'

In spite of her fierce words, no one knew better than Barbaik how to put her pride in her pocket when it suited her, and after receiving an invitation to a wedding, she begged the brownie to get her a horse to ride there. To her great joy he consented, bidding her set out for the city of the dwarfs and to tell them exactly what she wanted. Full of excitement, Barbaik started on her journey. It was not long, and when she reached the town she went straight to the dwarfs, who were holding counsel in a wide green place, and said to them, 'Listen, my friends! I have come to beg you to lend me a black horse, with eyes, a mouth, ears, bridle and saddle.'

She had hardly spoken when the horse appeared, and mounting on his back she started for the village where the wedding was to be held.

At first she was so delighted with the chance of a holiday from the work which she hated, that she noticed nothing, but very soon it struck her as odd that as she passed along the roads full of people they all laughed as they looked at her horse. At length she caught some words uttered by one man to another. 'Why, the farmer's wife has sold her horse's tail!' and turned in her saddle. Yes; it was true. Her horse had no tail! She had forgotten to ask for one, and the wicked dwarfs had carried out her orders to the letter!

'Well, at any rate, I shall soon be there,' she thought, and shaking the reins, tried to urge the horse to a gallop. But it was of no use; he declined to move out of a walk; and she was forced to hear all the jokes that were made upon her.

In the evening she returned to the farm more angry than ever, and quite determined to revenge herself on the brownie whenever she had the chance, which happened to be very soon.

It was the spring, and just the time of year when the dwarfs held their fête, so one day the brownie asked Jegu if he might bring his friends to have supper in the great barn, and whether he would allow them to dance there. Of course, Jegu was only too pleased to be able to do anything for the brownie, and he ordered Barbaik to spread her best table-cloths in the barn, and to make a quantity of little loaves and pancakes, and, besides, to keep all the milk given by the cows that morning. He expected she would refuse, as he knew she hated the dwarfs, but she said nothing, and prepared the supper as he had bidden her.

When all was ready, the dwarfs, in new green suits, came bustling in, very happy and merry, and took their seats at the table. But in a moment they all sprang up with a cry, and ran away screaming, for Barbaik had placed pans of hot coals under their feet, and all their poor little toes were burnt.

'You won't forget that in a hurry,' she said, smiling grimly to herself, but in a moment they were back again with large pots of water, which they poured on the fire. Then they joined hands and danced round it, singing:

> Wicked traitress, Barne Riou,
> Our poor toes are burned by you;
> Now we hurry from your hall—
> Bad luck light upon you all.

That evening they left the country for ever, and Jegu, without their help, grew poorer and poorer, and at last died of misery, while Barbaik was glad to find work in the market of Morlaix.

From 'Le Foyer Breton,' par E. Souvestre.

The Winning of Olwen

There was once a king and queen who had a little boy, and they called his name Kilweh. The queen, his mother, fell ill soon after his birth, and as she could not take care of him herself she sent him to a woman she knew up in the mountains, so that he might learn to go out in all weathers, and bear heat and cold, and grow tall and strong. Kilweh was quite happy with his nurse, and ran races and climbed hills with the children who were his playfellows, and in the winter, when the snow lay on the ground, sometimes a man with a harp would stop and beg for shelter, and in return would sing them songs of strange things that had happened in the years gone by.

But long before this changes had taken place in the court of Kilweh's father. Soon after she had sent her baby away the queen became much worse, and at length, seeing that she was going to die, she called her husband to her and said:

'Never again shall I rise from this bed, and by and bye thou wilt take another wife. But lest she should make thee forget thy son, I charge thee that thou take not a wife until thou see a briar with two blossoms upon my grave.' And this he promised her. Then she further bade him to see to her grave that nothing might grow thereon. This likewise he promised her, and soon she died, and for seven years the king sent a man every morning to see that nothing was growing on the queen's grave, but at the end of seven years he forgot.

One day when the king was out hunting he rode past the place where the queen lay buried, and there he saw a briar growing with two blossoms on it.

'It is time that I took a wife,' said he, and after long looking he found one. But he did not tell her about his son; indeed he hardly remembered that he had one till she heard it at last from an old woman whom she had gone to visit. And the new queen was very pleased, and sent messengers to fetch the boy, and in his father's court he stayed, while the years went by till one day the queen told him that a prophecy had foretold that he was to win for his wife Olwen the daughter of Yspaddaden Penkawr.

When he heard this Kilweh felt proud and happy. Surely he must be a man now, he thought, or there would be no talk of a wife for him, and his mind dwelt all day upon his promised bride, and what she would be like when he beheld her.

'What aileth thee, my son?' asked his father at last, when Kilweh had forgotten something he had been bidden to do, and Kilweh blushed red as he answered:

'My stepmother says that none but Olwen, the daughter of Yspaddaden Penkawr, shall be my wife.'

'That will be easily fulfilled,' replied his father. 'Arthur the king is thy cousin. Go therefore unto him and beg him to cut thy hair, and to grant thee this boon.'

210

Then the youth pricked forth upon a dapple grey horse of four years old, with a bridle of linked gold, and gold upon his saddle. In his hand he bore two spears of silver with heads of steel; a war-horn of ivory was slung round his shoulder, and by his side hung a golden sword. Before him were two brindled white-breasted greyhounds with collars of rubies round their necks, and the one that was on the left side bounded across to the right side, and the one on the right to the left, and like two sea-swallows sported round him. And his horse cast up four sods with his four hoofs, like four swallows in the air about his head, now above, now below. About him was a robe of purple, and an apple of gold was at each corner, and every one of the apples was of the value of a hundred cows. And the blades of grass bent not beneath him, so light were his horse's feet as he journeyed toward the gate of Arthur's palace.

'Is there a porter?' cried Kilweh, looking round for someone to open the gate.

'There is; and I am Arthur's porter every first day of January,' answered a man coming out to him. 'The rest of the year there are other porters, and among them Pennpingyon, who goes upon his head to save his feet.'

'Well, open the portal, I say.'

'No, that I may not do, for none can enter save the son of a king or a pedlar who has goods to sell. But elsewhere there will be food for thy dogs and hay for thy horse, and for thee collops cooked and peppered, and sweet wine shall be served in the guest chamber.'

'That will not do for me,' answered Kilweh. 'If thou wilt not open the gate I will send up three shouts that shall be heard from Cornwall unto the north, and yet again to Ireland.'

'Whatsoever clamour thou mayest make,' spake Glewlwyd the porter, 'thou shalt not enter until I first go and speak with Arthur.'

Then Glewlwyd went into the hall, and Arthur said to him:

'Hast thou news from the gate?' and the porter answered:

'Far have I travelled, both in this island and elsewhere, and many kingly men have I seen; but never yet have I beheld one equal in majesty to him who now stands at the door.'

'If walking thou didst enter here, return thou running,' replied Arthur, 'and let everyone that opens and shuts the eye show him respect and serve him, for it is not meet to keep such a man in the wind and rain.' So Glewlwyd unbarred the gate and Kilweh rode in upon his charger.

211

'Greeting unto thee, O ruler of this land,' cried he, 'and greeting no less to the lowest than to the highest.'

'Greeting to thee also,' answered Arthur. 'Sit thou between two of my warriors, and thou shalt have minstrels before thee and all that belongs to one born to be a king, while thou remainest in my palace.'

'I am not come,' replied Kilweh, 'for meat and drink, but to obtain a boon, and if thou grant it me I will pay it back, and will carry thy praise to the four winds of heaven. But if thou wilt not grant it to me, then I will proclaim thy discourtesy wherever thy name is known.'

'What thou askest that shalt thou receive,' said Arthur, 'as far as the wind dries and the rain moistens, and the sun revolves and the sea encircles and the earth extends. Save only my ship and my mantle, my word and my lance, my shield and my dagger, and Guinevere my wife.'

'I would that thou bless my hair,' spake Kilweh, and Arthur answered:

'That shall be granted thee.'

Forthwith he bade his men fetch him a comb of gold and a scissors with loops of silver, and he combed the hair of Kilweh his guest.

'Tell me who thou art,' he said, 'for my heart warms to thee, and I feel thou art come of my blood.'

'I am Kilweh, son of Kilydd,' replied the youth.

'Then my cousin thou art in truth,' replied Arthur, 'and whatsoever boon thou mayest ask thou shalt receive.'

'The boon I crave is that thou mayest win for me Olwen, the daughter of Yspaddaden Penkawr, and this boon I seek likewise at the hands of thy warriors. From Sol, who can stand all day upon one foot; from Ossol, who, if he were to find himself on the top of the highest mountain in the world, could make it into a level plain in the beat of a bird's wing; from Cluse, who, though he were buried under the earth, could yet hear the ant leave her nest fifty miles away: from these and from Kai and from Bedwyr and from all thy mighty men I crave this boon.'

'O Kilweh,' said Arthur, 'never have I heard of the maiden of whom thou speakest, nor of her kindred, but I will send messengers to seek her if thou wilt give me time.'

'From this night to the end of the year right willingly will I grant thee,' replied Kilweh; but when the end of the year came and the messengers returned Kilweh was wroth, and spoke rough words to Arthur.

It was Kai, the boldest of the warriors and the swiftest of foot-- he would could pass nine nights without sleep, and nine days beneath the water—that answered him:

'Rash youth that thou art, darest thou speak thus to Arthur? Come with us, and we will not part company till we have won that maiden, or till thou confess that there is none such in the world.'

Then Arthur summoned his five best men and bade them go with Kilweh. There was Bedwyr the one-handed, Kai's comrade and brother in arms, the swiftest man in Britain save Arthur; there was Kynddelig, who knew the paths in a land where he had never been as surely as he did those of his own country; there was Gwrhyr, that could speak all tongues; and Gwalchmai the son of Gwyar, who never returned till he had gained what he sought; and last of all there was Menw, who could weave a spell over them so that none might see them, while they could see everyone.

So these seven journeyed together till they reached a vast open plain in which was a fair castle. But though it seemed so close it was not until the evening of the third day that they really drew near to it, and in front of it a flock of sheep was spread, so many in number that there seemed no end to them. A shepherd stood on a mound watching over them, and by his side was a dog, as large as a horse nine winters old.

'Whose is this castle, O herdsmen?' asked the knights.

'Stupid are ye truly,' answered the herdsman. 'All the world knows that this is the castle of Yspaddaden Penkawr.'

'And who art thou?'

'I am called Custennin, brother of Yspaddaden, and ill has he treated me. And who are you, and what do you here?'

'We come from Arthur the king, to seek Olwen the daughter of Yspaddaden,' but at this news the shepherd gave a cry:

'O men, be warned and turn back while there is yet time. Others have gone on that quest, but none have escaped to tell the tale,' and he rose to his feet as if to leave them. Then Kilweh held out to him a ring of gold, and he tried to put it on his finger, but it was too small, so he placed it in his glove, and went home and gave it to his wife.

'Whence came this ring?' asked she, 'for such good luck is not wont to befall thee.'

'The man to whom this ring belonged thou shalt see here in the evening,' answered the shepherd; 'he is Kilweh, son of Kilydd, cousin to king Arthur, and he has come to seek Olwen.' And when the wife heard that she knew that Kilweh was her nephew, and her heart yearned after him, half with joy at the thought of seeing him, and half with sorrow for the doom she feared.

Soon they heard steps approaching, and Kai and the rest entered into the house and ate and drank. After that the woman opened a chest, and out of it came a youth with curling yellow hair.

'It is a pity to hid him thus,' said Gwrhyr, 'for well I know that he has done no evil.'

'Three and twenty of my sons has Yspaddaden slain, and I have no more hope of saving this one,' replied she, and Kai was full of sorrow and answered:

'Let him come with me and be my comrade, and he shall never be slain unless I am slain also.' And so it was agreed.

'What is your errand here?' asked the woman.

'We seek Olwen the maiden for this youth,' answered Kai; 'does she ever come hither so that she may be seen?'

'She comes every Saturday to wash her hair, and in the vessel where she washes she leaves all her rings, and never does she so much as send a messenger to fetch them.'

'Will she come if she is bidden?' asked Kai, pondering.

'She will come; but unless you pledge me your faith that you will not harm her I will not fetch her.'

'We pledge it,' said they, and the maiden came.

A fair sight was she in a robe of flame-coloured silk, with a collar of ruddy gold about her neck, bright with emeralds and rubies. More yellow was her head than the flower of the broom, and her skin was whiter than the foam of the wave, and fairer were her hands than the blossoms of the wood anemone. Four white trefoils sprang up where she trod, and therefore was she called Olwen.

She entered, and sat down on a bench beside Kilweh, and he spake to her:

'Ah, maiden, since first I heard thy name I have loved thee—wilt thou not come away with me from this evil place?'

'That I cannot do,' answered she, 'for I have given my word to my father not to go without his knowledge, for his life will only last till I am betrothed. Whatever is, must be, but this counsel I will give you. Go, and ask me of my father, and whatsoever he shall required of thee grant it, and thou shalt win me; but if thou deny him anything thou wilt not obtain me, and it will be well for thee if thou escape with thy life.'

'All this I promise,' said he.

So she returned to the castle, and all Arthur's men went after her, and entered the hall.

'Greeting to thee, Yspaddaden Penkawr,' said they. 'We come to ask thy daughter Olwen for Kilweh, son of Kilydd.'

'Come hither to-morrow and I will answer you,' replied Yspaddaden Penkawr, and as they rose to leave the hall he caught up one of the three poisoned darts that lay beside him and flung it in their midst. But Bedwyr saw and caught it, and flung it back so hard that it pierced the knee of Yspaddaden.

'A gentle son-in-law, truly!' he cried, writhing with pain. 'I shall ever walk the worse for this rudeness. Cursed be the smith who forged it, and the anvil on which it was wrought!'

That night the men slept in the house of Custennin the herdsman, and the next day they proceeded to the castle, and entered the hall, and said:

'Yspaddaden Penkawr, give us thy daughter and thou shalt keep her dower. And unless thou wilt do this we will slay thee.'

'Her four great grandmothers and her four great grandfathers yet live,' answered Yspaddaden Penkawr; 'it is needful that I take counsel with them.'

'Be it so; we will go to meat,' but as they turned he took up the second dart that lay by his side and cast it after them. And Menw caught it, and flung it at him, and wounded him in the chest, so that it came out at his back.

'A gentle son-in-law, truly!' cried Yspaddaden, 'the iron pains me like the bite of a horse-leech. Cursed be the hearth whereon it was heated, and the smith who formed it!' The third day Arthur's men returned to the palace into the presence of Yspaddaden.

'Shoot not at me again,' said he, 'unless you desire death. But lift up my eyebrows, which have fallen over my eyes, that I may see my son-in-law.' Then they arose, and as they did so Yspaddaden Penkawr took the third poisoned dart and cast it at them. And Kilweh caught it, and flung it back, and it passed through his eyeball, and came out on the other side of his head.

'A gentle son-in-law, truly! Cursed be the fire in which it was forged and the man who fashioned it!'

The next day Arthur's men came again to the palace and said:

'Shoot not at us any more unless thou desirest more pain than even now thou hast, but give us thy daughter without more words.'

'Where is he that seeks my daughter? Let him come hither so that I may see him.' And Kilweh sat himself in a chair and spoke face to face with him.

'Is it thou that seekest my daughter?'

'It is I,' answered Kilweh.

'First give me thy word that thou wilt do nothing towards me that is not just, and when thou hast won for me that which I shall ask, then thou shalt wed my daughter.'

'I promise right willingly,' said Kilweh. 'Name what thou wilt.'

'Seest thou yonder hill? Well, in one day it shall be rooted up and ploughed and sown, and the grain shall ripen, and of that wheat I will bake the cakes for my daughter's wedding.'

'It will be easy for me to compass this, although thou mayest deem it will not be easy,' answered Kilweh, thinking of Ossol, under whose feet the highest mountain became straightway a plain, but Yspaddaden paid no heed, and continued:

'Seest thou that field yonder? When my daughter was born nine bushels of flax were sown therein, and not one blade has sprung up. I require thee to sow fresh flax in the ground that my daughter may wear a veil spun from it on the day of her wedding.'

'It will be easy for me to compass this.'

'Though thou compass this there is that which thou wilt not compass. For thou must bring me the basket of Gwyddneu Garanhir which will give meat to the whole world. It is for thy wedding feast. Thou must also fetch me the drinking-horn that is never empty, and the harp that never ceases to play until it is bidden. Also the comb and scissors and razor that lie between the two ears of Trwyth the boar, so that I may arrange my hair for the wedding. And though thou get this yet there is that which thou wilt not get, for Trwyth the boar will not let any man take from him the comb and the scissors, unless Drudwyn the whelp hunt him. But no leash in the world can hold Drudwyn save the leash of Cant Ewin, and no collar will hold the leash except the collar of Canhastyr.'

'It will be easy for me to compass this, though thou mayest think it will not be easy,' Kilweh answered him.

'Though thou get all these things yet there is that which thou wilt not get. Throughout the world there is none that can hunt with this dog save Mabon the son of Modron. He was taken from his mother when three nights old, and it is not know where he now is, nor whether he is living or dead, and though thou find him yet the boar will never be slain save only with the sword of Gwrnach the giant, and if thou obtain it not neither shalt thou obtain my daughter.'

'Horses shall I have, and knights from my lord Arthur. And I shall gain thy daughter, and thou shalt lose thy life.'

The speech of Kilweh the son of Kilydd with Yspaddaden Penkawr was ended.

Then Arthur's men set forth, and Kilweh with them, and journeyed till they reached the largest castle in the world, and a black man came out to meet them.

'Whence comest thou, O man?' asked they, 'and whose is that castle?'

'That is the castle of Gwrnach the giant, as all the world knows,' answered the man, 'but no guest ever returned thence alive, and none may enter the gate except a craftsman, who brings his trade.' But little did Arthur's men heed his warning, and they went straight to the gate.

'Open!' cried Gwrhyr.

'I will not open,' replied the porter.

'And wherefore?' asked Kai.

'The knife is in the meat, and the drink is in the horn, and there is revelry in the hall of Gwrnach the giant, and save for a craftsman who brings his trade the gate will not be opened to-night.'

'Verily, then, I may enter,' said Kai, 'for there is no better burnisher of swords than I.'

'This will I tell Gwrnach the giant, and I will bring thee his answer.'

'Bid the man come before me,' cried Gwrnach, when the porter had told his tale, 'for my sword stands much in need of polishing,' so Kai passed in and saluted Gwrnach the giant.

'Is it true what I hear of thee, that thou canst burnish swords?'

'It is true,' answered Kai. Then was the sword of Gwrnach brought to him.

'Shall it be burnished white or blue?' said Kai, taking a whetstone from under his arm.

'As thou wilt,' answered the giant, and speedily did Kai polish half the sword. The giant marvelled at his skill, and said:

'It is a wonder that such a man as thou shouldst be without a companion.'

'I have a companion, noble sir, but he has no skill in this art.'

'What is his name?' asked the giant.

'Let the porter go forth, and I will tell him how he may know him. The head of his lance will leave its shaft, and draw blood from the wind, and descend upon its shaft again.' So the porter opened the gate and Bedwyr entered.

Now there was much talk amongst those who remained without when the gate closed upon Bedwyr, and Goreu, son of Custennin, prevailed with the porter, and he and his companions got in also and hid themselves.

By this time the whole of the sword was polished, and Kai gave it into the hand of Gwrnach the giant, who felt it and said:

'Thy work is good; I am content.'

Then said Kai:

'It is thy scabbard that hath rusted thy sword; give it to me that I may take out the wooden sides of it and put in new ones.' And he took the scabbard in one hand and the sword in the other, and came and stood behind the giant, as if he would have sheathed the sword in the scabbard. But with it he struck a blow at the head of the giant, and it rolled from his body. After that they despoiled the castle of its gold and jewels, and returned, bearing the sword of the giant, to Arthur's court.

They told Arthur how they had sped, and they all took counsel together, and agreed that they must set out on the quest for Mabon the son of Modron, and Gwrhyr, who

218

knew the languages of beasts and of birds, went with them. *So* they journeyed until they came to the nest of an ousel, and Gwrhyr spoke to her.

'Tell me if thou knowest aught of Mabon the son of Modron, who was taken when three nights old from between his mother and the wall.'

And the ousel answered:

'When I first came here I was a young bird, and there was a smith's anvil in this place. But from that time no work has been done upon it, save that every evening I have pecked at it, till now there is not so much as the size of a nut remaining thereof. Yet all that time I have never once heard of the man you name. Still, there is a race of beasts older than I, and I will guide you to them.'

So the ousel flew before them, till she reached the stag of Redynvre; but when they inquired of the stag whether he knew aught of Mabon he shook his head.

'When first I came hither,' said he, 'the plain was bare save for one oak sapling, which grew up to be an oak with a hundred branches. All that is left of that oak is a withered stump, but never once have I heard of the man you name. Nevertheless, as you are Arthur's men, I will guide you to the place where there is an animal older than I'; and the stag ran before them till he reached the owl of Cwm Cawlwyd. But when they inquired of the owl if he knew aught of Mabon he shook his head.

'When first I came hither,' said he, 'the valley was a wooded glen; then a race of men came and rooted it up. After that there grew a second wood, and then a third, which you see. Look at my wings also—are they not withered stumps? Yet until to-day I have never heard of the man you name. Still, I will guide you to the oldest animal in the world, and the one that has travelled most, the eagle of Gwern Abbey.' And he flew before them, as fast as his old wings would carry him, till he reached the eagle of Gwern Abbey, but when they inquired of the eagle whether he knew aught of Mabon he shook his head.

'When I first came hither,' said the eagle, 'there was a rock here, and every evening I pecked at the stars from the top of it. Now, behold, it is not even a span high! But only once have I heard of the man you name, and that was when I went in search of food as far as Llyn Llyw. I swooped down upon a salmon, and struck my claws into him, but he drew me down under water till scarcely could I escape him. Then I summoned all my kindred to destroy him, but he made peace with me, and I took fifty fish spears from his back. Unless he may know something of the man whom you seek I cannot tell who may. But I will guide you to the place where he is.'

So they followed the eagle, who flew before them, though so high was he in the sky, it was often hard to mark his flight. At length he stopped above a deep pool in a river.

'Salmon of Llyn Llyw,' he called, 'I have come to thee with an embassy from Arthur to inquire if thou knowest aught concerning Mabon the son of Modron.' And the salmon answered:

'As much as I know I will tell thee. With every tide I go up the river, till I reach the walls of Gloucester, and there have I found such wrong as I never found elsewhere. And that you may see that what I say is true let two of you go thither on my shoulders.' So Kai and Gwrhyr went upon the shoulders of the salmon, and were carried under the walls of the prison, from which proceeded the sound of great weeping.

'Who is it that thus laments in this house of stone?'

'It is I, Mabon the son of Modron.'

'Will silver or gold bring thy freedom, or only battle and fighting?' asked Gwrhyr again.

'By fighting alone shall I be set free,' said Mabon.

Then they sent a messenger to Arthur to tell him that Mabon was found, and he brought all his warriors to the castle of Gloucester and fell fiercely upon it; while Kai and Bedwyr went on the shoulders of the salmon to the gate of the dungeon, and broke it down and carried away Mabon. And he now being free returned home with Arthur.

After this, on a certain day, as Gwythyr was walking across a mountain he heard a grievous cry, and he hastened towards it. In a little valley he saw the heather burning and the fire spreading fast towards the anthill, and all the ants were hurrying to and fro, not knowing whither to go. Gwythyr had pity on them, and put out the fire, and in gratitude the ants brought him the nine bushels of flax seed which Yspaddaden Penkawr required of Kilweh. And many of the other marvels were done likewise by Arthur and his knights, and at last it came to the fight with Trwyth the board, to obtain the comb and the scissors and the razor that lay between his ears. But hard was the boar to catch, and fiercely did he fight when Arthur's men gave him battle, so that many of them were slain.

Up and down the country went Trwyth the boar, and Arthur followed after him, till they came to the Severn sea. There three knights caught his feet unawares and plunged him into the water, while one snatched the razor from him, and another seized the scissors. But before they laid hold of the comb he had shaken them all off, and neither man nor horse nor dog could reach him till he came to Cornwall, whither Arthur had sworn he should not go. Thither Arthur followed after him with his knights, and if it had been hard to win the razor and the scissors, the struggle for the comb was fiercer still, but at length Arthur prevailed, and the boar was driven into the sea. And whether he was drowned or where he went no man knows to this day.

In the end all the marvels were done, and Kilweh set forward, and with him Goreu, the son of Custennin, to Yspaddaden Penkawr, bearing in their hands the razor, the scissors and the comb, and Yspaddaden Penkawr was shaved by Kaw.

'Is thy daughter mine now?' asked Kilweh.

'She is thine,' answered Yspaddaden, 'but it is Arthur and none other who has won her for thee. Of my own free will thou shouldst never have had her, for now I must lose my life.' And as he spake Goreu the son of Custennin cut off his head, as if had been ordained, and Arthur's hosts returned each man to his own country.

From the 'Mabinogion.'